THE STAND IN

THE STAND IN

J. C. Arlington

To Susan—
The truth will set you free!

Jim A[signature]

Authors Choice Press
San Jose New York Lincoln Shanghai

The Stand In

Authors Choice Press
an imprint of iUniverse.com, Inc.

For information address:
iUniverse.com, Inc.
5220 S 16th, Ste. 200
Lincoln, NE 68512
www.iuniverse.com

This book is a work of fiction. Names, characters, and episodes (except those
sourced directly) are the product of the author's imagination
and are used fictitiously. Any similarity to actual persons,
living or dead is entirely coincidental.

Although this book is a work of fiction, all directly sourced material
is accurate. It has, however, been edited for dramatic content.

ISBN: 0-595-15728-9

As always, to my wife Linda.

Epigraph

History is based on whatever is available at the time it is written.

Foreword

On November 22, 1963 an event took place that will never rest in the mind of a nation. Notwithstanding the official findings, everything but the truth is history.

Prologue

Reclusive CIA spy Richard C. Nagell walked down Kansas street in El Paso, Texas at a nervous pace. He looked over his shoulder several times and checked to see that his handgun was securely fastened in its holster under his jacket. It was September 20, 1963. The day was a hot 93 degrees as it usually was in this western Texas town.

Nagell had a greasy look about him. His hair was always slicked back and his face had excess oil leaking from its pores. Dressed in a cheap suit and tie, he resembled a slippery lawyer.

Nagell's CIA dossier was as mysterious as his personality was eccentric. The dossier had scant entries regarding the operations he had been assigned to. It referenced assignments regarding meetings Nagell had with anti-Castro Cubans in New Orleans including Guy Banister. It also referred to Nagell's clandestine involvement in helping to provide support for the Fair Play for Cuba Committee and its sole member, Lee Harvey Oswald. Other entries included Nagell's connections regarding bizarre organizations such as the Anti-Communist League of the Caribbean, and The Friends of Democratic Cuba. The dossier also had scant reference about a trip Nagell had gone on to Mexico City. There he monitored cameras the CIA had outside the Cuban and Russian diplomatic missions. Several photographs were taken of a man the agency said was Oswald. It was later admitted that the man was not Oswald, but someone using his identity. Even FBI Director J. Edgar

1

Hoover, in a memo to the State Department in 1960, had said that someone might be using Oswald's identity. At the time, Nagell didn't know what the hell it all meant. Now, however, the pieces of this ominous puzzle had fallen into place and it greatly disturbed him.

Nagell, sweating profusely, entered the State National Bank. He looked around, but couldn't see any security guards. There were several patrons standing in a service line, three employees behind nearby desks, and a couple tellers at work either handing out money, or depositing customer checks.

Nagell stopped in the middle of the bank, pulled out his .38 caliber handgun, and discharged two rounds into the high ceiling. He dropped the gun onto the floor near his feet and waited for the police to arrive.

When the police arrived a few minutes later, Nagell offered no resistance. As he was being handcuffed, he said to his apprehending officer, "I'm glad you caught me. I really don't want to be in Dallas."

Albert Walker dragged deeply on his Pall Mall filter-less cigarette. When it threatened to burn his yellowed fingertip, he dropped it into the dirt and snubbed it out with his foot. Walker was white, slender, weighing about 165 pounds, about 5 foot 10 inches and in his early thirties. He wore a light colored jacket in the cool October air. As he went to light another cigarette, the real estate agent drove up, parked in front of him and got out of his car.

"Mr. Walker," said the agent, shaking Walker's hand.

"Mr. Siegel," said Walker in a distinctive Southern United States accent.

"Shall we?" Siegel opened his passenger door allowing Walker to enter and sit. Siegel got back into the driver's seat and drove off with Walker.

Siegel was an average looking man and an aggressive real estate agent who usually closed a sale. Most of his clients who came to this area already knew what they wanted. That made his job that much easier.

In the car there was silence until Siegel finally asked, "Are you looking for a summer home, Mr. Walker?"

Hesitantly, "No. No, I'll be living there."

"I see."

"I'm retiring, if you must know," mumbled Walker watching for Siegel's reaction. "I'm looking to get away from it all."

"Well, Beaver River is just what you're looking for. As you know, it's completely surrounded by the Adirondack State Park. There can never be any encroachment from development. The State of New York has preserved this area and Beaver River is as big as it will get."

"Then it sounds suitable. And the roads again?"

"There're no access roads, just a couple dirt ones that allow the few owners passage from the docks to their cabins."

"And this Lowville is how far?"

"About twenty seven miles to Stillwater, the last nine along a dirt road. From Stillwater, by boat or snowmobile, another nine miles to Beaver River. There's a railroad track from Big Moose, but that's not used anymore except by local merchants." Siegel looked out of the corner of his eye and saw Walker looking out the passenger window. Walker admired the thick forest that went by.

"You're not from around here?"

"You can tell?" Walker said sarcastically.

"I'm sorry, I shouldn't pry." Siegel concentrated on the road. Walker finished his drag and flicked the butt out the open window.

After the long winding dirt road to Stillwater, Siegel parked in the lot and went to find Ronny Richardson. Walker made his way down to the small dock at the Stillwater landing and looked out over Stillwater Reservoir. About 172 square miles, 11 miles long and one mile wide at its widest point, Stillwater Reservoir was becoming a popular summer camping destination and a winter-wonder-land for the burgeoning snowmobile enthusiast.

Siegel approached with a middle age man. "This is Mr. Richardson," announced Siegel, "who owns the taxi and the Beaver River Lodge. This is Mr. Walker."

Walker and Richardson shook hands. "Pleasure to meet you," said Walker.

"Nice to meet you. Shall we cast off?" Richardson boarded his water-boat taxi, a cross between an outboard and a steamboat. Ronny, dressed in overalls, had the look of a hard worker. His hands were rough, and his face parched and timeworn.

Walker followed Richardson aboard while Siegel cast off the lines and hopped on.

The ride was pleasant. Walker stood near the railing. He spotted a doe with her fawn near the south shore a few miles in. He admired the vast array of different colored leaves on the trees, from fire red to bright yellow. Siegel chatted with Richardson as Walker took in the vast blue skies and the dense forest of Regal White Pines, Spruce and other evergreens along the shoreline.

As they pulled into the Grassy Point Landing, Walker saw a half dozen boats docked there. Richardson pulled up and Siegel jumped off and secured the line. They walked a short distance and got into Richardson's beat-up 1945 Ford Pick-up. There were perhaps a dozen other rusty early model vehicles parked there.

"You bring these in by boat?" asked Walker.

"We have a small barge we hook up to the riverboat," said Richardson.

Walker nodded. They drove the short distance to the Beaver River Lodge. The Lodge was a rustic old building that housed a restaurant, bar, general store, gift shop and post office. It was quaint, with only 10 guestrooms.

"We'll go look at the property and come back for lunch," said Siegel.

"You brought the papers?" asked Walker.

Siegel threw Richardson a curious glance. "Yes," said Siegel, "We can fill out the papers if you like the property."

"If it's as you described over the phone, Mr. Siegel, I don't see any reason why I wouldn't want it."

"Yes, well." Siegel followed Walker, who followed Richardson to a small dock on the other side of the Lodge. There, they all got into a small boat with an outboard motor. Richardson started the engine and boated off across Norridgewock Lake.

Walker sat in the front of the boat, Siegel behind him. "As I explained over the phone, Mr. Walker," said Siegel, "the entire island is one lot. The cabin was built in 1947. I think you'll agree, that it's quite a reasonable deal."

Walker nodded and grunted.

A few minutes later the boat pulled up to a small dock on a remote island. The Island was near the South Branch, the opposite side of Norridgewock Lake from the Lodge. The main land was more than four hundred yards off the south shore.

Siegel secured the boat. Walker got out and headed toward the cabin that was slightly obscured by foliage. The island was a little more than one and a half acres in area. One cabin fit on it comfortably.

Siegel used his keys and opened the cabin door. Walker went in and looked around. There was a small porch, tiny kitchen, potbelly stove in the middle of the living room, and a small two-bed loft. "It's only had the one owner," said Siegel. "Mr. Roberts built it."

Walker went out and surveyed the rest of the island while Siegel and Richardson sat at the table in the kitchen.

"Young to retire, don't you think, Ron?" asked Siegel.

"For us maybe."

"Odd character."

"Yeah."

"But why here? He's from the south."

Ronny shrugged his shoulders.

Walker stuck his head in the door. "I'll take it." They motored back across the lake to the Lodge. Walker seemed satisfied. During the short boat ride, he admired the beauty of this remote, isolated area.

The Beaver River Lodge was a throwback to the early part of the 20th century. It had been rebuilt like the original Lodge, which burned down in 1956. It had that distinctive Adirondack feel, with its log cabin style walls and boarding house atmosphere. Pictures of rugged early 20th century Adirondack logging scenes hung around on several walls.

At lunch Walker signed the real estate forms that Siegel had brought in his briefcase. Walker lit a cigarette after lunch while Siegel crossed the t's and dotted the i's on the papers.

The television at the end of the bar reported the news of the day. The anchor came on and explained:

> In Dallas, Texas today, demonstrators shoved, booed, beat and spat in the face of Adlai Stevenson, the chief US delegate at the United Nations, following a speech he made there. A woman rushed forward and struck him on the head with her picket sign. In the Municipal Auditorium meeting, fistfights broke out several times as anti-United Nations members of the audience clashed with other spectators.

A newsreel showed Adlai Stevenson. He said:

> It becomes increasingly difficult, therefore, to understand the logic of these super-patriots who decry the United Nations; who talk of peace but who object to our institution for peaceful settlement; who decry every attempt at negotiation and conciliation and offer no alternative save weapons that will destroy friend and foe alike.

The anchor explained, "As he spoke, a light plane flew over Dallas towing a banner that said: 'Get US out of UN.'"

Another newsreel showed Stevenson who said:

The recently concluded nuclear test ban treaty, now signed by more than 100 countries, is the most important single step since the war in the field of arms control and disarmament.

Walker watched the story with pointed interest. He took a heavy drag on his Pall Mall and held it deep within his lungs.

"When did you say you were retiring, Mr. Walker?" Walker exhaled as he spoke. "In November. The latter part."

"I see."

One

Bill Clinton was finishing his second term as President. Although several lots had changed hands, a few more than once, Beaver River hadn't grown.

Judge Richard Bell, a US District Judge in nearby Syracuse, greeted Andy Bell at the Stillwater dock. Judge Bell was tall and stately, but with a rugged appearance, at the age of fifty-seven. He already had on that ridiculous fisherman's hat that he always wore that had fishing lures stuck in it. He resembled Colonel Blake from M*A*S*H.

Andy had just concluded his third year at the John F. Kennedy School of Government at Harvard University. At 22, he had his father's features and was just as tall at six feet. He was the only child that Rebecca and Richard Bell had. Rebecca had had two miscarriages before Andy and when they were successful on the third try, they counted their blessings and decided not to push their luck.

"We're all set," said Judge Bell. "Is Wendy coming this sum—?"

"No," said Andy abruptly cutting him off.

Judge Bell left it at that. He wasn't the prying kind.

Andy passed off his two bags with his belongings to his father and hopped into the boat. The boat was a former ski boat that his father had recently bought in Utica. Judge Bell motored out into the deeper water and accelerated towards Beaver River.

"This summer's been warmer than usual," said Judge Bell. "Average temperature has been eighty two. High humidity."

Andy nodded and looked at the passing shoreline. His mind was elsewhere.

The Judge pulled into the Grassy Point Landing and docked the boat. They walked the short distance to the parking lot and hopped in Judge Bell's 1979 rusted run-down Chevrolet truck. They drove through the woods to the Judge's cabin, which he had named the Osprey, after the majestic Adirondack bird, or fish hawk. The Osprey, his cabin, was not far from the Beaver River Lodge.

The Osprey was an A-frame design with a loft. It had a large main room downstairs with an old pot bellied stove, a spacious porch with a table, and a small kitchen. There were two beds in the main room and three more in the loft. The Osprey had a shed attached to its side where the firewood was stored and the generator was housed.

Norridgewock Lake was fifty yards from the front porch. Depending upon the season, the distance to Norridgewock Lake—because of the river level—could be far or close.

"Want some lunch?" asked the Judge.

"Yeah, thanks."

"I told Dusty we'd be in about now."

"Dusty running things?"

"Ronny had a stroke last fall. He's just about given up on working. He fishes and let's Dusty take care of everything."

Andy followed his father out and together they walked the short distance to the Beaver River Lodge.

Judge Bell had discovered Beaver River in the mid-eighties while snowmobiling with friends. He bought his small cabin in 1987 as a part his wife's therapy, but she only made it up here twice, both times with Andy. Judge Bell traveled here practically every Friday night since her passing shortly thereafter. He commuted back to Syracuse every Sunday night. Of course he stayed here whenever he could schedule a break in court action, mostly in the summer and a couple weeks here and there in the winter.

Judge Bell figured that something was wrong with Andy because he hadn't ever wanted to come here for even a few days. Now however, he wanted to spend the whole summer alone.

Inside the bar area of the Lodge, Andy and his father sat eating their lunch at a corner table. There were three patrons at the bar nursing drinks.

"Have you made plans about what law school you'd like to attend?" asked the Judge as he washed down his ham sandwich with a cool Molson's.

"No. Not yet," said Andy distantly.

"Since you're at Harvard, I'd think that would be the best choice."

"Yeah, I guess." He took a bite of his roast beef sandwich, not so much that he was hungry, but so that he wouldn't have to say anything. His father looked down at his plate as he bit into his sandwich. He sensed Andy wasn't telling him everything.

Walker shuffled in through the front door. Now in his late 60's (although he looked at least ten years older than he was) he walked with the aid of a cane. He had gained a little weight and looked sickly. He wore glasses now. He made his way past the Judge and Andy. "Judge," he nodded. He caught a glimpse of Andy who glanced back at him.

"Al," greeted the Judge.

Andy watched as Walker slowly passed by and sat at the far side of the bar. Walker looked back at Andy with a curious stare, then looked away.

"I've never seen him before," whispered Andy to his father.

"He's very reticent, a hermit so to speak."

"Where's he live?"

"On the island near South Branch."

"How long's he lived there?"

"Ronny told me he moved there in '63."

Andy finished off his sandwich. He drank a soft drink. He thought about this old and decrepit man. "No family?"

"Not that anyone has seen."

"Can I get you anything else, Judge?" asked Dusty Richardson appearing from the kitchen.

"Not for us, Dusty. Mr. Walker came in."

Dusty, Ronny's only son, was in his early forties, and wore an apron much like a pizza maker would. He was short, but physically well toned. He did everything from tending bar, cooking and handy work around the lodge. He had a young family, including three children ranging in ages from 4 to 9. "What can I get you today, Al?"

"Labatts and a turkey sandwich. Who's the kid?"

"Judge Bell's son. On vacation from college."

Walker nodded as Dusty went to prepare him his lunch. Walker lit up a Pall Mall and took a heavy drag. He noticed that Judge Bell and Andy had gotten up to leave. "Judge Bell?" He called out.

"Yes, Al."

Walker motioned for the Judge to come to him. "I'd come to you, but the body doesn't work as it used to."

"That's okay. What can I do for you?"

"Like I said, my body is giving out. I noticed your son there?"

"Andy."

"Yes, well, I suspect he's on vacation, but I was wondering if he would like a job. Chopping wood, odd jobs. I have a hole in my roof that needs patching."

"I'd encourage it, but let's ask him. Andy?"

Andy approached.

"This is Al Walker." Andy and Walker shook hands. "He's wondering if you could do a couple of chores for him."

"What kind of chores?"

"Chopping wood, clearing some brush," said Walker. "I got a hole in my roof."

"Yeah, sure."

"Come by tomorrow morning about nine? Do you know how to get there?"

"No."

"It's the only house on an island by the South Branch. You can't miss it."

"I'm sure I'll find it."

"Good."

"Take care of yourself," said the Judge.

"It ain't easy growing old."

Andy and his father went back to the Osprey. Andy decided to take out his father's old small rowboat that had a nine horse powered outboard motor on it and check out Norridgewock Lake. As he set out across the lake, he thought about how odd it was that Mr. Walker lived alone in such an isolated community. He had no family, or none that he had ever referred to according to Andy's father. Strange, with all of man's modern amenities, why someone would live like a frontiersman, Andy couldn't fathom. Nevertheless, Andy would welcome the chores that Walker offered. It would take his mind off of things.

He slowed the boat when he passed Walker's island. The place was run down. The cabin hadn't been painted in years. The front porch was drooping on one side, and twigs and other dead tree parts littered the roof. A tree actually enveloped half the cabin. Some chores thought Andy. The place was a mess! He sped up and circled around the island. He shook his head and headed towards the Osprey.

Later that night, Andy and the Judge went over to David Kirby's cabin. Kirby reminded Andy of a weasel. He was short, skinny and bald. Kirby was in his late fifties and was a former stock broker from New York who had a nervous breakdown several years back when he lost much of his life savings in junk bonds and the stock market crash of 1987. He took what little he had left and moved to Beaver River.

Ronny and Dusty Richardson stopped by and together, with Andy, the Judge and Kirby, played poker. Everyone drank his own preferred alcoholic beverage.

"I saw Walker's place today. It's not a pretty sight." Andy rearranged the cards he had been dealt.

"He hasn't done anything to fix it up in twenty years or more," said Ronny. "You get inside?"

"Not yet. What'd he retire from?"

"No one knows," said Dusty. "I still say he ran drugs, guns or something like that."

"He was only in his thirties I would say when he moved in there," said Ronny. "I'll take two."

Judge Bell slid Ronny two cards. "Must've made a fortune to retire that early," said the Judge. "I still have three years before I'm eligible."

"Come to think about it," Dusty said to Andy, "you'll probably be the first to set foot on his property since that day dad and the real estate agent did in '63."

"No one thinks that's odd?" Andy asked.

"Sure."

Everyone nodded or grunted.

"Maybe he was Mafia," Andy said.

"How so?" Dusty asked.

"Like witness protection or something."

"Maybe."

"I think we should leave it at that then," said Andy's father being the legal eagle. "He has his right to privacy. If you mess around, his protection or whatever if it is related to that, could be blown and get him killed."

Andy played his hand. At any rate, his curiosity had swelled. It did unnerve him a little that he'd be the only one in years to set foot on the island. Maybe he could find out something about Walker. Then again, perhaps it was better left alone.

They played cards and drank until one O'clock in the morning.

At Nine O'clock in the morning Andy boated over to Walker's island. He docked his father's boat and walked up the short path to Walker's front porch door. He knocked three times and stood waiting.

Walker appeared at the door several seconds later. He steadied himself with his cane and hobbled down the steps. He wheezed from a bad cough, then lit up a smoke. "The hole's on the East Side, in the middle on the main room. We should fix that first. There's a ladder out back." He took a deep drag and blew the smoke out and down away from Andy. "Clear the twigs and leaves off so we can see what we're dealing with. There're roofing materials in the shed."

Andy fetched the ladder. He wondered what he was getting himself into. He did, after all, plan to take it easy this summer. He had brought his laptop computer along and wanted to work on his senior thesis.

Walker stood at the bottom of the ladder while Andy climbed up and slid along the roof. He carried a small handsaw Walker had given him from the shed. He cut a few branches from the encroaching tree and scrapped off some brush. He located the spot where Walker had suspected the leak, right where a branch from the tree had scrapped and dug for several years. The area was just before where the loft sloped down. He peeled up a shingle and stuck his finger right through the roof. He tore off some tarpaper and shingles that were rotted. He cleared off the tar and gunk.

"You're right," said Andy peering over the edge. "It's a hole that goes clear through. I'll need to clear off the rest of the roof and trim back this tree first. And a hammer or paint scraper to make an area for a patch."

Walker grunted and headed into the shed. Andy cut back the tree while Walker organized his materials.

After he had considerably trimmed back the tree, and dropped the branches off over the side, Andy scraped away more of the shingles and tarpaper. He made the hole larger by cutting out the rotted wood making an eight-inch radius.

Walker dropped something in the shed. Andy heard him cussing.

Andy put his eye down and peered into the main room. What he saw sent shivers down his spine. Stacked against the front wall in olive drab military gun racks, he saw several rifles and guns. He noticed stacks of newspapers against the sidewall. He changed his line of sight and saw some kind of an altar on a table against the back wall. There was a candle burning on a cloth on the table and he could make out the bottom of a photograph and its frame, but couldn't see who was in the picture. The entire interior of this main room wasn't a mess, but could use a serious cleaning.

"How's it going?" said Walker from below.

"Fine. I'll be right down." Andy descended the ladder and retained the roofing materials. A short while later he had patched the hole.

During the lunch hour Walker brought out a card table and placed a loaf of bread and some cold cuts on it. "I have beer or lemonade."

"Lemonade, please." Andy sat on the porch step and ate a sandwich while Walker got him lemonade from his refrigerator. Walker sat in a folding chair near the table.

For the longest time they ate in silence. Andy helped himself to the bag of chips Walker had placed on the table. "What else did you have in mind, Mr. Walker?"

"Perhaps finish clearing more of that tree and cutting up the wood. It stacks in the shed."

Andy nodded and looked at the small-dilapidated porch. "I spent one summer working for Habitat for Humanity. We built houses for the poor, and I was thinking that you could use a new porch."

Walker scanned his porch. "Suppose you're right," he said after a tense silence. "What organization you say?"

"Habitat for Humanity. Mostly in the South, but they build houses everywhere. I was actually on a site one summer with former President Carter."

"Carter?" Walker said like he didn't know who that was.

"Carter. You know, President Jimmy Carter. 77 to 81?"

"Oh. Yeah. I've sort of lost track over the years."

Andy thought that either this man had Alzheimer's, or had been out of touch.

They ate in silence again. Andy began to feel relaxed that this man wasn't some kind of a madman, but he didn't feel totally at ease. Walker had some kind of an arsenal in that cabin, much like either a member of a fanatical militia, or a survivalist doomsday nut would. He was obviously a hermit and didn't care too much about what was going on with the world outside Beaver River.

"Well, I'll finish up on the tree and see you when, Mr. Walker?"

"I think you're right about the porch. Hang on a minute." He went into his cabin.

Andy stood awkwardly and wondered what Walker would emerge with. A minute later Andy's question was answered.

"Here's four hundred dollars," said Walker. "Keep some for yourself and use the rest to get some lumber and supplies for the porch. You can come–n–work on it whenever you're ready. There's no hurry." He handed the wad of twenties to Andy.

Now that was odd that Walker had this kind of money lying around, Andy thought, but then who was around to steal it? He stuffed the cash in the front pocket of his shorts. "Thanks, Mr. Walker." Andy finished trimming back the tree then cut it up into firewood.

Walker picked up the lunchables and went back into his cabin. He had to stop and catch his breath. When he put his hand up against the wall for support, he went into a rough coughing spell. He had to struggle against the spell to get over to his bed to lie down. For the longest time he lay there and tried to regain his breath. He was light headed. The eerie glow of the candle from the shrine nearby illuminated a crucifix that sat behind it. The picture of the man on the wall looked down at the floor, his arms folded.

A few minutes later after the room stopped spinning, Walker sat up and lit a cigarette. He felt fine now.

Andy picked up the tools and stacked the wood. When he finished he walked down to the dock, got into the boat and boated back to the Osprey.

Andy pulled up to his father's dock. Judge Bell was there to secure the line.

"How'd it go?"

"Good. He's odd, but friendly." Andy climbed out of the boat. "I'm gonna fix his porch. It's severely rotted."

"I'll need you to run me over to Stillwater after dinner. Pick me up there Friday night at about seven."

They walked up the path to the Osprey.

Two

Cheryl Taylor had buried her grandmother three days ago. Grandmother Jackson had had a heart attack at the age of 67. Death was swift and at least she didn't suffer that long. The doctor said that she had probably died within five minutes of the attack.

Cheryl was now on her own at the young age of 21. Her grandmother had raised her since the age of 7 when her mother had died in an automobile accident caused by a drunk driver. Cheryl's father had died earlier in a military helicopter crash at Fort Benning, Georgia.

Cheryl had the lonely and intricate task of closing her Grandmother's affairs. She had a few minutes before meeting with the attorney, so she started sorting through grandmother's memorabilia. Her grandmother had old photographs, newspaper clippings and assorted knickknacks packed in boxes in a hall closet.

Cheryl found a picture of her Grandmother at about the same age that Cheryl was now. There were striking similarities. It almost made her think she was looking in a mirror. She had her grandmother's soft shoulder length tan colored hair and her face was smooth, perfectly symmetrical and slightly tanned. Cheryl was an attractive woman, and always had men flirting with her.

Cheryl had to put the picture down beside her. A tear welled up in her eye. She had never seen this picture of her grandmother before. She had always obviously known her at an older age. It was too creepy to look at the picture again, so she put it back in the box.

She reached into the back of the closet and pulled out a shoebox. In it, Cheryl found some old letters and photographs of her grandmother, a man, and some pictures where the both of them were together, mostly smiling, hugging or kissing. Cheryl hadn't ever seen these pictures before either and just thought that perhaps the man was an old boyfriend she hadn't told her granddaughter about. The man in the picture reminded Cheryl of someone, like she had seen him somewhere before, but she couldn't think for the life of her where.

She opened the letters and soon discovered that they were love letters. At the conclusion of each letter the man signed his name: John.

Cheryl set the box aside and decided to read the letters thoroughly later. She saw several large brown shopping bags on the other side of the closet. She had to get up and close the side of the closet she was at and slide open the other side. She pulled out one of the bags—she could see at least five there—and looked in it. The bag was stuffed full of unopened envelopes. She took out one envelope and looked at the address. It was addressed to her grandmother, Leonora Jackson, but there was no return address. The postmark on this envelope was too faded to make out where it was mailed from.

Cheryl ripped open the envelope and took out an 8x11-folded piece of white paper. Inside the paper, to her obvious surprise, but bewilderment, were 25 twenty-dollar bills. There was no writing on the paper and nothing else in the envelope.

Cheryl dropped the money on the floor beside her and promptly searched several more envelopes from the bag. Each envelope that she ripped open she found 25 twenty dollar bills. She opened at least ten envelopes before she kneeled down and sat on her feet. She drew in a deep breath and exhaled loudly. "Oh my God! There's got to be thousands."

An hour later at the reading of her grandmother's will, Cheryl sat across the desk from her grandmother's attorney. She was the only survivor.

Grandmother's lawyer, Herbert Rothstein, had known Cheryl's grandmother the better part of thirty years and she trusted him completely. "I know I don't have to tell you, Cheryl," said Rothstein, "that your grandmother cherished you above and beyond everything in this world."

Cheryl smiled as Rothstein continued with the accolades. Her mind was elsewhere, thinking about the 200,000 dollars that she had counted in the bags in grandmother's closet. She'd have to open several bank safe deposit boxes to spread the money around. She certainly couldn't open regular bank accounts and have the Internal Revenue Service stepping into the picture.

"So it should come to you as no surprise," continued Rothstein, "that she left the house to you, all her possessions contained therein, and her savings account containing one hundred and fifty thousand."

Cheryl drifted off in thought. Who had sent all that money? Why hadn't grandmother deposited the money, invested it, much less opened the envelopes? She'd have to know the answers. She'd have to try and trace these mysterious envelopes somehow.

"What're your plans?

"To finish college."

"That's right, what're you studying?"

"I was studying teaching," she said disengaged.

"Well, I wish you luck. Just sign here, and here." Rothstein pointed to where he wanted her to sign.

She signed the papers and was on her way. She had far too many questions to find answers to.

A couple days later Walker got up early and took his boat over to the dock behind the Lodge. Ronny Richardson had said back in 1963 that

Walker could tie his boat there anytime he needed to, which was only when Walker had to go shopping in Lowville and run other errands. At the dock he secured his boat and meandered down to the Grassy Point Landing where his larger boat that would take him across the reservoir to Stillwater was docked. Walker didn't have a vehicle to drive him from the lodge to the landing like most had. Actually, this was always good exercise and he didn't mind the leg stretch. He usually only took this journey once a month, sometimes twice, so he didn't really need a car. Walking at a much slower pace now with his cane, he pulled a small luggage holder that carried his reusable cloth grocery bags.

The summer days in this part of upstate New York, in the outback, were usually pleasant. The humidity at times could become quite intense; it was this morning, as evidenced by the sweat that had accumulated upon Walker's brow. He had to stop and catch his breath when he got to the landing and shoo away the flies that circled his head. He lit up a cigarette to regain his equanimity. He had started smoking when he was in the service, many years ago. Damn soldiers, he chuckled. They'd go on physical training runs and have to light up a cigarette immediately thereafter to catch their breath.

Leaning against his boat, he went into a coughing spell. He spit up thick mucus mixed with blood. He'd never done that before. He wiped his mouth with his handkerchief and untied his craft. He motored out past grassy island and into the reservoir.

He'd made this trip so many times over the past three decades. This time however, the trip was for more than one reason. Oh sure, he'd had appointments with Doc Bergholtz, but those were usually routine ones. Now, it was for pain he'd been experiencing in his chest for some time. Nevertheless, for a man of his age, it wasn't uncommon to have aches and pains.

He sat down and piloted his craft and thought about death. He had prepared for death. He welcomed his waltz with the grim reaper after what he had done for so many years, so many years ago. The only thing that remained uncertain for him, he now realized, was what waited for him on the other side of the door.

In Stillwater at the parking lot, he did have an old 1973 Buick Electra. After docking his boat in Stillwater, he cranked up the Electra and headed into Lowville.

Walker was finally called into Bergholtz's examination room after a long thirty-minute wait. He had scanned through the recent issue of *Adirondack Life*.

Bergholtz, a slightly overweight man in his sixties, who tipped the bottle regularly, greeted Walker, "What's the problem, Al?"

"Pain in my chest. A cough, some blood this morning."

The Doc looked at him in a concerned way. "Did you quit?" He took his vital signs.

"Now? What's the point?" He shifted on the exam table.

"To buy you a little more time."

"A little more time won't mean much for an old crust like me."

Bergholtz jotted down some orders on a professional pad. "I'm ordering some tests. You'll have to go to the clinic for these."

"How long will it take?"

"Al, you're not well. You need to have this done."

"It's cancer isn't it?"

"Not necessarily."

"Don't, Doc. Just spell it out."

"My first guess, yes. But let's not jump to conclusions." Bergholtz ripped off several sheets from his pad and handed them to Walker. "The results will take a few days. Schedule an appointment one-week from today with Louise. And stop smoking for Christ's sake."

Walker threw the Doc a 'yeah right look' and slid down from the exam table. He scheduled another appointment and drove over to the clinic.

Andy just about had the entire porch torn down. He had dragged over to the door a couple of stones that Walker could use as a step temporarily until he had built the new porch. Andy took the initiative and cut up the old porch for firewood. He stacked it in Walker's shed.

Walker's cabin was certainly a wreck, Andy concluded. There was a lot of work that could be done to it if Walker wished it. In any event, he would build Walker his new porch first. He certainly could use the extra money back at the university. Even with his father's generous loan, Andy, like most young men his age, always needed more money.

Andy had brought his own refreshment. He sat down on the stone steps for a drink and thought about what he had seen through the roof. He knew Walker was supposed to return at any moment. The note Walker had left said four hours. It was actually now four and a half. He was overdue.

Andy looked around and scanned the lake. He listened. He neither saw a boat nor heard one, so, with drink in hand, he tried to look in through the front window. The curtain was drawn and he couldn't see anything.

Andy walked around to the side window and could barely peer through the opening in the crack through the white curtain. He couldn't see the back wall that he had seen the other day because this particular window was behind that wall and to the side.

Andy walked to the back window and luckily could see into the cabin. Obviously he couldn't see the back wall, but he did see the front wall near where the old porch was, and the new one would be. He could see more clearly the arsenal stacked there.

Stacked in those military gun racks against the wall, as if for hasty combat, were: 2 Winchester double barreled 12 gauge shotguns; 1 Browning single barrel 16 gauge shotgun; 2 high intensity model 88 Winchester .243 rifles; 1 Spanish 28 gauge double barrel shotgun; 3 5.56mm AR-15 assault rifles (the civilian equivalent of the military M-16); 1 40mm M203 grenade launcher attached to a regular military

M16; 1 M2 .50 caliber Browning machine gun sitting on a tripod facing the front window (capable of shooting 500-650 rounds per minute); 1 .221 IMP sub-machine-gun/rifle; and 1 Cobray M11 9mm short automatic sub-machine gun (capable of shooting 1,200 rounds per minute). Below, on the floor, were several military style, OD green, ammunition cans and a couple crates that had US Army markings on them.

This guy was indeed, thought Andy, some kind of a survivalist nut case.

The sound of Walker's boat motor abruptly coughed and quit. Startled like a kid caught with his hand in the cookie jar, Andy plodded around to the front of the cabin. Fortunately, he was at the back and the dock was in the front so there was no chance that Walker had see him snooping.

Andy helped Walker unload the supplies. They headed for the cabin. Walker lost his breath and had to struggle to get out his words. "I see you're productive. I didn't expect this much so fast."

"I cut up the wood and piled it in your shed." Andy opened the cabin door for Walker.

Walker stopped at the door and gently blocked Andy's entry in a polite, not so obvious way, or so Walker tried to make it seem. Walker placed the two grocery bags he was carrying on the floor just inside the door. He then took the other two from Andy and did the same.

Andy was well aware that Walker didn't want him to go in, so Andy waited at the bottom of the step. "I'll pick up the wood tomorrow, Mr. Walker and get started the day after."

"That's fine," said Walker. He nodded and went in his cabin closing the door behind him.

Andy picked up the tools he had been using and stored them in the shed. During the several trips to the shed, Andy's mind whirled with crazy scenarios about this Walker and his behavior. What was it that Walker had in that cabin, besides the weapons, that he couldn't even let someone like Andy, a kid who could care less, see? He thought about the weapons and decided not to tell anyone what he saw.

Inside the Osprey, Andy grabbed a Molsons Ale from the refrigerator. His father had the Osprey decorated with antique Adirondack logging tools. Some hung on walls, others adorned tables and desks. Some tools dated back at least a century, when logging in this area was the way of life. Thank God, Andy's father had said, that the State had stepped in and saved this part of New York for generations to come.

Andy lay down on the couch on the porch. The porch, facing Norridgewock Lake, had several chairs and a kitchen style table. The porch was separated from the main part of the cabin by a sliding glass door and was enclosed by a fine screen to keep out all those pesky New York insects.

Andy lay there for the longest time thinking about everything. He wanted to call Wendy, but decided against it because he was sure that she wouldn't want to talk with him since she broke it off. It was over, he concluded, at least from a romantic perspective, (if it had ever truly been one).

He thought about his mother. She had died from breast cancer, despite early treatment. It had apparently spread just enough to the point of no return before the mastectomy. It was a long and horrific passing. Andy's father handled it well on the surface, but inside, Andy concluded, really did take it hard.

Andy heard a Loon wail in the distance. It certainly was tranquil up here. He thought it was nice for a short stay, a month perhaps, maybe this whole summer, but he had to get back to civilization and its cornucopia of modernity eventually. He fell asleep.

Three

Winston Franklin, his name for the past forty years, got out of his Dodge Ram and hobbled up the sidewalk with the aid of a cane. Almost completely bald, in his early eighties, he shuffled across the driveway and into his small house that was just outside Sierra Vista, Arizona. Arizona over the last twenty years or so has grown much like that of Florida. With retirees living longer, they sought out the warmer climates to at least feel a little more comfortable in their latter years.

Franklin, like Walker, now realized that with these more frequent visits to the doctor, death was close at hand. Nevertheless, he would also ride it out as long as he could. He still drove, although he had had a recent accident, only a fender bender, but in any event, it was his first accident ever. It was his fault; he didn't see the oncoming car.

Franklin's small home was decorated with Southwest Native American artifacts and paintings, mostly Apache, some ironically Papago, a few Hopi designs. Franklin sat down to read the newspaper, *The Tucson Citizen.*

As he scanned the paper, Franklin mumbled aloud to himself. He read an article about Clinton pushing for more gun control. "Damn Clinton." He crumpled up the paper and set it aside. He grabbed some medication from a table by his side, popped several pills and washed them down with bottled water.

Franklin's thoughts rambled. He remembered the agency, and the glory days, and reminisced about how he had been an agent within an agency within an agency. He laughed when he saw a recent interview given by Richard Helms, former Director of the CIA, whereby Helms had said that it was virtually impossible for rogue elements to be running around within the CIA. What did that reporter expect? That Helms would say yes? Reporters; what bastards, stewed Franklin.

Franklin remembered what Allen Dulles had said about how an agent would lie to protect the agency and its secrets no matter what, even under oath. The agent might, Dulles had said, tell his superior, maybe the president, but that might not always be the case.

Franklin has been an active member of the Association of Former Intelligence Officers for the past twenty years. He loved to travel to Washington once a year for the annual luncheon and reminisce with old contacts, such as Helms and David Atlee Phillips, the former Chief of Western Hemisphere Division. Phillips was actually in charge of the Mexico City operation and had sent a photograph to the FBI on November 22, 1963 of Lee Harvey Oswald entering the Russian embassy in Mexico City on October 1, 1963. The photograph didn't even closely resemble Oswald and the CIA had to later admit that it wasn't Oswald.

Franklin thought about Iran-Contra—which was long after his retirement—and how the players had been amateurs. "You don't run an operation out of the White House basement like that," Franklin laughed to himself. Didn't they learn from Nixon?

No, in his day professionals like him knew how to run covert operations, hide them from the White House, Congress, and even the agency at large for that matter, despite what Richard Helms had said. He had known Helms and knew that Helms would never, like Dulles said, admit agency secrets, or protocol. Notwithstanding our free and open (some would say liberal) press, they could, as in the case with Reagan, be used and toyed with.

Franklin had learned by way of the best possible means, on the job training in World War II. He and the boys always cleaned up after themselves after each operation so no loose ends would unravel and rear their ugly heads down the line. Even after having been out of the business for all these years in retirement, a loose end from time to time would pop up.

One such loose end was Richard Nagell, although Franklin thought Nagell was nuts. Nagell always threatened to spout off whatever little he might have picked up, despite never having been involved or evidence that he claimed he had. To this day Franklin hadn't seen the evidence. And it hadn't turned up at Nagell's sister's house like Nagell said it would upon his death. If he had this evidence, why hadn't he turned it over to either the FBI or the media? Nevertheless, when Franklin found out where Nagell was, Franklin made a phone call and Nagell turned up dead in a run down shack along the 101 freeway in Los Angeles in late 1995.

Franklin's mind wandered back to another loose end that had never been tied up. He thought about it for the longest time. Unlike Nagell, this other loose end had never turned up anywhere to say anything. He had just disappeared into the Pandemonium that day. After all these years, Franklin figured that it didn't matter anymore. If this loose end hadn't said anything yet, he never will. Yet, it dug at him that he and the boys were never able to locate the final loose end. Apparently, he reasoned, this man was too clever and had already made plans before that tumultuous day. Franklin had to give him that much, but he still considered the case open until he heard word as to his whereabouts, or Franklin himself was dead.

Cheryl decided to keep her Grandmother's house for herself. It would take the system a couple months to formalize the paper work, so she decided to take a trip to where all those letters she had found in her grandmother's closet had been post marked: Syracuse, New York.

She had already opened up several safe deposit boxes at several different Huntsville, Alabama area banks and stuffed in as much cash as she could in each box. She paid the rent on each box for several years in advance.

She had the cash on hand, so she decided that she would utilize it as often as she could, instead of using her credit card. Sure enough, unbeknownst to Cheryl, the authorities at the airport notified the Feds as soon as she bought her ticket in cash. They followed her to her gate and watched her for several minutes while she waited for her plane.

The two federal agents looked puzzled but they had to stick to SOP and search her.

The taller agent signaled to a uniformed airport security officer who was standing nearby waiting for the word to move in. He approached.

"Excuse me ma'am, could you come with us please?" asked the security officer.

Cheryl was apprehensive. "What's wrong, officer?"

"We'll talk in the office."

The agents followed Cheryl and the officer to the security office.

Cheryl was led into an office that was just off the concourse. The agents closed the door behind her. She sat in front of the desk.

"May I see some identification, Ma'am?" asked one of the agents not so much as a request, but as an order.

Cheryl handed the agent her driver's license.

"It's standard procedure when anyone buys a ticket in cash, Miss Taylor. We just need to search your bags."

The other agent took that remark as his authorization and snatched up Cheryl's carry-on bag. He rummaged around through her bag but didn't find anything that would signal to him that she wasn't anything but an average law abiding citizen. He shook his head at the other agent.

"My grandmother just died," said Cheryl nervously. "I need a vacation and am using some cash she had rolled up and pinned to her bra for emergencies."

"I'm sorry for the inconvenience, Miss Taylor." The first agent handed Cheryl her identification. She secured it in her purse and collected her bag. She looked around at the agents.

"You're free to go."

Cheryl promptly got up and returned to the passenger waiting area. She had to take several minutes to regain her composure. She felt she had been treated like a criminal. God, she stewed. They thought I was a drug smuggler or something. She boarded her flight shortly thereafter.

Judge Bell couldn't wait for the weekends anymore. He couldn't wait to retire to the Osprey permanently, which would be soon. He only wished that his wife, Rebecca, could have lived to enjoy the elder years. Damn, he cried internally, she was robbed, like so many are, of a long life and to enjoy the golden years after all the hard work. She had been a court reporter, where the Judge had met her, thirty-five ago. He could never love another he decided after her death.

He sat on the bench this day and let his mind wander. The case was about some hood in a slick suit—they all looked the same to the Judge after a while—who was being prosecuted by the federal government for interstate drug smuggling. The laws had gotten tougher, which meant longer stiff sentences, even in plea bargains, so therefore the accused had to plead not guilty and hope that his shifty lawyer could get him off.

Judge Bell knew very well that the drug war would continue forever, so long as there was demand, there would be supply. It kept everyone employed, even the DEA, he chuckled to himself. Look at how much money was spent on law enforcement, court proceedings; this drug business kept everyone going around in circles.

"I've heard enough for today," said Judge Bell slamming down his gavel so hard that it took most by surprise. "Court adjourned. Monday morning, nine A.M." He sprinted for his chambers.

He quickly tidied up his chambers and just before rushing out the door, went over to turn off his computer. The computer screen showed the emblem for the United States Federal court system.

Judge Bell drove the long drive to Stillwater where Andy was waiting near the landing. Andy had already refueled the boat cans and had made reservations at the Stillwater eatery, The Black Bear.

"I just got in. You're early," said Andy.

"I closed court early."

"You can do that?" asked Andy as they walked over to the Black Bear.

"It's my courtroom. I'm the Judge. I can do what I want."

"I thought it was the people's court?"

"I'm not Judge Wapner."

"I meant, the court is federal, it belongs to the American people," said Andy seriously.

"Yeah, something like that," said Judge Bell as he opened the door to the restaurant to let Andy pass.

Andy and the Judge sat at a table and each ordered fish-n-chips.

"I started building Walker's porch yesterday," said Andy trying to engage his distant father in conversation. "I'm going to build a larger one, much like the Osprey so Walker can sit outside and enjoy his final years."

"His final years?" The Judge laughed.

"He went to Lowville and has to go again next week."

"He's sick?"

"He has coughing spells with blood."

"He smokes like a chimney," said Judge Bell pouring his beer into its frosty glass after the waitress had set it down. "I have a case coming up where a smoker dying of lung cancer is suing a tobacco manufacturer. Poor bastard will die before it gets to the jury."

"And the case you're on now?"

"More drugs." Judge Bell looked past Andy thinking about his deceased wife again.

"So nicotine is a drug, it's addictive."

"One expert says it is, another say it's not. How do you weigh their expertise? I still think it killed your mother. Her father smoked two or more packs a day and your mother breathed that crap in for all those years as a kid."

"Isn't that a conflict of interest? Shouldn't you, what's the term, recuse yourself from the case?"

"No, because the cause of your mother's cancer wasn't ever established. It's only conjecture."

There was a long tense silence while both father and son remembered their wife and mother.

"There's something really strange about him," said Andy breaking the silence, "Walker, I mean. He's a really nice guy, but he doesn't say much." Those weapons were right on the tip of his tongue, but he bit it to keep himself quiet.

"It's none of our business. Perhaps something traumatic happened in his life and he left it behind. People crack, Andy. Like I said, this is America and the man is entitled to his privacy. You're a student of government and should realize that."

Andy pondered and organized his thoughts as their fish-n-Chips arrived. Somberly, he said, "I'm not sure about my plans."

Judge Bell crunched on his fish and waited for Andy to continue.

"I've decided not to go on to law school."

His father took in a deep sigh.

"I just don't think it's as noble as it was."

"Okay." The Judge looked down at his plate. Andy knew his father was disappointed since he had almost entirely paid Andy's way.

"I want to do something else, but am not sure what. Maybe help people or something."

"Lawyers don't help people?"

"Some do. The truly down trodden, I suppose. But it doesn't seem perhaps as rewarding as it must've been in your day."

Judge Bell spoke while he ate. "What did Shakespeare say? Kill all the lawyers. It's not exactly a novel concept."

"Yeah, but I want to do more. Something else."

"Perhaps you should take a year off after you graduate and think things over."

"You know I watch you and hear you grumble about the courts these days."

His father stopped eating. "I've not been a good influence in that regard. You shouldn't listen to all my ramblings."

"So I shouldn't listen."

"I didn't say that."

There was a long silence, save the sound of his father eating. Andy had never been close with his father. The Judge obviously had always been too busy. Before being appointed to the federal bench by President Ford, he had been a justice department prosecutor and before that a deputy DA for Onondaga County. He wasn't there for Andy as a child, wasn't there to really give advice when a young kid needed it most. Although, because his father wasn't so demanding and overbearing, Andy turned out all right. The Judge knew how that when some parents were strict, their kids sometimes rebelled and got into trouble. He let Andy do what he wanted and Andy never got into serious trouble like so many kids today did.

"You're anticipating retirement more and more."

His father finished his drink. "It's even more political these days, if you can believe that. We're second-guessed, overturned, now more than ever. The courts convict criminals who go free on technicalities later on. Usually because we allowed this, didn't allow that. It's subjective. That's the great American legal conundrum. The law means whatever those above us say it means at that particular time, and it should be flexible to the times in which we live, but they get ridiculous, political appointees. Don't think for one moment that a federal judge isn't a political appointment."

"And you?"

His father shrugged his shoulders. He looked at Andy who sat quietly. "Look, don't take what I say. You have to do what you have to do. You have to go out and figure things out for yourself. It's just that I'm tired, I miss your mother, and I live for nothing but all this." He waved his hand around. "I've worked fourteen, sixteen hour days for almost forty years, from school to the DA's office to the bench. I'm not a political animal who seeks a higher office. I've worked hard for my retirement and want to enjoy it."

The Judge tossed his napkin onto his empty plate. "You're young, idealistic. That's what this country needs. Do what you want. If you want to work in government to help make this country or world a better place, it's still a worthwhile endeavor. If not, that's your choice too." He could see Andy thinking. "Well, I've said enough."

Andy knew he was displeased. He didn't care, however. They were silent after dinner when they boated over to Beaver River. Andy looked out at the setting summer sun as the waves splashed up against the boat. His thoughts went back to Walker as he focused on the wake behind the boat.

Four

Cheryl had no idea what she was doing. She checked into a motel in Syracuse and lay down on the bed. Every one of the envelopes that her grandmother had received was post-marked from the same post office. She would start there, but had no idea how to go about her task. She had to try, otherwise this mystery would eat at her forever. Her grandmother had a secret and she apparently had told no one. Cheryl had to find out who was sending this money, why, and why for over thirty years.

After sleeping for nine hours, Cheryl got up the next morning and made her way over to the post office shortly after it had opened. It was a small post office and had four windows, but only two tellers on duty at present. There were three people in line so she waited her turn. When called, she took out one of her grandmother's envelopes.

"I have an unusual question," Cheryl said to the woman who threw back a pleasant smile.

"Yes?"

"I have this envelope. It's post marked from here. You see, my grandmother recently passed away and I wanted to find out who was sending them."

The woman examined the envelope and handed it back to Cheryl. "I'll have to let you speak with my supervisor."

The woman went into the back room. A moment later a man appeared. The manager took Cheryl aside. She explained the situation and handed the post-marked envelope to the supervisor.

"Well, ma'am," said the supervisor, "there's no way to tell. As long as the mail is deliverable, we deliver it. If it's not, then we are allowed to open it and find out if we can send it back to the party who sent it."

"But there's nothing inside that indicates who sends these," explained Cheryl frustrated. "My grandmother died and they're all post-marked on or near the first of each month."

"I don't know what to tell you. There's really nothing we can do. It could be dropped in any box within this office's area of operation."

Cheryl sighed deeply. "There's no way you could alert your letter carriers to be on the look-out so we can find out where they're dropped off?"

"We're treading on sensitive grounds. Besides, we don't have the time to do special searches."

"There's nothing criminal going on here."

"I don't know."

Cheryl looked down at the floor and acted distressed.

"Let me keep this and I'll alert my carriers. Where are you staying?"

"Here." Cheryl wrote down where and the phone number. She handed it to the man. "Thanks. It means so much to me. Thank you."

The man watched her leave.

She went back to her motel room and lay on the bed. She stared at the ceiling wondering if perhaps she was wasting her time.

Andy was indeed building Walker a spacious porch. Walker didn't know what to make of it. He thought it was large enough to live on.

"Don't you think you're building it too big?"

"I don't mind, Mr. Walker." Andy rested to chat.

"I mean, it's too big for my use." Walker unfolded a lawn chair and sat nearby.

"Well, this way you could sit outside and enjoy the air and scenery. You do have one of the most beautiful spots in Beaver River, you know, being on an island and all." Andy tried to engage Walker in conversation, but Walker was distant.

After a long uneasy moment, Andy said, "You have one of the most isolated places here."

"So you're saying I'm strange for being a hermit?"

"No, I just think—"

"Don't think, kid. It's dangerous." Walker coughed a spell, then lit a cigarette. Andy studied him out of the corner of his eye.

"We're encouraged to think in a democracy, Mr. Walker."

"Huh?"

"Thinking. In a democracy."

"What did you say you're studying?"

"Well, at present, political science."

Walker took a heavy drag on his cigarette and stared Andy down. "Political science?" Walker said that like it was a joke. "Why?"

"Why what?"

"Why study political science?"

"To…understand it and make things work better. Most go on to law school."

Walker laughed in between another coughing spell. "Make what work better?"

"Society, government."

"You're wasting your time."

"I don't think so."

"Have you discovered just what government is the best form of government?"

"Well…a democracy, of course."

"You think the people pick the best government?"

Andy thought it over. "Perhaps…not always." Andy now felt defensive. He'd gotten the old man to open up for a debate about the state of affairs, which to Andy it seemed that he hadn't followed for many years, and now Walker went on the attack.

"Democracy is make believe," said Walker.

"I don't follow."

"Money."

"Money?"

"Money is the government. Everything else, the president, congress, the courts, is window dressing." Walker took a deep drag on his cigarette and held it deep.

"Yes, money is power," countered Andy trying to get in a lick and sound important.

"You're kidding," Walker grinned.

Andy knew it sounded pedestrian as he said it, but he had to say something.

"It doesn't matter what window dressing you use," continued Walker, "monarchy, autocracy, democracy, socialism, money is what rules over us; money is the government, under any arrangement. How it's collected and distributed, again, that's all idiomatic to the time in which it's used. Communism, well I think all would agree now that it's impossible because of the human animal. Marx was wrong. He was a pathetic, bitter and poor exiled newspaperman. They're creatures of the night."

Andy didn't know what to say. He was taken back by Walker's outburst, and at the same time interested now about Walker's insights, or rather, outlook. "I didn't know you were interested in philosophy."

Walker threw Andy an annoyed glance, got up and folded his lawn chair. "I used to work for the government."

Andy watched him as he hobbled up the newly built platform.

Walker stopped and sensed Andy's suppression. "Forget what I just said, kid. I don't want to discourage you."

Walker went into his cabin and closed the door.

Andy sat there for a few moments. What the hell had gotten to this guy? He thought about what his father had said at the Black Bear. Had old age made him sour too, or realistic? Something or someone had shafted him.

It was getting late, so Andy picked up his tools and stored them in Walker's shed. He couldn't wait to pick at Walker more when he got the chance. He's got to know what drove this old angry man into isolation and why he's so contemptuous.

When Andy learned the truth, well, he'll have wished he had never pried.

The weekend went by uneventfully. Andy worked on Walker's porch, Walker moped about, and Judge Bell went fishing on the reservoir. When Sunday night came, Andy took his father back to Stillwater so the Judge could get back to the bench for his Monday morning session.

On Monday morning Walker got up early and headed out across Norridgewock Lake. He docked at Richardson's Lodge and went down to the landing on the reservoir. He certainly wasn't moving as fast as he used to, so the trip took longer. Surely he would be late for his appointment he stewed to himself. He used his cane to push off from the dock at the landing. He throttled his boat and gently boated out onto the calm morning waters.

Andy got up when he heard Walker's boat pass by on the lake, although he didn't know who it was, nor did he look to see. He took his time getting breakfast and then headed out towards Walker's asylum about 45 minutes later.

When Andy got up to the porch, he saw a note stuck to the front door. It read: "I have to go into Lowville. Be back in short order. Walker."

Andy worked on the porch as his mind raced with thoughts of being a snoop. Walker would be gone for hours, he reasoned. Why not? Although he should wait, he agreed, just a little while longer to give Walker time to be far enough away so that Walker couldn't double back and catch him by accident.

He'd finish the wall for the porch he was working on, then he'd look around. He had to. Curiosity about this old creep was eating at him.

The annoying ring of the motel telephone awakened Cheryl.

"Miss Taylor?" A voice over the phone said.

"Yes?"

"This is Mr. Kamp, at the post office. I have something for you."

"Thanks. I'll be right there." Cheryl sprang into action and hurried on over to the post office.

The supervisor, Mr. Kamp, whom Cheryl spoke with yesterday, stood behind the counter. He saw Cheryl rush in and signaled for her to go to the back.

"This is Mrs. Kenyon," said Mr. Kamp. "She may be able to help you, but I must tell you again, Miss Taylor, this all stays within this room. Understand?"

"Yes, sir," said Cheryl in her polite Southern accent.

The supervisor disappeared into a back office leaving Cheryl and Mrs. Kenyon standing there. "I've worked the same route for eleven years now," said Kenyon. "Let me tell you, they better switch my route or promote me soon or I'll—well, never mind. Anyway, this envelope," she handed the envelope Cheryl had given the supervisor back to Cheryl, "I've noticed it in the same box. Sometimes there's very few letters in that box, and that's why I've noticed this one. I of course think nothing of it, except that it never has no return address, but if it's deliverable, we deliver it."

"Where's the box?" asked Cheryl politely.

"Here," said Kenyon pointing to a map she had in her hand. "This is my route."

"Today's the first. It should be dropped off about now. If I watch the box, can you alert me when it's dropped?"

Kenyon gave her an uncertain look and raised her eyebrows.

"Please. This is for my dead grandmother. I've got to know."

"Okay, I'll keep an eye out. But I didn't do this."

"I understand. Thank you," said Cheryl turning to go.

"What're you going to do? Stake it out?" asked Kenyon calling out.

"If that's what it takes." Cheryl darted out of the post office.

She walked to a nearby convenient store and purchased cheap binoculars, a baseball cap, a notebook and a couple of pens, and some bottled water. She then walked across the street and rented a two-door sedan, then drove the five blocks to where the mailbox was located.

The box was on the corner opposite a bank. She parked the car on the opposite side of the street from the box near a driveway to a house. She slightly obscured herself from the point of view of the box. There she waited and watched.

"We have to start treatment right away, Al," said Doc Bergholtz.

"And if we don't?" asked an uneasy Walker shifting in a chair in front of the doctor's desk.

"You'll be dead in six months."

Walker shrugged his shoulders.

Doc Bergholtz shook his head. "What the hell's the matter with you? With treatment, we can buy time."

"Time?" Walker looked down at the tip of his cane.

"I can't guarantee anything, but we could be talking a years at least, and if we're completely successful, you could just die of old age."

Walker laughed. "Doc, look at me. What's old age?"

"In the minds of many, it doesn't exist. George Burns was one hundred."

"He died?"

"You don't follow the news?"

"Not lately." Walker stared out the window while the doctor studied him.

"You want to die, don't you, Al?"

Walker looked back at the doctor.

"I know it's none of my business, but why?" asked Bergholtz.

Walker's eyes seemed to look right on through Doc Bergholtz as he slowly spoke. "I've cheated death for over thirty years. But I've lived each and every day in my own hell. Hiding from my past, left the ones I loved, for their safety I must say." He paused and seemed to snap out of his trance. "This treatment, how's it work?"

"We'd have to admit you for each round of therapy. A few days for each round. We'll have to remove a part of your lung."

"I don't know yet. What's the use, I say?" He raised his hand to stop the Doc from responding. "You've made your point. I appreciate it. I'll let you know in a couple days. A couple days won't matter will they?"

Bergholtz shook his head. "But not more than a couple. Everyday we wait it gives it more time to spread."

"Okay." Walker got up to leave, but stopped and turned at the door. "Oh, I almost forgot. Here's Syracuse." He walked back to Bergholtz and handed him an envelope with a Huntsville address. There was no return address.

Bergholtz took the envelope and stuffed it into his lab coat. Walker closed the door behind him after leaving.

Andy had checked the back door and windows, but they were all closed and locked. Here it was, the hottest time of the year for this part of New York State, and Walker had the place sealed tighter than a sardine can.

He went back to the porch and began to work, but stopped and looked at the front door. "No. There's no way," said Andy out loud disbelieving.

He walked across the platform and stopped at the front door. He looked at the knob. It was as old as the cabin, it's original one, never been replaced. He turned the knob. The door opened. Andy just stood there dumfounded. "I don't believe it! The old man forgot to lock the front door?"

Andy slowly entered. The cabin had a distinctive old and musty smell, like it hadn't been aired out for centuries. He left the door open so he could hear if a boat was to approach.

The front door opened into the kitchen. The main room with the loft was to the right. Nothing odd or unusual about the kitchen, so Andy sneaked into the main room.

The pot belly stove was there in the middle of the room, but what interested Andy immediately, was the shrine, or whatever it was against the back wall. Andy passed the boxes of army ammunition and assault rifles that decorated the front wall. He was transfixed and focused on the shrine.

The candle on the table in front was extinguished, but next to it was a statuette of what Andy thought must be Mary, the mother of Christ. Andy wasn't really religious, but his family background was Protestant. He didn't know too much about the Catholic faith, but he did realize that the catholic faith usually displayed the crucifix, as opposed to the Protestants who usually displayed the cross. Walker displayed a crucifix behind the candle. Rosary beads hung around the crucifix.

This shrine was certainly spooky. The picture above the table fore-shadowed the whole scene in an ominous way. There, hung on the wall, was a copy of the famous painting of President Kennedy by Aaron Shikler, the one where Kennedy is standing with his arms folded look-ing down at the floor. Andy had taken the tour of the White House a few years ago, and was certain that this was a copy of the one that hung there.

How odd, he thought. He backed up and looked around. He saw a couple of large chests against the sidewall. He moved slowly towards them, thinking that something was about to jump out at him. They were dusty, and locked. He looked around for a key, but couldn't locate one.

He heard a boat approaching. "Shit!" Andy darted out the door and closed it behind him. Off in the distance he could see Walker approaching. Distance hell, he thought. It was too close. Perhaps Walker's eye sight wasn't that good anymore. "Damn," he mumbled grappling with some lumber.

Walker docked and made his slow trek up the path. He carried a bag of groceries. "Looks good, but I don't know who'll use it," he said huffing under his breath.

"I'm sure you'll enjoy it when it's finished," disputed Andy.

Walker climbed the newly built steps and approached his door. Andy watched out of the corner of his eye while he aligned a 2X4 for the saw.

Walker tried to put his key into the lock, but it wouldn't fit. He tried jamming it in, but it still wouldn't go in. He turned the knob and opened the door instead. He turned to Andy.

Andy started sawing to hide his red and embarrassed face.

"I keep forgetting," said Walker. "Are you going into Lowville soon?"

"I could go tomorrow," said Andy nervously not looking at Walker.

"I've been meaning to get a new door knob. This one's rusted through. Could you pick one up?"

"UH, sure," said Andy relieved but still not looking at him.

Walker went into the kitchen and returned to the porch a minute later. "Here's a twenty. Keep the rest for yourself." He passed off the twenty to Andy who took it and jammed it into his pocket.

Walker went back inside and closed his door.

"Whew." Andy let out a little air. He finished the final wall to the porch. All he had left to do was put the screen around the porch and affix a door. He picked up his tools for the day and went back to the Osprey.

Andy collapsed on the couch on the porch. What's with this guy? Andy wondered. Some kind of a shrine to JFK? Had the death of JFK sent him over the edge? Sure it hurt a lot of people, but they didn't run away from the world. They went on with their lives and everything went back to normal. And what's with all those weapons and ammunition? Was it for a small war, perhaps to defend Beaver River from an invasion?

From whom? He didn't belong to one of those secret militias? No. He never went anywhere. He couldn't be involved in any. Andy's mind ran around in circles for awhile until he drifted off for a nap.

Five

Cheryl had kept a log of everyone who made a drop the first day. She meticulously described in detail the people, their cars, their license plate numbers, (actually, most drop-offs were from people on foot), and anything else notable. She noted the time, their ages, everything.

There were only fourteen people on day one and no one looked unusual. The letter carrier opened the box at about 4:30 and shook her head at Cheryl indicating that the letter was not there. No one dropped off a letter after the pick-up. Cheryl went back to the motel shortly after seven P.M. The thought did cross her mind that the person doing this could drop the letter off when she wasn't there. Nevertheless, she couldn't sit around in this car all night.

Cheryl still didn't know how she would know if and when the person she was looking for made the drop. It could be today; it could be a few days from now. But it would happen soon, since the postmark was always about this time of the month. She realized that she would have to sit for a few days, see if the letter showed up in the letter carrier's bag, and then when it did, she would come back next month and see who on her log showed up to make the drop when the letter turned up in the carrier's bag next month. Could she really go through with this? It could take months! She only hoped Mrs. Kenyon would cooperate next month. Cheryl realized that Kenyon and her supervisor could get into trouble or something. There probably was some federal law or regulation that was at issue, she figured.

Cheryl parked in the same spot this day and worried that someone might get suspicious seeing this car parked with a girl inside using binoculars spying on people dropping off mail. She'd deal with it when and if caught.

By 3PM this day there had been only six drop-offs. Four were on foot, and two by car. Cheryl logged what she could.

Doc Bergholtz drove up in his pick-up and parked in the bank. He got out of his truck and crossed the street at the corner. He walked towards the mailbox. When he got there, he quickly dropped Walker's letter in. He walked back to his truck, got something out of it and went into the bank.

Cheryl noted the whole episode. She didn't notice him coming, but she did watch through her binoculars as he went back to his truck.

She got out and quickly went over to the Doc's truck. She noted that the dealer's advertisement around the rear license plate said Lowville, NY. She also noted the Doctor's advertisement on the side doors of his truck: DOCTOR BERGHOLTZ, MD, GENERAL PRACTITIONER, LOWVILLE, NY.

Cheryl returned to her car and waited until Bergholtz came out of the bank. As he headed to his truck, Cheryl took out a picture of her grandmother standing hand in hand with the mystery man over thirty or more years ago. She compared Bergholtz to the man in the picture. So long ago, Cheryl thought, but the features seemed wrong.

Cheryl watched Bergholtz drive off. She waited to almost five O'clock. She got hungry and had to go to the restroom. There was a cafe next to the bank that she had used, and she hoped that that wouldn't be the time when she missed the drop. Perhaps, she thought, this was a wild goose chase after all.

As she was getting out of her car, she saw Mrs. Kenyon pull up in her mail jeep. Kenyon saw her and nodded. Cheryl decided to walk over and talk with her.

Kenyon opened the mailbox and pulled out that distinctive white plastic United States Mail crate that the letters inside a mailbox dropped into.

"I don't know, Mrs. Kenyon," said Cheryl approaching, "perhaps this is crazy."

"I can understand." Kenyon handpicked up the few letters that were there. She threw them one at a time into another box that she used to collect the bulk of the boxes she emptied. Near the top of the pile, there it was; the mystery envelope. "Oh my God!" She handed it to Cheryl.

"That's it." Cheryl handed it back to Kenyon. "There were seven people. Thanks. Thank you very much." Cheryl turned and started back towards her car.

"Remember our deal, Miss Taylor."

Cheryl waved at Kenyon. Kenyon finished loading her mail, got into her truck and drove off. Cheryl studied her log. She could definitely discard her log from yesterday, and concentrate on the seven entries for today.

The more she sat there, the more Cheryl concluded that the out-of-town Doctor Bergholtz made the most sense. Here these letters had been dropped mysteriously all these years, and if someone were going to all this trouble to conceal their identity, they wouldn't live around the corner from the mailbox. This person certainly drove in from out of town! Her other two entries that drove cars this day didn't stick out like Bergholtz had.

Cheryl looked at her map and saw that Lowville was a long drive. That's got to be it! She decided to get some rest at the motel and a fresh start in the morning. She drove off hoping her sleuthing was correct. Life was indeed, concluded Cheryl, a lot of hard work, and much more than that, luck.

It was mid-morning the next day when Andy walked out of the hardware store in Lowville with hardware supplies including Walker's new doorknob. He hopped into his Jeep and sat for a moment looking at the purchase. It was, he thought, unethical, not to mention illegal, but there was something that this old kook was hiding, and by God, Andy had to satisfy his curiosity.

Andy got out of his Jeep and returned to the store. He had an extra key of Walker's new doorknob made. He put the extra key on his own ring and started up his Jeep. He drove out into the street and passed Cheryl who was driving in the opposite direction.

Andy drove back to Stillwater while Cheryl drove up to the service station. She checked the phone book. She wrote down the address of Bergholtz, got back into her rental, and checked her map. Luckily, Bergholtz's practice was on the main drag, State Street.

Cheryl drove to Bergholtz's office and parked. She was nervous. Somehow she hoped she had the wrong guy. At the same time, however, she knew that this man was going to deny that he had been sending these envelopes all those years. She realized her detective work wasn't over. After he denied it, then what? She didn't know.

Bergholtz was with a patient. His receptionist, Betty, champing on a wad of gum, looked up when Cheryl entered. "May I help you?"

"AH, yes. I'm obviously from out of town," said Cheryl referring to her accent, "but I have this unusual pain in my chest. I saw that this was a doctor's office and decided to stop."

Betty looked her over. "I guess we could squeeze you in. Do you have medical insurance?"

"Well, it's an HMO in Alabama, but I can pay in cash." Cheryl took out a wad of twenty-dollar bills and dropped them on Betty's desk.

Betty's eyes went wide. "That's not necessary, Ma'am." Betty picked up the money and handed it back to her. "Just fill out these forms please," Betty said as she handed Cheryl a clipboard full of forms.

Cheryl sat in the waiting room for twenty minutes before Doc Bergholtz emerged from his exam room with a patient. The Doc saw Cheryl sitting there so he smiled and nodded.

Betty handed the Doc the clipboard that Cheryl had filled out. "Miss Taylor," said the Doc motioning for Cheryl to come into the exam room.

Cheryl got up. Her mind raced with trepidation. When he denied it, would he get angry? Her palms were sweaty and her heart jumped around in her chest.

The Doc closed the door. "So, Miss Taylor, you're having some sort of chest pain?" said the Doc looking at the clipboard. "Please, sit on the exam table."

"I can't sit." Cheryl stood and faced Bergholtz to record his reaction. "I saw you drop an envelope similar to this one," she handed one of the envelopes to him, "in a mail box in Syracuse."

Bergholtz's own heart leapt out of his chest. "I don't know what this is, Miss." He handed the envelope back to Cheryl.

"My grandmother, Leonora Jackson, died last month."

Bergholtz turned to hide the sweat that had begun to build upon his upper lip like Nixon's when he lied. He blotted it with his handkerchief.

"You don't need to send them anymore."

The Doc turned to face Cheryl. "I'm sorry ma'am, but I don't know what you're talking about."

"Were you an old boyfriend or something?"

"I think you're going to have to leave now."

"Is this you in the picture?" Cheryl tried to hand Bergholtz the photograph of her grandmother and this man, but he wouldn't take it. He went over to open the door.

"It doesn't look like you," continued Cheryl. "I mean, even though it's many years ago, this man I think looks different."

"I'm sorry, ma'am, you'll have to leave."

"Your act was less than convincing, Doctor. I saw you drop off the letter and I now know you're covering for someone. I can see it in your eyes." Cheryl dropped the photograph on the exam table and walked past Bergholtz. "I'll be in town for a while." She went back out to her car and sat.

Doc Bergholtz closed the door to his office. He wiped the sweat from his face. Walker had never told him what was in the letters, except they were for family. He placed a phone call.

"Beaver River Lodge," answered Dusty over the phone.

"Hey, Dusty, how are you?" asked Bergholtz. "Its, Doc Bergholtz."

"Fine, Doc, thanks."

"Could you get a message to Al Walker for me?"

"Sure. What is it?"

"Just have him call me as soon as he can. It's about some tests we're running."

"Okay, Doc."

"Thanks." Bergholtz hung up the phone. He leaned back and caught his breath. After all these years, for once a month to run errands for his practice, pick up supplies, visit family, and drop off those envelopes. For more than thirty years and nothing. Bergholtz realized, as did all of Beaver River, that Walker was a mysterious man with no history known in these parts. Better left alone they figured.

But now this young woman shows up, as smart as she is to figure this out. She looked harmless. This Cheryl Taylor, whoever she was, acted determined to find Walker. That would be up to Walker, not him, he said to himself.

Dusty ran the note down to the Osprey and caught Andy who was loading up the small craft to head over to Walker's. Andy buzzed on over and docked the boat on the opposite side of Walker's rickety dock. Another project that he could build perhaps, or so he thought.

Andy strolled up to the newly built front porch that did look good, he thought proudly. He rapped on Walker's door.

There was no answer. He turned and looked at Walker's boat docked behind him on the lake. He knocked again. No answer.

He walked around to the side of the cabin and looked. "Mr. Walker? Its, Andy."

Nothing. He returned to the front door and knocked again. Still nothing. Damn, he thought. Did the old man go and die on him now just as he was increasing the value of his property?

He tried the doorknob. Sure enough, it turned. He looked out over the front yard. "Mr. Walker?" Well, he won't mind, I'm sure, Andy figured. He slowly opened the front door and entered the cabin. "Mr. Walker?"

He worried again about finding a dead man. He set the bag on the kitchen table and crept into the main room.

There, in the corner of the room, lying on a bed, was the body of Mr. Walker. "Mr. Walker?" Andy called out one more time.

Walker sprang up out of a deep sleep and sat in a sitting position. He instantly engaged an AR-15 assault rifle that he had next to him. He quickly pulled the cocking handle back and chambered a round. His finger was on the trigger and he was ready to cut Andy in half at the torso when Andy threw up his arms and screamed, "Its, me Mr. Walker, Andy!"

Walker had had a nightmare and was soaked in sweat. He dreamt that someone, after all these years, was going to find him.

Walker quickly apologized. "I'm....Jesus, I'm sorry, Andy." He put the rifle down and struggled to stand up. "I'll meet you on the porch."

Andy backed out the front door and stood on the lower set of steps. What the hell had just happened? His hands trembled.

Walker emerged from the door and closed it behind him. He wiped sweat from his face with a handkerchief.

"I put your new door knob on the kitchen table," said Andy under a nervous voice.

"Good. Well...I'll AH, let you get back to work then." Walker just began to realize what he had done to this poor boy. Would he now suspect something? He was surprised Andy hadn't run off. In truth, Andy really couldn't have engaged his legs to run if he had tried.

"Dusty Richardson sent a message." Andy stepped forward slowly and handed the folded paper to Walker.

Walker read the simple note and put it in his pocket.

Andy had naturally peeked, but all it said was, "Call Doc Bergholtz immediately."

Walker retrieved the new doorknob and gave it to Andy to install.

"Put this on for me. I have to make a phone call."

Andy watched out of the corner of his eye as Walker shuffled on down to his boat. The guy doesn't even have a telephone! No television, from what Andy could remember either. He thought he saw an old radio in the kitchen, however.

He installed the new doorknob then worked on putting the new porch door in place. He couldn't believe what had just happened. Walker was a time bomb, survivalist, nut case, something! This man almost killed him! Why? Would Andy really want to know?

Judge Bell had heard enough. This slick drug peddler, Tommy Scardino, sat in that chair dressed in his Armani suit looking cocky that this Judge would be intimated enough to give him an easy sentence. Tommy Scardino was a handsome hood in his late twenties. Getting all the girls, it's a shame he was a piece of shit.

Tommy's lawyer, up from the bowels of New York City, Attorney Jerry Goetherd, sat next to Scardino looking just as smug. Goetherd was notorious for representing the underworld. His gold Rolex and necklace glistened in the florescent light.

"Mr. Goetherd?"

Goetherd stood with a swatch of forms. "I move to dismiss on the grounds that—"

"Sit down and shut up," said Andy's father angrily. He had had enough of Goetherd's sneaky courtroom maneuvering. "The Supreme Court has already ruled that the confiscation of property in the commission of drug related offenses is constitutional. It's not double jeopardy."

Goetherd stood to protest once again. "I must object and move—"

"Once more, Goetherd and I'll hold you in contempt. Now, shut your trap." Judge Bell shifted authoritatively in his chair behind that rather large federal bench on high looking down like an eagle ready to snatch up its prey. "The property will remain confiscated," continued Bell. The property in question was a house, one Ferrari, one Lexus and other smaller, but not necessarily less expensive items.

Tommy Scardino's face twisted and changed its color to red. Goetherd sat defeated.

"Mr. Scardino, please rise," said the Judge breaking the repose.

Tommy rose from his seat defiantly, his body swaggering at his hips. Goetherd stood next to him.

"I am imposing the mandatory maximum sentence as allowed by law. Mr. Thomas Scardino will serve twenty-five to life. Parole will not be considered until twenty five years have been served." Bell slammed his gavel down.

Tommy nudged Goetherd's arm with his own. Goetherd shrugged his shoulders and whispered to Tommy, "We'll appeal."

"What good does that do me now?"

"Excuse me, Mr. Scardino. You wish to address the court?" asked the Judge.

"You won't get away wish this! You son-of-a-bitch!"

"Bailiff, get him out of my courtroom!"

Tommy struggled with the bailiff and another had to be called in.

In the back of the room, Jimmy Scardino stood and rushed forward. "Tommy, we'll get you out!" He was stopped and held back by yet another bailiff who had just entered the courtroom. Jimmy Scardino, Tommy's younger brother, was a young hood who worked for Donny Rossetti, their uncle. Jimmy was short, but muscular. He almost looked like a dwarf on steroids. Despite working out on weights feverishly to impress the women that came through his uncle Donny's nightclub in Brooklyn, he usually only attracted neighborhood girls looking to be a gangster's gal.

Tommy yelled at Judge Bell as he was being handcuffed on the floor in the prostrate position. Goetherd stood by in shock.

"I'm coming for you Bell. You son-of-a-bitch! You're a dead man!"

"Tommy, shut up," insisted Goetherd.

The Bailiffs got Tommy to his feet.

"I'm adding on six months to be consecutively served for threatening a federal judge," blurted out Bell quickly. "Mr. Scardino, you will not be eligible for parole until you're past your prime!" Judge Bell slammed his gavel down hard. "Get him out of here!" Judge Bell went into his chambers and slammed the door. He could still hear Tommy hollering from the courtroom as he was dragged away.

Jimmy angrily stood in the courtroom listening to Tommy being dragged off. Jimmy looked over at the door to the Judge's Chambers. He stood there scowling for several minutes, his face contorted in anger.

Andy's father hung up his robe and sat at his desk. He stared at a picture of his deceased wife.

Walker's face turned ashen. "Who?" he asked over the phone.

"Says she's Cheryl Taylor, from Huntsville," said Bergholtz over the phone. "She's sitting in a car in my lot and says she won't go away. She has a picture of you as a young man with some woman."

Walker sat on the stool that was under the phone in the main dining room of the lodge. He massaged his forehead. "It could be a trap," said Walker sounding muddled. "Get rid of her."

"What?" asked Bergholtz confused.

"I don't know any Cheryl Taylor."

"Look, Al, I've done this for you for what, more than thirty years. I never asked questions. You had to expect that this would happen sooner or later."

Walker hung up on Bergholtz. He stood up with cane in hand and scanned the dining room. Ronny was the only one there. Walker looked away and headed for the door.

"Everything all right, Al?" asked Ronny.

"I…I don't know." Walker stumbled out the door and down the path to his boat. He had another coughing spell and almost fell overboard when he started the motor. Half way across Norridgewock Lake he passed Andy who was heading back to the Osprey.

Andy waved from a distance, but Walker never acknowledged him. Andy shook his head. Old wacko!

Back at the Osprey he made himself a roast beef sandwich for his dinner. After dinner, Andy took out his laptop computer. He started to work on his senior thesis. His thesis focused on the presidential primary process. His premise would be that such a sparsely populated state, New Hampshire, with problems and concerns usually disparate than that of the rest of the country, had too much power in selecting nominees for the two major parties. He would show that more then half of the prospective presidential primary candidates over the last 40 years had dropped out of the race after New Hampshire and therefore the rest of the country was stuck with little choice. He would argue as many have for years now, that the system, by which Americans chose their nominees for their respective parties, needed reform.

Later Andy couldn't concentrate on his project. He closed his thesis file and created a new one. He named it Walker. He decided to make a journal. He recorded the strange near death event with Walker. He turned out the lights around midnight.

Six

Walker loaded up. He strapped the Cobray M11 sub-machine-gun under his arm in a leather shoulder holster. He wore a light jacket. He placed his cane beside him and motored across Norridgewock Lake. He docked at the Lodge.

Dusty heard a boat pull up and dock. He looked out his bedroom window and saw that it was Walker. After midnight? Strange. Certainly Walker was engaged in more activity than he ever had in the time he'd been in Beaver River. Dusty went back to bed while Walker headed down to the Grassy Point Landing.

By the time Walker got to Lowville it was well after two O'clock in the morning. He drove up and parked a couple blocks from Bergholtz's house. He hobbled over to Bergholtz's house staying in the shadows of the alley. He saw no one around, so he jimmied open Bergholtz's lock and sneaked into the house. In Bergholtz's bedroom, he flicked on the light and called out, "Where is she?"

Bergholtz sat up and screamed, "Jesus Christ, Al!"

Walker had his finger on the trigger and had it pointed at the doctor. He was frantic enough that he wouldn't hesitate a second to shoot off rounds at Bergholtz if Walker thought Bergholtz was not forthcoming.

"Where's the woman?"

"Al, she's a child. Twenty, twenty one at the most." Bergholtz was still getting his bearings in the dimly lit room, but could see that Walker looked demented.

"That's just who they'd send," said Walker scanning the room.

"Who who'd send?"

"Where is she, Doc, Goddamnit!"

"At…at the Hass Motel. She drove a rental."

Walker left as fast as his old legs could carry him. Bergholtz sat there in his bed stunned.

In room 7, at the Hass motel, Cheryl laid sleeping. She had turned out the lights around 12:30 after having surveyed several maps and her notes, plotting her next move. Clearly, Bergholtz was not the source of the envelopes, but was covering for who was. She thought she might have to harass this guy until he broke, or the real man showed up, since this Doc would certainly alert the man he was covering for. Cheryl had come this far; she wouldn't go back to Alabama until she had the answers to her questions.

Walker located the only new car in the lot. It must be the rental, since most were usually new cars. It was parked in front of room 7. There were only five other cars there. This had to be the one.

Inside, there was a loud THUMP against the door, like someone had run into it. Cheryl awoke, then froze. Silence. More than a moment passed.

At last, in a split second, the doorknob exploded in a quick succession of rounds. Cheryl cringed.

Walker stood on the other side looking like an old wretch from Hell, his face frozen in resolve. With his cane in one hand, and his other hand holding the gun, he stumbled just inside the door.

Cheryl sat absolutely still; there was no where to go. The horror registered on her face. She plainly saw the gun that he was holding.

Walker flicked on the light and got a visual fix on her. He hesitated on the trigger. He had come here to kill this woman, because she was clearly sent here to take him out! But, he stood there and stared at her.

An eternity passed by. She swallowed hard and said, "I've come from Alabama."

"Nora?" He barely had the breath to form the word. He thought he was seeing a ghost.

Its him, she knew. But, he's delusional. He thinks she's her grandmother. "No. I'm Nora's granddaughter, Cheryl Taylor."

He slurred his words. "I'm…I'm sorry, Nora."

She slowly edged up off the bed and towards him. She was certainly terrified and clearly understood that he was holding the gun on her, but she had to approach him. "I just had to find you after all these years."

"You look like when we first met. I'm an old man." He was bewildered.

"Grandmother Nora is dead. I'm Cheryl, her granddaughter."

"No. No, this is a trick."

"No. It's the truth."

"You look like Nora."

"Who are you?"

His hands trembled slightly. "You shouldn't have come here." He started to come out of his trance. "Go back to where you came from." He lowered the gun to his side.

"John, isn't it?"

He froze.

"John."

He shook his head. "No. No. Go back to where you came from." He re-holstered his weapon and slowly turned and limped back out into the parking lot.

She followed after him. "Who are you and what did you have to do with my grandmother?" She was right behind him. He turned and caught her off guard, pushing her away. He got into his car. He couldn't focus on the key. It wouldn't go into the ignition switch. He had to get a grip. He had never been in such poor shape.

Cheryl quickly ran back into her room and grabbed the keys to the car. She ran to the parking lot just as the man started his car. She hopped in and started hers, dressed in her light nightgown.

Walker drove off. Cheryl followed.

He turned down River Street heading East.

Cheryl pushed down the accelerator and saw Walker's old rusted out Electra as it made the turn. Even though it was an eight cylinder and in its time could have out run Cheryl's rental, there had been no need for Walker to keep it in top shape. That was evident as it coughed and spit like the old man who drove it.

Cheryl kept her distance and drove with her parking lights, not her headlights. Luckily the moon provided a bright ray and Cheryl wanted to follow this guy as far as she could. For about five miles Cheryl kept her distance along Number Four Road. At the Hamlet of Bushes Landing, she followed Walker as he turned left. For several miles she followed him until the Electra abruptly stopped. She stopped and kept her distance.

For five minutes they waited in this position. She had turned off the parking lights and let the car idle.

Three more minutes passed before Walker turned off his lights.

She didn't know what to do, or what he was doing. With the aid of her back-up lights, she slowly backed up as best she could without going off the road. She stopped the car and waited.

And she waited. She got more and more scared, until she turned on her headlights. Walker's Electra was no where to be found. "Damn it," she said. She had better turn around and head back knowing the way in which she came. Any further without maps and she would get lost.

Back at the Hass Motel the Sheriff's Deputy was waiting with the motel manager. Cheryl pulled up and parked. She got out and approached the two men. They were shocked to see her in her nightshirt. "Someone tried to rob me."

Cheryl told a story, not the true story. The deputy took the report. She gave a false description of a burglar.

She moved her things to another room for the rest of the night. She laid there thinking. She knew what this old man drove and what road she lost him on. She would continue the hunt tomorrow. Hopefully, the direction in which they had headed, was the true direction where this mystery man lived. Now more than ever she had to find out who he was, why he was hiding and running around with guns. He didn't kill her, she said over and over reassuringly to herself, despite the fact that she now realized that that was his original intention.

The fact was that Walker hadn't seen Cheryl's parking lights following him until they had passed Bushes Landing. He had sat there and agonized over the situation. He couldn't kill her. She was, swear to God, a young Leonora. The resemblance was astounding! She was Nora's granddaughter. Nevertheless, he couldn't have anything to do with her. He went back to his cabin, arriving there at almost five in the morning after sitting in his car in the darkness at Stillwater. He had wanted to cry, for this Cheryl, for Nora, for himself. No, he could never cry for himself. He had done what he had done. He was at peace with the consequence of his actions. As almost anyone who has ever lived has realized, but nevertheless dreamt, was that you can't change the past, no matter how much one wanted to.

Winston Franklin answered the door and saw Henry Seine standing there looking like he had one foot in his grave. Seine was, like Franklin, in his eighties. He had a driver drop him off at the door. He too had a cane to steady his move. Overweight, and taller than Franklin, he had permanent red cheeks. He wore thick Coke bottle glasses. Both men were frail, but could still get around fairly well.

Henry Seine had been an ardent cold warrior in his day. Like so many of his generation, he had fought on the front line in Europe during the war. He rose in the ranks quickly, like many had, after his superiors had been killed in combat. Soon, Seine found himself working for the CIA's precursor, the Office of Strategic Services, or the OSS. Even before the official surrender of the Nazis, Seine was helping the OSS smuggle out former Nazi officials that the United States would need in the developing Cold War. Before the end of World War II, the powers in the super-government of the United States had recognized the emerging cold war with the Soviets and saw the necessity of those Nazi officials who had intelligence on the Soviets. Seine personally, in his own mind, took accolades for winning the cold war against the Soviets. He laughed when the Soviet Union fell apart. Despite the trillions that were spent, or borrowed (that future generations will have to pay for), he felt it was all worth it. They had won! And had emerged even stronger!

Like William Colby, the former CIA Director, Seine also had no ill feeling about the tactics employed by the CIA following World War Two through the 50's and beyond. He knew how all those radicals in the 60's felt about their freedom in this country! What the hell did all those bastards think that the CIA and the Pentagon were ultimately protecting? That's right, their freedoms. Their freedom to rebel! All those cry babies carrying on about what Seine and others did during that time, was short sighted. Even though Seine had been fired, along with many following the disastrous Bay of Pigs, he continued working for the agency running operations covertly though front companies worldwide. Although most of his former contacts were dead now, he still had connections. He was, indeed, one of the last of the lasts. Suffering from sight loss, hearing loss, arthritis, and diabetes, Seine still felt he had to protect his operation; an operation that was never over until all of those loose ends had been tied. He always finished a job.

"You look pathetic, Hank," said Franklin. "Come in."

"Yeah, same to you, you old shit." Seine pushed past Franklin. He made his way into Franklin's living room and sat on a hard chair. "How quaint, we almost have matching canes."

"Drink?"

"Yeah," answered Seine.

Franklin dumped straight bourbon into a cocktail glass. He passed it off to Seine.

Seine gulped it down. "Yeah, I'm almost dead. Diabetic and heart disease. Give me another." He finished the bourbon. "I'm bored. I wish we were still in action."

"What part's that?"

"Everything," Seine said receiving his second drink. He set the glass on an end table.

"For Christ's sake, Hank, you're an old bastard. What could you do?"

"Put an operation together for someone."

"I've often thought about it, but it's not like the old days," explained Franklin. "You can't control people like you used to. What, with everyone running around writing a goddamn book and the media sticking a fucking television camera in your face nowadays, you'd have to kill them all."

Seine sat there and thought it through for a moment. "You writing a book, Winston?"

"What're you crazy?" Franklin looked away from Seine as he said that.

"What'd you write?"

"I didn't write anything, you paranoid old son-of-a-bitch."

"A journal? You kept a fucking journal," Seine stood up and confronted Franklin. "A memoir?"

"You're nuts, Hank. Jesus, we've known each other for over fifty years." Franklin put his hands on Seine's shoulders to calm him down. "Now get a Goddamn grip."

Seine shook his head and sat back down. Franklin guided him.

"It's just that Nagell," Seine said. "I'm still worried that something will show up."

"If nothing has shown up by now, nothing will." Franklin poured himself a drink.

"I still say we find his sister or whoever he said. She could be just hanging on to whatever Nagell said he had until the right time." Seine huffed under his breath. He had some trouble breathing.

"Nagell was a lunatic. He had nothing. It's just more crap that'll lead people in the wrong direction." Franklin sat down and sipped his own drink, rum. "I haven't seen you all worked up like this for years."

"It still could come apart," Seine mumbled.

Franklin sighed. "After all these years? We've covered all our tracks."

"Except O'Connell!"

"He hasn't done anything all these years. He's not going to. We picked him because he was apolitical."

"They all were."

"That's my point," Franklin said sipping his drink again. "It's clear that he didn't give a shit. He took his loot and ran. He was entitled to that."

"So were the rest. But they were dealt with accordingly."

"He was smarter than the rest, that's all. He knew the severity of the hit. He was one step ahead of us."

Seine grunted to himself and downed his drink.

"He just figured it out," Franklin said.

"But how? We kept those teams isolated. I've analyzed this for years."

"I don't know. We've beaten this to death. It doesn't matter now. Forget it." He studied Seine. "You can't stand it to this day that he was one step ahead."

"He was just an operative. He shouldn't have had that jump."

"Well, he did. Perhaps it was a wild guess, that's all."

"He was only enlisted for Christ's sake," Seine grumbled.

"Come on, Hank, being an enlisted man never meant you were any less. You were in the big one. You know how they made things happen under the worst of conditions in the damnedest situations." Franklin shook his head. "O'Connell hasn't said anything. He won't now. If he's alive, he's practically an old fart just like us."

Seine shook his head. He wasn't yet convinced. After all these years, it still dug at him.

"Besides," said Franklin, "don't you think that whoever hired us are all dead now themselves?"

"We never completely mopped up."

"They don't know that. They never knew any of the details."

"You never worried that they'd find us and mop up?"

"You, I was out of the inner loop if you remember. They never knew I worked for you."

"Yeah, you're right."

"It bothered me for many years. Look, Hank, I don't loose sleep over this anymore. We were the best at what we did. We kept our distance and cover from them, and they from us. There's no way ever anyone will be able to trace this to us, through us, and to them. It's over. This chapter is closed. History has been written."

Seine thought about that remark. "Yeah, well we wrote it, didn't we?"

"And you know as well as I do, that history is whatever those who write it says it is."

"Now you're philosophical, Winston. History is whatever the truth is, but what we're talking about is not history."

"And therefore history is not really history, because it's not true. History isn't necessarily the truth."

"You're loosing me."

"What the kids are taught, and what the people know, is anti-history."

"An interesting term. And does it really matter?"

"Not from my perspective," said Franklin. "Not from my perspective."

Seven

Andy had worked on his journal, a little on his thesis, and then he went fishing on Stillwater. He didn't have any luck so he toured the reservoir. He went up and down each inlet and around every island. This was, after all, only his third trip to Stillwater and had never really seen it all.

As he witnessed the beauty of this corner of the world pass by from the comfort of his father's boat, he couldn't help but let his mind wander back to Walker yet again. Walker had almost killed him! Again he didn't think it was necessary to inform his father, since he wanted to get to the bottom of this old man's story. How and when he got back in there when Walker was away would be a challenge.

By the time he had made his way along the north shore, he was near the Stillwater landing, so Andy decided to dock and eat at the Black Bear.

Cheryl had already driven up and down several roads. Many turned to dirt or gravel at various points and remained so until usually a dead end. She had never realized that there was such a remote and isolated place in New York State. After all, when most people thought of New York, they thought of a city-state, after the reputation of New York City, a concrete jungle. New York, she now realized, was much like Alabama; that is, when you got out of the city, you were in the country!

She took the turn and ended up in Brantingham, but that didn't seem right either. She decided to back track and ended up at Bushes Landing, where she knew she had been the night before. She noticed that the road turned to the right so she went that way. At the hamlet of Number Four, she turned right and drove the 8.6 miles to Stillwater.

When she drove into Stillwater, she realized that it was another dead end, but there was a hotel there, a Ranger Station, a parking lot with several cars, and boat trailers parked in their own respective lot. She parked in the car lot and walked over to the Stillwater Reservoir sign and map that showed and explained the reservoir area.

At the sign, a group of campers where assembling their gear for a camping expedition. She listened to their accent and realized that it wasn't an accent, but they were speaking Russian! Wow, Cheryl thought. The Russians had invaded after all!

She went back to the parking lot and walked up and down each row. Cheryl didn't see the Buick Electra that the man who had almost killed her the night before was driving. Walker had hid it in the boat trailer lot and it was obscured from her point of view.

Another wrong turn, she thought. She sat there near the reservoir sign thinking through her next move. Obviously, the Doctor back in Lowville knew this man. She could always go back and harass him. There was that connection that she had established and she couldn't give up now. She looked at the hotel, thought a moment about asking questions, and decided that it was worth a try.

Inside the Black Bear, Cheryl saw a bar and a small dining room off to the side. A young family, the father, mother and four kids sat at a table in the dining room eating their dinner (the kids fighting with one another), and a young man, Andy, sat eating his at the bar. Cheryl walked up to the bartender. "Hi. Diet Pepsi, please."

"Would you like to see the menu ma'am?" asked the bartender, Top he's called.

"No thanks." Cheryl looked at Andy just as he looked at her.

His adrenaline ignited. She was breathtaking. Andy had to look away so as not to be caught staring, or blushing. He sipped his soft drink. He heard her Southern accent.

Top, actually his nickname because he was a retired First Sergeant from the Army, had purchased the hotel and Black Bear and settled down with a comfortable pension. He brought Cheryl her drink. "Anything else I can get you?"

"Well, I have a question if you don't mind."

"Not at all." Top wiped the bar down with a rag.

"I was looking for this car I saw heading, I think, this way last night. It was an old big blue Buick, I think early seventies."

"Yeah. Al Walker's. It's usually parked in the lot."

Andy's ears perked up.

Jackpot! Cheryl said to herself. "Where's he live?"

"In Beaver River."

"Beaver River? Where's that?"

"It's across the reservoir."

"Across the reservoir? What road do you take?"

"There're no roads that go there from here."

"From where then?"

"You have to take a boat to six mile road or all the way in to Grassy Point Landing."

"A boat? Can I rent one?"

"They're all rented out, but there's a taxi that can take you there. It's run by the Beaver River Lodge. They have two trips daily. I'm sorry but the second one already left for today."

"Okay. Thanks. Thank you."

Top nodded and went about his business.

Andy thought about Wendy. The hell with her. She was the one who broke up with him. He worked up his courage. This girl has a southern accent, Andy reflected. Funny thing, no matter how much Walker tried to get rid of his southern accent, it was still evident. Andy decided to go for it.

"Excuse me?"

Cheryl had hoped he would talk with her. "Yes?"

"I'm sorry to pry, but I overheard your conversation about Al Walker's car."

Cheryl excitedly moved closer. "Do you know him?"

"Well, sort of. I've worked for him."

"Doing what?"

"Just around his cabin, fixing things up." Andy could smell her perfume.

"Do you have a boat?"

"Yeah."

"I could pay you."

"What is your connection with Walker?"

"He knew my grandmother."

"How so?"

Cheryl paused a moment to think how she would handle this. "To tell you the truth, Mr.?"

"Andy Bell." He stuck out his hand and she shook it. His palm was slightly sweaty and butterflies fluttered around inside his stomach.

"Cheryl Taylor," she said. "I'm not sure how he knew her. I assume he was an old boyfriend."

"Your grandmother didn't tell you?"

"I learned of this man after her death."

Damn, thought Andy. This Walker and his shadowy past were getting foggier.

"I must tell you, Cheryl," said Andy, "that Mr. Walker is sort of a hermit."

"Somehow that doesn't surprise me."

"Why?"

"He doesn't want anything to do with me and wants to leave my grandmother in his past, although for many years he's been sending her…notes…in the mail. So, I've got to know what it's all about." She took out a picture.

He looked at it and nodded. "I think that's a young Walker." Andy stared at the photograph. For some strange reason, he thought he had seen this man, the young Walker, or his picture someplace before. It resembled someone he knew. He shook it out of his head and returned the picture to Cheryl.

"Can you take me to him?"

"Yes," Andy blurted out.

"Thank you. I want to pay you."

"No. I'm going that way anyway. I'm staying at my father's cabin."

"Thanks. I'll wait for you outside."

"There's a lodge in Beaver River. You could stay there."

"Good. I'll get my bags." She went to get her things.

Andy Grabbed two quick bites off his sandwich and left at least a third of it there on his plate. He swigged down as much soda as he could, threw enough money to cover the meal and tip onto the bar, then sprinted for the door.

Outside, he saw Cheryl retrieving her bags from her rental. She had one typical sports bag and a knapsack.

"Can I help you with that?"

"No, thanks. I've got it." She followed him to the boat.

After she was in the boat, Andy pulled the two ropes that held the boat to the dock. Cheryl sat in the passenger seat next to the driver. He took it steady so that he could converse with her.

"I have a lot of questions about Walker that I'd like answered too," said Andy just loud enough above the sound of the 50 Horse Powered outboard.

"Like what?" asked Cheryl looking up at Andy.

"Well, it's not easy for me to say this, not knowing his relationship with your grandmother and all, but he really doesn't want anyone in his cabin. He has many weapons and he almost shot me once."

Cheryl perked up. "Really?"

"I awakened him from a dead sleep when he wouldn't answer. I went inside and he sat up with an assault rifle and pointed it at me. A second or two later and I could've been hamburger."

"I see." Cheryl thought it best that she keep her incident to herself for the time being. "How do you think I should approach him?"

"Has he met you?"

"In a way, but he told me that he didn't want to see me again. He said to go home."

"Where's home?"

"Huntsville, Alabama."

"I've never been there."

"It's really nice, much like here, right now, but I have to admit I didn't think New York looked like this. I was expecting skyscrapers."

"Many think that way." Andy accelerated and the boat picked up speed. The motor was too loud to continue the conversation so each watched the shoreline pass by.

Andy realized that he would have to take this Cheryl over to Walker's island and probably go up to the door with her. If he didn't, well he didn't want to think about what could happen.

At the Grassy Point Landing, he docked and tied up the boat. Cheryl followed. They walked the short distance to where Andy's father's truck was parked.

"How'd they get these cars in here?" asked Cheryl.

"Everybody asks that," he chuckled. "On a barge." He drove to the Lodge. The ride was bumpy and Cheryl had to hold onto the door handle, lest she topple over onto the front seat.

"It's getting late. I think we should wait until the morning to go see Walker," Andy said.

"Why we?"

"Walker lives on an island on Norridgewock Lake. I'll have to take you over by boat."

"On an island?"

"Yeah, on an island. He's quite the mystery. And, as I told you, unpredictable."

"Then he is hiding from something. Out here, all this way, on an island?"

"Yeah. Seems so."

Cheryl wondered what kind of a madman she was getting involved with. Nevertheless, like Andy, her curiosity was eating at her even more.

Inside the Lodge, Cheryl waited while Andy went and got Dusty.

"Your girlfriend, Andy?" Dusty asked.

"Not yet."

Dusty threw Andy a devilish grin.

"This is Cheryl Taylor. She's from Alabama," Andy said introducing Cheryl. "This is Dusty, Cheryl. He'll set you up. I'll see you in the morning, how about nine?"

"Fine," Cheryl said nodding her head.

Dusty checked her into a room. Cheryl's room looked out over Norridgewock Lake. The sun was getting weak in the sky, and as Cheryl threw her bag onto the bed, she peered out over the calm evening water. She could see a small bridge that ran over a dam nearby that obviously helped regulate the water lever. She couldn't see an island from her view.

She unpacked. Her room had a small nightstand next to a queen-sized bed and a table by the window. A little bathroom was on the side. Like the main lodge building, the rooms were built in the Adirondack log cabin style. She plopped down on the bed and threw out a long sigh. He's cute, she thought about Andy. Not bad for a Yankee.

When Andy got back to the Osprey, there was a message on the answering machine. He played it.

"Andy? Hi, its, Wendy." Her voice had that innocent, yet razor sound to it. "I'm at my folks' house in Cape Cod. I got to thinking about us and thought about seeing you before the summer was out, maybe patch things up. Give me a call." The machine beeped.

Andy stood there dazed. Now?! Why right now? He erased the message and slouched down onto the couch on the porch. He visualized Wendy's face hovering in front of him, smiling and wanting to make love with him one moment, then arguing about nonsensical things the next. Shit. I can't call her back now he steamed. Not now!

He sat there on the porch for a while longer. Who was this Cheryl? Damn, he wanted to know her.

Andy heard knocking at the side door early the next morning. He groggily got up.

"Its, Dusty, Andy."

Andy opened the door.

"Doc Bergholtz is concerned about Walker. Walker was supposed to call Bergholtz back. Can you check it out?"

"Yeah. What time is it?"

"Seven thirty. And call the Doc first. Here's his number." Dusty handed Andy a slip of paper.

Dusty trotted back to the lodge. Andy placed the call.

"This is Andy Bell," he said into the phone.

"Andy, listen," said Bergholtz over the phone. "Al Walker has cancer, in his lungs. He knows it and is being stubborn. He needs treatment but is hesitant about coming in. Can you go over there and get him to come in to see me?"

"Why would he listen to me?"

"He talked about you the other day. Said you're a good kid, a little naive, but trustworthy."

"You think he wants to die?"

"Yeah, but I'm not Jack Kevorkian."

"I don't know, Doc. I'll try."

"Thanks, Andy." The phone clicked off.

Cancer? Andy paced around the room. This could be his chance to get in there. Andy plotted.

He got dressed and hurried over to the lodge. Cheryl was already up and eating a light breakfast of juice and toast in the dining room.

God, she looked good. Andy smiled and waved at her as he approached. "It's a little early, but we can get started when you're ready."

"Let's go," said Cheryl dabbing her lips with her napkin.

Out the door they flew. Across the lake Andy gave the little outboard full throttle. The ride took five minutes.

Andy docked on the opposite side of Walker's flimsy little boat. He noticed that it had a small leak and that Walker kept an old soup can in the back to shovel out the water that seeped in.

Getting out on the dock, Cheryl's foot broke through a plank. Luckily, it wasn't serious and she pulled her foot right back up through the hole.

"I was going to ask him if he wanted me to build him a new dock," Andy said. "Let's go, but stay behind me and hit the deck if I say."

Cheryl nodded when Andy was looking, but shook her head when he wasn't. She followed him up the path.

"Mr. Walker," yelled Andy. They stopped at the outer porch door that Andy had just assembled. He looked at her and she shrugged her shoulders in a signal saying let's go.

Andy opened the porch door and they crept in.

"Nice porch. Your work?"

Andy nodded. At least she's perceptive, a quality Wendy lacked.

"Mr. Walker?" Andy knocked on the inner door.

Silence.

"This is just what happened to me before," Andy said nervously.

Cheryl pushed past him. She rapped on the door. "Mr. Walker! We know you're in there."

Andy looked at her like it wasn't a good idea to say that. "I told you, he's not exactly got it all together."

Cheryl tried the doorknob. It was locked.

Andy sighed and said, "Here." He pulled out Walker's key from his key ring.

"You have your own key?"

"It's a long story."

Cheryl took the key and opened the door. She pushed it all the way back into the kitchen. "After you," she said looking at him.

He gave her a distressed look and edged in. "Mr. Walker?" Andy spoke softer so that he wouldn't get his head shot off.

Cheryl followed close behind. They stopped at the entrance to the main room. She almost gagged on the stale air.

They saw Walker on his bed in the corner. He lay there stiff as a board. Andy turned his head and whispered to Cheryl, "You don't think he's..."

"I don't know. Find a pulse."

"Thanks. Why don't you while I cover you?"

"All right." Cheryl moved closer, took a deeper than usual breath, and reached for Walker's wrist. He was cold.

Andy nervously scanned the cabin.

"He's alive," Cheryl uttered. "Shallow breathing, or wheezing, slow pulse."

"We've got to get him to a doctor. His doctor's in Lowville."

"Yeah, I know."

Andy paced aimlessly. "You stay here. I'll go call Doc Bergholtz."

Cheryl wasn't too thrilled about this. "Leaving me?" She was half joking to calm her nerves.

"I'll be back in a flash." Andy burst out through the door and ran as fast as he could to the dock. He opened the boat full throttle back to the Osprey.

Cheryl had that queasy feeling. She took Walker by the wrist again and felt his pulse. Alive, but weak. She dropped his wrist to his side. She stood up and looked around the cabin.

She became mesmerized by what Andy had seen days earlier; the Shrine on the wall. The candle was out, but the other items hung or sat there in a gloomy light. She had no idea what to make of it. She then examined the army arsenal against the wall, on the floor, and scattered about. Cheryl had seen guns before, her grandmother had a couple guns, most do in Alabama. But Cheryl had never seen hand grenades and other bombs or whatever they were.

About ten minutes later she heard Andy returning in his boat. He sprinted up to the house.

"We've got to get him out onto the lawn," Andy said.

"My God, he must weigh a hundred seventy or so."

"Find a sheet and we'll just have to drag him."

"Then what?"

"Bergholtz is having a helicopter flown in from Watertown. It should be here in minutes."

"Wonderful."

Bergholtz had actually told Andy to stand by Walker and that the paramedics would come in and get him and put him in a rescue basket, but Andy didn't want them to see all the guns.

Cheryl found a sheet and the two of them together struggled to roll Walker over. They eased his body onto the floor and into the sheet. The keys in his pocket fell out. It appeared that there was his cabin key, a boat key and the key to the Electra. A couple other nondescript keys were on the ring.

Walker mumbled, but didn't wake up. Andy and Cheryl froze in fear.

Andy threw the keys on the couch and pulled on the sheet. He dragged Walker across the floor to the kitchen. "Hold his head as we go down the steps," said Andy.

Cheryl kneeled down and took Walker's head in her hands. Walker still had hair, mostly white, but he hadn't washed it in several days. It gave Cheryl a moment to pause.

Andy pulled on the sheet and slowly Walker's body went down the steps. They got him out on the ground and dragged him out into the opening in front of the cabin.

"Get me some blankets. We need to wrap him up."

Cheryl ran back to the cabin.

Andy stood over Walker and searched the sky.

"What the hell are you doing, kid?" Walker muttered.

"I'm getting you to a hospital."

Walker tried to speak but went into a bloody coughing spell. Andy had to use the sheet to wipe the blood from Walker's chin. "No," Walker said barely.

"I don't understand. You're dying. You need medical attention."

"Let…" Walker coughed and more crap came out of his mouth, "me die."

"What," Andy pretended. "I can't hear you, Mr. Walker. It'll be all right. Just hold on."

Cheryl arrived with two heavy blankets. Together, they wrapped Walker as he tried to curse out Andy through his coughing spells.

Cheryl stood with Andy. They waited a few minutes until they heard the helicopter approaching. Andy tore off a chunk of the white sheet and held it up as a flag.

The helicopter came in and hovered nearby. Two paramedics jumped out with a rescue basket. With Andy's help they got Walker into the basket and shoved it into the helicopter.

"I'm a relative," yelled Cheryl to one of the paramedics above the onslaught of noise caused by the helicopter blades that churned above her.

"Get in," said the medic.

Andy looked at Cheryl like what was she doing? Cheryl gave Andy a quick hug. "It's okay," she said in his ear. She gave him a quick kiss on his cheek then hopped into the helicopter.

Andy stood there for a moment taking in what had just happened, not with Walker, but between Cheryl and himself. The helicopter departed and swooped away a second later leaving Andy standing there alone. He couldn't believe it. Walker's almost dead. Cancer was eating away at him from the inside out and she kissed him.

Andy realized that he had the run of the mill. They had left the door wide open! It was wrong what Andy planned to do, but he had to look around. Probably, he thought, there was nothing. There was nothing to Walker and he was just an eccentric old hermit. Andy would soon find out that he was wrong, however.

Eight

Walker was admitted to the hospital in Watertown. Bergholtz arrived shortly thereafter. Immediately Walker was put on life support and stabilized. Bergholtz gave the authorizations for radical cancer treatment. It was a life-threatening situation and Walker hadn't ever made out a living will, so as his physician, Bergholtz took responsibility.

A surgical cancer specialist was chosen and Walker was operated on. They removed a portion of his left lung. Black was an understatement. Walker never regained consciousness before the medical attention began.

Bergholtz saw Cheryl sitting in the waiting room. He knew he couldn't avoid her. He wasn't surprised when he had heard that she was on the helicopter.

"Miss Taylor," Bergholtz said sitting down next to her.

"Doctor Bergholtz," she said coolly.

"You saved his life."

"Yeah, but he doesn't want to live apparently."

"I'm an old fashioned doctor. I believe in saving the lives of my patients."

Cheryl shrugged.

"I really don't know what he had to do with your grandmother. I just dropped off the envelopes. I never once opened one and never knew what was in them."

"I think he's my grandfather," Cheryl said distantly.

Bergholtz nodded. "I thought perhaps that was the case the other day."

"My grandmother was married. I only learned after her death that she had changed her name sometime in the early sixties, about the same time my grandfather supposedly died. She moved from Birmingham to Huntsville. She told me that her husband had died in a car crash. She never went into details and was always distant on the subject. I never had any reason to disbelieve her so I never checked it out, that is until after her death and I found clues. I don't think she thought I would go to all this trouble to find out the truth. I have to admit, that I didn't know how to go about finding out, but for thirty years, Doctor?"

"Yeah. In the beginning, Walker asked me as a favor, then every month it was the same so I just did it. I have relatives in Syracuse and usually picked up supplies and things like that, it saved on shipping charges. So I never questioned Walker. You say envelopes. No letter?"

"He sent money. My grandmother never deposited it or apparently used any. She obviously knew I would find it and it would be mine. But you can understand the curiosity?"

Bergholtz nodded and got up to go. "Well, we're going to buy your grandfather just a little time so you can work things out with him."

"You know he doesn't want anything to do with me."

"Perhaps you can bring him around."

"I hope. How long do you think he has?"

"If he comes through this and they cleaned it all out, and if he's really lucky, a couple years at most, six months at least."

She nodded. Bergholtz walked off down the corridor leaving Cheryl alone.

Andy tried the keys from Walker's key ring. Not one fit the lock to the chest by the wall. He dropped Walker's keys into his own pocket. He searched around, first in the main room, then in the kitchen. He finally found some keys hanging on a key rack in the kitchen.

He had to open up a couple windows to let in some air, so the musty smell could begin to dissipate. Beyond that, he didn't want to disturb too much just in case Walker lived and came back.

He stuck the key into the chest and it opened. He was amazed by what he saw. It was nothing but military memorabilia from the Korean War. There was Walker's web belt, canteen, dress uniform and fatigues neatly folded, and photographs of him and buddies in the war. There was an assortment of newspaper clippings, some from the *Stars and Stripes*, others from the *New York Times*. Nothing about Walker was mentioned in the clippings, just overall military movements and victories.

He dug deeper in the chest and found a Purple Heart and other medals, still in their original cases. Under the medals Andy located the orders that corresponded with the medals, making them official. However, something striking about each and every order came to light. The name wasn't Walker's but someone by the name of John O'Connell.

Andy was making a mess as he searched through all the papers and documents he could find. He looked over his shoulder expecting Walker to be standing there ready to shoot him dead.

Each and every paper, document, commendation, orders; the name was John O'Connell! Andy sat back on the floor after kneeling at the chest all this time. He held some of the papers in his hand. "John O'Connell? Who the hell are you?" He must be a fugitive from justice, Andy thought. The military must be looking for him, or something. But for—Andy had to do mental math—for almost 50 years? Korea was 50 years ago!

Andy finished digging through the chest and found more of the same about O'Connell and his war memorabilia. That's all there was. He took several minutes to re-pack the chest the best way he could remember it was packed when he had opened it.

He closed and locked the chest. He paced around the kitchen for a minute, then the main room for several more. There has to be something else.

He froze. Then, he looked straight up. The loft was above him. Andy climbed the ladder, but realized that the trap door to the loft was secured with a padlock. He tried the keys on the key ring but none would open the loft. He climbed back down. He found more keys on the rack in the kitchen, but not one fit the padlock. He replaced the keys and searched around. Nothing.

Andy searched under, over and around everything in the whole down stairs of the cabin. Nothing. Damn it, he couldn't just break it! "Wait a minute," Andy said out loud.

He reached into his pocket and pulled out Walker's key ring. "What an idiot."

He climbed the ladder to the loft. There were two padlock keys on the ring. He tried one. It didn't work. He tried the other. The lock popped open. Andy's palms became sweaty. He took a deep breath and opened the trap door.

It was too dark to see anything up there. Maybe something would jump out at him! He remembered that there was a window at the front of the loft, but it was boarded up from the inside. He searched around for a light switch, but realized that Walker rarely used electricity. In most cabins in Beaver River there was no electricity! If one wished to use juice, they had to buy their own generator and make it. Walker had an old generator in the shed, but Andy didn't think that Walker used it. His refrigerator probably ran on gas, like his father's. Walker used candles for the most part, he remembered.

He climbed back down the ladder and located a candle and grabbed a hammer from the shed. He returned to the cabin and climbed up to the loft.

From the shadowy glow of the candle Andy could see an antique desk in one corner. It had candles on it so he lit them. There were tables that lined the walls of the loft and just enough room to walk down the middle isle to the window at the front of the cabin. He told himself the hell with it and he used the hammer to pry open the board that was nailed over the window.

The hot afternoon sun was streaming in and illuminated the entire loft. It almost blinded him. He opened the window to let the stale air out and the fresh air in. He blew out the candle he was holding and set the board from the window down in front of it.

He turned around and felt a rush of uneasiness pass through him. He had to lean up against a table and catch his breath. He'd found the treasure!

There were pictures of people and newspaper clippings plastered all over the walls and the ceiling, almost like wallpaper. There were vintage official-looking government dockets and papers piled high on the tables. Everything was covered with thick dust.

He reached over and lifted the nearest folder off the table next to him and saw that it was stamped: DIRECTOR'S EYES ONLY. The files there on that table were labeled: OPERATION MONGOOSE, ALPHA 66, PHOENIX PROGRAM, EXECUTIVE ACTION PROGRAM, SAIGON MILITARY MISSION, JM/WAVE and etc. Andy placed them back onto their respective pile.

He looked above him and saw old faded black and white 8 x 10 pictures of people…no, all men. What stirred the fire of Andy's curiosity was that most of the pictures were of Asian or Latino men. "What's all this?" Andy had the shakes. "He's going to kill me for sure. Maybe he died already." He got nervous, but wanted to see more.

He looked at newspaper clippings and files. They didn't register with him one way or another. Either Walker was in on these operations, or he was some kind of a lunatic. This bizarre loft or depository now explained, in part, Walker's odd behavior.

Andy sat at the desk on the other side of the loft. There was a newspaper clipping sitting there. It was only a couple years old. It was a clipping from *The New York Times*. *The Times* was available in Lowville,
Andy recalled.

He picked the clipping up. It was an article attributed to the
Associated Press and apparently Walker had scribbled the date 11/95
across the top of the article because of the way in which Walker had
clipped it, the article didn't show the paper's printed date. The heading
read: "FORMER CIA AGENT RICHARD C. NAGELL FOUND DEAD."
The subheading read: "CLAIMED HE KNEW OF KENNEDY CON-
SPIRACY."

Andy read the article. It explained that Nagell had worked for the
CIA, was arrested in El Paso in '63 for shooting at the ceiling of a bank,
and in his later years was a sort of a recluse. It also said he was believed,
according to the CIA, to be mentally ill. "Like anyone I know," Andy
joked aloud. The article went on and said that Nagell always claimed he
had evidence about the conspiracy, but that he never provided any. He
said that after his death the evidence would surface. The Justice
Department's Office of Special Investigations looking into the assassination even to this day, as requested by the House Select Committee on
Assassinations, had nothing from Nagell and eagerly awaited anything
that might turn up. The article said that Nagell was found dead in a run
down bungalow along the 101 Freeway in Los Angeles. It listed no cause
of death.

Andy put the article back in its original spot. There was a small bookcase on the opposite side of the desk from that of the newspapers. Andy
rolled the office chair over slightly to get an angle on the bookcase. He
was astounded by what he saw. The bookcase contained the Warren
Commission Report of the Assassination of President Kennedy, *The
New York Times* Edition, and the entire 26 volumes of testimony and
exhibits. There were several clippings and bookmarks in most of the
books that stuck out slightly, marking their spots.

Andy grabbed a book from the case and opened it to a section that was marked with a newspaper clipping. The section marked dealt with the magic bullet theory as theorized by a young lawyer appointed to the commission; Arlen Specter from Pennsylvania. Sections of Specter's theory were underlined. Apparently Walker had scribbled a word on the side near Specter's name. The word Walker had scribbled was "clever!" The clipping that marked this page was about a Jim Garrison who disputed the theory in a court case in 1969. "The guy from the movie," Andy said out loud.

What stuck out for Andy about the clipping was a note that Walker had scribbled on the side of the Garrison clipping. The note read: "Smart-ass!"

Andy closed the book and returned it to the shelf. He hoped he would have more time to look through these books. Sure he could go to a library and read the entire set, but the set he had to go through was the one that had dozens of clippings and notes marking pages throughout it; Walker's set.

Walker also had the complete set of the House Select Committee on Assassinations from the late seventies. He picked up a book that was marked. A section about Kennedy's autopsy in the final report section was highlighted. It read:

> The secrecy that surrounds the autopsy proceedings, therefore, has led to considerable skepticism toward the Commission's finding. Concern has been expressed that authorities were less than candid, since the Navy doctor in charge of the autopsy conducted at Bethesda Naval Hospital destroyed his notes....

Andy didn't know what to make of all this. Did Walker have something to do with this? Andy was well aware of all the conspiracy theories out there, and the fact that the House Select Committee on Assassinations concluded in 1979 that President Kennedy was "probably killed as a result of a conspiracy," but they left it at that. Andy had seen the movie that Oliver Stone had made, *JFK*, but thought that it was too broad. The conspiracy couldn't have involved everyone from everywhere. Too many people knowing about something of that nature, someone would have come forward. Like most Americans, Andy went back to his life and it was again soon forgotten. After all, people had wasted their entire lives running around in circles about this.

He found a clipping from the *NY Times*. It was a story about, and it had, the complete text of Eisenhower's farewell speech. Walker had circled excerpts from that speech. Andy read:

> Our military organization today bears little resemblance of any of my predecessors in peacetime, or, indeed by the fighting men of World War II or Korea.
>
> Until the latest of our world conflicts, the United States had no armaments industry. American makers of plowshares could, with time and as required, make swords as well.
>
> But we can no longer risk emergency improvisation of national defense. We have been compelled to create a permanent armaments industry of vast proportions. Added to this, three and a half million men and women are directly engaged in the defense establishment. We annually spend on military security alone more than the net income of all United States corporations.
>
> Now this conjunction of an immense military establishment and a large arms industry is new to the American experience. The total influence—economic, political, even spiritual—is felt in every city, every state house, every office of the federal government. We recognize the imperative need for this development. Yet, we must not fail to comprehend its grave implications. Our toil, resources and livelihood are all involved; so is the very structure of our society.

In the councils of government, we must guard against this acquisition of unwarranted influence, whether sought or unsought, by the military industrial complex. The potential for the disastrous rise of misplaced power exists and will persist.

We must never let the weight of this combination endanger our liberties or democratic processes. We should take nothing for granted. Only an alert and knowledgeable citizenry can compel the proper meshing of the huge industrial and military machinery of defense with our peaceful methods and goals, so that security and liberty may prosper together.

Andy sat for a moment and wondered why Walker had highlighted this section of the speech. An army general had said this? What did he know that no one else did?

He found a file that was labeled: ROCKEFELLER. He opened it and realized that it was from the Rockefeller Commission of the middle seventies. Walker had highlighted a section. The Commission reported that the CIA had committed "plainly unlawful and...improper" acts. The Commission said that the CIA had been involved in "domestic break-ins, mail openings, testing mind-altering drugs on unsuspecting victims and spying on thousands of Americans." The Commission also said that the tramps arrested in "Dealey Plaza might have been E. Howard Hunt and Frank Sturgis."

Andy heard a boat approaching. "Shit." He ran to the window and saw that it was Dusty, just about to dock his boat.

On the way to the trap door, just above the desk on the wall, Andy noticed a newspaper clipping of JFK smiling. Faded somewhat, it was the same size as all the other pictures that were affixed there in the loft.

Andy hurried down the ladder, closing, but not locking the trap door. He ran out and met Dusty half way up the path. Andy stopped so that Dusty had to stop there also.

"Walker's alive and stable," Dusty said. "Miss Taylor called from the hospital. And your father tried the Osprey, then called us. He's coming in about dinnertime. 'Says he's taking an extended weekend.'"

"How's Cheryl?"

"Miss Taylor? Fine. Sounded fine. Who is she, Andy?"

"I think she's related to Walker."

"You're kidding? What's it look like inside?" gestured Dusty wanting to go inside Walker's cabin.

"Nothing unusual," Andy said doing a good job at lying. "He's just an old hermit, like everyone said. A little messy, nothing beyond that."

"Well, I guess you can lock up his place?"

"Yeah, he left me in charge. He wanted a couple more things fixed up so I'll putter around and finish it all up before he gets back. When do they expect him to be released?"

"Days, a week at least. He had a serious operation."

"Okay. That'll give me time to get this old shack in top shape for his recovery."

"Oh, Cheryl said that Bergholtz told her two years at the most, six months at the least."

"Damn. The tobacco companies made a mint off that guy."

"You aren't kidding," chuckled Dusty. "Ain't that the truth? Okay, catch you later." Dusty departed in his boat.

Andy looked at his watch. He didn't have a whole lot of time, yet he had to see more. He went back up into the loft.

He found a book there on the shelf. It was titled *Portrait of the Assassin*, 1965, by Congressman Ford, a Warren Commission member. Andy opened to a page that Walker had marked. He read from page 13:

No sooner had the Commission investigating President Kennedy's assassination assembled its staff and tentatively outline methods of operation that it was plunged into an astounding problem. On Wednesday, January 22, the members of the

Commission were hurriedly called into emergency session by the chairman. Mr. J. Lee Rankin, newly appointed General Counsel of the Commission, had received a telephone call from Texas. The caller was Waggoner Carr, the Attorney General of Texas. The information was that the FBI had an 'undercover agent' and that that agent was none other than Lee Harvey Oswald, the alleged assassin of President Kennedy!

Prior to that day the newspapers had carried an inconspicuous article or two speculating on whether Oswald could have been an agent of any United States Government agency. Mrs. Marguerite Oswald had made statements that she thought her son must have been tied in with the CIA or the State Department. But now the alarm had been sounded by a high official; and the Dallas prosecutor, Mr. Henry Wade, who had also reported the rumor, was himself a former FBI man....

On the arrival of the members, each took his place around the eight-foot oblong table. The late hour and the complete disruption of everyone's personal plans added to the atmosphere of tension....

J. Lee Rankin...then reported the startling allegations to the members. They looked at one another in amazement.

The session [starting at 5:30] that followed lasted until after seven. I cannot recall attending a meeting more tense and hushed.

The Commission made the decision to ask the Texas Attorney General, District Attorney Wade and any other Dallas officials who had knowledge of these allegations to come at once to Washington and secretly present what they had heard. There should be absolutely no publicity.

The Texas officials slipped into the nation's capital with complete anonymity. They met with Lee Rankin and other members of the staff and told what they knew. The information was that

Lee Oswald was actually hired by the FBI; that he was assigned the undercover-agent number 179; that he was on the FBI payroll at two hundred dollars a month starting in September 1962 and that he was still on their payroll the day he was apprehended in the Texas Theatre after having gunned down Officer J.D. Tippet! The officials returned to Dallas after their visit on Friday, January 24. Their presence in Washington was unknown to the press or the public....

The Commission itself had no grounds at the moment for rejecting or accepting. Members knew that the whole business was a most delicate and sensitive matter involving the nation's faith in its own institutions and one of the most respected federal agencies....

Andy saw a reference Walker had marked there in pencil on the page. It read: "WRC 22, 327, 840 + V27, 742." Andy read how the Commission concluded that "Oswald was not an informant or agent of the FBI, that he did not act in any other capacity for the FBI, and no attempt was made to recruit him in any capacity." As Andy read, he learned that the Commission based its finding entirely upon the affidavits of J. Edgar Hoover, his assistant and three FBI agents. It also included an affidavit from agent Gordon Shanklin of the Dallas office.

Andy flipped back to Ford's book and on page 19, and then 20, read how Rankin said that Wade had told him that he (as an FBI agent) "had paid off informers and undercover agents in South America, and that he knew that it wasn't revealed on any records he ever handled who he was paying it to."

Andy read the following exchange, however, between two Commission members, Boggs and Dulles (the former CIA Director), as reported by Ford:

Boggs: Let's take a specific case. That fellow Powers was one of your men [Andy remembered that Powers was the U2 pilot shot down in Russia, that subsequently derailed the peace talks between Eisenhower and Khrushchev].

Dulles: Oh yes, but he was not an agent. He was an employee.

Ford went on to say in his book, "The problem was far more difficult with a true undercover agent, where there is nothing in writing."

Andy closed the book and set it down. What the hell? Like Hoover and his boys (his boys? Andy laughed to himself) would admit something so explosive. It would certainly prove that either the FBI knew of, or had clues to support the fact that Oswald was planning or capable of this act beforehand, or that they were involved. Andy still couldn't except the latter; he always believed the former, however.

Andy found a file sitting there next to where the book was. It was a transcript from a House Subcommittee chaired by Representative Don Edwards in 1975. He learned that Special Agent of the FBI, James Hosty, admitted under oath that he had received a handwritten note before the assassination from Oswald. However, after the assassination, he was told to destroy the note by Gordon Shanklin. Shanklin had been told, according to Hosty, to get rid of the evidence by J. Edgar Hoover.

Andy couldn't believe this. 1975? The Warren Commission report was concluded in 1964, and Ford wrote his book in 1965! Therefore, not only had the FBI destroyed evidence, according to agent Hosty, it had lied to, and misled the Commission. "One of the most respected agencies," according to Ford! If Hosty destroyed this note, what else had the FBI withheld or destroyed?

Wait a minute! Andy looked at Walker's notes and discovered that a note was found in Oswald's possession that had Hosty's name and telephone number at his FBI office.

He found a peculiar newspaper article in the back of the file. It was from the *Philadelphia Inquirer* of December 8, 1963. It reported

"Oswald's mother said an 'agent named Hosty' came to the Irving house and talked to the young man at length in his car."

Andy closed the file and returned it to the shelf. He opened a small notebook there and saw a reference to an Officer Tippet that Walker had written in a notebook. It said, "V22, page 481."

He decided to see what it was all about.

Andy learned in that volume how a witness to the Tippet killing, Warren Reynolds, who after chasing the killer for one block, failed to identify Oswald as the man he was chasing.

Walker's scribble there said, "See V11 437."

Andy found the section. It was Reynolds's testimony and he talked about how he was shot in the head with a rifle two days after he had given the information to police.

Walker's next note said, "See V25 870-872."

Andy located it. It was about how Darrell Wayne Garner was picked up for the shooting after he had confessed to his sister-in-law. However, he was released after a woman provided an alibi by the name of Nancy Jane Mooney, a former striptease artist who had worked for Jack Ruby at the Carousel Club. Garner was thus released and never heard from again.

Walker had a folded newspaper article there in between the pages. It was an article from *The Dallas Morning News* dated February 14, 1964. The article explained that Mooney, after being arrested for a domestic disturbance with her roommate, had, alone in her cell, hung herself in the Dallas Jail house.

Another newspaper article folded there was from the *San Francisco Chronicle* dated December 3, 1963. In the article, Oswald's mother said, "the FBI had shown her a picture of Jack Ruby 17 hours before the Dallas striptease club owner killed her son Lee." The article explained the FBI denied showing her a picture of Ruby.

Andy then followed Walker's notes to Volume 6 page 443-444. It was the testimony of Oswald's landlord at his boarding house. She said that

Oswald returned at 1PM and a police car pulled up shortly thereafter, before Oswald left.

> Mr. Ball. Where was it parked?
> Mrs. Roberts. It was parked in front of the house.
> Mr. Ball. Did this police car stop directly in front of your house?
> Mrs. Roberts. Yes—it stopped directly in front of my house....
> Mr. Ball. Where was Oswald when this happened?
> Mrs. Roberts. In his room.
> Mr. Ball. Were there two uniformed policemen in the car?
> Mrs. Roberts. Oh, yes.
> Mr. Ball. And one of them sounded the horn?
> Mrs. Roberts. Just kind of a 'tit-tit'—twice.

Andy was dumbfounded. Why would two policemen in a patrol car, just after Oswald had returned to his boarding house after the assassination, come by the house and honk the horn? Some kind of a signal?

Damn. It was late. Andy had to go get his father. He closed up and hurried on over to Stillwater.

A doctor informed Cheryl that Walker was coming around. After he had been admitted to a room, she went in to see him.

Walker had the usual ubiquitous medical devices stuck in every possible wrinkle of his skin, including an IV. He had a small oxygen tent around his head. He was barely conscious, and groggy when Cheryl stood over him.

"I don't think you can deny it and it doesn't take a genius to figure it out that you're my grandfather, Mr. Walker," said Cheryl passively, "although I suspect that that isn't your real name either."

Walker turned his head slightly and stared at her. He tried to speak but all that came out was raspy air. He pursed his lips, closed his eyes tightly and rolled his head over away from her.

"I'm not leaving until you recover and tell me the whole story. I'm going to be in here every day all day until you can talk again." She took a seat by the window and waited.

Andy picked his father up at Stillwater. They went into the hotel for dinner.

"What happened?" Andy asked.

"I had to get out of there. I postponed a hearing of the tobacco case until Monday."

They sat at a dining room table. "But I thought you said the man who brought the suit is in bad shape, and probably couldn't wait."

"Worse. He died, so it doesn't matter that I postponed it."

"What happens now?"

"His family continues the case, his lawyers see to that."

Top appeared. "Andy, what happened to your girlfriend from yesterday?"

"Wendy's here?" Judge Bell inquired excitedly.

"No, it's not Wendy, Dad. It's a long story. She's staying at the Lodge, Top."

"I thought you turned as red as a ripe tomato."

Andy gave him a cross look.

"What can I get you guys?"

"The steak and fries, and a Molsons," Judge Bell said.

"The chicken dinner and a Sprite."

Top went about his business while Judge Bell looked over at Andy.

"Well, what happened?" asked Judge Bell.

"Her name is Cheryl Taylor. I think she's Walker's granddaughter."

"You're kidding?"

Top arrived with their drinks.

"In all these years, nothing, not a peep, then his granddaughter shows up?"

"Walker has cancer," Andy said. "We found him this morning unconscious and he was flown out by helicopter to Watertown where the both of them are now."

"The only excitement in Beaver River in perhaps decades and I miss it. So you've seen the inside of Walker's place. What's the verdict?"

"Nothing really. He's a hermit, has very little. A couple guns." Andy sipped his soft drink. "The other trial's over?"

"The drug king-pin case. The defendant had an unruly outburst and threatened to get me after I threw the book at him. No respect anymore. These hoodlums think they can do whatever they wish with no repercussion."

"Can he get you?"

"It'll be in the transcript. He'd be crazy."

"You're not worried?"

The Judge shook his head.

Andy's mind wandered back to this Cheryl Taylor. He didn't want to small talk with his father anymore about this. Andy realized that his attraction to this young woman only complicated the situation, but what the hell; if he got the chance to romance her, he certainly would. Although, despite being treated badly by Wendy, he still had feelings for her, however, her irrational behavior, selfishness and wealthy family, did turn him off. He realized that his father liked the fact that he had a relationship with the daughter of a member of Congress from the Boston area. Andy understood that his father probably thought that this connection could in time be beneficial in furthering his career. Andy agonized about this, and about what he had seen in Walker's loft. What did it all mean? Damn, he had to get back over there as soon as possible and find out.

Nine

Walker was more alert when he awoke early the next morning. They had removed the oxygen tent and he was breathing through a tube placed up his nostrils. "Nurse," he barked in a coarse voice.

He fumbled around for the button to call the nurse. He found and pressed it. He located the bed controls and raised the head up so that he was almost sitting.

A young nurse came in. "Good, you're up, Mr. Walker."

"Cut the pleasantries, nurse. I want to see Bergholtz."

"Doctor Bergholtz?" The nurse asked while checking Walker's IV tube, bag and flow.

"No, Bergholtz the butler. I want to see him now!"

"I don't think he's due in until this afternoon."

"I don't give a damn when he's due. Pass me the goddamn telephone!"

The nurse figured that she should heed his request after being warned that he was an irascible soul.

Walker grabbed the phone from the nurse and punched in a number.

"Bergholtz," answered a voice over the phone.

"Bergholtz?"

"Al?"

"What the hell have you done to me?"

"Saved your life."

Walker had to catch his breath. He felt dizzy. "I don't want saving."

"You can also thank those two kids."

"Get me the hell out of here."

"You need to stay there for a few days. You had major surgery."

Walker slammed the phone down into its cradle. He almost hyperventilated. After he caught his breath, he punched in another number. "Yeah, Bell in Beaver River. I don't know the Goddamn number, why the hell do you think I called you? Patch me through." He waited. "Judge Bell?"

"Yeah," the Judge said over the line.

"Its, Al Walker."

"Al, how are you?"

"Cheerful. Can they keep me here against my will?"

"Well, no, but for your own good, you should listen to your Doc…"

"Forget it. Is Andy in?"

"Sure, hang on."

"Hello," said Andy over the line.

"Its, Walker. Did you lock up my cabin?" He wheezed slightly.

"Yeah, right after you left, sir. I have your keys."

"Good. Don't let anyone in there. Go by and check to see that it's secure."

"When you coming back?"

"Just as soon as I fire my doctor and can walk out of this prison."

"Okay."

Walker hung up. He tried to get up out of bed, but couldn't do it. His body just wouldn't perform the commands he demanded.

Cheryl entered carrying a fast food breakfast. She saw Walker trying to get up. Here it goes, she said to herself, taking a breath.

"Grandpa," she said in a teasing way.

Walker threw her an agitated glance.

Cheryl pulled the chair by the window closer to the bed. "I think you're only on a liquid diet, so I hope you don't mind if I eat this in front of you?"

"You've got to help get me on my feet."

"Sorry, I don't think so."

"Dammit, they can't keep me here!"

"You're sick."

"And that's my business."

Cheryl munched on a croissant.

He was about to explode.

"Since you're not going anywhere right now, let's chat."

"I can't talk with you. Go back to where you came from."

"You know exactly where I come from."

Walker didn't say anything. Defeated, he turned his head away.

Cheryl took out a picture of Walker with her grandmother. She held it up in front of his face. He wanted to look away, but focused on the picture instead. He stared at it for several seconds until he closed his eyes and turned his head away again.

Cheryl dropped the picture on his chest. He pushed it aside. It slipped off of him and on to the floor on the opposite side of the bed.

"My grandmother, you knew her as Nora of course, said you had died in a car accident. I never questioned the story, never had any reason to, except until she died and I found everything, all the money still in the envelopes you sent. A few were opened, but for the most part, the bulk of them weren't."

"You haven't told anyone about what you found?" Walker blurted out still looking away from her.

Cheryl sensed his concern and thought through her answer. "And, what if I did?"

"You could get us all killed," he snapped.

"Chances are you're going to die sooner than you might." Cheryl sipped her tea and set it down on the side table. She knew she was getting nowhere with Walker so she figured she'd have to get at him directly. She walked around to the other side of the bed. She picked the picture up and got in Walker's face.

"I'm usually a well mannered southern girl, grandfather, but you leave me no choice."

He turned his head in the opposite direction. She got so angry that she grabbed his head and turned it back to face hers, almost yanking his out of it's socket. "Why did you leave her? Why did you come up here and hide in the woods all these years? Why won't you talk to me?!"

He shook loose her grip on his head. "I was right, you're trying to kill me." He massaged his sore neck from the jolt. "I still don't know if you are who you say you are."

Cheryl huffed and got her purse from the stand. She took out some more photographs and fingered through them. She threw one at Walker, then another, then yet another. They landed on his head and chest.

He slowly reached for one and brought it down to just in front of his face.

"That's my mother with my grandmother. My mother, your daughter, was actually killed in an automobile accident. I was young and naive and thought everyone died in car crashes, not to say that many don't, but not apparently in this family."

Walker set the picture down on his chest. Silence.

There was too much silence for Cheryl. "Talk to me. Talk to me damn it!" Tears rolled down her face. She grabbed Walker by his hospital gown around the collar and tightened her grip. If anyone were to enter the room at this moment, they might think she was going to beat it out of him. She tried shaking him, but he said nothing. Tears dripped off her cheek and onto his gown. "What's the matter with you?! You ran out on my grandmother, didn't you!" She wanted to slap him, but let go. She backed off and sobbed.

Walker wanted to reach for her head to stroke her hair and he wanted to cry, but he was too old and too tired to start caring now.

She plopped down into the chair, knocking her breakfast onto the floor accidentally.

He couldn't let his emotions take over. He hadn't ever let that happen. This still could be a trick. She still could be a setup. If he were younger, he'd have killed her that night and not have let this gone as far as it had.

She sniffled and dried her tears with a napkin. She regained her composure. She figured she'd have to outsmart him, maybe trigger him some way to answer her questions. She waited several minutes until she felt she could continue. He stared at the wall opposite her.

"Did you love her?"

"Huh?" He snapped his head around.

"Love her. Nora?"

Walker almost fell for the trick. However, he thought about playing senile. "Where?" He turned his head away again.

"In Alabama."

"Nora?"

She remembered the name from the back of the photographs and on the letters. "John?"

Walker's head spun around so fast that it almost didn't stop at the point at which it should have. Then he realized that she was testing him, so he slowly turned his head straightforward.

"Its, John, isn't it?"

"You'd better leave before you get us all killed."

"You keep saying that. What are you, a fugitive or something?"

"No!"

"Well what is it then, John?"

He got so upset that he started coughing and had quite a spell. Cheryl called for the nurse.

The nurse gave Walker a sedative. He didn't say anything else. He drifted off into a mid-morning slumber. Cheryl sat there by the window determined to get more answers, all the answers. She wasn't going to leave until she found out the truth.

"What did he say?" Judge Bell asked as he swept the kitchen floor.

"That if I wanted," Andy said with a straight face, "I could clean the place and fix some things. What're you going to do?"

"If you're going over there, I'll go fishing on Stillwater."

Andy nodded. After the Judge finished sweeping, he got his gear together, put on his `Colonel Blake' hat, and set off.

Andy tracked down Cheryl in Walker's room and placed the call.

"He's being a real ass," Cheryl said over the phone.

"How long will he be there?"

"If he gets his strength back, he's going to just walk out of here, but I can't see that happening for several days yet."

"Good," said Andy.

"That's not so good. He needs to stay here a couple weeks," rebutted Cheryl, "maybe more."

"I mean that he's getting the care that he should've had long ago. I'll check in each morning, maybe try to stop by soon. If you need me, the number is 555-3243."

"Okay," she answered.

Neither hung up the phone yet. There was a long pause. Finally, Andy said, "Okay. Bye."

"Bye," Cheryl said.

They hung up and thought about the other and hoped that there was a mutual interest.

Andy set sail for Walker's island.

At Walker's dock, he nailed in the loose board that Cheryl had dislodged. Andy said the hell with building a new dock right now; he had more important investigative work to do.

He opened the window in the loft so that he could see and hear if anyone was coming. He began to rummage around.

Andy was more interested in the files that were labeled and stamped by intelligence departments: The CIA, FBI, DIA, NSA. "How many intelligence agencies are there?" Andy mumbled. He obviously had heard of the CIA and the FBI, who hadn't? But the DIA? Andy opened a manila folder and discovered that the DIA was the Defense Intelligence Agency. Another folder explained that the NSA was the National Security Agency.

What Andy found interesting about all the files was that they were classified, but so old that perhaps they were declassified by now. They were copies of originals.

He fingered through a dusty file from a pile on a table near the window. It was labeled: PHOENIX PROGRAM.

He read through the two-inch file and discovered that this operation was run out of the CIA, primarily in South Vietnam, by then CIA station chief, William Colby. Andy was shocked at what he read. The CIA to rid South Vietnam of communists described it initially as a pacification program that spiraled into a mass murder campaign! There were names all over these pages that Andy didn't recognize: Colonel Edward G. Lansdale; General Henri Navarre, a French commander; R.G.K. Thompson, a British civil servant with the British Advisory Mission; Juan C. Orendain; Colonel Napoleon D. Valeriano. He read how many Vietcong and other communist insurgents were either assassinated or captured and tortured.

Andy found another file labeled: CIA ANTI-QUIRINO TEAM. The file outlined the policy: "Headed by a man named Ramon Magsaysay, his task was to divide up his special forces into Communist HUK's and loyal military to attack communist strongholds and villages throughout South East Asia, including the Philippines. They would exterminate with 'EXTREME PREJUDICE.'" One name near the end of the document that sent a chill through Andy's body, listed with several others, was John O'Connell.

He set the file aside and found a peculiar looking pamphlet. It was labeled: AGENCY ASSASSINATION MANUAL. AGENCY EYES ONLY. DESTROY. There was a newspaper clipping stuck in its pages. Andy pulled it out and read how a third party in Nicaragua had discovered a CIA Agency assassination manual in 1984. He fingered through the manual and read how an assassin was to conduct his business, including tactical support, cover, assassination and disposal, and extraction.

Andy was overwhelmed. He had to set it down. He took a deep breath and grabbed another file.

This one was labeled: ANTI-COMMUNIST LEAGUE OF THE CARIBBEAN. More names popped out that Andy didn't recognize: Guy Banister; David Ferri. Another file there was labeled: JM/WAVE. The names of Sergio Arcacha Smith; Antonio Veciana; and Maurice Bishop were listed. He skimmed through it and didn't see anything else, that was, not until the last page. There, he saw the name John O'Connell. The name had a sloppy circle around it and the word: Get!

Andy opened a book from the HOUSE SELECT COMMITTEE ON ASSASSINATIONS, Volume 10. He read the sections Walker had apparently highlighted:

> (484) According to FBI files…Banister also became excessively active in anti-Communist activities after his separation from the FBI…. The CIA file on Banister indicated the agency considered in September 1960 using Guy Banister Associates for the collection of foreign intelligence….

> (486) It was probably a result of such anti-Castro activities that Banister became acquainted with David Ferri. Ferri, an Eastern Airlines pilot, was also extremely active in Sergio

Arcacha Smith's anti-Castro group. Ferri shared Banister's anti-Communist and anti-Castro fervor.

(488) In the fall of 1963, Ferri and Banister worked together again with [attorney] G. Wray Gill for the defense of new Orleans organized crime head Carlos Marcello on a deportation case.

(489) Ferri became a suspect in the Kennedy assassination soon after it had occurred.... The Committee found evidence of a possible association between Ferri and Oswald.

(495) Newman [the building owner in New Orleans where Banister rented his office] theorized that if Oswald was using the 544 Camp Street address and had any link to the building, it would have been through a connection to the Cuban Revolutionary Council or Banister's office.

(496) Sergio Arcacha Smith and David Ferri...[were] all heavily involved in Cuban exile activities.

(498) [Delphine] Roberts [Banister's volunteer secretary] stated that she saw Oswald come into Banister's office on several occasions.

(500) Martin...[Banister's associate] went to Banister's office [the night of the assassination] and, in the heat of the quarrel, Banister said something to which Martin replied, "What are you going to do—kill me like you all did Kennedy?" Banister drew his pistol and beat Martin in the head. Martin believed Banister would have killed him but for the intervention of Banister's secretary, who pleaded with Banister not to shoot Martin.

(502) Martin has also told the committee he saw Lee Harvey Oswald with Ferri in Guy Banister's office in 1963.

(505) Oswald's name was included [in Banister's files] among the main subjects of the file on the Fair Play for Cuba Committee.

(509) The primary import of the 544 Camp Street address must be analyzed within the context of evidence of a Ferri-Oswald link. Unfortunately, the precise nature of their relationship may never be known.

(510) As can be seen by the Committee investigation into Ferri's association and activities throughout his life especially during the summer of 1963, there are several factors which explain why Ferri and Oswald could become closely associated....

(514) C. Significant to the argument that Oswald and Ferri were associated in 1963 is evidence of prior association in 1955 when Ferri was captain of a Civil Air Patrol squadron and Oswald a young cadet. This pupil-teacher relationship could have greatly facilitated their re-acquaintance and Ferri's noted ability to influence others could have been used with Oswald.

Andy put the file down and picked up another that was labeled: BANISTER. This file explained how Banister had been a radical member of the John Birch Society and was a former FBI agent. He ran a private investigators service out of a New Orleans office, the same building where the Cuban Revolutionary Council was located.

Another file was labeled: OPERATION MONGOOSE. It went on in detail how weapons were smuggled to Anti-Castro Cubans and how logistics were arranged for the training of those Cubans. The training grounds included areas in Louisiana and Mississippi. The policy objective was stated: OVERTHROW CASTRO GOVERNMENT! The file explained extensively about the group's planned re-invasion attempt of Cuba with CIA support. Again, what caught Andy's eye, was that the name O'Connell was listed there, this time as a trainer.

Another file had the name of Antonio Veciana, founder of Alpha 66. Again O'Connell's name was listed as a trainer.

As he picked up a file from the tops of each pile, and replaced it after scanning through it, Andy realized that his fingerprints were all over them, imprinted and visible to the naked eye because of the dust. Perhaps Walker, or O'Connell if that's who he was, didn't come up here much anymore. How could the old bastard climb the ladder? He was in bad shape and could barely walk around.

Andy rubbed his eyes and coughed the dust out of his lungs. He looked up at the A-frame ceiling above him and slowly scanned each photograph. He didn't recognize anyone. The pictures weren't labeled in any way. What he realized was, however, that none of the men in the pictures were smiling. Each photo seemed to be an impromptu one, like it was secretly taken.

Some of the men were Asian, others Latino, some maybe Cuban. A handful were Anglo.

Andy sat down in the creaky old office chair. He swung around and stared up at the JFK picture. His breathing rate increased and he felt like passing out, but maintained his equilibrium. The picture stared back at him and gave him the creeps, like a ghost was looking back at him from its grave. The late president had a cheerful smile, not like the rest. This photograph was from a newspaper, and was taken unlike the rest.

He felt queasy and became nervous. He swiveled around in the chair and looked at all the other photos again. "They're all dead! They must be all dead." His mind went on overload. Walker had worked for these guys, these agencies, he thought. That's got to be it, considering the arsenal in the main room like he was defending Fort Knox! He was defending himself from all these people and agencies and organizations. Why else would he have all these files and be listed in them? They wanted him dead for some reason. That's why he's hiding!

Andy realized that he was the only one who'd been in this cabin for over thirty years. He sat and thought this through. He couldn't just ask Walker. Yeah, right. Walker would shoot him for sure and bury him by the back shed. What did these groups, both official government ones and private ones, have on him? He knew too much? But surely he hadn't revealed this to anyone, and why would he now?

He started to dig through more files. He found more obscure operations that had been conducted all over the world. He saw names of Asian and Latino men and those words again: EXTERMINATE WITH EXTREME PREJUDICE. There were more operations that had been conducted in South East Asia, with dates in the 1950's and 60's, all labeled: BLACK OPS. There were files relating to operations in Latin America: Guatemala, Nicaragua, and El Salvador, again dating to the 1950's. There were files on Greece, in the late forties! Iran! Africa!

Andy's head spun. He couldn't think. There was too much information here, nothing that made much sense. Andy's emphasis for his degree in Political Science was American Government, not world affairs, so he didn't know all that much about some of these countries and their histories. He had had some related subjects involving this topic, and he had heard or studied vaguely some of the events that had taken place in these areas of the world, but he didn't have the whole, or an accurate picture. Actually, who did? Sure, he was well aware of the fact that the CIA had overthrown other governments, been involved in the internal politics of these other countries, including political campaigns and intimidation, coercion and outright assassinations of the opposition, but he didn't know the details.

He went back to the desk. He grabbed a book from the voluminous Warren Commission. He opened to a page that was marked with a piece of white paper and a newspaper clipping.

He had opened to the section that had the entire testimony of Mr. Lee Bowers, the Railroad switchyard operator who worked in the railroad yard behind the grassy knoll of Dealey Plaza.

Andy noticed that some of Bower's testimony in the book was underlined. The part underlined was about what Bowers saw that day, November 22, 1963. Andy read the underlined testimony:

> Mr. Ball. Did you notice any cars around there?
>
> Mr. Bowers. Yes; there were three cars that came in during the time from around noon until the time of the shooting....
>
> Mr. Ball. And the first came along that you noticed about what time of day?
>
> Mr. Bowers. This was approximately 12:10....
>
> Mr. Ball. And the car you noticed, when you noticed the car, where was it?
>
> Mr. Bowers. The car proceeded in front of the School Depository down across 2 or 3 tracks and circled the area in front of the tower, and to the west of the tower, and, as if he was searching for a way out, or was checking the area.... The first car was a 1959 Oldsmobile, blue and white station wagon with out-of-state license.
>
> Mr. Ball. And, it had something else, some bumper stickers?
>
> Mr. Bowers. Had a bumper sticker, one of which was a Goldwater sticker....
>
> Mr. Ball. And, did you see another car?
>
> Mr. Bowers. Yes, some 15 minutes or so after this...there was another car which was a 1957 black Ford, with one male in it that seemed to have a mike or telephone or something....
>
> Mr. Ball. Did you see it leave?

Mr. Bowers. Yes; after 3 or 4 minutes cruising around the area it departed the same way. He did probe a little further into the area than the first car.

Mr. Ball. Did you see another car?

Mr. Bowers. Third car, which entered the area, which was some seven or nine minutes before the shooting...was a 1961 or 1962, Chevrolet, four door Impala, white, showed some signs of being on the road. It was muddy up to the windows, bore a similar out-of-state license to the first car I observed, occupied also by one white male.

Mr. Ball. What did it do?

Mr. Bowers. He spent a little more time in the area. He tried—he circled the area and probed one spot right at the tower in an attempt to get and was forced to back out some considerable distance, and slowly cruised down back towards the front of the School Depository Building.

Mr. Ball. Then did he leave?

Mr. Bowers. The last I saw of him he was pausing just about in—just above the assassination site.

Mr. Ball. How long was this before the President's car passed there?

Mr. Bowers. About 8 minutes.

Mr. Ball. You saw the President's car coming out of Houston Street from Main, did you?

Mr. Bowers. Yes.... It came in sight after it had turned the corner of Elm and Houston.

Mr. Ball. Were there any people standing on the high side— high ground between your tower and where Elm Street goes down under the underpass toward the mouth of the underpass?

Mr. Bowers. Directly in line, towards the mouth of the underpass, there were two men. One man, middle-aged, or slightly older, fairly heavy-set, in a white shirt, fairly dark trousers.

Another younger man, about mid-twenties, in either a plaid shirt or plaid coat or jacket.

Mr. Ball. Were they standing together or standing separately?

Mr. Bowers. They were standing within 10 or 15 feet of each other....

Mr. Ball. In what direction were they facing?

Mr. Bowers. They were facing and looking up towards Main and Houston, and following the caravan as it came down.

Mr. Ball. Did you see any other people up on this high ground?

Mr. Bowers. There were one or two people in the area.... Each had uniforms....

Mr. Ball. Did you see any activity in this high ground above Elm?...

Mr. Bowers. At the time of the shooting there seemed to be some commotion....

Mr. Ball. Were the two men there at the time?

Mr. Bowers. One of them was.... The darker dressed man was too hard to distinguish from the trees. The one in the white shirt; yes....

Mr. Ball. When you said there was a commotion, what do you mean by that? What did it look like to you when you were looking at the commotion?

Mr. Bowers. I am just unable to describe rather than it was something out of the ordinary, a sort of milling around, but something occurred in this particular spot which was out of the ordinary, which attracted my eye for some reason.... [Afterwards, I] sealed off the area, and held off the trains until they could be examined, and there was some transients taken off at least one train.

Mr. Ball. Is there anything that you told me that I haven't asked you about that you think of?

Mr. Bowers. Nothing that I can recall.

Walker had scribbled a note next to this ending. It read, "Great questioning! Leaves a lot open!"

A photograph was folded next to another piece of paper. The photo was the famous "tramp" one taken by William Allen of the *Dallas Times Herald*. It showed the three tramps, who were just taken from the train like Bowers said. The picture was snapped in front of the Texas School Book Depository. Two officers who have never identified are escorting the three tramps in the picture. Walker had written the following across his copy of this photograph: Howie and Frank! What a pair, you assholes...

Andy thought a moment. Wait a minute! Howie and Frank? Howie and Frank? The Watergate plumbers? E. Howard Hunt and Frank Sturgis?

Walker had scribbled the words: No police record of this event. You guys were good!

Andy remembered that E. Howard Hunt had worked for the CIA and later Nixon as a White House plumber and that when Nixon during Watergate had paid off Hunt to keep him quiet, Nixon had said on the Watergate tapes that Hunt could open up "the whole Bay of Pigs thing again."

Jesus! Andy thought. He opened the folded piece of paper. It was from a transcript taken from a filmed and taped interview that Lee Bowers had given to lawyer Mark Lane on March 31, 1966. It read:

Lee Bowers. There was some occurrence—a flash of light or smoke or something which caused me to feel like something out of the ordinary had occurred there.

Further, Andy read:

> Lee Bowers. He [Mr. Ball] seemed to be satisfied with the
> answer to that one and did not care for me to elaborate.... I was
> cooperating by telling them what I knew and not attempting to
> be difficult in any manner, but simply to go along with the ques-
> tions that they were asking. When he changed the subject, well, I
> had no choice but to answer his questions....

Andy skimmed down the page, where Bowers was talking about
being interrogated in a small room at police headquarters following the
assassination:

> [I told the police that the shots were] almost on top of each
> other.... They made no comment other than the fact that when
> I stated that I thought the second and the third shots could not
> have been fired from the same rifle, they reminded me that I
> wasn't an expert, and I had to agree.

There was a newspaper clipping stuck there in between the pages of
Bowers' testimony, which had yellowed with age, but Andy could clearly
read it. It described the mysterious death of Bowers in a single car accident on an empty road in Midlothian, Texas on August 9, 1966. The doctor who performed the investigation reported that Bowers had died of
some kind of shock, or trauma. That was it. The clipping didn't elaborate.

The guy died a few months later after his elaboration! Andy
scratched his head.

Walker had written a note there on the clipping. It read: "V19, p. 483."

Andy quickly found the section. Walker had highlighted portions of
an affidavit, signed by Julia Ann Mercer, on 22 November 1963. It was
taken at the Sheriff's Department, County of Dallas, Texas.

On November 22, 1963, I was driving a rented White Valiant automobile west on Elm Street and was proceeding to the over-pass in a westerly direction and at a point about 45 or 50 feet east of the overhead signs of the right entrance road to the over-pass, there was a truck parked on the right hand side of the road. The truck looked like it had 1 or 2 wheels up on the curb.... The truck was a green Ford with a Texas license.

A man was sitting...slouched over the wheel [and he was] a white man and about 40's and was heavy set.... Another man was at the back of the truck and reached over the tailgate and took out from the truck what appeared to be a gun case.... It was brown in color. It had a handle and was about 3 1/2 to 4 feet long.... He then proceeded to walk across the grass and up the grassy hill which forms part of the overpass....

I had been delayed because the truck which I described above was blocking my passage and I had to await until the lane to my left [sic] cleared so I could go by the truck.

During this time that I was at this point and observed the above incident there were 3 policeman [sic] standing talking near a motorcycle on the bridge just west of me.

The man who took what appeared to be the gun case out of the truck was a white male, who appeared to be in his late 20's or early 30's.

Walker had scribbled there on the page the words: Never called to testify! Commission never investigated! Thanks...Andy skimmed through other sections. Some passages were underlined but many were not. Andy figured he'd have to bring a notebook next time to take notes, perhaps his laptop. What would he note? He could note these particular passages that were marked and underlined, what they referred to, and whom they dealt with. Too much information buzzed through Andy's head now to make any sense of all this. He'd wrap it up for today and come back tomorrow with his laptop. He made sure that everything was put back the way he had found it. He nailed up the board for the window and locked the trap door on his way down.

During his boat ride back to the Osprey, his mind whirled. Walker certainly must be O'Connell, and had been involved in these operations somehow. But what was his involvement, if any, with the assassination? A conspirator? Andy couldn't believe it. Impossible! He hadn't seen any direct connection of O'Connell to this. However, it was clear that this O'Connell was directly connected to all those secret operations. This can't be, he said to himself. This was Beaver River, New York. Montana was were they all went!

Ten

Judge Bell puttered around the Osprey that night doing the dishes and repairing a leaky sink pipe. Andy worked on his laptop. He logged in what he had seen and done this day in the file named Walker. Then he created a new file and called it: O'Connell. This file would list those specific locations in the Warren files that Walker had marked.

The phone rang just as Andy was going to unplug it and plug in his computer to go on-line.

"Osprey," Andy said into the phone.

"Its, Cheryl."

"How is he?"

"Stubborn as ever. I really think he's my grandfather. I can see it in his face."

Andy paced by the phone. He wanted to see her. "What's the update on when he's leaving?"

"No one's willing to discharge him. But, he thinks just as soon as he can get out of bed. His hospital doctor ordered that he be given drugs to keep him sleepy."

"I see." Andy was relieved. This should give him time to gather more data from Walker's loft. "I have to take my father over to Stillwater tomorrow night, I can drive in and maybe we could have dinner?" Andy waited nervously twirling the telephone cord. His father heard that from the kitchen.

After a pause, Cheryl said, "Sure. I'll meet you here at the hospital. If he's awake maybe you can talk some sense to him."

"I doubt that, but see you tomorrow night, about seven O'clock?"

"Okay."

"Bye."

"Bye." She must like me, he hoped. He looked out through the front porch screen and across the lake. His mind wandered from Cheryl, back to Wendy, then to that cabin on that island and the secrets it held.

Andy snapped out of his dreamlike state, plugged his laptop into the phone line and went on-line to the Internet. He prepared an e-mail message to a friend, Patrick Hennelly, who was taking summer classes at Harvard. Andy turned to Pat whenever he needed help with anything computer related.

For this e-mail, Andy asked Pat to leave him a message when he would be in so they could talk. Andy clicked on send. The short letter was sent on its way.

Andy went off-line and reconnected his father's phone line. Although he knew his father wouldn't mind his hook-up, he didn't want to run up the phone bill too much, since the access phone number he used was the one from the university in Massachusetts.

Judge Bell poked his head in through the door from the kitchen. "Kirby's having a game. He invited you."

"Okay," Andy said closing his computer.

Together they walked to Kirby's cabin.

The usual gaggle of card players had already gathered there: Kirby, Ronny and Dusty.

"Open bar gentlemen, as usual," Kirby announced. "Help your-selves."

Everyone did and sat for a game of Poker. They played with quarters.

"So, Andy," Ronny jumped in, "you, this girl and Walker are the talk of the town."

"You're kidding," Andy said sarcastically. "You call this place a town?"

"Is she Walker's granddaughter?" Kirby asked dealing the first hand.

"Seems so, but obviously they don't know each other."

Everyone checked his hand. "Three," Andy asked for. Kirby slid him three cards.

"And here after all these years," Dusty joined in. "Where'd she come from and how'd she find him?"

Andy didn't want to discuss the matter so he shrugged his shoulders. "I don't know."

"Everyone comes from somewhere," said Dusty. "Everyone's got a past."

"Yeah, and a government file," chided Kirby.

"Fold," Andy said throwing his cards down on to the table. "What do you mean, like FBI or something?"

"Some do, but everyone has an IRS file," Kirby said.

"Duh, of course," said Andy chastising himself. "Even I have one with my measly income."

"Government's got a file on everyone."

"Raise it a buck," said Andy's father throwing four quarters in the pot. "You have a questionable IRS file, Dave?"

"You think I'd tell you, Judge?" Kirby said throwing in five quarters. "Raise five."

"Call." The Judge revealed his hand. He had three jacks.

Kirby threw down his flush.

"What about Walker's cabin, Andy?" Ronny asked.

"What about it?"

"What's it look like? I know he has some guns. Heard him shooting before, usually in the winter when not very many residents are around."

Andy drank a gulp of his beer. "Yeah, I saw a shotgun."

"Shotgun, hell! He was shooting a semi-automatic assault weapon."

"I don't know much about guns," Andy said rearranging his new hand that his father had dealt, "but there were a couple rifles there. I've watched movies. One looked like an M16 or something."

"I still say he ran guns or drugs," said Ronny.

"I still think the Mafia angle," Kirby said.

"His cabin is pretty much like anyone else's," Andy said, "except it's not as tidy." That part was relatively true.

"Yeah, but weird," continued Ronny. "He hasn't had anything to do with the rest of us, except pleasantries, small talk. Eats occasionally at the lodge."

"Don't you wonder about this guy, Judge?" Kirby asked. "Two, please."

Judge Bell slid Kirby two cards. "Yeah, I have to confess."

"Get the stenographer," said Dusty.

"I was just as curious," said the Judge. He looked at his son who watched him as he spoke. "I ran a check on him through the Justice computer, oh, more than five years ago or so. Nothing turned up."

Because you had the wrong name! Andy's cymbal went off, thinking to himself. The name O'Connell played over and over in his head. Andy challenged the hand and took it this time with a straight. "Justice computer, dad?"

"Yeah, every federal judge has one in his chamber to enter and extract related court matters. Computers, how did mankind get along without them?"

Andy shook his head, swigged his beer. "Who sold Walker his land?"

"It was the old Roberts place," said Ronny dealing a new hand. "He died and his daughter sold it."

"No, I mean who was the agent that sold the land?"

"That was ah, Aaron Siegel, poor bastard," said Ronny.

"Why do you say that?"

"It must've been a couple months later, I believe, he was shot to death and his office burned to the ground."

"Damn," Andy let slip. His heart sank to his knees.

"Police said it was a robbery," continued Ronny. "The robber or robbers—the police wrote up in their report—burned the place down to hide any evidence. Can you believe it? All this in Lowville. The last murder was over a hundred years ago. Couple of loggers fighting or something."

"You remember that too?" Dusty asked.

"Ha, Ha," said Ronny jesting.

As the hand was played out, Andy's mind gyrated. To hide any detailed evidence of the real estate transaction, Andy deduced. Sure the county records and local paper would report the transaction, but more detailed long forms and papers would have been destroyed in the fire. The town or county would have filed the transaction, under the name Al Walker, of course. But there would have been duplicates somewhere, with the seller perhaps. Oh no, Andy dared to ask.

"Where's the seller now?" Andy folded his hand.

"I believe she lived in Watertown," Ronny said taking the hand this time.

"Was her name Roberts?"

"What are you going to do, sleuth this out, Andy?" Ronny asked.

"Just interesting, sounds bizarre considering Walker's behavior." Andy figured he should cover his inquisitiveness somehow.

"Roberts. Yeah, at the time the property was listed as Roberts, under the daughter's name, I believe was, Jeanne."

Andy now feared Walker, rather O'Connell, had her done in too. He would have to find out.

"You have it in for the girl?" Dusty asked.

"None of your damn business."

"I saw how you looked at her the other day when she was checking in."

Andy gave him a mind your own business look, but it didn't work.

"Be careful with those southern women."

"What the hell does that mean?"

"I dated one when I was in the Army, in Louisiana."

"Yeah, and what happened?"

"She couldn't get enough! It almost killed me."

"How so?"

"Her estranged husband came back from the field and almost caught us."

"Fooling around with a married woman?" Ronny asked.

"They were separated."

"What's with our military corrupting the young men?"

"Knock it off."

"Yeah, so never mind about Cheryl," Andy interjected.

"I'm just foolin.'"

The guys continued playing poker well into the morning until most were either out of quarters, too tired to carry on, or too drunk.

Andy and his father stumbled back to the Osprey.

"You're thinking about Walker and his hermit-like lifestyle and mysterious past, right?" Andy's father asked.

"In a way. After all, I'm working for him. I should know some background."

"Well, forget it. He obviously wants to be left alone. There's nothing to the mystery, I checked, remember? He probably had a tragic life and ran away from the world, or is under the witness protection program. It's really none of our business. This is America, need I remind you."

"No, Judge, your honor."

They walked the rest of the way in silence. Not if he was O'Connell and was a fugitive who ran from justice! Andy said to himself. He had to leave the discussion where it was, and not discuss anything with his father until he had more evidence. It was clear that his father would disapprove of what he was doing, it was perhaps illegal, even though his father had done it. However, his father hadn't dug deeper, like Andy just had to do. Private detectives did this kind of stuff all the time. The only difference was perhaps they were registered or licensed. Andy looked up at the night sky that was clear, save full of stars. He just had to find out. However, when the truth was known, he'd have wished he hadn't pursued this.

Andy didn't have an opportunity to go over to Walker's place the next day. He helped his father, who had asked him, to cut an old Spruce tree down that was threatening to collapse onto the Osprey's shed nearby. Although majestic for more years than even the Judge's age, the way in which the tree was leaning, it had to go. Its roots had been weakened and it would certainly tip over next winter under the weight of ice and snow.

By the time Andy and his father had cut the spruce down, buzzed it up into firewood and cleaned up the twigs, it was mid-afternoon. They cleaned up and prepared to head on over to Stillwater.

Andy was anxious to go. He wanted to see Cheryl. He actually had butterflies when he thought of her. He hadn't had this feeling for a girl for years. He had dated Wendy for almost three years, and come to think of it, he couldn't ever remember having butterflies over her.

"Andy, its, Wendy on the phone," his father called out from inside the Osprey as Andy threw an overnight bag into the truck.

Andy traipsed inside and reluctantly took the phone from his father. "Wendy." He looked at the floor.

"Didn't you get my message?" Wendy asked.

"Yeah, but a lot has been happening here."

"You don't want to see me?"

"I need some time alone."

"Alone? Why?"

"Just because."

"Andy, I'm offering to make up with you. I still have feelings."

Andy didn't answer. He wanted to end the call.

"Can't I come see you?" Wendy asked impatiently.

"Maybe in a few weeks."

"Weeks? I'm not going to wait for you forever, Andy."

"It's just not a good time."

"Well, then. I'll wait for your call." She slammed the phone down.

Andy sighed and dropped the phone into its cradle. He had no intention of calling her back. He joined his father who waited in the truck outside.

They drove in silence down to the landing and got into the boat. Andy sat in the back letting the breeze blow at his face.

Judge Bell looked back at him. Andy had his eyes closed. "It's not any of my business, but do you want to talk about it?"

Andy opened his eyes. "Not really."

His father maneuvered through the Grassy Point area, avoiding the large stumps that were just beneath the surface of the water in particular spots. The speed of the boat in this area was slow, and one had to know the exact route to take, otherwise they'd crash their craft.

"I know you like the fact that Wendy's father works in the halls of power," said Andy finally, "but she's too much of an unpredictable silver spoon princess."

Judge Bell hid his amusement by looking out at the approaching main area of the reservoir.

Andy closed his eyes again. His father hadn't ever given any advice before, solicited or unsolicited, so the discussion ended there.

At Stillwater, they docked the boat. Judge Bell went to his car and Andy to his.

"Next Friday, same time," the Judge called out.

Andy signaled him with the okay sign and a wave. He got into his Jeep and peeled out. He was gone and up the dirt road a couple minutes ahead of his father, and given the speed that kids drove compared to their parents, Andy would be several minutes ahead of his father when he reached civilization.

The drive to Watertown took just under an hour and a half. Andy pulled in early and went straight to Walker's room. There, Cheryl sat waiting. Walker was in and out of consciousness.

She stood up, and, for some impulsive reason, he went right up to her and gave her a quick salutatory hug. After he had done it, he couldn't believe he had. He blushed. She was surprised he did it, but she didn't protest.

"How is he?" Andy asked backing off, giving her some space.

"We haven't talked today," she said with perhaps too much space, wanting Andy a little closer than he was. "Bergholtz came by and still has him drugged up so he won't just get up and walk out of here."

"Since he's not going anywhere, shall we?" He waved his arm toward the door. He followed her out.

Andy drove to a nearby Pizza Hut. They sat opposite one another in a booth. He ordered a large pizza, certain he could eat most of it by himself, and a pitcher of beer that came to their table promptly.

"What're you thinking?" Andy asked.

"I don't know yet. Grandmother said very little about my grandfather and I didn't ask. I have no idea why he left." She felt somewhat nervous looking him straight in the eye. She knew for sure that she was attracted to him and that made it harder to look at him for some odd reason.

He obviously suspected why Walker had left, but kept it to himself. If Walker, or rather O'Connell, was Cheryl's grandfather, then Andy certainly couldn't tell her or what he suspected.

"Perhaps they just had a falling out or something," he said coming up with the obvious answer.

"There's got to be more to it. It's too bizarre. He talks nonsense, like we're all gonna get killed. What's that about?"

He shrugged his shoulder and sipped his beer.

"My grandmother must've changed her name when she moved from Birmingham to near Huntsville in 1963 a few years after my mother was born. My grandmother said my mother was born in Birmingham, but there's no birth record under her name. The county records in Huntsville listed my grandmother's property under her name, Jackson, but nothing in Birmingham."

"Jackson?" Andy said thinking aloud.

"Why do you ask it like that?"

"It's one of the most common names in America. There're millions of Jacksons."

"And?"

"A needle in a haystack."

"You're right. There's no birth certificate for a Leonora Jackson in Birmingham either, where she said she was born too."

They sat silent for a moment.

"What're you thinking?" She asked.

Nothing he could tell her at this time, so he played along. "Walker, or your grandfather, must've still cared for her to send those notes."

She decided to tell the truth. "They were more than notes. He sent money. Much of it she never used."

He nodded. Natural impulse was to ask her how much, but it was entirely inappropriate and he actually didn't care.

"So the money was to take care of not only her, but my mother."

"I don't get it," he said sipping his beer again.

"He must've felt guilty and obligated in some way."

Andy admired her intelligence, but his mind wandered to the flesh. He was attracted to her perfectly rounded and well-developed breasts. He had to almost shake it out of his head and get back to the subject.

"Tell me about yourself," she said changing the subject.

"Not much to tell, actually. My father is a federal judge, I begin my senior year at Harvard."

"That's not much? It's impressive. So, then what's your degree in?"

"Political science, American Government."

"What can you do with a degree in political science?" Their pizza arrived. "Usually, most go on to law school," he explained while pulling off a slice of pizza. "Or work in government, which is shrinking and doesn't have as many opportunities as there used to be."

"So what're you going to do?"

"I don't know. I don't want to be a lawyer. I thought I'd go work in government, FBI or something if they'd have me. I know it sounds idealistic, but I want to work for the people and make this country a better place. Although, as everyone must be well aware of, government is more despised than it used to be. The second half of this century has seen a dramatic turn around in the people's attitudes about their government. Not long ago it was seen as a worthy calling. Back in the times of Jefferson, he thought it was honorable for a citizen to go to Washington, serve his country, then go home. Now, with career politicians and the all powerful dollar, it's not so revered."

She was impressed at his dissertation, and at the same time surprised at his cynicism. She blew on her pizza to cool it. Andy watched her and she caught him watching her. He looked away.

"Now, it's your turn," he said. "About you."

"Well, most of it you know, except I was studying teaching in college for an elementary credential."

"That's admirable."

"But not respected as it should be. The pay is so low, no one wants to do such hard work for so little. People have no idea how difficult it is to teach children today with all the distractions, gangs, even in Huntsville, drugs and broken homes. We even have gangs in Huntsville with guns shooting people and the kids see this stuff every day. I was interested in history, but there're too many history teachers."

"And too many Americans don't know their history, like the Ziggy Marley song, 'Don't know your past, don't know your future.'"

"Yeah, but I don't know my past, if this guy is my grandfather. What did he run from?"

"His past," he let slip out.

"That's what I'm here to find out. He can die after he tells me everything."

"You think he'll talk? I mean, he ran from it probably to hide from it."

"I'm not afraid of him. I'm not going away until he does talk."

Good, he said to himself. He nodded and chewed on a piece of pizza.

After dinner Andy drove her back to her motel near the hospital. She sat there in his Jeep.

"I had a good time," she said.

"Me too." Andy sprang from his seat and ran around and opened her door.

She was surprised. "You're not the stereotypical Northerner."

"And what is that?"

"Stereotypes. Forget it." She got out of the Jeep.

Andy walked her to her door. He felt like a high schooler on a first date. "Good night," he said.

She turned. "Thanks." She bent forward and kissed him lightly on his cheek. He melted.

"It's late," she said. "Are you going back to Beaver River?"

"Ah, no. I was going to get a room and check something out in town tomorrow," he said uncomfortably.

"There's an extra bed, here. It'll save you the trouble."

"I don't think it's a good I...."

"I do." She found her motel key and opened the door. She took him by the arm and led him in and closed the door.

Inside, she locked the door, threw her handbag onto the chair, and moved closer to him. She kissed him and his hormones exploded.

He put his arms around her and together they submerged one another in young passion. They undressed each other and after intense sex, slept in the same bed.

The next morning Cheryl got out of bed first. She looked at Andy lying there on his side, completely nude because of the sweltering humidity. She had had sex before, even had a steady boyfriend with whom she made love, but what she had last night, she felt, was more than casual sex. She made her way into the shower.

He heard the shower a few minutes later and rolled over onto his back. He had a similar retrospection that she had had moments ago. With Wendy, it had been okay, but last night with Cheryl had been ferocious. Perhaps, he reasoned, it was just animal attraction. It wasn't love; he didn't know her.

She came from the shower as he was getting up out of bed. He was completely exposed while she was wrapped in a towel.

"What happened?"

"I don't know," she said. "You look cute."

He took her hands in his. "Let's not let it stop at last night." He kissed her on her lips.

She reached around behind his head and held him close for a kiss that lasted an eternity. In doing so, she pulled his body closer.

Later they shared breakfast together in a nearby coffee shop. For the most part, they small talked.

After breakfast Andy got in his Jeep and headed for the county records office for Jefferson County. Cheryl went back to the hospital and sat with Walker.

By the time Andy asked one clerk, then another, he was searching through a microfiche file. He couldn't believe what he read in the county death records. Jeanne Roberts died in May of 1964! She was run over in a hit and run accident. The perpetrator was never identified or captured. "He killed her!" Andy felt the blood run out of his face.

He drove down to Herkimer, the county seat for Herkimer County; the county Beaver River was located in. He dug through real estate transactions for the year 1963 and located the sale of the Roberts cabin in Beaver River.

The executor of the Roberts' estate, Jeanne, the daughter, sold the land. Albert Walker bought the land. Andy copied down Walker's Social Security Number.

He searched through the local newspaper and found the story on microfiche about the death of real estate agent Aaron Siegel. Just like Ronny had said.

Andy searched the databases of several sources and couldn't find anything more about an Albert Walker. Nothing in the birth records, nothing in the death records. He remembered he had read stories about how people had assumed the identity of dead people using their Social Security Numbers, and thought that Walker probably had done this. It was becoming more evident to Andy that Walker must be this mysterious O'Connell and that he had covered his tracks so that no one would know where he was. It was all beginning to make sense, sense to Andy that now gave him cause for alarm. Walker was hiding in Beaver River. He was hiding from what was up there in that loft. Andy certainly had to keep a computer log of his events, just in case Walker found out what Andy had done and was doing, and did kill him, then there would be a story for the authorities.

Andy went back to the Osprey in Beaver River. It was late afternoon by the time he arrived. There was a message from Pat. "Andy, just call. I'm in all day."

He called Cheryl first. "Anything?"

"He comes in and out of it. But nothing."

"Okay, I just got in."

There was a long silence.

"I hope we can see each other soon," Cheryl finally said.

"Well, I could come in every couple of days or so."

"Isn't that too inconvenient?"

"No. Not at all. I'll call you and let you know."

"Okay. Bye." Cheryl hung up the phone.

Andy hung up and dialed Pat. "Its, Andy."

"How's vacation?"

"Interesting. Can you do me a favor?"

"What?"

"Hacking."

"Depends. Where?"

"A Social Security Number."

"Oooohhhh." Pat thought about it for a moment. "Yeah. What is it?" Andy told him the number. "I need something else."

"Yeeessss?" Pat said in a teasing manner.

"A mysterious man by the name of John O'Connell. Can you check on that name?"

"I'll see what I can come up with."

"Thanks, Pat." Andy hung the phone up. He sat there a minute staring at his notes. He then entered the information he had gathered today into his computer.

Patrick Hennelly sat in his cramped dorm room at Harvard University. He was the typical computer geek. He wasn't bad looking, but he did in a way remind Andy of Bill Gates. Pat would sit at his computer and spend hours on the Internet, and mess around with every software program available. He wrote his own programs. Pat could computer-hack just about anything.

His dorm room looked like the Unabomber's shack, and was just as small. There were papers piled high in several spots and dirty clothes thrown in the corner. The obvious center of Pat's universe was his desktop computers and the endless stockpile of software and disks strewn about.

He had written down the Social Security Number and the name John O'Connell on a pad. "This shouldn't take long," Pat said aloud as he pointed and clicked, and tapped on his keyboard.

He got an access denied message across his screen.

Pat swiveled around in his chair and found a loose-leaf notebook behind him on a bookcase and fingered through it. He found some formulas and numerical notations scribbled down there in pencil. He hammered away at his keyboard and pointed and clicked several times until his computer began bombarding the Social Security Administration's database with possible access combinations.

Pat spun around and grabbed a half-eaten peanut butter sandwich that was sitting on a nightstand near his bed. He took a bite from the sandwich and placed the remains back down next to the keyboard.

The message access denied popped up and disappeared within a split second and his computer entered a new sequence just as fast. A total of ten thousand possible combinations had already been tried within the span of two minutes.

Finally, a message stopped the process. It read: "Social Security Administration." It was superimposed over the emblem of the Administration. A line requested a command.

Pat looked in his notebook. He turned back to his computer and entered a string. A directory popped up. He searched the directory and found a search by SSN command line. Pat entered the Social Security Number that Andy had given him.

A second later the file for that number popped up on screen. Pat quickly ordered up a printout and exited the file.

He then promptly searched the directory and found a search by name line. He entered that area and typed in John O'Connell.

A second later the computer responded with search results. It read: "Search results, 8,465 John O'Connell's found." Pat popped in a floppy diskette and down loaded the list within seconds. He closed the file and got out of the Social Security Administration's database.

He called Andy at the cabin.

Andy answered the phone. "Osprey."

"Its, Pat. How's your vacation?"

"You asked that already," said Andy knowing that Pat was serious. "You can't be done already?"

"I got it. The number you gave me is for an Albert Walker."

"That's it."

"But there're more than eight thousand John O'Connell's."

"Damn," Andy said. "I guess I'll have to get a number on him."

"I can send you the info on Walker and a copy of the O'Connell list."

"Yeah. I'll hang up and plug in."

"I'll scan the Walker info into my computer and send you two files."

"Thanks, Pat."

"What's this all about?"

"I don't know yet," Andy lied.

"All right," said Pat, "give me a minute. Call me only if you don't get it." He hung up.

Andy disconnected the telephone and plugged in his computer. He opened the software that would transfer the data.

About three minutes later the computer modem rang and Andy's computer answered. After computer protocol was established the linkup was completed with Pat's computer. Andy hit a command and his software downloaded the files that Pat's computer sent. The process took three minutes and a status bar reported that the files were transferred successfully. Andy went off line immediately thereafter. He checked and saw that the two files were listed. One was Walker, the other O'Connell.

Andy unplugged his computer from the phone line and reconnected the telephone. He then opened the Walker file.

The file wasn't even one page long. It showed that Albert Walker was born in Houston, Texas in 1930. He was abandoned and left on the doorstep of the county—an orphan.

Walker had been a truck driver and worked for the Mason Trucking Company of Houston, Texas from 1949 until 1963. Regular Social Security taxes were paid on his behalf until 1963 when they stopped.

Andy realized that no further taxes were ever paid to his account. Nothing else was listed here. There's that coincidental year, 1963, Andy said to himself.

The Walker file concluded with the words: Nothing follows.

"Holy shit," Andy said. No record of an application for benefits. Nothing follows. Walker had killed Walker too!

Andy closed the Walker file and opened the O'Connell one. It was just a list of John O'Connell's and their Social security numbers, nothing else. Andy would have to get a number. There had to be a number in that old cabin somewhere.

Clearly, Andy concluded, Walker had assumed the identity of this Albert Walker, rather O'Connell had, Andy corrected himself. He decided that he would just have to accept that fact and concentrate on who O'Connell was. The real Albert Walker was probably dead, killed by O'Connell and the body either buried or destroyed. Even if Andy did go to Houston and look through records, there probably wouldn't be any, or they'd be inconclusive. Walker was an orphan and had no family. No one but his employer would miss him and even they might not have filed any missing person's report. O'Connell obviously had chosen a person who had no family, as an adult either.

In any event, Walker was history, he told himself, and it didn't matter how O'Connell assumed this man's identity, just the fact that he had. O'Connell was the mystery where Andy's attention needed to be focused.

Andy sat there for the longest time thinking about what secrets he had yet to learn about O'Connell. If all that he now assumed was the truth, how could he explain this to Cheryl? He still didn't have the facts, he reminded himself. He'd better learn the facts first before he made any definitive conclusions. However, after he had learned the facts, he'll have wished he hadn't.

Eleven

Andy got up early and headed out across the lake by eight thirty the next morning. He had his computer with him in its Velcro carrying case and had recharged the internal battery last night.

He stopped in the main room of Walker's cabin and glanced at the chest he had searched through before. He got the key and went through it and found the commendations that O'Connell had received during his time in Korea. The commendations listed no Social Security Number, but the outmoded service number that military personnel had been issued in those days, which was well before the military converted to the current Social Security Number system.

Andy entered the service number into his O'Connell file. He searched through the entire chest and found a small picture near the bottom. The picture showed a group of men in a bunker, probably in Korea. The men were relaxed and smiling. Andy studied the photo and realized that one of the men in the picture closely resembled the man in the picture with Cheryl's grandmother. And again, the man closely resembled someone Andy had seen before, but he couldn't remember who, or where he'd seen him.

He replaced everything in the chest as he had found it. He wondered if Walker ever looked in here anymore. There was a thick coating of dust on the chest top, so probably not. Andy returned the key and decided to get to work up in the loft.

Walker was aware that Cheryl was sitting in the chair by the window looking at him, but he didn't acknowledge her. After all these years of hiding, his granddaughter, if that's who she was, finds him? He couldn't believe it!

Cheryl stared him down. She became impatient. "I'm not leaving here, Watertown, or Beaver River, until I get the truth, grandfather."

"Don't call me that," Walker shot back looking over at her.

"I think it's clear."

"You don't know for sure."

"I know for sure that it was you sending Nora those envelopes full of money for thirty years. You know she didn't use much of it."

"Then it's yours. Take it and go live your life." He rolled his head away from her.

"So you admit that much."

He didn't answer. The nurse came in with his breakfast. She opened the cover.

"I got it," said Cheryl intervening. The nurse left.

Cheryl opened Walker's juice.

He used the automatic controls and raised the head of his bed. "I can get it," he stewed.

She backed off and he grabbed his dry toast. He crunched on it and took a sip of his juice.

"So why did you really leave?"

"'Can't tell you that."

"You won't or you can't?"

He didn't answer.

"Just tell me the truth."

"The truth?" He snickered. "There's no truth."

"Now what does that mean?"

"It means nothing." He sipped his black coffee then nibbled on some fruit.

"Did you love her?"

"What?"

"Love her. Nora, my grandmother."

He stopped eating and stared at his coffee. She saw that she had hit a nerve. He let his mind wander and he let it slip. "Always made good coffee."

"What?"

He continued to stare at the coffee. "The coffee." He paused. "She always had it ready in the morning and knew how to mix it just right."

"She didn't drink coffee."

"Yeah, but she knew how to make it."

She had him opening up. If she could small talk him, perhaps she could get the answers she wanted after she had gained his trust. "She always loved to cook, too."

"Yeah, I loved everything she cooked up." He paused, then snapped out of his daydream. He cut up his omelet. "Not like this crap."

"It's expected for hospital food."

He took a mouth full and chewed away. "She's gone?" He asked the question as a matter of fact.

"Heart attack."

He continued to chew and stare straight ahead. He sipped his coffee again.

"I don't care what it is that you may have done in your past," she said, "all I want to know is…"

"What are you talking about?" He snapped at her.

"Nothing." She knew she had stepped over the line and the stare that he gave her could have turned her into stone. She backed off and sat down in her chair. She knew that she would have to take this slower and chip away at him in sessions.

"You're talkin' about a federal judge, Jimmy," said Donny.

"So. I don't give a fuck. The asshole has it comin'," said Jimmy Scardino.

Donny Rossetti's nightclub, including the parking lot, filled an entire city block in Brooklyn. A swanky joint, at present the day crew cleaned up from the previous night.

In his early fifties, short, stocky and mostly bald (it seemed he only had one strand of hair that he combed across his forehead) Donny Rossetti had run the family business for the last five years. His father, now in his late seventies, had moved to their Florida estate with his thirty-year-old bride.

Donny's only remaining son, Michael, ran the import business. Donny's other two sons had been killed in small-time local turf wars. The Rossetti family had its tentacles in several businesses that stretched all along the eastern seaboard of the United States. The import business imported many food products from Europe, but had also imported drugs that the nephews handled, including Tommy, who had spread his distribution network throughout upstate New York. Jimmy had worked mainly as a thug for his older brother Tommy.

Jimmy paced in front of the bar by Donny who sat on a barstool smoking a cigarette.

"I told him not to be so goddamn conspicuous," said Donny. "He was always reckless and didn't listen."

"So we leave him there?" Jimmy stopped pacing in front of his uncle.

"We appeal. Goetherd said there're grounds."

"Grounds? Goetherd's an incompetent fuck."

"He's worked for the family for years." Donny took a drag on his cigarette.

"I can't do nothin,' Tommy's my brother, your nephew."

"You do what I tell you and keep your nose out of this."

Jimmy looked at him squarely, yet said nothing.

"Do you hear me?" Donny demanded.

Jimmy nodded his head.

"A fuckin' federal judge. I don't need that crap. Now get the hell outta here."

Jimmy strode off pompously. He couldn't let his older brother sit in prison while years went by appealing, and then if his sentence were upheld, he'd be there forever. But how could he get him out? He'd figure something out. On his way out the door, he bumped into a man who was sweeping the dance floor. "Watch what you're doing you stupid shit!" Jimmy said as he stormed off.

Andy found an interesting CIA document that apparently Walker had gotten as a result of a Freedom of Information Act suit filed by a Washington attorney, Bernard Fensterwald. The document was CIA Document No. 632-796. The date of declassification was 1977. He read the document:

> 8. Jean SOUTRE AKA Michel Roux AKA Michael Mertz—on March 5, [1964] the FBI advised that the French had [withheld] Legal Attaché in Paris and also the [withheld] had queried the Bureau in New York City concerning subject, stating that he had been expelled from the US at Forth Worth or Dallas 18 hours after the assassination. He was in Fort Worth on the morning of 22 November and in Dallas in the afternoon. The French believe that he was expelled to either Mexico or Canada. In January he received mail from a dentist named Alderson...Subject is believed to be identical with a Captain who is deserter from the French Army and an activist in the OAS [a right-wing French militant group.] The French are concerned because of DeGaulle's planned visit to Mexico. They would like to know the reason for his expulsion from the US and his destination. Bureau files are negative and they are checking in Texas and the INS...

Andy then read a clipping attached to the file. It was from *The New York Times* and it reported on the Senate Intelligence Committee from 1975. He read how the CIA's assassination program, nicknamed Executive Action Program, had used many expert rifle teams composed of persons around the world to assassinate political opposition in Foreign countries. Andy learned that all the declassified documentation was either blackened out, or that the participants in the program were referred to in code. No names were mentioned, only their code-names such as: WI/ROGUE or QJ/WIN.

Down the page, Richard Helms was quoted in the CIA file. He said, "If you needed somebody to carry out murder, I guess you had a man who might be prepared to carry it out."

Andy scratched his head and set this file aside. He then fingered through a section in volume 6 of the Warren Commission where Jean Hill, who was wearing the red raincoat, and was standing with Mary Moorman opposite the grassy knoll, testified about the events of November 22, 1963. Andy had to read it:

Mr. Specter. Where were you the day of November 22, 1963 at about noontime?

Mrs. Hill. I was standing directly across from the Texas School Book Depository on a grassy slope and the triangle toward the underpass....

Mr. Specter. How many shots were there altogether?

Mrs. Hill. I have always said there were some four to six shots.... They were rapidly—they were rather rapidly fired.

Mr. Specter. How will you describe the sequence?

Mrs. Hill. Quicker—more automatic.

Andy turned a couple pages and continued where highlighted:

Mrs. Hill. I ran across the street.... I saw a man up there running, or getting away....

Mr. Specter. Where was the man when you first saw him?

Mrs. Hill. He was right up there by the School Depository, just—not at the corner where they say the shots came from, at the other end, right up on the slope at the top of the slope.

Mr. Specter. Would that be in front of the School Book Depository Building?

Mrs. Hill. Yes.

Mr. Specter. At the west end?

Mrs. Hill. More to the west.

Mr. Specter. And where did you see him going?

Mrs. Hill. I saw him going toward the tracks, toward the railroad track to the west.

Mr. Specter. What did you observe about the man, if anything?

Mrs. Hill. That he just had on a brown overcoat and a hat.

Mr. Specter. Why was your attention attracted to him?

Mrs. Hill. Because he was the only thing moving up there.

Mr. Specter. Now, did you have a conscious impression of the source of the first shot that you heard, that is, where it came from?

Mrs. Hill. I had always thought that they came from the knoll.

Mr. Specter. And what, if anything, did you do next?

Mrs. Hill. There was a man holding Mary's arm and she was crying and he had hold of her camera trying to take it with him.... [He was] telling her she had to go with him, I started trying to shake his hand loose, and grab the camera and telling him that "No, we couldn't go, we had to leave.... He kept telling me—he insisted we go with him and he just practically ran us, and he got—they were throwing up a police net around that building at the time, and he just practically ran us up to the court house, I guess it is, and put us in this little room and I don't know why…it was just the sequence of events, that everything was just happenings so fast…. He kept standing in front of the door…and he wouldn't let us out.

Andy skipped to page 220 where the highlighting continued:

Mrs. Hill. I talked with this man, a Secret Service man…. He said, "Mrs. Hill, we were standing at the window and we heard more shots also, but we have three wounds and we have three bullets, three shots is all that we are willing to say right now…." Then, he asked me—I was asked did I know that a bullet struck at my feet and I said, "No; I didn't." And he said, "What do you think that dust was?" And I said, "I didn't see any dust…." The Secret Service man said…it struck at my feet…. I was told not to…mention the man running…. It was an FBI or Secret Service that told me not to…. He said, "You know you were wrong about seeing a man running…. You didn't."

Andy rubbed his eyes with closed fists. His head was spinning. Why had Walker selectively highlighted these sections? Did he know something that others only suspected?

Andy read Walker's highlighted sections in volume 6, where S.M. Holland, who was standing with several men on the triple overpass, explained what he saw:

Mr. Stern. Did you hear a third report?
Mr. Holland. I heard a third report and I counted four shots and about the same time all this was happening, and in this group of trees—[indicating]…. There was a shot…and a puff of smoke came out about 6 or 8 feet above the ground right out

from under those trees. And at just about this location from where I was standing you could see that puff of smoke, like someone had thrown a fire-cracker, or something out, and that is just about the way it sounded.... There were definitely four reports.

Mr. Stern. You have no doubt about that?

Mr. Holland. I have no doubt about it. I have no doubt about seeing that puff of smoke come out from under those trees either.

Mr. Stern. Did you tell them [FBI] that you heard distinctly four shots at that time?

Mr. Holland. Yes.

Mr. Stern. You were certain then?

Mr. Holland. I was certain then....

Mr. Stern. What did you do then?

Mr. Holland. Well, immediately after the shots was [sic] fired, I run around the end of the overpass, behind the fence to see if I could see anyone up there behind the fence.

Mr. Stern. That is the picket fence?

Mr. Holland. That is the picket fence.... I ran on up to the corner of this fence behind the building. By that time I got there there were 12 or 15 policemen and plainclothesmen....

Mr. Stern. Mr. Holland, is there anything you might add to this?

Mr. Holland. I remember about the third car down from this fence, there was a station wagon backed up toward the fence, about the third car down, and a spot, I'd say 3 foot by 2 foot, looked to me like somebody had been standing there for a long period. I guess you could count them about a hundred foot tracks in that little spot, and also mud up on the bumper of that station wagon.

Mr. Stern. Tracks you saw in the mud?

Mr. Holland. It was muddy.... It would have been a hundred tracks in that one location.

Mr. Stern. And then you saw some mud on the bumper?

Mr. Holland. Mud on the bumper in two spots.

Mr. Stern. As if someone had cleaned his foot, or-

Mr. Holland. Well, as if someone had cleaned their foot, or stood up on the bumper to see over the fence.

Mr. Stern. You thought the officers there would take care of that?

Mr. Holland. I thought that the officers would take care of it because there were so many there, I thought they would take care of everything, and a layman didn't have any business up there, and I went on back to my office.

Mr. Stern. When you ran behind the picket fence after the shots were fired, did you come near the area where the station wagon was parked?

Mr. Holland. Went up to behind the arcade as far as you could go.

Mr. Stern. So, you would have passed where this station wagon was?

Mr. Holland. Yes.

Mr. Stern. Or, that area?

Mr. Holland. I walked back to the car and noticed the tracks there in one little spot.

Mr. Stern. When you first came around, that was quite soon after the shots were fired?

Mr. Holland. Yes.

Mr. Stern. And that was later you came behind the station wagon?

Mr. Holland. Oh, maybe 3 or 4 minutes after I got up there, and 3 or 4 minutes after I got up to the end of the fence.

Mr. Stern. A parking area for the School Book Depository?

Mr. Holland. No; it is a parking area for the Sheriff's department and people over at the courthouse. They park in there.

Mr. Stern. I see.

Mr. Holland. Sheriff's department parks in there. District attorneys' cars park in there. It is railroad property, but they let them park in there and save them 25 cents. Don't put that down. Might get in trouble.

Andy stopped and thought about what he had read so far. Each section was marked with either a related newspaper clipping, or a piece of notebook paper that had scribbling thereupon. Some of the clippings reported the mysterious deaths of some of the spectators and officials over the span of just a few years following that day.

Andy had to stretch. He got up out of the office chair and saw that several hours had passed. He had brought a sandwich to eat, so he started in on that. He paced back and forth until he finished his sandwich. He stopped at one of the side tables and saw a clipping upon a stack there. It was a report about a man who had apparently killed himself by a gunshot to the head in May of 1964. Andy saw nothing in the article that clicked in his mind, except the fact that his name was Gary Underhill, and that he had been a CIA agent. Walker had scribbled a note in the margin that read: "Poor Gary. They got you. RIP."

Andy dug through more articles there and saw names of men from the military and/or intelligence agencies that had eventually retired and took up either detective jobs or business related ones, usually connected with the defense industry. What struck Andy as curious was the fact that all these men had died in the middle nineteen sixties. Most had died in accidents, or were the victims of crimes.

Andy listed the names, writing down a total of 11. He went back and sat at the desk.

While he ate his sandwich, he found a file near the bookshelf. He opened it and saw a declassified copy of NATIONAL SECURITY ACTION MEMORANDUM NO. 263. It was dated October 11, 1963 and was declassified on July 6, 1976 by Jeanne W. Davis of the National Security Council. Walker had highlighted the following:

THE WHITE HOUSE
WASHINGTON

To: Secretary of State
    Secretary of Defense
    Chairman of the Joint Chiefs of Staff

Subject: South Vietnam

At a meeting on October 5, 1963, the President considered the recommendations contained in the report of Secretary McNamara and General Taylor on their mission to South Vietnam.

The President approved the military recommendations contained in section I B (1-3) of the report, but directed that no formal announcement be made of the implementation of the plans to withdraw 1,000 U.S. military personnel by the end of 1963....

McGeorge Bundy, National Security Advisor, signed the memorandum and a copy was sent to the Director of Central Intelligence and the Administrator for International Development.

Attached to the back of the memorandum was another. This one was No. 273. It read:

THE WHITE HOUSE
WASHINGTON

November 26, 1963

NATIONAL SECURITY ACTION MEMORANDUM NO. 273

TO: The Secretary of State
    The Secretary of Defense
    The Director of Central Intelligence
    The Administrator, AID
    The Director, USIA

The President has received the discussions of South Vietnam which occurred in Honolulu.... He directs that the following guidance be issued to all concerned:

5. We should concentrate our efforts.... This action should include not only military but political, economic, social, educational and informational effort....
6. Programs of military and economic assistance should be maintained....

8. With respect to Laos, a plan should be developed...for military operations up to...50 kilometers inside Laos....

McGeorge Bundy signed it. Andy realized that it essentially reversed Kennedy's policy of withdrawing 1,000 military personnel by the end of 1963!

He grabbed volume 3 of the Commission and opened to a section that was marked; pp. 212-241. It was the testimony of Roy Truly, the Texas School Book Depository Superintendent. The testimony read:

Mr. Belin. Mr. Truly, when did you first hear the name of Lee Harvey Oswald?

Mr. Truly. I heard the name on or about October 15th.

Mr. Belin. Of what year?

Mr. Truly. Of 1963.

Mr. Belin. And from whom did you hear the name?

Mr. Truly. I received a phone call from a lady in Irving who said her name was Mrs. Paine.

Mr. Belin. All Right. What did Mrs. Paine say, and what did you say?

Mr. Truly. She said, "Mr. Truly...you don't know who I am but I have a neighbor whose brother works for you. I don't know what his name is. But he tells his sister that you are very busy. And I am just wondering if you can use another man."...and I told Mrs. Paine that—to send him down, and I would talk to him—that I didn't have anything in mind for him of a perma- nent nature, but if he was suited, we could possibly use him for a brief time.... So he came in and introduced himself.... I gave him an application to fill out, which he did....

Mr. Belin. Did he fill it out in front of you, or not?

Mr. Truly. Yes; he did.... He looked like a nice young fellow to me—he was quiet and well mannered. He used the word "sir," you know, which a lot of them don't do at this time.... He came to work the next morning.

Andy skipped to other sections that Walker had highlighted. He read, continuing with Truly's testimony:

Mr. Belin. Would you classify Lee Harvey Oswald as an aver- age employee?

Mr. Truly. Above average.

From page 218:

Mr. Belin. Now I want to take you to the morning of November 22nd. First let me ask you when you heard your employees discussing the fact that the motorcade would be going by the Texas School Book Depository? . .

Mr. Truly. I don't recall hearing any particular discussion about him coming by.

Andy skipped to the next highlighted section on page 223:

Mr. Truly. I pressed the button and the elevator didn't move. I called upstairs "Turn loose the elevator."

Mr. Belin. What did you call?

Mr. Truly. I said, "Turn loose the elevator."

Mr. Belin. First of all, did the elevator come down?

Mr. Truly. It did not.

Mr. Belin. All Right. Then what did you do?

Mr. Truly. I went up on a run up the stairway.

Walker had scribbled a notation there on the side of the page. It said: V7 p 386.

Andy located volume 7 and flipped to page 386 that had a marker in it. There he read more highlighted testimony of Truly:

Mr. Ball. Mr. Truly, when you came into the building with Officer Baker, you tried to look up the elevator shaft, didn't you?

Mr. Truly. Yes; I sure did.

Mr. Ball. And where did you see the elevators?

Mr. Truly. On the fifth floor—both of them on the same floor.

Mr. Ball. They were both on the fifth floor?

Mr. Truly. Yes.

Mr. Ball. Are you sure of that?

Mr. Truly. I am sure, because their bottoms were level.

Andy followed Walker's notes back to volume 3.

Mr. Belin. Then what did you do?

Mr. Truly. I came back to the second floor landing.

Mr. Belin. What did you see?

Mr. Truly. I heard some voices, or a voice, coming from the area of the lunchroom, or the inside vestibule, the area of 24.

Mr. Belin. What did you do then?

Mr. Truly. I ran over and looked in this door.... I opened the door back and leaned in....

Mr. Belin. What did you see?

Mr. Truly. I saw the officer almost directly in the doorway of the lunchroom facing Lee Harvey Oswald.

Mr. Belin. And where was Lee Harvey Oswald at the time you saw him?

Mr. Truly. He was at the front of the lunchroom.... When I reached there, the officer had his gun pointing at Oswald. The officer turned this way and said, "This man work here?" And I said, "Yes."

Mr. Belin. And then what happened?

Mr. Truly. Then we left Lee Harvey Oswald immediately and continued to run up the stairway until we reached the fifth floor.

Mr. Belin. Did you hear Lee Harvey Oswald say anything?

Mr. Truly. Not a thing.

Mr. Belin. Did you see any expression on his face?

Mr. Truly. He didn't seem to be excited or overly afraid or anything....

Andy skipped to page 227.

> Mr. Belin. Where did you think the shots came from?
>
> Mr. Truly. I thought the shots came from the vicinity of the railroad...west of the building.... [I said to the officer] "I think we are wasting our time up here...I don't believe these shots came from the building."
>
> Mr. Belin. About how long after these shots do you think it took you to go all the way up and look around the roof and come all the way down again?
>
> Mr. Truly. Oh we might have been gone between 5 and 10 minutes....

Andy skipped to the next highlighted text on page 239:

> Mr. Dulles. Anything about his appearance that was startling or unusual?
>
> Mr. Truly. No, sir. No, sir; I didn't see him panting like he had been running or anything.
>
> Mr. Dulles. Was there any discussion, as far as you know, among your employees, of the fact that the procession would go near the School Depository?
>
> Mr. Truly. No, sir....
>
> Mr. McCloy. You did not see him on November 22 with any package or bundle?
>
> Mr. Truly. No, sir.
>
> Mr. Dulles. You do not think he used any elevators at any time to get from the sixth to the second floor?
>
> Mr. Truly. You mean after the shooting? No, sir; he just could not, because those elevators, I saw myself, were both on the fifth floor...it would have been impossible after the assassination. He had to use the stairway as his only way of getting down....

Walker had another note scribbled down there. V7 p. 384. Andy found it.

> Mr. Truly. Chief Lumpkin told Captain Fritz that Mr. Truly had something to tell him, which I would like to tell him, so he stepped over 4 or 5 feet to where I was, away from the other men—officers and reporters....
> Mr. Ball. What did you tell him?
> Mr. Truly. I told him we had a man missing—I told him what his name was and his Irving address and he said, "All right, thank you Mr. Truly.... While I was up there, just as I left Captain Fritz, a reporter walked over and said, "What about this fellow Oswald?" And I said, "Where did you learn the name Oswald?"...I don't know who it was.

Andy found a paper folded there on this page. It was a stenographic recording taken from the executive session of the commission on 22 January 1964. It read:

> Mr. Dulles: Why would it be in their [FBI] interest to say he [Oswald] is clearly the only guilty one?
> Mr. Rankin: They would like to have us fold up and quit.
> Mr. Boggs: This closes the case, you see. Don't you see?
> Mr. Rankin: They found the man. There is nothing more to do. The commission supports their conclusions, and we can go home and that is the end of it....
> Mr. Boggs: I don't even like to see this being taken down.
> Mr. Dulles: Yes. I think this record ought to be destroyed.

There was a clipping from the *New York Times* attached to the note. It explained how Representative Boggs, a member of the Warren Commission, who had expressed doubts about the commission's findings, disappeared on an Alaskan plane flight. His body and the plane were never found.

Andy drew in a deep breath.

He didn't have too much time to sit here and read everything, as interesting as it was, so he noted the volumes that were marked and those page numbers of text that Walker had highlighted.

He found another paper marking a section in volume 7, that of the testimony of Dallas patrolman Joe Smith whereby he ran over to the fence behind the knoll immediately after the shooting because a witness said she saw shooting from the bushes. Andy noted the testimony that was underlined and moved on. He located the testimony of James Tague, the man who had been near the triple underpass in Dealey Plaza who was struck either by a fragment of a bullet or piece of cement caused by one of the bullets fired that day. He read a clipping Walker had there from an article in the *Dallas Morning News* how the Warren Commission had to reluctantly include this episode, and account for one of the three bullets, then had to show how one bullet made seven wounds.

There wasn't much from Tague's testimony that Walker had underlined, so Andy quickly skimmed it:

Mr. Liebeler. How long after did you feel yourself hit by anything?

Mr. Tague. The deputy Sheriff looked up and said, "You have blood there on your cheek."

Walker had scribbled: "OOPS!"

Mr. Liebeler. Do you have any idea which bullet might have made that mark?

Mr. Tague. It was either the second or third.

Mr. Liebeler. Did you hear any more shots after you felt your-self get hit in the face?

Mr. Tague. I believe I did.

Mr. Liebeler. Did you have any idea where these shots came from when you heard them ringing out?

Mr. Tague. Yes; I thought they were coming from my left.

Mr. Liebeler. Immediately to your left?...

Mr. Tague. Up but the, whatever you call the monument....

Mr. Liebeler. Behind the concrete monument?...

Mr. Tague. Yes.

Mr. Liebeler. Did you look up near the railroad tracks in that area after you heard the shots?

Mr. Tague. I looked around.... I ducked down back here.

Mr. Liebeler. Under the railroad tracks?

Mr. Tague. Right.... When I stuck my head outside, the Secret Service car was just starting to pass under the underpass.

Mr. Liebeler. There was a considerable echo in that area?

Mr. Tague. There was no echo from where I stood. I was asked this question before, and there was no echo....

Mr. Liebeler. Do you remember seeing anything else or observing anything else that day that you think would help the Commission, that I haven't asked you about?

Mr. Tague. I felt very strongly that the third shot hit down there....

Mr. Liebeler. Is there anything [else]?

Mr. Tague. The only thing that I saw that I thought was wrong was that there was about 5 or 6 or 7 minutes in there before anybody done anything about anything.

Mr. Liebeler. That was after the shots were fired?

Mr. Tague. That was after the shots were fired.

Mr. Liebeler. What do you mean, "Before they did anything?"

Mr. Tague. There was no action taken except for the one policeman that I could see that stopped his motorcycle, and it fell over on him at first, and he got it standing upright and drew his gun, and he was the only one doing anything about it.

Mr. Liebeler. You didn't see any other policemen around the area?

Mr. Tague. Not for 4 or 5 minutes. If Oswald was in that building, he had all the time in the world to calmly walk out of there.

Mr. Liebeler. Apparently that is just what he did do.

"Or anyone could have done," said Andy to himself. It's almost like they intended to allow him, or whomever, the opportunity to escape, he thought. Either that or it was the Keystone Cops! Walker had another note there that read: "Thank God!"

Andy then found a transcript from the Jim Garrison/Clay Shaw trial in New Orleans where steelworker Richard Carr, a witness on November 22, 1963, said that he saw a "heavyset man wearing a hat, horn-rimmed glasses, and a tan sport coat standing in a sixth floor window in the Depository moments before the shooting." Carr said he later "saw the man walking down Commerce Street in a hurry." A note scribbled in the margin of the article said: "Jack again, dumb ass!"

Andy just had to read more Warren Commission testimony. It was from witness Howard Leslie Brennan. Brennan said:

Mr. Brennan. I looked up at the building. I then saw this man I have described in the window and he was taking aim with a high-powered rifle. I could see all of the barrel of the gun. I do not know if it had a scope on it or not. I was looking at the man at the time of the explosion. Then this man let the gun down to his side and stepped out of sight. He did not seem to be in any hurry.... I believe I could identify this man if I ever saw him again.

There was a notation made there that said that Brennan failed to identify Oswald in the line-up.

Andy also noted a FBI statement from witness L.R. Terry, who said: "There was a man with him." Walker had scribbled the word yes with an exclamation point suggesting the Commission discount this testimony. Andy realized that that's just what they did after he read further.

Later that afternoon Andy had noted many sections that Walker had highlighted of the Warren Commission. There was too many and it was too exhaustive. To think that the average person could weigh through all this, quipped Andy. He hadn't read every section he found that Walker had highlighted, but only skimmed them. He got up and sifted through more files that he hadn't seen yet from another table.

He found another file labeled: BANISTER. On the second to last page, Andy found a list of names that sent a shock wave throughout his body. Name for name the list included all the names that Andy had listed earlier from the clippings on the opposite table, one was Underhill.

However, there were 12 names on this list, one more than Andy's list. The twelfth name on this list, and not Andy's was the name: John O'Connell.

Andy fell into the office chair and read the file, word for word. The file referred to a program run by the CIA called: EXECUTIVE ACTION. Near the end of the file, one page before the list of names, was the following: CLASSIFIED EXPERT RIFLEMEN, LIST FOLLOWS:

The last page had the list. If Walker was indeed John O'Connell, then, as Andy discovered, he was the only one who was alive from this list! He felt light-headed.

Andy thought about the fact that so many files and Volumes of the Commission had notes and clipping stuck in them. Dammit! He said the hell with it. He was convinced that Walker hadn't been up here in a long time, and that it would almost be unlikely that he could climb the ladder anymore, so he decided to grab a few volumes to aid in what passages he noted in his computer. He loaded up with ten volumes to get started. Hopefully, he could sneak them back in.

He finished loading up after a couple trips up and down the ladder and secured the loft. He looked around the main room and decided to log in the types of weapons he saw stacked there. It took him several minutes.

He opened a smaller crate and was astonished! It was full of M67 fragmentation hand grenades. He searched the other ammunition there and realized that it all uniformly corresponded to the weapons.

He studied Walker's shrine. "He must be Catholic." Andy shook his head slowly. Is this for some kind of atonement? Andy stood there disbelieving the thoughts running through his head.

It was now time for dinner and Andy was getting hungry. He closed the cabin and returned to the Osprey. There, he saw two messages waiting. He pushed the button on the answering machine and grabbed a snack from the refrigerator.

"Andy, your old man. Pick me up Thursday. Usual Time. Thanks." Beep, the machine went.

"Andy, its, Cheryl. He's loosening up a little. They walked him today and he did better than expected. He's determined more than anything to just walk out of here on his own. Call me when you can." Beep, the machine ended the messages and re-set itself.

Andy dialed the hospital.

Cheryl answered. "Room two ten."

"Its, Andy."

"Hi. He thinks he's leaving tomorrow."

"Can he?"

"Legally, yes. Physically, possibly. I'm trying to convince him that he needs a nurse. I offered to stay at the lodge and come over and take care of him."

"What'd he say?"

"Nothing."

They were silent. Finally, "I'll wait here," said Andy. "Call me with what's going on tomorrow."

"Okay. I hope to see you tomorrow."

"If you're coming back in, tell Walker I'll pick both of you up in Stillwater."

"I'll try. Bye."

"Bye." Andy hung up the phone and thought a moment, then dialed Pat.

"Yeah," Pat answered.

"Its, Andy. I got a new number and another favor to ask."

"I'm listening."

"If I send you a list with the sections I want from the Warren Commission, can you get those sections on disk and send them?"

Silence. "Warren Commission?"

"Yeah," said Andy detecting Pat's apprehension in the favor at hand.

"How many sections?"

"About thirty."

"Thirty! Warren Commission? How does that have anything to do with your thesis?"

"You'll be surprised when you read it."

More silence.

"Anything, you ask, I'll get it for you," said Andy placating him.

"All right. I'll try to get this all over the computer. It might be easier if I tap right into the National archives," said Pat thinking it through as he spoke.

"Wherever. One more thing."

"What?"

Andy detected a restive tone. "Last thing I should need."

"Listening," said Pat again waiting for the task.

"I didn't get a Social Security Number on O'Connell, but an old military service number."

Dead silence from Pat's end of the line. "How old?" he finally asked.

"Probably Korean war."

"Korean war!"

"Can you do it?"

"I don't know."

"There's got to be a list of the soldiers in that war somewhere."

"I'll give you one guess where."

"Pentagon," agreed Andy.

"I'll try other places first, like the Korean veterans of America, or even the achieves again. I don't know, Andy. You're going to get me in trouble."

"You're too good. They won't catch you. Anyway, they must have a historical branch, the Pentagon I mean. A list of veterans or something that's not top secret."

"The way the government is, certainly the Pentagon would lock away their records for centuries."

"Well, whatever you can get. I'll send the sections I need of the Commission."

"Okay, I'll switch over and wait for your call."

"Give me a minute to hook up." Andy hung up and plugged in his computer. A minute later he was sending his request telephonically, via LabLink—software that computers used to send data to each other—to Pat's computer.

Andy shut down his computer and plugged his father's phone line back in.

Pat loved to work in cyberspace. He had been either playing with computers or working with them almost since he was a baby. His father had been a computer programmer and had worked with many different computer companies. Presently, his father was an executive with a company that was overseeing the National Sheriff's Organization. Their goal was to be linked up and on-line so that sheriff departments nation wide could share data instantaneously; More of Big Brother.

Pat's father, needless to say, had shared data and computer secrets with Pat over the years. He taught Pat well. Pat had programs that weren't available to the public.

Pat fingered through an Internet yellow page directory and found a listing for the National Archives. He figured that since much of the information there was public, certainly the Warren Commission, he would start his search there.

And it was. It took some computer tricks, and he got around having to pay a fee, but he got in and quickly found the report, all 26 volumes, and the actual report. He called it up, then down loaded each section that Andy's file called for.

Twelve

Later that night Andy was restless. He couldn't wait for Pat. He realized it could take some time. It was eating at Andy. He had to read more.

He got into the boat and went back to Walker's cabin. It was a dark and cloudy night.

He took his flashlight with him, but lit up the candles in the loft so he could see.

He found a notebook wedged in between two volumes. He opened the small pad and saw notation printed there. He decided to follow Walker's research trail labeled: RIFLE. See WCR p. 179.

He opened and found the highlighted section and read how Oswald, while in the Marine Corps in May of 1959, had "scored 191, which was 1 point over the minimum for ranking as a 'marksman." The scale, in the military thus being, marksman (the lowest rating)—sharpshooter (intermediate)—expert (the highest rating).

Walker then directed the reader to page 193. Andy read how the Commission chose three riflemen, "rated as master by the National Rifle Association." These men were chosen to fire the Mannlicher-Carcano rifle that said, "made in Italy" on it.

Walker's notes said V3 p. 441-445.

Ronald Simmons, Chief of the Infantry Evaluation Branch of the Ballistics Research Laboratory, said:

Mr. Simmons. All three riflemen are rated Master by the
National Rifle Association. Two of them are civilian gunners in
the Small Arms Division of our Development and Proof
Services, and the third is presently in the Army, and he has a
considerable background as a rifleman, and also has a Master
rating.

Mr. Eisenberg. Was it reported to you by the persons who ran
the machine-rest test whether they had any difficulty with sighting the weapon in?

Mr. Simmons. Well, they could not sight the weapon in using
the telescope…. We did adjust the telescopic sight by the addi-
tion of two shims…. We had rather unusual coincidence with
respect to this target….

Walker had a note there that said "See V26 p. 261-262." Andy located
those pages.

They were photographs of the targets the "Masters" had used in their
tests. They were standard firing range targets. Walker's note there said:
"Stationary targets at that!"

Back in V3, page 446, Simmons Continued.

Mr. Simmons. This involved the displacement of the weapon
to a sufficient angle that the basic firing position of the man had
to be changed…. And for the first four attempts, the firers
missed….

Andy looked at the pictures of the targets again. Chalk marks circled
there showed that the shots had all been low. Not one hit the enlarged
head or neck area of the target.

Back in V3, page 446, Andy read how only one master had gotten off
three shots in the required time.

Mr. Simmons. Specialist Miller used 4.6 seconds on his first attempt, 5.15 seconds in his second attempt, and 4.45 seconds in his exercise using the iron sight.

Walker's notation there said: "Commission concluded 4.8-5.6 seconds." Walker's scribble there said: "Back to V3 p. 447."

Andy went back there and found that Simmons said they had made "several comments" in reference about the weapon. Walker's note said: "See V1 p. v."

Andy did. It read, "Brief deletions have been made of material which might be considered in poor taste and is clearly irrelevant to any facet of the Commission's investigation."

"I wonder why Walker highlighted that?"

At the end of this, Walker's note said: "But they devoted several pages to Ruby's mother's 'fishbone delusion?'"

Andy learned that that was where she thought she had a fishbone stuck in her throat.

Walker had written: "Pages of supporting evidence! How silly!"

Andy felt as though he was on a treasure hunt with which the way Walker's notes pointed him all over the massive 26 volumes and the final report itself.

Walker's notes then said: "V3 p. 447."

Simmons said the experts had concern about the rifle, "particularly with respect to the amount of effort required to open the bolt."

Next, Walker pointed him to WCR p. 182-183. There, he learned that, despite the fact that the rifle sight was not lined up to the line of fire when found, and the difficulty in operating the bolt on the obsolete weapon, the Commission concluded:

> The various tests showed that the Mannlicher-Carcano was an accurate rifle and that the use of a four-power scope was a substantial aid to rapid, accurate firing...Oswald had the capability to fire three shots, with two hits, within 4.8 and 5.6 seconds.

In V26, p. 103-104, Andy found a letter written by J. Edgar Hoover to J. Lee Rankin. Walker highlighted the following:

It is to be noted that at the time of firing these tests, the telescopic sight [on the alleged assassination weapon] could not be properly aligned with the target.... The weapon is presently grouping high and to the right with respect to the point of aim.

Andy was now over-tired. His head seemed to buzz. Nevertheless, he followed Walker's clues. He next turned to Volume 18 p. 640. From Marina Oswald's affidavit, Andy read:

I went into the garage where Lee kept all of our things to see if his rifle was in its place. But the rifle which was wrapped in a blanket was there....

Then all of a sudden some policemen came and began to search....

They went into the garage and...the rifle was not there.

In Volume 1, page 74, Andy followed Walker's trail:

Mrs. Oswald. They began to search the apartment. When they came to the garage and took the blanket, I thought, "Well, no, they will find it...." I thought the police had simply come because he was always under suspicion.

Mr. Rankin. What do you mean by that—he was always under suspicion?

Mrs. Oswald. Well, the FBI would visit us.

Mr. Rankin. Did they indicate what they suspected him of?

Mrs. Oswald. They didn't tell me.

Andy then followed Walker's markers to, and compared, V1, pp. 74 and 164-165; V4, p. 211; V24, p. 219. There, he learned that Marina failed to identify the alleged assassination weapon while at the Dallas police station. She said that she couldn't identify it as her Husband's.

Andy then followed Walker's trail to Volume 24 p. 228. It was an affidavit signed by Seymour Weitzman, a Deputy Constable. He said:
> Yesterday November 22, 1963 I was standing on the corner of Main and Houston....

> I was working with Deputy S. Boone of the Sheriff's Department and helping in the search. We were in the northwest corner of the sixth floor when...[we] spotted the rifle about the same time. This rifle was a 7.65 Mauser.... The rifle was between some boxes near the stairway. The time the rifle was found was 1:22 PM.

"What the hell's going on here?" Andy said out loud. He was getting tired and his eyes were straining at nearly two o'clock in the morning, yet he read just a little more.

Andy found a copy of a letter written to a Mr. Galanor in Riverdale, New York. It was dated July 14, 1965. It was a small reproduction and Walker had scribbled something in the bottom right corner that read: "Lane p.411." Nevertheless, the letter revealed:

> Dear Sir:

> Concerning your inquiry on the 6.5-millimeter Mannlicher-Carcano cartridge, this is not being produced commercially at this time.

> Any previous production on this cartridge was made against Government contracts which were completed back in 1944.

Therefore, any of this remaining ammunition which is on the market today is Government surplus ammunition.

I trust the above information answers your questions.

It was signed by H. J. Gebelein, Assistant Sales Service Manager, Winchester-Western Division, of the Olin Mathieson Chemical Corporation.

Near the bottom, Walker wrote the word: OOPS again!

A sudden crash was heard downstairs! Andy thought his heart had stopped! He froze. The candle flickered softly on the breeze that whooshed through the cabin, up the ladder and into the loft.

It's an island. There can't be any animals here. He grabbed his flashlight and stuck his head down through the trap door.

He shined the light around and realized that he had left the door from the kitchen open and that a giant raccoon had pushed open the screen door to the porch. "Damn, you scared me," said Andy as he went down, shooed it off and closed the porch door. His heartbeat resumed a normal beating rate a few moments later. He went back up to the loft and continued.

Andy looked in Volume 24 again and followed Walker's trail to Volume 1, page 119, he read:

Mr. Thorne. Exhibit 141 is an envelope that contains a bullet [the one taken from the Mannlicher-Carcano].

Mr. Rankin. Have you ever seen bullets or shells like that that your husband had?

Mrs. Oswald. Lee's were smaller.

Walker's next note there was peculiar. It said: "Archives No. 344."

Andy looked around and didn't know what that meant. He searched a couple of file folders and finally on the third try found some copies of materials from the National Archives.

He searched through several until he found Number 344. It was a copy of a Secret Service transcript from an interview with Marina Oswald conducted on December 1, 1963. In it, she said that Lee's rifle "had no telescopic sight on it."

Andy was dumbfounded and exhausted. All this conflicting testimony and documentation made his head spin even more. He just couldn't think anymore. He just couldn't read anymore either, so he closed up and returned to the Osprey where he fell fast asleep.

Pat had searched through a Korean War section and found no individual information about soldiers who had served. He exited the Archives and ran a search command for the Korean War on the Internet at large.

He found a couple sites but nothing about individual soldiers. He surfed the Net for a while and got no where.

Next, Pat went to his notebooks. He searched there for a few minutes, then turned back to his computer. He ran several sequences, but kept getting the words: access denied.

He tried more numbers and commands, but couldn't get in. He turned back to the stack of files behind him and searched there for several minutes until he found a file. He turned back to his computer and called up software that wrote programs. It was a design that went above and beyond the C++ program that was readily available at any PC store.

For several hours into the night, Pat sat there and wrote a program. He improved upon a design originally written by Kevin Mitnick, who had been arrested in 1995 for computer hacking government databases, most notably the North American Air Defense Command; hence the movie *War Games* was based on him. Pat altered and enhanced Mitnick's design and protocol.

At nearly three in the morning, Pat was ready to try. He took out the diskette that had the Warren Commission information on it and inserted a blank diskette. He backed up his new program that he had just written onto the new diskette.

Next, he ran some commands and his computer dialed its modem and went to work. Pat sat back and watched.

The computer automatically routed its telephonic call all over the world and got several public phones. Finally, after several seconds, the line ended at the Department of Defense (DOD) database. The computer started running hundreds of access codes.

Pat sat and watched for nearly a minute and began to sweat, becoming nervous at how long this was taking. He timed the "At the door knocking but you can't come in process."

A minute and a half. "Shit," he mumbled.

Thousands of numbers ran past his screen almost instantaneously. They almost blurred together as they flashed by.

Two minutes.

At last, the computer got in! The DOD emblem popped up on screen and an "Enter search command" showed.

Pat entered the category: Service Numbers.

The database asked for the number.

Pat quickly typed in the number Andy had found in Walker's chest.

The computer shot back the message: John O'Connell, Served Korean War 1950-52. File omitted.

Pat hit the print command on his computer and quickly got the hell out of there.

An Army Specialist sitting at a desk in the Pentagon's database computer room had noticed that someone was downloading information a couple minutes after the search had begun. The specialist wasn't looking at his station, rather he was small-talking with the duty sergeant when the search had begun. When the Specialist finally noticed an illegal access entry, he feverishly began hitting keys on a computer keyboard.

His supervisor, Army Captain Moody, stood behind him. "What've you got?" The Captain asked impatiently.

"I traced the call to Lisbon. A phone booth. From there the line was open and came from Munich, another public phone and from Munich from Mexico City, same thing. That's when it cut off."

"Did they get anything?" Moody asked.

"Yeah. I got it right here." The Specialist called up what Pat had just downloaded and printed out. "It's printing."

Captain Moody walked over to the printer and tore off a sheet. He saw the same information that Pat had just acquired: John O'Connell, Served Korean War, 1950-52. File omitted.

Captain Moody walked back to the Specialist at the computer. "Another hacker. The Colonel's gonna explode. I'll need a full report." The Captain shuffled off while looking at the printout.

Thirteen

Andy was awakened for the second time in almost a couple hours. The first call, at four thirty in the morning, was from Pat with the information. Andy had downloaded the files and fallen back asleep without having looked at them.

The second call came at seven o'clock.

"Hi," said Cheryl cheerfully.

"Hi," Andy said groggily.

"After breakfast he's discharging himself. He spoke with Bergholtz over the phone and they had a big fight."

"He wants to get back here and die." Andy stretched.

"I told Bergholtz I'd be looking after him. He gave me some instructions and medication and I told Walker I was driving him back to Stillwater."

"And?"

"He sort of grunted. I guess that meant yes."

"Well I guess we both get to play taxi today. My father comes in tonight."

"Judges don't work on Fridays?"

"Apparently not this one anymore. I'll wait for you in Stillwater."

"We'll be there. Bye." Cheryl hung up.

Andy dragged himself about the cabin and got breakfast and took a shower. He should still beat them to Stillwater.

Just before he was to go out the door, Andy called up the file from his computer that Pat had made from the printout last night.

Andy stared at it: John O'Connell, Served Korean War, 1950-52. File Omitted.

"File Omitted. File Omitted?" Andy clicked his computer off and headed to Stillwater.

Captain Moody had submitted his report to Colonel Garner at the Pentagon. Garner brought the matter up during the morning staff briefing. He handed the report and the computer tear-off of the information that Andy now had to Sergeant Hadder.

"Find out who this O'Connell was," said Garner, "and why someone would be trying to access his service record."

Hadder scanned the report from Moody.

"We need a complete review of our computer security," said Garner. "How many times have we been through this?"

After the briefing had been dismissed, Sergeant Hadder got to work. He spent the greater part of the day searching through every possible file and database that the DOD had, going back to before its inception in its present form in 1949. To be thorough, he searched files that had long since been either put into computers or on microfiche going back before 1949. He found nothing. The only entry was the one in which Andy's computer hacker Pat had found and that was listed as omitted.

Sergeant Hadder reported to Garner and Garner sat at his desk perplexed. He decided to make an inter-agency request for information. He put together a report and asked the intelligence community, primarily the CIA, if they had anything on this O'Connell, since many military personnel in those days routinely did double duty with other agencies.

Andy picked up Cheryl and Walker at Stillwater and took them both to Beaver River. Walker didn't look good. Cheryl dragged an oxygen cart along and the tubes ran from the tank to underneath Walker's nostrils feeding him oxygen. Cheryl whispered to Andy that Walker had leaned up against the passenger door and slept the whole way. During the boat ride Walker sat in the back with his eyes closed.

At Beaver River they loaded Walker into Andy's smaller boat and took him to his cabin. Cheryl had to steady Walker by holding his arm as he walked.

When Cheryl followed Walker into the cabin, he tried to push her away with his arm.

"I'm coming in," she huffed at him. "I've already seen the guns and don't care what you have them for."

Andy raised his eyebrows at Cheryl's tenacity and followed them into the main room. She helped Walker into a chair by the window. "I'm going to make your bed and get you in it."

Walker looked up at Andy helplessly. Andy shrugged his shoulders.

Walker looked around the room. Everything looked in order. "I'm just an enthusiast," Walker said to Andy.

"Hey, this is America. I've read the second amendment."

Walker grunted and looked at the floor. Actually, he didn't give a damn what they thought.

Cheryl made the bed and put Walker's medication on the counter in the kitchen. He gasped as she helped him into his bed. She undressed him except for his underclothing and got him settled.

"I'm going to have Andy bring me over here a couple times a day to look after you."

"Just let me go," Walker wheezed.

"I can't do that. You're my grandfather."

Walker waved his hand at her to go.

"Don't shoot us when we come back," Cheryl said as she was leaving. Andy followed her to the door.

Walker heard the boat pull away. He rolled over onto his side and struggled to get up, but couldn't. He removed the oxygen tube from his nose and then slowly slid down onto the floor and caught his breath.

He crawled over to the table that held the shrine. He opened a secret panel in the floorboard. The panel was only one foot square. He reached into the floor and pulled out a bomb. It had a unique timer that could be set on a 48-hour clock. He turned it on, set the timing device so that the bomb would go off in about 31 hours. He replaced the bomb in the floor. The bomb sat atop a fifty-gallon drum that was buried beneath the floor. It was full of fuel oil and fertilizer.

He replaced the floorboard and crawled back to his bed. He got a pad and pencil off the stand next to his bed and noted the time. He grabbed an alarm clock and set it so that it would go off each morning at 6:30. That way, the alarm and his note were set to remind him to reset the bomb each day, with at least a twenty four-hour window of safety.

Walker then got back into bed. He didn't plan to kill himself, never did, never will. He was Catholic. In his heart he had attained atonement with his God. It was certainly against God's law, he believed, for one to kill himself.

What he now planned to do was to allow the cabin to blow up and burn to the ground after he died. He certainly felt that the end would now come at any time. He would insure that nothing would survive for anyone to look at. He had already written his will and placed it in a canister in the shed. Just in case the shed caught on fire from a spark that might travel its way, the will would survive. It was simple and straightforward.

The fire would hopefully be described as a probable accident. After all, why would the authorities perform an intensive investigation for an old hermit? There wouldn't be much left after the ammunition blew up and this old wooden cabin raged into a fireball.

Walker felt at ease with his plan. He had it all figured out.

Andy and Cheryl sat in the lodge eating lunch. The more she talked, the more Andy found himself attracted to her. Likewise, she felt comfortable with him, and enjoyed his company after dealing with Walker the past few days.

"I've come this far," said Cheryl sipping her soda. "I can't leave until I know why."

Andy was glad she didn't want to leave, yet he was uncomfortable with what he had learned and with not telling her. How could he now? If this Walker was indeed her grandfather, then he was a murderer! How would she react? How would she feel?

"You're not saying much," Cheryl pointed out.

"I'm just thinking how I could help you with Walker. I don't think he'll want anymore repairs. He's planning on dying and what's the point?"

"I'd like you to stay with me while I'm over there."

"Yeah, that's no problem." Andy finished his sandwich.

Cheryl yawned. "I need a nap. I'm going to turn in for a couple hours."

"I have to get my father later. We usually have dinner in Stillwater."

"I'll hang out here around the lodge, maybe take a walk."

She stood to go. Andy followed her to her room at the lodge.

"Bye," Cheryl said first. She hugged and kissed him gently on the cheek.

He returned the kiss and walked back to the Osprey. There, he got his computer and the volumes he took from Walker and sat on the porch. He opened the Warren Commission Volume 7 pp. 531-539 where Patrolman Joe Smith talked about what he saw, heard and did.

Mr. Liebeler. While you were standing here and the motorcade went by, tell us what happened at that point.

Mr. Smith. I heard the shots.

Mr. Liebeler. Did you turn to watch the motorcade? Did you turn to watch the President as the motorcade went by?

Mr. Smith. Yes, sir;…Then I heard the shots, and I immediately proceeded from this point…. I started up towards the Book Depository after I heard the shots…. This woman came up to me…she told me, "They are shooting the President from the bushes." So I immediately proceeded up here.

Mr. Liebeler. You proceeded up to an area immediately behind the concrete structure here that is by Elm Street and the street that runs immediately in front of the…Depository, is that right?

Mr. Smith. I was checking all the bushes and I checked all the cars in the parking lot…. I looked into all the cars and checked around the bushes. Of course, I wasn't alone. There was some deputy sheriff with me, and I believe one Secret Service man when I got there…. I pulled my pistol from my holster…. Just as I did, he showed me that he was a Secret Service agent.

Andy saw a clipping from a *Dallas Morning News* article that Walker had there in between the pages, quoting the Secret Service, that no agents were stationed around Dealey Plaza, but were in fact all assigned to the motorcade, and had gone on to Parkland Hospital. Mr. Smith must have been mistaken about a Secret Service agent there behind the fence that day concluded the Commission.

Andy sighed and continued with Smith's testimony:

Mr. Liebeler. Did you have any basis for believing where the shots came from, or where to look for somebody, other that what the lady told you?

Mr. Smith. It sounded to me like they may have came from this vicinity here.

Mr. Liebeler. Down around the—let's put a No. 5 at the corner here behind this concrete structure where the bushes were down toward the railroad tracks from the Texas School Book Depository Building on the little street that runs down in front of the Texas School Book Depository Building.

Mr. Smith. Yes.

Mr. Liebeler. Now you say that you had the idea that the shots may have come from up in that area?

Mr. Smith. Yes, sir; that is just what, well, like I say, the sound of it....

Mr. Liebeler. What did you do after you had searched this area?

Mr. Smith. Well, it was, I don't remember whether this was a deputy sheriff—I don't know his name—he was in civilian clothes—he said they came from the building up here....

Andy took a swig from his hand-held cooler. He stopped and looked out over the lake. It was a hot summer day. The lake was relatively calm with occasional ripples. Locals went by in their boats; children swam in the water nearby.

It was becoming more obvious to Andy the pattern that was developing in the files he was reading. That pattern had to do with the activity on or around that damn grassy knoll, what witnesses saw, heard or did before, during and after the shooting.

The theory as to why Walker had underlined the sections that he did worried Andy. He didn't want to say it, or even think it. If Walker was O'Connell, and O'Connell was an expert rifleman, and the conspiracy is true—like the House Select Committee on Assassinations concluded was "probable"—then O'Connell was there behind the fence that day, probably one of the shooters.

Andy went back to his file. He scanned down to the testimony of Mrs. Robert Reid:

Mr. Belin. What is you occupation, Mrs. Reid?

Mrs. Reid. I am a clerical supervisor [for the] Texas School Book Depository....

Mr. Belin. Let me ask you this.... Before you turned and went back into the building [after the shooting] did you—did Mr. Campbell say anything to you?

Mrs. Reid. He said,..."It came from the grassy area down this way...."

Mr. Belin. All right. When he said "this way" which direction was he pointing?

Mrs. Reid. In the direction of the parade was going, in the bottom of that direction....

Mr. Belin. Did you see anything else...?

Mrs. Reid. No; because I ran into the building.... I ran up to the office.

Mr. Belin. You went into the building in the main lobby?

Mrs. Reid. Yes; I did.

Mr. Belin. All right. You went up through the stairs and then what did you do?

Mrs. Reid. I went into the office....

Mr. Belin. And then what did you do?

Mrs. Reid. Well, I kept walking and I looked up and Oswald was...in the back door of the office.... I had no thought of anything of him having any connection with it at all because he was very calm. He had gotten a coke and was holding it in his hands.

Mr. Belin And when in Dallas, we started the stopwatch from the time that the last shot was fired, is that correct?

Mrs. Reid. That is right.

Mr. Belin. And then you went through your actions, what you saw, your conversations that you had, and your actions in going back into the building and up to the point that you saw Lee Harvey Oswald?

Mrs. Reid. That is right.

Mr. Belin. Do you remember how long by the stopwatch it took you?

Mrs. Reid. Approximately 2 minutes.

Mr. Dulles. I didn't hear you.

Mrs. Reid. Two minutes.

Mr. Belin. From the time of the last shot the time you and Oswald crossed?

Mrs. Reid. Yes….

Mr. Belin. Was he moving fast?

Mrs. Reid. No;…he was moving at a very slow pace.

Andy stretched. He left his computer on the table and walked down to the water's edge. He took his shoes off and waded into the water. Knee deep, he looked out over the lake. He saw Walker's island in the far distance. He also could see the front edge of the cabin through the trees that were in front of it.

It bothered him that he didn't know what this meant. He couldn't just ask Walker. He'd never admit to this. Even the people who had been duped, wouldn't admit that they had been wrong, or duped, because it would not only make them look like fools, but would send a shock wave through this country that indeed rouge elements had been involved. Even given Watergate and Iran-Contra, where rouge elements within the government ran around and did what they did, some people still couldn't believe that this was possible. Some people were so naive as to how things really worked, and why. Even so, many didn't care.

Even Andy doubted what he had found. Nothing in Walker's cabin proved that Walker was O'Connell. Having old military artifacts from a war long ago didn't prove that. Nothing there proved that O'Connell was there that day. Nothing Andy had found proved O'Connell was involved. Andy turned his mind over and over thinking of a plan of how best to proceed with Walker. He knew he probably couldn't get back up there in the loft now that Walker had returned. He'd have to study what he found.

Andy sat down on the boat dock and dangled his feet in the water. If O'Connell had been an expert rifleman, and had worked for Banister, then O'Connell was surely well known in intelligence circles. Andy remembered reading that it wasn't until President Ford, or was it Carter, who signed an executive order making it illegal for the CIA to use assassination as a political tool anymore. That meant, Andy was well aware, that the CIA regularly all through the 50's and 60's used assassination as a political tool. Perhaps O'Connell had worked for them. Andy also had read where the CIA had hired and worked with the American Mafia to assassinate Castro more than once. Even many declassified documents showed that, and McNamara and President Johnson admitted it.

Andy went back to the porch. He scanned the Walker highlighted sections in volume 6 of the testimony of Miss Victoria Adams:

> Mr. Belin. What is you occupation?
>
> Miss Adams. I am employed as an office survey representative...[on] the fourth floor of the Texas School Book Depository....
>
> Mr. Belin. Where were you when the motorcade passed?
>
> Miss Adams. I was inside the building...[on] the fourth floor.
>
> Mr. Belin. Did you watch the motorcade through a window?
>
> Miss Adams. Yes, sir.... From our vantage point...we were obstructed from the view.
>
> Mr. Belin. By what?
>
> Miss Adams. A tree. And we [Sandra Styles, Elsie Dorman, and Dorothy May Garner] heard a shot.... It seemed as if it came from the right below rather from the left above....
>
> Mr. Belin. You went back into the stockroom which would be to the north of where your offices are located on the fourth floor, is that correct?

Miss Adams. Yes, sir; that's correct.

Mr. Belin. When you got into the stockroom, where did you go?

Miss Adams. I went to the back stairs.

Mr. Belin. Are there any other stairs that lead down from the fourth floor other than those back stairs in the rear of the stockroom?

Miss Adams. No, sir.

Mr. Belin. Now, you were running down the stairs, did you encounter anyone?

Miss Adams. Not during the actual running down the stairs; no, sir.

Mr. Belin. Then you got to the stairs and you started going down the stairs. You went from the fourth floor to the third floor?

Miss Adams. That's correct.

Mr. Belin. Anyone on the stairs then?

Miss Adams. No, sir.

Mr. Belin. Let me ask you this. As you got to the stairs on the fourth floor, did you notice whether or not the elevator was running?

Miss Adams. The elevator was not moving.

Mr. Belin. How do you know it was not moving on some other floor?

Miss Adams. Because the cables move when the elevator is moved, and this is evidenced because of a wooden grate.

Mr. Belin. Did you look to see if the elevator was moving?

Miss Adams. It was not....

Mr. Belin. It was not moving?

Miss Adams. No.

Mr. Belin. As you got off the stairs on the third floor, did you see anyone on the third floor?

Miss Adams. No, sir.

Mr. Belin. Then you immediately went to the stairs going down from the third to the second?

Miss Adams. That's correct.

Mr. Belin. As you ran down the stairs, did you see anyone on the stairs?

Miss Adams. No, sir.

Mr. Belin. All right. You got down to the second floor. Did you see anyone by the second floor?

Miss Adams. No, sir.

Mr. Belin. Did you immediately turn and run and keep on running down the stairs towards the first floor?

Miss Adams. Yes.

Mr. Belin. Now when you were running down the stairs on your trip down the stairs, did you hear anyone using the stairs?

Miss Adams. No, sir.

Mr. Belin. Did you hear anyone calling for an elevator?

Miss Adams. No, sir.

Mr. Belin. How long do you think it took you to get from the window to the bottom of the stairs on the first floor?

Miss Adams. A minute at the most.

Mr. Belin. So you think that from the time you left the window on the fourth floor until the time you got to the stairs at the bottom of the first floor, was approximately 1 minute?

Miss Adams. Yes.

Mr. Belin. You heard no one else running down the stairs?

Miss Adams. Correct.

Mr. Belin. During the trip down the stairs on the way down did you ever encounter Lee Harvey Oswald?

Miss Adams. No, sir.

Mr. Belin. No one stopped you from getting out of the building when you left?

Miss Adams. That's correct.

Mr. Belin. That is helpful information. Is there any other information that you have that could be relevant?

Miss Adams. There was a man that was standing on the corner of Houston and Elm asking questions there.... Later on television, there was a man that looked very similar to him, and he was identified as Ruby.

Walker's notation there at that point read: "See WCR p. XL."

Andy scanned to that page and found that Walker had highlighted a section to A Guide to the Commission Exhibits, No. 2424. It read:

Jack Ruby at press conference in basement assembly room about midnight November 22, 1963. (Jack Ruby is the individual in the dark suit, back row, right-hand side, wearing horn-rimmed glasses).

Andy found the page with the photograph and saw the picture of Ruby standing in the back of the room at the press conference that had Oswald in the front of the room answering questions for the reporters.

Walker's remark there said: "Got around that day didn't you, Jack?"

Stuck there in-between the pages, were several newspaper clippings. The first was from the *San Francisco Chronicle*, dated December 3, 1963. It was a photograph taken by photographer James Altgens, an *Associated Press* photographer. It was taken from the south side of Elm Street and showed the presidential limousine in the foreground at the time of the shooting. In the background was a circle of a man standing in the doorway of the Texas School Book Depository.

Andy looked at the man in the picture. Walker had scribbled the words: If not Oswald, then his twin!

The article went on at length about how the man in the background of the picture closely resembled Oswald. The man in the picture has on an undershirt and another dark shirt open in the front.

However, Andy learned that the Commission said on page 137 that, "The Commission has determined that the employee was in fact Billy Nolan Lovelady...."

Walker's note said: "V22 p. 794."

Andy learned that Lovelady said he wore "a red and white striped sport shirt buttoned near the neck."

Walker had a photocopy of a document there. It read: "National Archives, Basic Source Materials in Possession of Commission: Commission No. 457, FBI interview of Lovelady, Dallas, February 29, 1964. Lovelady said that he had on 'a red and white vertical striped shirt.'"

Walker's notation said: "V22 p. 794."

There, Andy read that Lovelady told the *Herald Tribune*, that on the day of the assassination he wore "a red and white striped sport shirt buttoned near the neck."

Walker's note said: "V22 pp. 793-794."

Andy discovered that Oswald had on an undershirt and a dark shirt open to the waist when photographed after his arrest.

Walker's note there said: "Lovelady never questioned before Commissioners—inconclusive questions asked by junior counsel..."

Andy stopped and thought about a plan. He knew he was pushing his luck, or rather Pat's, but he had to see if Pat could dig there. He had another plan that he was also considering. He had to be careful, yet, like Cheryl, Andy had to have answers to questions.

He placed a call to Pat.

"Yeah?" Pat answered.

"You always in?"

"Not always."

"You know why I'm calling."

"One guess, O'Connell."

"Can you get into the CIA files?"

"Are you fuckin' crazy?"

"Maybe."

"What I did with Defense was illegal."

"You've hacked many places, all illegal."

"Yeah, but now you're talking about the CIA!"

"I knew you could do it."

There was a long pause. Pat sighed deeply. "I'll do one search. If I get in I stay for no more than five minutes, no matter if I get something or not. Those people can trace at least that fast."

"Thanks." Andy hung up and went back to the porch. He turned his computer off and got ready to pick up his father in Stillwater.

Colonel Garner was almost finished with his report and request for information. He knew many people who worked for the CIA, however, even though Garner had a top secret security clearance, he knew he could be denied information based on that elusive term known as national security.

He pushed the report to the side of his desk and would fax it over to Langley just as soon as he finished an unrelated report that required his immediate attention.

Pat sat back in his chair and rubbed his eyes. What the hell was Andy getting him into? He had known Andy for three years and knew Andy's father was a federal judge, so maybe there could be some protection if things got out of hand.

Pat knew he could do it, but that he would have to cover his tracks more than he had with the Pentagon, because, when it came to the CIA, he knew you were dealing with an almost separate, or super-government. They operated under their own rules. Certainly in the past they at times answered to no one. Five minutes, he kept repeating over and over in his head.

He got to work. With any luck, he could have this finished in minutes, because he was using the program he had made for the Pentagon search. Pat took care and made sure that he re-routed the call all over the world going through four dozen phones in fifteen countries, including places like South Africa and Russia!

He hit a few keys, and clicked his mouse a couple times, then his computer did the rest. Pat leaned back and watched as the call was placed. If someone in Israel tried to use the public phone at the same time that he was using it, the person in Israel would hear a busy signal. They most likely would hang up and try another phone. Nevertheless, they couldn't interrupt Pat's link-up.

The call took fifteen seconds to hook up and dial the CIA's computer database. Pat's hacking program took over and began running access codes after the computer in Langley answered.

Pat's heartbeat picked up speed. He watched his on-screen stopwatch and was ready to hang up if he went over five minutes.

It was taking too long. Thirty seconds and Pat saw thousands of numbers spin by and thousands of messages that countered his request for access that read "access denied." Pat perspired more than usual.

Garner started faxing the report and request to his counterpart at Langley. After the five pages were faxed, Garner closed up his office and headed home.

At Langley, in his office, Gordon Krup noticed the fax waiting there in the basket of his fax machine. He took the papers and put them in numerical order, ran a photocopy immediately so the papers were easier to handle, and sat down to read the report from Garner.

Krup was in his middle forties, looked older than he was, and was always dressed impeccably. He was a dedicated CIA bureaucrat who ran agency security.

Krup knew nothing of a John O'Connell. More disturbing, however, was the fact that someone hacked into the Pentagon and the hacker could be anywhere in the world. Part of the CIA's new responsibility in the post cold war era was to keep on top of the developments in the computer world so that hacking like this was prevented. They were supposed to spy on foreign companies and know of the very latest in computer technology, including hacking. However, there was always some whiz kid out there that figured out a way around things.

Krup went to alert his staff.

Finally, after more than 90 seconds with Pat squirming in his seat, his computer was in. The emblem of the Central Intelligence Agency showed on his screen.

He typed in a request for archival information.

The computer gave several options.

He chose: By name.

The computer asked for the name.

He typed in the name of John O'Connell.

The computer began its search. Pat looked at his stopwatch and saw two minutes fast approaching.

"Come on, come on," Pat said nervously.

Krup was standing over a computer specialist in the mainframe computer database room. The specialist hit a few keys and responded, "You're not going to fuckin' believe it." He stared at his screen that showed an outside line had a search in progress. "He's doing it at this very moment!"

Krup put his hand on the man's shoulder. "Let him. He's after information on a man named O'Connell. I don't know what that means yet, but it's more important that we trace this."

The specialist got right to work. He pointed and clicked his mouse.

A file number popped up on screen! Pat quickly scanned it and saw that it was cross-referenced with another name: Henry Seine.

He instantaneously ordered a printout and then typed in the file number. He waited. His stopwatch showed that three minutes had now passed.

The file appeared on screen. Pat ordered a printout and quickly scanned the information there as it was printing. It was short:

FILE NUMBER: 59AU74I032: O'CONNELL, JOHN. REPORTED MISSING 631203. FILE OMITTED.

The CIA computer specialist sat watching his computer do its own work. Krup, and now a half dozen people, stood there observing. The anxiety level increased.

On the computer screen everyone saw the hacker's phone call being traced. There was a world map and a line going out from Langley. The line crisscrossed all over the map: from Berlin, to Mexico City; from Mexico City to London; From London to Hong Kong. The line stopped at one site for a of couple seconds, then a telephone number showed in a database line on the lower left of the screen, then the line shot out across the map, usually on the other side of the world.

Pat saw that four minutes had passed. He had to do one more search. He requested a cross-reference on: Seine, Henry. He waited.

Four minutes forty two seconds had passed. Pat's fingers shook slightly.

Six seconds later his computer showed:

FILE NUMBER: 61HN93MO9R: SEINE, HENRY. RETIRED AGENT. FILE OMITTED.

Pat hit the key for a printout, turned and noticed the stopwatch showed five minutes three seconds. He turned back to his computer and disconnected the call.

"Got it!" exclaimed the CIA computer specialist. "A number in Cambridge, Massachusetts. He just cut it off."

"Harvard University," said Krup. "I knew it. Damn kids. Get me a printout, including exactly what he got. I'll get someone on this."

The computer specialist ordered a printout of the entire episode, including Pat's number. Everything was also automatically recorded in the computer.

"Shit," Pat mumbled under his breath. "Took too long." He scanned the printouts onto a diskette, then called Andy, but got the machine. "Its, Pat. I got it. Call me."

He emptied his trashcan and burned the printouts. He placed the diskette on top of his computer.

Andy had picked up his father, they had dinner as usual at the Black Bear, and went back to the Osprey. During dinner they small-talked. Andy had explained that Cheryl would be looking after Walker and that he would take her over there and hang out.

Although he hadn't met Cheryl, Judge Bell suspected that Andy had something going with her by the way that he avoided talking about her, yet sounded eager to hang out with her.

Needless to say, Judge Bell was beginning to become concerned with Andy's lack of interest in a law degree, his separation with Wendy and her father's connections, and Andy's involvement with this girl, Walker's granddaughter. What could he say, however? Andy was far too independent to take any advice, so the Judge bit his lip and kept his disappointments to himself.

Andy picked up Pat's message and listened to another message that Wendy had left. She was waiting for his call and wanted very much to visit him. He didn't call her back. He placed his call to Pat while his father unpacked behind him.

"Its, Andy."

"I don't know what you're getting me into," said Pat, "but there's nothing here."

"Nothing?"

"References to omitted files again."

"Send me what you've got."

"I'm ready."

"Give a minute." Andy hung up the phone and plugged in his computer.

His father looked over at him and Andy sensed it. "Research for my thesis."

"It's okay," said his father reassuringly.

Andy was plugged in and got set up when Pat's computer called. Andy's computer downloaded the file and Pat's computer hung up when the transfer was complete. Andy plugged his father's phone back in and checked the file. He scanned what little information there was. He sighed and shook his head. The new name listed with O'Connell's only added to Andy's intrigue, but the lack of information frustrated and agitated him more, adding to the mystery.

Andy turned the computer off and set it aside. "I'll be back in a little while," he said to his father as he rushed out the door.

Pat erased the diskette and buried it in a pile of other blank diskettes. He erased his e-mail phone numbers and logs. He insured that there was no information about where the files could have gone, or that he had had them.

He tensely looked around his small dorm room. His roommate had gone home for the summer. It was almost the weekend, Pat didn't have classes on Fridays, so he decided to get out of here and go somewhere, anywhere away from here. He knew what he had done could get him into trouble, and that thought made him worry for the first time since he had begun hacking years ago. Then again, he recollected, he hadn't hacked the CIA and the Pentagon before!

Pat stuffed some clothes into a bag, grabbed a nearby laptop, and departed. He went into Boston and checked into a cheap hotel.

Andy met up with Cheryl and together they walked to the bridge that crossed over the small dam that separated Norridgewock Lake near Beaver River Station. There they stood silently looking at the full moon. The moonlight reflected off the lake that had calmed down for the night. They could smell the White Pines and Spruce trees that swayed gently in the warm breeze.

"Look at that," she said pointing at a mother duck and her ducklings that paddled by. The mother squawked at them to keep up.

They watched as the duck family headed for a bed of reeds in a nearby marsh.

"What're you thinking?" he said breaking the stillness that pervaded the area.

"The grandfolks. It's eating at me."

"It's not going to be easy to get him to answer questions he's obviously tried to bury for three decades." He thought to himself about the irony in that statement.

"I know, but, you understand?"

"Yeah. To know our past, it's a need that many have to know; should know; must know." What the hell did I just say? He thought.

"It's like all those adopted people who search to find out who their parents were, no matter how painful their discoveries may be."

He nodded. When he looked at her, he felt this intense energy flow from her to him. He watched her shoulder length tan hair gently blow in the soft warm breeze.

"I'll help you. We'll work on him together."

"Thanks." She felt that same energy that he did.

They looked at one another simultaneously and their eyes locked. He told himself to move. He literally thought of that stupid damn crab singing that song from *The Little Mermaid*, "Kiss the Girl!"

And he did. They latched onto each other. She ran her fingers through his hair. They embraced tightly while they kissed.

It seemed like an eternity, but they pulled back an inch. His hormones had already kicked in, so had her's.

"Let's go," she whispered leading him back to her room. He made sure that no one was around or saw him when he went in with her. After all, Dusty had a policy that a single person paid a lower rate. One night for a couple was five dollars more.

They slowly undressed one another and sensually made love. It was just as delicious as the first time.

A few minutes later she fell asleep snuggled up to him, her head resting on his chest like a pillow. He lay there for a while thinking about Cheryl, Wendy, Walker, and the crime of the century, and how he would find the answers to all these burgeoning questions.

Fourteen

Judge Bell got up before the sun to go fishing. He now knew full well that Andy was involved with Cheryl. None of his business, he figured, yet, again, he reflected on his disappointment that Andy didn't hit it off with Wendy. Unfortunately, Judge Bell knew all too well, that in America as elsewhere, it still meant something to have connections. Having connections did open doors and Wendy's father could have given Andy that break.

He left a short note on the table for Andy that said, "Went fishing." He got his gear together and headed down to the Grassy Point Landing. Out on the reservoir, Judge Bell sat back and enjoyed the solitude. He had to get out here every weekend. If he didn't, he'd either have been corrupted by now, or insane.

Walker awoke to an enormous coughing spell about four in the morning. He struggled, but couldn't get out of bed. He was too weak. He rested for a while, then rolled over and fell off the bed. He tried to crawl, but didn't get far. He lay there trying to catch his breath. His oxygen tank and the tube from it were too far for him to reach.

After several minutes, he caught his breath and managed to sit up and lean against the wall. It took him awhile, but he was able to finally get up with the aid of a chair and pull the picture of JFK off the wall. He dismantled the shrine and cleared the table, putting everything under it. He then shuffled across the room and found a blanket in the cabinet. He had to stop and catch his breath after another coughing spell. He clutched his chest. The pain was intense.

After a few minutes, he slid onto the floor by means of the chair and covered the things from the shrine with the blanket. He reset the bomb for 48 hours. He covered the trap door with the edge of the blanket.

He tried to get up, but was too dizzy. He coughed and passed out on the floor.

Andy awoke first. Cheryl was half-awake as she rolled over to greet him. They kissed and embraced.

"I gotta to sneak out of here," Andy said. "Hungry?"

"A little."

"Meet you in the lodge in twenty minutes?"

"Thirty," Cheryl said. "I have to shower."

Andy affectionately kissed her again, then got up. He went back to the Osprey and showered. He saw his father's note and now worried that his father was becoming like Walker, a weekend recluse.

He met Cheryl for breakfast. Dusty smiled and went about his business, but suspected that there was more going on than Andy just being a nice guy.

After breakfast they headed out across the lake for Walker's asylum.

Andy docked the small boat. They approached the cabin. "We should go in carefully," he said.

At the main door inside the porch, Andy knocked loudly. "Mr. Walker? Its, Andy and Cheryl. We're coming in."

There was no answer. He looked at her. She signaled to go ahead. He opened the door and crept in. They saw Walker on the floor in the middle of the room.

"Mr. Walker?" Andy said shaking Walker's shoulder.

Walker groaned.

Andy rolled him over. "Let's get him into bed."

Together, they struggled and lifted Walker back into his bed.

Cheryl covered Walker with his sheets. She strapped on his oxygen tube over his head and adjusted it under his nose.

Andy had to catch his breath. He looked up and noticed that the shrine had been taken down. The wall where the picture of JFK had been hanging showed that the paint there was darker than the rest of the wall. Andy saw the blanket under the table and knew that Walker had hidden everything there.

Cheryl gave Walker medication from the kitchen. He was conscious, but inattentive. She returned the medication to the kitchen. Andy followed.

"What do you think?" Andy asked.

"Well, Bergholtz said it would be rough. He should recover for now, but he could die at any moment. Could live a couple years."

"We should clean up. This place hasn't been for years."

"I agree."

Bolt was his name. He was told to find out who this kid was, how he had hacked his way in, and what he wanted with John O'Connell. Technically, the CIA should have gone to the FBI, but Gordon Krup wanted this information before the Bureau was brought in and complicated the situation. Krup had already tracked down exactly what dorm the phone number that they had traced to Harvard came from. Today, for the most part, the university was deserted, considering it was the summer and a weekend.

Bolt was an even six feet, and solid muscle at the age of 45. A henchman, and unnaturally bald so he could assume disguises (much like E. Howard Hunt had done), he was dressed like a homeless man and wore a wig with long hair, a fake beard and mustache.

Bolt's job was easy. The hallway was clear, no one in sight. He located Pat's dorm room and rapped on the door several times with a small tool he had in his hand. After no one answered, with tight fitting rubber gloves, he used that small tool and unlocked the door. A twist of the knob and Bolt was inside. He closed the door behind him.

He glanced around the room and realized this kid was indeed the hacker he had been sent to find. There were two computers, side by side, computer diskettes piled around the room in several locations, and software programs stacked in waist high mountains. He sifted through manuals and notebooks.

Bolt turned on both of Pat's computers. He sat there and waited for them to activate. Both computers came on and asked for access codes. Bolt took out a diskette and shoved it into the first computer. He rebooted the computer and waited for the diskette to kick in and take over the process.

The diskette bypassed the access code in seconds. Bolt checked the directory. He activated the communications software, which included the modem, hit a few keys, clicked the mouse a couple of times, and sent the entire contents of Pat's computer on-line to a CIA computer in Langley. The whole process took five minutes.

Next, bolt conducted the same procedure with the other computer. That one also took about five minutes.

The entire contents of both computers had been sent to the computer in Langley, which included the files, software, e-mail addresses, Internet numbers, computer games and college papers of Pat and his roommate, Harry Morris.

Bolt removed the diskette and put it in his pocket. He turned the computers off and searched the room. He found portions of uneaten food items including half a Snickers bar, a couple bites of a sandwich, an open peanut butter jar. He opened and looked through dresser drawers, desks and the closet. He fingered through papers and notebooks on the table. He found several papers that had Pat's name on them. Bolt jotted down any names he saw. He found other software manuals and notebooks with software programs. He found an address book with many names and numbers, but not many addresses.

Bolt took a small camera out of his pocket. He photographed the contents of Pat's address book. He then flipped the pages of four note-books one at a time and took a picture of each page. The process took several minutes. When he was finished, he noted the names of the man-uals and software programs.

Bolt had been in Pat's room for two hours when he had searched through everything. He was good at what he did and had insured that everything was as he had found it. He prowled out the door.

Walker had slept almost the entire day. Cheryl was able to feed him some bread and soup later that afternoon. Just before they left, Cheryl had told Walker to stay in bed and not to get out. He moaned. They had brought all the plastic paraphernalia from the hospital including the bedpan, water pitcher and urinal, and had placed them on a stand near Walker. He whimpered during Cheryl's instructions and fallen asleep again shortly thereafter.

Andy and Cheryl got back into the boat. He took her around the lake. They got out near the northeast inlet of South Branch and walked up the river embankment. There, Andy showed Cheryl a sizable dam that beavers had built. The dam was almost shoulder height, stuck together with thick twigs chewed off as a beaver would! A small amount of water trickled over the top. There was even a beaver home in the river in back of the dam.

"I've never seen one before," she said. She picked up a twig and examined it. "Its amazing how clever animals really are."

They waded around the dam for several minutes until they walked back towards the inlet. Andy lay down on the sandy shore. Cheryl sat up next to him.

"What's going to happen if you find out his past and he does die?" Andy asked. "Then what'll you do?"

"It depends on what I learn, I guess." She played with the sand, letting it sift through her fingers. She was hoping this new relationship would lead to something, that is if Andy felt the way she did.

"You could come and visit me in Huntsville," she said. "I've decided to keep my grandmother's house. It's large, but houses like that aren't built anymore."

"I could. I'd like that. I want to graduate, then go somewhere else, get away and see what's out there."

They were quiet a long moment.

"Did you notice," she said, "that Walker removed the picture of Kennedy and that other stuff?"

Andy knew she would ask sooner or later. "Yeah."

"It's like he doesn't want us to see it, although we already have. What does it mean?"

Andy thought it through as he spoke. "Perhaps he's sentimental or something and doesn't want us to think he's softer than he lets on."

"He's Catholic. My grandmother was Southern Baptist. No connection there. We weren't extremely religious, but we did go from time to time." She lay down next to him on her back. "I wonder what's in that chest."

Oh no, he thought.

"And up in that loft he keeps locked."

Andy closed his eyes tightly. He didn't want to speak and have to keep lying. He couldn't tell her yet. He just couldn't. "I don't know," he said. "I guess we should take it slow with him, if he ever opens up at all."

"You're right. I think he's slightly senile, I guess you could say. A little has come out. I think if we outsmart him, work around the edges, we can get it out of him."

Andy rolled to his side. He placed his hand on her abdomen. She responded by placing her hand atop his. He moved closer, lowered his head and kissed her.

Gordon Krup sat at his desk in his office at Langley. His assistant, Jack Riles, sat across from him. They searched through a massive printout of the entire contents of Pat's computer. The stack of papers comprising the printout totaled over a thousand pages. Most of the information there involved computer software, games, student papers and downloaded Internet files. Those files were thrown in the recycle basket after each man quickly scanned them.

"Here's something," said Riles. "His phone records have him calling several locations within the past few days. I'll run these numbers and see what we get." He left the room.

Krup continued to look through the papers. So far, neither he nor Riles had found the information that was extracted the other day by this kid. He obviously knew the extent of what he had done and erased the information.

Riles entered. "They're running a check on those numbers." He sat down and continued to look at the stack of papers in front of him.

Another diligent assistant, James Burham, entered the office. "I've got some interesting details on O'Connell and Seine." He closed the door behind him.

Krup and Riles looked up and listened.

Burham sat next to Riles across from Krup. "Get a hold of yourselves, you're not going to believe this," Burham said. "O'Connell was an expert rifleman who had worked for Guy Banister on several occasions."

Krup leaned back in his high-top chair. "Jesus Christ," he said. "Where'd you get this?"

"In the archives, cross referenced. This stuff isn't on line for obvious reasons. We have no direct files on O'Connell or Seine. They're missing. All this comes from Banister and other cross-referenced files."

"Continue," sighed Krup.

"Banister had hired Seine for arms smuggling operations throughout Latin America during the 1950's," explained Burham looking at the file. "Seine had hired O'Connell to train guerrillas in the use of those arms.

They had the support and cover of this agency for their front in Guatemala.

"O'Connell's name also came up in another file," continued Burham glancing at Krup who massaged his forehead with his right hand. "O'Connell was involved in training anti-Castro Cubans for the Bay of Pigs. He was contracted for the JM/WAVE operation."

"I don't like where this is going," Krup interrupted.

"O'Connell's name also came up with a former agency front company, the Vietnamese Metal Works in Saigon." Burham looked up from the file. "He was a mechanic and did several hits, all South Vietnamese targets, communists, sympathizers etc. All of this run out of the Saigon Military Mission."

"Fuck," bemoaned Krup. "I know of the program, but fill in the details."

Reading from the file, Burham continued. "Let's see, blah, blah, blah, oh. The Military Assistance Advisory Group ran the precursor to the Phoenix Program out of the Saigon Military Mission. The Phoenix Program was later conducted by the agency whereby communists or other sympathizers were pacified. Director Colby estimated as many as 20,000 Vietcong had been pacified.

"O'Connell's name popped up cross-referenced in several other files," continued Burham. "Again, all hits. Many in Latin America and Southeast Asia. All of the hits were contracted through front companies."

"How many hits have you found?" Krup asked.

"I count thirty two in just these files. There may be more."

"Quite the killing machine," jested Riles.

"The Pentagon has nothing on Seine or O'Connell," recommenced Burham. "Again their files are missing. I checked with the Bureau, and they sent over a missing persons report on O'Connell from late '63. The report was filed by retired agent Winston Franklin. There was never a report filed on Seine. His whereabouts are unknown."

"Then he could be still out there," interjected Krup. "We need to find him, or if he's dead, get that. Anything else?"

"Just more operations, many the same."

"Okay. When you get everything you can from the archives, chronologically list everything that each man was involved in and a brief summation of that operation."

"On it," said Burham exiting.

Krup looked back down at the printout on his desk. "This kid's working for someone," he said. "We need to get Bolt on it and find out what's going on."

The next morning Walker disobeyed Cheryl's orders. He felt better and had more strength. He pulled off his oxygen tube and crawled over to the bomb and reset it. He realized that these two kids weren't going to leave him alone. It was now a mistake, he fumed to himself, that he had hired Andy. Although, this Cheryl, his granddaughter he now admitted, could have still found him.

Since they planned on showing up, Walker reset the timer on the bomb to four in the morning. He reset his alarm for that time and wrote the time down on his pad.

He crawled back to his bed and struggled to get in it.

Cheryl met Andy at the Osprey. Andy's father was resting in a lounge chair on the porch reading the latest John Grisham novel. He found Grisham's novels quite accurate, but disagreed with some of his positions. He saw Cheryl walking his way.

He opened the door to the porch. "Come in. I'm Andy's father."

"The Judge. I'm Cheryl Taylor."

They shook hands. "Andy, Cheryl's here."

Andy burst out from the shower with a towel wrapped around him. She smiled and his father was embarrassed that he was so dressed.

"Dad, this is Cheryl Taylor. Cheryl, my father, the honorable Judge Richard Bell."

"We already met, Andy," said his father.

"Oh. Okay. I'll just get dressed and..." He darted into the main room and grabbed his shorts and a T-shirt.

"Something to drink? Juice, tea?" Judge Bell said.

"Ice tea, please."

"Sure. Please, sit."

She sat at the table on the porch. Andy returned promptly already dressed with his wet hair slicked back over his head. His father returned with ice tea and two glasses. He poured the tea.

"How's Walker?" Judge Bell asked.

Andy looked at Cheryl to respond.

"He really should be in a hospital," she answered. "We found him on the floor yesterday." She drank a sizable portion of her drink, seeing how the humidity hadn't subsided over night.

"Andy tells me he's your grandfather."

"He left way before I came along, but I think there's no doubt." She took out the photograph of Walker sitting with her grandmother and showed it to him. "My grandmother and Walker I believe."

"He hasn't admitted it?"

She shook her head.

Judge Bell studied the picture carefully. He thought that the young Walker looked like someone he had seen before, but couldn't think who. "I first met him in eighty nine. I'd been here two years and hadn't seen or heard of him. Then, he walks into the lodge and Ronny introduces me. I'd see him occasionally and we'd small talk, which is all it's ever been, but I think he was suspicious of me in the beginning."

Andy suspected why. "You think its him?" Andy asked.

"I think so. You can see it in his face." He handed the picture back to Cheryl. "I'm sorry."

She took the picture and put it back in her wallet. "It's okay. You're probably wondering how I found him. I traced some envelopes he had Doc Bergholtz mail for him in Syracuse. My grandmother probably could have done the same, but she didn't, or knew where he was and didn't care. I had to know who sent them, and why. I guess she thought I wouldn't make the effort, or wouldn't know how to go about finding him. Luck had something to do with it."

"You haven't found the why yet," Judge Bell sensed and said as a statement.

Cheryl shook her head.

"He hasn't kicked you out, though."

"In a way, but I'm not leaving here until I get the truth."

Judge Bell wasn't going to say anymore. The picture Cheryl had showed him proved that it was a much younger Walker sitting with a woman Cheryl said was her grandmother, and he didn't have any reason not to believe her. If Walker was her grandfather, then, in a way, she did have some right to be here. On the other hand, Walker's entitled to his privacy, including his past. There's no law that says a grandfather has to accommodate his granddaughter.

"In a strange way it works out," said Andy. "You're here to look after him. Otherwise, he'd probably just die of neglect over there in that cabin."

"And we all know that's what he wants," she said.

They were silent in their own thoughts for a moment.

"Well, I had a good catch yesterday. If you agree to come back for dinner, Cheryl, I'll cook up some bass."

"Yeah. Thanks. I'd like that."

Judge Bell finished his tea and went into the kitchen.

Fifteen

Bolt sat on a bench in Cambridge and was disguised like he was the day before in long hair and a beard. It was later that morning when he heard the phone ring in the booth on the corner. He walked over and answered. "Yeah?"

"We found the program he used," said Krup over the phone. "Good work."

Bolt waited for his instructions.

"We traced his credit card to the Patriot Motel in Boston. He checked out thirty minutes ago. Call me when you get something, but remember, don't hurt him."

"I'll be waiting," said Bolt hanging the phone up. He went up into the dorm and waited for Patrick Hennelly to show.

Two hours later Pat entered the dorm hallway and approached his room. Bolt peered around the corner and saw him coming.

As Pat dug in his pocket for his keys, Bolt stepped out from the shadows. "Patrick Hennelly?"

Pat turned and dropped his keys.

"We need to talk," said Bolt approaching.

Pat panicked. He dropped his backpack and fled down the hallway from the direction he had just come. Bolt ran after him.

"I'm not going to hurt you," shouted Bolt running after him. "Stop!"

But Pat was incredibly fast. He was down the stairs and out across the green in seconds.

Bolt was just as fast and began to close in on him. "You're over reacting," yelled Bolt. "I won't hurt you."

Pat wouldn't hear of it. He knew what he had done was serious. He had read all about the CIA and the world of spies. He feared the worst. Huffing and almost out of breath, he turned a corner and ran across a street.

Bolt was only a few yards behind him. "We just want to talk."

Pat knew how they liked to talk with rubber hoses and electric shock! He turned a corner and started to run across the street when a transit bus broadsided him. The bus was going forty miles an hour and Pat was thrown several yards.

Bolt came to a quick stop. He took cover behind a building.

The bus stopped. The driver and several passengers came running.

The driver felt for a pulse. Nothing. He took off his jacked and covered Pat's head.

"Fuck," Bolt muttered to himself. He sneaked off.

Andy and Cheryl had already been at Walker's cabin for an hour. They came early and found Walker fast asleep in his bed. They took a walk around Walker's small island and returned to find him awakening. Cheryl stood over Walker and Andy behind her.

"Go away," said Walker closing his eyes again.

"Sorry, we're here to stay," said Cheryl going into the kitchen to get him some medication.

Walker looked at Andy who stared back at him.

"What're you looking at?" Walker snapped.

"Can't you just go easy on her?"

"I don't know who she is."

"She's your granddaughter."

"Ah…"

"I saw the pictures. I think there's no question. You and her grand-mother are in the same picture affectionately hugging. And, if you look at Cheryl next to a younger you, there's a resemblance."

"You're the smart ass college kid, aren't you?"

"Here you go," said Cheryl returning with some pills and clean water for his pitcher.

Walker looked up at her and sluggishly opened his hand for the pills. She dropped them into his hand, poured water into a cup and handed it to him.

He sat up slightly and took the medication. She took the cup from him after he had washed the pills down.

"I want to get up and walk."

She looked at Andy who nodded. Walker sat up and swung his legs over to get into position. "Get me that robe," he said pointing to the wall where his robe hung on a hook.

Andy got the robe and they put it on him. Walker tied it in front.

"Let's go," directed Walker.

Andy and Cheryl grabbed him from each side and together they lifted him up on to his feet. They walked him around the room.

"I want to sit on the porch," he barked.

They did as instructed and led him to the porch. They sat him down in his folding lawn chair. Walker was out of breath, but would live, Cheryl presumed.

Andy got two chairs from the kitchen. He set one chair down for Cheryl and one for himself. They were all in a row looking out at the still Morning Lake.

Walker wheezed a little and coughed into his handkerchief.

Andy finally broke the lull. He said, "Anything else you need for me to do around here, Mr. Walker?"

"You've done enough," he uttered. "I'm sure to die soon and this is all for nothing."

"Someone would buy it, besides, I don't think you'll die for a while. I had a grandmother who said she was going to die every day for fifteen years."

Walker grunted. Cheryl cracked a smile.

"You have to understand," said Walker, "that I'm an old man who's been alone for many years and I'm not comfortable with you two being here."

"We understand," said Andy. Cheryl listened. She wanted to let Andy loosen him up for her.

"I'm a survivalist," continued Walker, "who fled to the hills during the height of the cold war."

"The cold war's over," said Andy.

"I read the papers."

"I didn't see a television, or a radio. The newspapers you got are weeks old."

"It's still news to me."

"'Suppose you're right."

"Television, not religion, is the opium of the masses. Marx was wrong again."

"Eye candy they say today," said Andy thinking that Walker wasn't unintelligent. Then again, neither was Ted Kaczynski.

They were silent for a couple minutes.

"What do you do?" Walker asked turning to look at Cheryl.

She was startled. "Work?"

Walked nodded.

"I was studying to be a teacher."

"Was?"

"No. I'm planning to go back in the fall. My mother was a nurse. Her name was Sue."

"Susan?"

Cheryl knew she had hooked a cord with him, because that's how her mother was always addressed, even when Cheryl could remember. "Yeah, Susan," she said.

Walker stared out at the lake. "What happened to her?"

"She was killed in a car accident coming home from work late one night. A drunk driver. He spent one night in jail, was fined and released. A few years later the same man killed a family of four early one morning, got six months for manslaughter, was released and was shot to death by the grandfather the next day. The grandfather got life in prison."

"Justice, Huh, Andy?" Walker asked provoking him.

"You could say in the end, yeah."

"Not for the grandfather."

"The laws have been changing. Drunk driving offenses are getting tougher."

"A little too late for the old man, though."

"Not too late here," said Cheryl.

"What?" Walker snapped.

"Well, it's not so much justice, so to speak, than what is a right."

"What?" Walker didn't follow.

"That I know my past."

"The past is over," Walker rebuffed.

"Perceptive," said Andy under his breath.

"What?" demanded Walker. "You getting flippant with me?"

Now there's a word no one says anymore, thought Andy. "No sir." Andy recoiled.

"But it's important we know our past; where we come from," continued Cheryl applying the pressure.

Walker didn't answer her.

"You're part of my past," she said.

Walker grunted, and wheezed. "Many of us would be better off not knowing our past," Walker finally said spitting into his handkerchief.

"That's up for the individual to decide. It's not fair that anyone deny someone else the right to know."

Walker glanced over at Andy. "Perhaps Lenin was right."

"What the hell're you talking about?"

"The people need to be led, told what to do, and as long as they don't know the details, are given their daily bread, they're happy and won't bother the master."

"What? She's talking about a person's past, you're talking political philosophy."

"It's all comparative, kid."

"Comparative to what?"

"To what's going on in this country."

"And what's going on in this county?"

"Look at all the white angry males who can't handle the truth about this country's past." He paused. "They don't want to know the past."

Andy knew he was muddled, but at least he was talking more than he had. "I'm listening."

"You read the papers," Walker went on, "at least I hope you're one of the few who still does?"

"More than the papers, but go on."

"Look, kid, people can't handle the truth. This country can't handle the truth. It was government policy to break treaties with the Indians. After all, who was the government going to side with? The Indians who were primitive and stood in the way of progress? Or the expanding white man and his settling family that brought in revenue, in one way or another, for the government. Growth gives the government more power. And slavery? And world domination? I was a part of that last concept, insuring the survival of Capitalism so those Multi-national corporations would rule the world as they do today. Look at the World Trade Organization that everyone is afraid of now. If the people really knew how we, in part, achieved that, they'd be abhorred, despite the benefits that it has achieved for them. There're better off not knowing the details."

Holy shit! Andy said to himself. It's just like the last time he went off the handle. "I hope you don't mind my asking you?"

Walker waved his hand indicating that it was all right to go ahead.

"Do you have a degree?"

Walker laughed under his breath. What the hell, he thought. "No."

"You must have been in the service, since you know so much about weapons. I mean, some of those weapons are military ones."

Walker chuckled slightly. "Smart ass, aren't ya?"

"A guess, I guess."

"You guess. Yeah, I was in the Marines."

It's coming, ever so slowly, Andy believed. "Really? You must have been in the service, well, at least forty years ago?"

"Good at math, are you?"

"Not really."

"Yeah, Korea."

Hello, John O'Connell! Andy tried to maintain his composure. "So what happened?"

"What do you mean what happened?"

"You got out."

"Yeah like millions."

The Marines! Andy's suspicions were being delivered to him incrementally. "Ever in Vietnam?"

Walker turned toward him and barked, "What do you know about it?"

"You were in the military. We fought a war there too. Were you there?" Hello, Andy said to himself.

"I just told you I got out after Korea."

"No, you said that you got out, like millions. You didn't say when."

"Well, I got out after Korea."

"So you've never been to Vietnam?"

"What makes you think I've been to Vietnam?"

"I thought perhaps, that…"

"Well don't think, Goddamnit."

Answer my question, Andy said to himself. "So you didn't go to Vietnam?"

"I didn't say that."

Andy had him. "What did you say?"

"I didn't say that I wasn't in Vietnam."

"So, were you?"

"Well, no, yes, no."

What the hell was that? "I don't understand," said Andy. Actually he did, but he had to play the situation unknowingly.

"Well I was there, but after I left the military," said Walker now uncomfortable with continuing this line. Damn it, he shouldn't have said that!

Andy didn't want to push it too much, so he backed off. They sat silent for a few minutes.

"Did you love her?" Cheryl finally jumped in.

"Huh?" Walker growled. He was truly having trouble following the conversation from Andy to Cheryl.

"Nora, my grandmother."

"Ah, yes, I loved her," he said distantly.

She nodded her head slowly to hide her excitement. She could see that he was drifting. "Do you want anything to eat?"

Walker looked at her. He seemed to stare right through her. She did indeed remind him of Nora, his ex-wife.

Cheryl looked back at him but became uneasy by his vacant look.

"Something to eat, sir?" She asked again.

"Toast. Coffee." He looked out at the lake again. Cheryl went into the kitchen.

Andy watched Walker out of the corner of his eye. Walker twirled his cane between his legs.

They didn't say anything to each other. Cheryl returned a few minutes later with Walker's toast and coffee. She found a small folding tray by the door and set it up in front of him. He nibbled on the toast and sipped the coffee. She sat back down beside him.

"Still detect a slight accent," said Cheryl to her grandfather.

Walker didn't answer.

"So you loved her. Why did you leave?"

"I told you, it's better one leave the past where it is."

"You can't trust me with the truth?"

"No! You two can come here and assist me until I am up and around on my own. But don't come any sooner than seven o'clock in the morning."

Cheryl looked at Andy and he shrugged his shoulders. He could see that she wanted more information, but thought that it was time to settle with what they got so far and perhaps more would follow a different day. He shook his head at her. She nodded.

Cheryl cleaned up after Walker had eaten his toast and finished his coffee. She and Andy got Walker back to bed shortly after noon. He rested while they went back to the Osprey and had lunch. They had told Walker they would return later and get him up again for dinner.

Andy and Cheryl went swimming. The day was one of the hottest yet. It was only in the low eighties, but the humidity in these parts can melt your frame away. They small-talked and frolicked together most of the afternoon.

Krup and Riles had the phone numbers identified that Pat had used. Most were to family or computer related, and one number was traced to Federal Judge Richard Bell in Beaver River, New York.

Krup instructed Bolt to tread on sensitive ground when approaching the Judge. The mystery, Krup concluded, was that some of the calls were during the workweek, unless the Judge was on vacation.

Riles had already gotten public records from Herkimer County and located the Judge's property. The details had been relayed to Bolt.

Bolt, dressed like an amateur fisherman, had driven a rental to Stillwater. He quickly learned that he would have to take a boat to Beaver River, and was hooked up with Dusty's run and went over on the second trip that day. In fact, Dusty and Bolt passed Andy and the Judge in the middle of the reservoir going the other way.

Bolt checked into the lodge at Beaver River and then took a walk around.

He located Judge Bell's cabin and realized that no one was there after surveying the area. However the place showed that someone was around because a bathing suit and towel hung on the clothesline. He walked down to the trestle that separated the reservoir and the lake. Nice isolated place, he reflected. Bolt had been told that Patrick Hennelly had been digging into the archives and had accessed information on a John O'Connell, but he wasn't told the extent of O'Connell's activities, or that he was reported missing in 1964. Krup only told him that O'Connell had worked for the agency and that his files were omitted. Bolt was to find out who wanted information on O'Connell and why.

Later that evening, Andy returned and picked Cheryl up. They hopped in the boat and went back to Walker's cabin. They marched him around the cabin and fed him. Nothing in the way of substance was discussed, but Walker was getting more congenial with each visit. He was even beginning to accept the fact that Cheryl was his granddaughter, and that neither one of these kids were after anything, or couldn't be trusted.

Bolt was prowling around when he noticed that the boat at the dock in front of the Judge's cabin was not there. Someone was here! He waited near the neighbor's idle cabin, hiding behind a tree. He wore no wig, or any other disguises. His shiny bald head, looking like G. Gordon Liddy's, glistened in the moonlight.

Andy and Cheryl went by in the boat.

Bolt could see that it was the same one he saw docked here earlier. He watched as the boat docked at the lodge. The girl got out, then the boy. They embraced, kissed, and then released one another. The girl walked up to the lodge while the boy got back into the boat and headed this way.

Andy docked and walked up to the Osprey. He went inside and threw his cap onto the bed. It landed on top of his laptop computer that lay there.

Bolt knocked on the outer door to the porch.

Andy went to the door and saw an athletic looking middle aged man dressed like a fisherman in a fly jacket.

"I'm looking for Judge Bell?"

"He's not here," said Andy after he had cracked open the door.

"Oh, you must be his son."

"Yes, Andy."

"Nice to meet you." Bolt extended his hand.

Andy reluctantly shook it. "And you?"

"Oh, I'm sorry. James Fowler. I knew your father years ago. May I come in?"

"Well…"

Bolt invited himself in. "Nice place you have here." Bolt went into the main room behind the porch and looked around.

Andy became a little concerned with this man's forceful intrusion. "Where do you know my father from?"

"Oh, from court." Bolt had already put two plus two together and figured that Hennelly and Andy, the same age, were accomplices.

Andy became more suspicious, and more nervous. "Could you be more specific?"

"Yes, but I'm afraid…" Bolt turned and flashed his credentials in Andy's face. "I'm not going to hurt you, Andy. I'm CIA and only want to talk. You give me the correct answers and I'll be on my way."

Andy backed up abruptly and bumped into the sliding glass door. Bolt kept his distance, but was closer. Damn, Pat was caught!

"We'd be crazy to do anything to a federal judge's son, besides, we don't do much of what we used to."

"That's not very reassuring." Andy kept cool on the outside, but was scared to death on the inside.

"We can sit and talk like two intelligent and civilized human beings," said Bolt.

"I don't know if I can sit."

"Okay. We'll stand." Bolt backed off giving Andy more space. He continually scanned the cabin as he spoke. "We only want to know what you want with O'Connell's files."

Andy felt like he was going to urinate in his pants. He came up with a quick response. "I befriended his granddaughter."

"The girl in the boat."

"Yes. She never knew him. Her grandmother just passed away. Cheryl, the granddaughter, never knew him and her grandmother never told her about him. My friend, I guess that's how you traced me here, is good at computer hacking, so I asked him to check some databases and see if he could come up with something."

Bolt listened. He knew better than to tell Andy about his friend Hennelly.

"We're just trying to see if her grandfather is still alive and where he might be."

"Does your father know you're breaking into Pentagon and CIA computers?"

"No," said Andy defeated.

"We haven't gone to the FBI yet, but what you've done is a serious crime."

"We're not after state secrets. We're harmless."

Bolt studied him. He was good at interrogations, and either this kid was telling the truth, or was a good liar. "What did your friend tell you?" Bolt would know if he were lying.

"That O'Connell had been in the military, and his file was omitted."

Good answer. Bolt knew when Andy used the term OMITTED that Andy did indeed get the same information that Hennelly had extracted. "His granddaughter is your girlfriend?"

"Well, I guess. Yes, yes she is."

"What have you learned besides the information you got from the Pentagon and CIA?"

"Nothing. Dead end." Andy didn't like his own choice of words.

"Nothing?" Bolt moved around slowly.

"We've tried all over; county records, state files. O'Connell just disappeared."

"When?"

"Sometime in the middle sixties."

"Why?"

"We don't know."

"What was his occupation after the military?"

"We'd like to know that too."

Bolt glanced past Andy's bed and looked Andy straight in the eye. "You're not lying to me?"

"No sir. If you can help us find out what happened to O'Connell and why, Cheryl would greatly appreciate it."

"We're not in the business of private investigation."

"Yeah, but obviously O'Connell had a CIA file."

"You're treading on dangerous ground, kid. Why would he?"

"I just figured that many in those days did double duty, with different agencies."

"How would you know that?"

"I'm a political science major, well read, and the way in which he disappeared indicates spy work or something." Andy thought he sounded pretty good.

"Yeah?"

"You can understand that when a girl's grandmother dies, and she finds out that her grandfather didn't die, but was listed as missing, then this is all quite innocent."

"Kids aren't so innocent these days."

Andy didn't dignify that remark.

"So where do you search now?" Bolt asked.

"I don't know."

Bolt stared him down, making Andy shake slightly.

"There's nothing you can tell us?" Andy asked.

Bolt walked past him and onto the porch. Andy turned and slowly followed.

Bolt turned and faced Andy. "I hope you told me all that you know."

"Yes, sir," Andy said straight out like a private in the Army.

"I'm going to report what you told me. If you're lying, they may report this to the FBI. I don't think your father would be too thrilled."

"My friend, Pat, who you must have talked to…"

Bolt nodded his head.

"…is really quite harmless. He never did it before, and he'll never do it again."

Only Bolt knew the significance of that statement. "You stick your nose in places where it doesn't belong, you can get it cut off."

"So does this mean my government career is over?"

"You're thinking about going into government?"

"It's on my list."

"What's Cheryl's last name and where's she from?"

"Taylor. Huntsville, Alabama."

"Alabama? How'd you meet her?"

Andy was quick under pressure. "You know Habitat for Humanity?"

Bolt nodded.

"We met last summer in the South building homes."

"Her grandmother has the same last name?"

"No. Jackson."

Bolt nodded slowly.

"You're not going to bother Cheryl? She doesn't know I had my friend search those files. I just had a hunch."

"I don't know yet. If I don't like what you've said, I may."

Andy nodded.

"Like I said, we'll go to the Bureau if..." Bolt raised his index finger and pointed it at Andy like a disciplining parent. He exited the porch and went back to the lodge.

Andy collapsed into a chair and caught his breath. His heartbeat did double-time.

Bolt placed a call to Krup's home outside Langley. He reported what Andy had said. It seemed to satisfy Krup for the time being. Krup already knew that they had gone too far, especially with the death of Patrick Hennelly. They had found the program that Hennelly had designed and were already reviewing their computer security. They had already run a check on the Judge and his son and found nothing that would indicate anything subversive. Yet, Krup wanted to find out what had happened to this O'Connell, considering the activities he had been involved in. He decided to tract down this Henry Seine, and see what he had on O'Connell.

Andy placed a call to Pat, but only got his answering machine. He left a message for Pat to call him back as soon as he could. Andy was curious why Pat hadn't called to warn him that this Bolt was coming, and why he had given Andy up so easily. Pat must've cracked under the torture.

Andy sat down in his bed and opened a book from the Commission. He realized that if the CIA wasn't finished with him, he'd have to conceal his computer, for it certainly had the real story, just in case they did him in.

Andy read James Simmons' FBI report (another witness that day). The FBI said that "Simmons said he thought he saw...smoke near the embankment in front of the School Book Depository...."

Andy read the section that Walker had highlighted in volume 3 of the testimony of Howard Leslie Brennan:

> Mr. Brennan. Well, as it appeared to me he was standing up....

Walker had scribbled a note there that read: "The windows were too low to the floor to stand up and shoot!!!"

> Mr. Belin. Could you tell whether or not it had a scope on it?
> Mr. Brennan. I did not observe a scope.

Andy scanned down to page 145 where Brennan was testifying about talking with a policeman a few short minutes after the shooting:

> Mr. Belin. And then what happened, sir?
> Mr. Brennan. He said, "Just a minute."...And then he had me to, I believe, Mr. Sorrels, [a Secret Service Agent from the Dallas office] an automobile sitting in front of the Texas Book Store.
> Mr. Belin. And then what happened there?
> Mr. Brennan. I related my information and there was a few minutes of discussion, and Mr. Sorrels had taken me across the street to the Sheriff's building.

Walker had another note there: See p. 158. Andy skimmed forward.

Mr. Dulles. Did you give any estimate—was it a matter of 5 minutes, 6 minutes, 7 minutes? In general, how long did it take you from the time that you left where you were protecting yourself to the time you were on the front steps? What order of magnitude? 10 minutes?

Mr. Brennan. No; it was shorter time than that....

A note made by Walker said: "See V7 p. 347." Andy located that section. It was from Agent Sorrel:

Mr. Stern. What happened next, [after the shots] Mr. Sorrels?

Mr. Sorrels. We proceeded to Parkland Hospital as fast as we could.

Mr. Stern. Just a minute. How much time do you think elapsed from the time the shots were fired until the time you returned to the Book Depository?

Mr. Sorrels. About 20 minutes....

Mr. Stern. So you estimate about 20 minutes?

Mr. Sorrels. It could have been more than 20 or 25 minutes at the very most....

Andy flipped over to page 354 where Sorrels explained the lineup later that night.

Mr. Sorrels. So I took Mr. Brennan, and we went to the assembly room, which is also where they have the lineup, and Mr. Brennan, upon arrival at the police station, said, "I don't know if I can do you any good or not, because I have seen the man that they have under arrest on television," and he said, "I just don't know whether I can identify him positively or not" because he said that the man on television was a bit disheveled and his shirt was open or something like that, and he said "The man I saw was not in that condition...." They did bring Oswald in in a lineup. He looked very carefully, and then we moved him closer and so forth, and he said, "I cannot positively say...." Then he repeated that the man he saw was not disheveled....

Mr. Stern. At that time, did Mr. Brennan say anything else to you that you have not told us, or to anyone else?

Mr. Sorrels. Not that I recall. He says, "I am sorry, but I can't do it. I was afraid the television might have messed me up. I just can't be positive. I am sorry."

Another note Walker had there said: "Back—V3, p. 147." Andy went back and continued with Mr. Brennan's testimony:

Mr. Belin. By the way, Mr. Brennan, I note that you have glasses with you today. Were you wearing glasses at the time of the incident that you related here?

Mr. Brennan. No....

Mr. Belin. How is your eyesight today?

Mr. Brennan. Not good.

Andy rubbed his eyes and ran his fingers from his left hand through his short hair. "Jesus! The Commission's star witness?"

Mr. Belin. In the meantime, had you seen any pictures of Lee Harvey Oswald on television or in the newspapers?

Mr. Brennan. Yes, on television.

Mr. Belin. About when was that, do you believe?

Mr. Brennan. I believe I reached home quarter to three or something of that, 15 minutes either way, and I saw his picture twice on television before I went down to the police station for the lineup.

Mr. Belin. Now, is there anything else you told the officers at the time of the lineup?

Mr. Brennan. Well, I told them I could not make a positive identification....

Mr. Belin. What is the fact as to whether or not your having seen Oswald on the television would have affected your identification of him one way or the other?

Mr. Brennan. That is something I do not know.

Mr. Belin. About how far were you away from the window at the time you saw him, Mr. Brennan?

Mr. Brennan. Well, at the time, I calculated 110-foot at an angle. But closer surveillance I believe it will run close to 122 to 126 feet at an angle....

Mr. Belin. Well, I hand you Commission Exhibit 477, where you marked a "B" at the point there you first said you saw the Negro men. Is this the one you now say you might have been mistaken?

Mr. Brennan. Yes; I believe I was mistaken....

Mr. Belin. You are pointing to the window to the east of where you have now marked "B"?

Mr. Brennan. That I am not positive of....

Mr. Belin. Are you pointing to the fifth-floor now?

Mr. Brennan. But I don't recall this window at the time of the shooting being that low.

Mr. Belin. Now, by this window you are pointing to the window on the sixth floor?

Mr. Brennan. Right....

Mr. Belin. You saw the motorcade turn?

Mr. Brennan. No; not after I saw the motorcade, I did not observe a man or a rifle in the window.

Mr. Belin. Did you observe the window at all until after you heard that first sound which was a backfire or firecracker, at least you thought it was?

Mr. Brennan. No.... But I glanced up or looked up and I saw this man aim for his last shot. The first shot and the last shot is my only positive recollection of two shots.

Mr. McCloy. Did you see the rifle explode? Did you see the flash of what was either the second or the third shot?

Mr. Brennan. No.

Mr. McCloy. Could you see that he had discharged the rifle?

Mr. Brennan. No. For some reason I did not get an echo at any time. The first shot was positive and clear and the last shot was positive and clear, with no echo on my part.

Mr. McCloy. Did you see the rifle discharge, did you see the recoil or the flash?

Mr. Brennan. No.

Mr. Dulles. But could you see what he was firing at?

Mr. Brennan. I could not see the President or his car at that time. And I still don't know what was obstructing my view, because I was high enough that I should have been able to see it. I could not see it.

Mr. Belin. Mr. Brennan, on one of your interviews with the FBI, they record a statement that you estimated your distance...did you make that statement to the FBI—and this would be on 22 November. To test the best of your recollection?

Mr. Brennan. There was a mistake in the FBI recording there.

Mr. Belin. In that same interview, you stated that you attended a lineup at the Dallas Police Department.... You stated that you could not positively identify Oswald as the person you saw fire the rifle. Now, is this an accurate recording of the statement you made to the FBI on or about November 22?

Mr. Brennan. Yes....

Mr. Belin. You had observed his picture on television prior to the time of identification, and that that tended to cloud any identification.... Now, does this December 17 interview accurately record what you told the FBI with regard to that matter of identification?

Mr. Brennan. I believe it does.... He looked much younger on television than he did from my picture of him in the window....

Mr. Belin. Do you remember the specific color of any shirt that the man with the rifle was wearing?

Mr. Brennan. No, other than light, and a khaki color—maybe in khaki.... I remember them [the trousers] at the time as being similar to the same color of the shirt or a little lighter. And that was another thing that I called their attention to in the lineup.

Mr. Belin. What do you mean by that?

Mr. Brennan. That he was not dressed in the same clothes that I saw the man in the window.

Mr. Belin. You mean with reference to the trousers or the shirt?

Mr. Brennan. Well, not particularly either. In other words, he just didn't have the same clothes on.

It was getting late. Andy rubbed his tired eyes. He closed the book and cut off his computer and turned out the light. He laid there thinking about all this. He couldn't believe all the contradictory statements, facts and confusion.

Another disturbing aspect to this conundrum, was that Walker had clipped articles on the unusual and premature deaths of many witnesses, participants or alleged conspirators, such as: Guy Banister in June of 1964; Lee Bowers in August of 1966; David Ferri in February of 1967; and William Whaley, the cabdriver who drove Oswald to Oakcliff after the shooting, in December of 1965. The list went on for four pages.

The odd thing about all these deaths was that most were killed in automobile accidents, or as the result of suicide.

Andy felt uneasy as to where this was all leading, however, at the same time, it made him more curious. Despite everything he had discovered thus far, again, he kept reminding himself, nothing still proved that O'Connell was there that day, or was involved. He knew that the real truth had to come from Walker, or rather O'Connell himself.

Sixteen

Jimmy Scardino sat fidgeting in his late model Camaro in Brooklyn. He took a drag on his cigarette and flicked the butt out the window onto the street.

Louis Gravino opened the passenger door and slid into the seat. He closed the door and turned to Jimmy. "What's up?"

Louis, or Lou as he's called, was one of Jimmy's cohorts in the local car-stealing ring that Jimmy operated—another side business of the Rossetti family. They'd steal the cars and sell them to Mexican smugglers. Before one knew it, and the police got on the case, one's car was south of the border.

"We're gonna put some pressure on someone."

"Yeah? Who?" Lou followed orders without question. The same age as Jimmy, Lou was just as dumb. Like Jimmy, he too had dropped out of school at 16. Average looking with his hair slicked over his head with gel, he thought the women were attracted to him because of his looks. They were, however, like Jimmy, attracted to the money, and the gangster life. "I love this part of the business."

"The judge who put Tommy away."

Lou was smart enough however to know the seriousness of this activity. "Jimmy, a judge?"

"You fuckin' work for me, Lou. You do what the goddamn I say." Jimmy took out another cigarette and lit it. He nervously blew the smoke out in Lou's direction. "We're going up to Syracuse this week."

Lou sighed and looked out through the windshield. "How do you do that? Ain't the guy a fed?"

"What difference does that make? We go up and put the squeeze on him. Threaten his family. Tell him if he goes to the police, or doesn't cooperate, we whack someone from his family."

Lou sat quietly. He didn't like this at all. Although not related to Jimmy, Lou's family had been taken in under Jimmy's family organization well over forty years ago. In fact, Lou's father and uncles had always worked for Donny Rossetti's family since they had been kids. Tragically, Lou's father and three of his four uncles had all been killed in turf wars. How could Lou say no to Jimmy? He had never said no to anything. If he ever said no, he'd lose his job, perhaps his life.

"Okay, Jimmy."

"Get some ski masks and clothes we can ditch. Make 'em big."

Lou looked over at Jimmy. He had serious reservations about this, but had to do it.

"Go. Go on."

Lou opened the door and set off in search of the items Jimmy had just ordered. Jimmy sat there dragging on his cigarette. He was well aware of the dangers. But Tommy was his older brother. The rage he felt for this judge took over and blinded all sense. How dare this arrogant son-of-a-bitch mess with his family, a family, Jimmy figured, brought in jobs and revenue to this country!

Krup had flown into Tucson and rented a car. He drove out to Winston Franklin's house in nearby Sierra Vista. In not being able to find any substantive files on Seine or O'Connell, he had found files on Franklin that connected him to Seine. Several files under Franklin listed Seine's name.

Krup knocked on the door. He waited and knocked again after more than thirty seconds.

"I'm coming, I'm coming, hold on," said Franklin from within his house.

Several seconds later Franklin opened the door. Krup saw an old decrepit man standing there.

"Yeah?"

"Winston Franklin?"

"Yeah, was is it?"

Krup showed him his identification.

"Oh, come in. Come in. Yes, nice to see you again, Gordon."

"Thank you. It's been what, about ten years since we last talked." Krup walked past Franklin and stood inside. Franklin closed the door.

"Yeah, at the Association dinner. How's the old department?"

"Sorry to say, Winston, they've seriously cut back. Budget cuts."

"Figures." Franklin had been at one time the Chief of the Directorate of Operations—the person who oversaw covert espionage around the world. In the old days his duties included the hiring of assassins to deal with the political opposition to the governments that the United States supported around the world. Franklin was a Deputy Director when Kennedy fired Franklin's boss Allen Dulles and several others following the Bay of Pigs. "What can I do for you?"

"We're looking for Hank Seine."

Franklin felt a wave of heat flash through his face. He had to hide the shock at hearing that name.

"We came across files that had your name linked to his."

"I have to sit," Franklin said avoiding the questioning.

"Do you know where we may find him?"

"I haven't seen him for over thirty years. Longer actually. He disappeared, if I recall." Franklin regained his poise.

"But you knew him?" Krup sat on the couch opposite him.

"We worked together, yeah. What's this all about?"

"His name came up on an inquiry connected with a man by the name of John O'Connell."

Franklin almost died! He thought at any moment he'd fall over. "O'Connell?" Franklin managed to say.

"A hacker broke into our computer archives searching for information related to John O'Connell. O'Connell was a mechanic for the company in the fifties and early sixties. He was reported as missing. You filed a missing person's report with the Bureau."

"O'Connell. O'Connell," said Franklin thinking out loud, pretending not to know. "No, I don't remember that name."

"We found a memo written by you to Seine. In it, you requested the services of O'Connell for an operation in Saigon."

Franklin was sweating profusely. He took out a handkerchief and wiped it from his brow. "Arizona," he chuckled. "Always hot."

"Beautiful country," offered Krup. "I can understand why we went to war to get it."

"Yeah. Yeah," said Franklin trying to shift the conversation.

"So, O'Connell?" Krup asked.

"Ah, I might recall the name. He was a mechanic you say?"

"The best, according to our files."

"Yeah, I guess I remember him. Just seemed to have disappeared. I think I was looking to contract him."

"Why you? His family didn't miss him?"

"My memory fails me. I can't recall the particulars." Franklin shifted uncomfortably in his seat. "I may have met him, there were many in those days, you know. Nothing I can really remember to detail for you."

"You have no idea why O'Connell and Seine's files were destroyed?"

"No."

They were silent for a moment.

"Who's doing the hacking?" Franklin asked.

"Nothing serious. A couple of college kids."

"College kids?" Franklin couldn't believe this after all these years. "How would they get O'Connell's name?"

"Seems his granddaughter is trying to find out what happened to him."

"No kidding." Franklin looked away. "Where's the granddaughter?"

"Her boyfriend's father is a federal judge in New York. They're staying at the Judge's cabin in a place called Beaver River."

Franklin nodded. "I see. A judge's son hacking the CIA files?"

"Well, it was a college friend of his at Harvard."

"Harvard?" Goddamn Kennedy's backyard again, stewed Franklin to himself.

"Unfortunately, the kid was killed when he ran from our agent, right into an oncoming bus."

"Shame." Franklin thought Krup meant it was business as it was in the old days. "The kids have anything on O'Connell's whereabouts?"

"Not that we can determine. They might keep digging though. I'll have an agent run a follow up, but we're treading on sensitive ground here, especially with a federal judge."

"What's his name?"

"Bell. His son is Andy."

"I see."

They were silent, Franklin plotting. Krup had hoped to find out what had happened to this O'Connell and why he had disappeared. Franklin had hoped that it was over, forever. The past did come back to haunt you!

"O'Connell," said Franklin thinking out loud. "Interesting."

"What about Seine?"

"Like I said, I haven't seen him in years."

"You don't know where he lived, or may have gone after the company?"

"No."

"Well…"

"Now that the cold war is over, what're you guys up to these days?"

"It's not like it used to be, Winston. It's more corporate."

"How so?"

"We spy on foreign companies, make sure they're not stealing secrets from ours. A lot of trying to keep tract of nuclear weapons, raw materials, things like that."

"Terrorists?"

"And that."

"And Clinton?"

"You'd be surprised."

"How so?" Franklin asked curiously.

"Well, you know the Republican presidents we had never interfered, and of course Reagan let Casey—an old boy whom you worked with—Casey ran it any way he wanted. The Democrats? Carter left us alone for the most part, and of course Johnson gave you guys free reign. Clinton, unlike Kennedy, knows better than to mess with us. Actually, we made some deals with him when he was Governor during the Contra days, so we've got him where we want him. Its Congress more than anyone who tightens the screws."

"Damn Oversight."

"That's it."

"Bastards never knew what was good for them. They wanted us to do the job that they needed us to do, but when they found out how dirty the business was, they didn't like it, they didn't like or want to know the details. We were on top of the cold war and kept things under control. Of course we made mistakes, but did we contain the Soviets?"

"Revisionists are working on that."

"Respect and appreciation. That's what this is all about. My generation stopped the Nazis, contained Communism, and preserved American democracy."

Krup was taken by Franklin's outburst. He didn't need to be taught a history lesson. His father had fought in World War II and had retired from the military. He was a military brat and had been proselytized by his father on the prevailing military view of that time.

"Would these revisionists rather have the Soviet's run the world, and this country now?" Franklin asked. "They need to go back and look at Khrushchev's speeches. What did he say? 'We'll bury you.' What the hell do these assholes think he was talking about?"

"You don't need to tell me, Mr. Franklin. I understand."

"I'm glad someone does."

Krup figured that he should get out of here and let Franklin enjoy his retirement, his memories, and his senility. "Thank you for your time," said Krup standing to go. "We'll keep in touch."

"If you find out where O'Connell is, I'd be curious," said Franklin.

"I'll see what I can do."

Franklin shuffled over to the door and saw Krup out. He watched as Krup drove off.

Andy and Cheryl had gone to see Walker over the next two days. Each trip they walked him to the porch and had minor discussions. Walker was getting better and could make the trip to the porch almost on his own.

Each time they stayed for a couple hours and went back later in the day. Walker didn't say anything of substance. Andy wanted to go gradually, but at the same time feared that when Walker did fully recover with this medical episode, he would not want them back.

Andy taught Cheryl how to operate the small outboard boat so that she could go over and visit Walker on her own this day. Andy wanted to go visit his father in court, and hopefully get a chance to run a search on his father's computer. In fact, Andy had only been to his father's courtroom two times, and then only once in his chambers.

Andy drove down to Syracuse. He entered the courtroom and saw one bailiff at a desk looking like he was ready to crash. His father sat at the bench, and looked up at Andy as he entered. An attorney for the tobacco company sat at one side of the table in front of the Judge and the attorney for the family of the victim on the other. An associate attorney for the tobacco company cross-examined a witness for the plaintiff.

Andy took a seat in the back and felt like he was in a room that most there wished they weren't. He studied his father who looked down at the papers on the bench in front of him. If one had been spying on the situation here, they might get the impression that the Judge was sleeping by the way the angle of his father's eyes were cast down. Maybe he was, because at times he didn't move for the longest time. Sometimes he would lean back in his high-top chair and close his eyes. Andy listened for several minutes to tedious questioning by the attorney, that to Andy, seemed to go around in circles, or off on a tangent.

Luckily, Andy had brought his laptop, and did open up a file and read more that Walker had highlighted. He sat there while the attorney went on questioning for more than an hour.

Andy wasn't at all comfortable with what he planned to do, but felt he couldn't inform his father yet of his suspicions until he confirmed at least some of them in part.

Judge Bell kept looking at his wristwatch and at 12 O'clock straight up he called for a lunch break. The court was to return at 1:30. Andy walked up to the gate that separated the public area from the court floor. "May I approach, your honor?"

Judge Bell got up and walked down the three steps that led from the bench down to the floor and waved at Andy to follow. "In chambers," said the Judge.

Andy followed his father into his chambers behind the courtroom. Andy closed the door behind him and set his computer down in a chair across from his father's desk.

"What going on?" Judge Bell asked.

"Research. I was wondering if I could look through your law books."

"Of course. What's the thesis on?" Judge Bell took his robe off and hung it in a closet.

"It's about the presidential primary process, but I wanted to see if there were any federal court decisions that have effected the process in any way."

"Sounds interesting. I'm having lunch with another judge, you're welcome to come along."

"I had a late breakfast. If you don't mind, could I stay and look through your books?"

"Sure. I'll inform the bailiff."

"Thanks."

"These books are reference, pertaining to federal appeals cases and their rulings," said the Judge pointing to a group of books against the wall in a bookcase, "and these are cases involving Supreme Court decisions. Now, of course, all these books are not in detail, that you'd have to go to a law library for. For a more in depth analysis, as to the history and so forth."

"Great," said Andy. He noticed the computer on the desk against the wall.

"I'll be back at 1:30."

"Thanks."

The Judge exited through the back door to his chamber and into a hallway. Andy was left standing there like the kid in front of the cookie jar.

He grabbed a few books from the shelves and spread them out on a table near the computer, which was on, and had a screen saver of fish swimming by. Andy touched the mouse and the screen saver disengaged. The emblem of the federal court system showed. At the bottom of the screen there was a blank line that asked for a user ID.

Andy went to his father's desk and opened the top drawer. He was careful not to disturb things in a way that his father would notice. He searched through the drawer and found nothing. He opened another drawer and searched, but found nothing. He sat a moment thinking where the number could be written, since he knew all too well that his father wasn't the best at remembering numbers.

He then looked at a picture on the desk of his mother taken when she was a woman in her late twenties. He stared at it as she beamed back a warm smile. There was another picture next to this one showing the three of them together, about ten years ago. He had to shake loose the grip that the pictures had on him and concentrate on the access code. He had a thought!

He darted over to the computer and typed his mother's birthday in. The computer spit back the message: Access Denied. "Damn." He sat there thinking for the longest time, until he remembered another date. Of course!

He typed in his parents' wedding day. The screen changed and up popped a menu. Andy saw several categories listed including, Justice Department and FBI. He scrolled through the menu until he found the Justice Department's archives. He accessed them and ran a search for John O'Connell. He waited a moment until the computer shot out the message: None matching.

He went back to the main menu and found the sub category: FEDERAL BUREAU OF INVESTIGATION.

He accessed it and scrolled through another menu and found a search command. He typed in the name John O'Connell. He waited.

A moment later the computer showed at least a dozen John O'Connells. Andy scrolled down the list and found the one he was looking for. The computer revealed: John O'Connell, missing persons, 1964. The file number was 64-O'Connell-M64.doc.

Andy typed the file number in on the line at the bottom of the screen. He waited.

A moment later the complete missing persons file popped up. Andy knew he couldn't download it into his father's computer and leave a record, so he ordered a printout. Just as soon as the computer had sent the data to the printer, Andy exited the complete system until the emblem of the federal court system showed again. Two minutes later the screen saver kicked in and fish were swimming across the screen again.

Andy waited next to the printer and grabbed the sheets as they came off. He sat down at the table and read the file that was only three pages long.

The file listed O'Connell's name, Social Security Number and service number. It outlined his service record, stating that O'Connell had served in the Marines during the Korean Conflict. It said that after Korea he had received an honorable discharge. Following his discharge, his employment was listed, from 1953 until 1963, as a gun shop owner in Birmingham, Alabama. The report said he sold his shop in middle 1963 and no further employment was listed.

The next part blew Andy away as the printer finished the third page of the file. The file read: "O'Connell had married Leonora Everett and together they had one child, a girl, Susan." The file went on to explain that "O'Connell and his wife were divorced in 1961. Leonora O'Connell moved away with Susan and no further information follows."

The file continued to report that "O'Connell disappeared in 1963 and someone by the name of Franklin, Winston, former CIA agent and administrator, had filed a missing persons report, first in Birmingham, then with the FBI."

The FBI did follow up by trying to find Leonora O'Connell, in connection with trying to find John, but reported that she had sold her house in Birmingham that she had gained in the divorce. The FBI investigated further and reported that like John, Leonora and her daughter Susan had disappeared: "WHEREABOUTS UNKN..."

Andy sat back and took a deep breath. He agonized over the information he now had. Leonora, Susan, the contents of the chest in Walker's cabin; everything pointed to the fact that Walker was indeed O'Connell. There was no longer any dispute!

Andy wished he could tell Cheryl, but knew he still couldn't, not yet at least. He folded the printout and put it into the pocket of his laptop computer's carrying case.

His father returned at 1:20. They small talked about Andy's thesis until it was time for court. Andy exited the chambers into the court and closed the door. He whispered to the court clerk that his father was ready. Andy walked out into the public area.

Standing just outside the courtroom doors, looking in through the windows like two peeping Toms stood Jimmy Scardino and Lou Gravino. They were dressed in oversized pants and white T-shirts. They saw Andy come from the Judge's Chamber and whisper in the clerk's ear. They watched as Judge Bell exited his chambers and waved good-bye to Andy who waved back as he walked through the gate.

Jimmy realized that Andy closely resembled the Judge. When Andy exited through the front doors and passed right by them, Jimmy nudged Lou. They followed Andy out into the parking lot.

They watched as Andy got into his jeep and drove off. They quickly got into Jimmy's car and followed.

Minutes later, as they were leaving the city limits, Lou asked, "Where's he takin' us?"

"How the fuck should I know? But we follow him." They kept their distance and followed Andy all the way to Lowville.

Andy had thought of the possibility that the CIA wasn't finished with him and could at any time be following him, keeping surveillance. However, he didn't pay attention to the Camaro that followed from a distance.

In Lowville, Andy got some supplies for the Osprey, and using some of the money that Walker had given him, he bought the old man some provisions also.

Jimmy and Lou sat in their car across the street waiting and watching.

They followed Andy down one road, then another. The road turned to a dirt one, and the dust kicked up onto Jimmy's immaculately well kept Camaro.

"Shit!" Jimmy muttered. "Where the fuck are we?"

Lou looked over at him, shrugged his shoulders, then back at the road. They followed Andy all the way into Stillwater and parked in the parking lot. Andy had driven up and parked near the boat. He unloaded the supplies into the boat as Jimmy and Lou walked over to the large wooden map of the entire Stillwater area. Lou watched Andy while Jimmy looked at the map.

"Come on," ordered Jimmy. They walked down towards Andy.

"Hey," Jimmy called out.

Andy looked up from the boat.

"We're campers, never been here before," said Jimmy.

Andy noticed his distinguishable Brooklyn accent.

"And we're wondering where you're going."

"Beaver River. They're many campsites spread all around. You saw the map?"

"Yeah. Beaver River, what's that?"

"A small village, private cabins. There's a lodge there where you can rent a room."

"Really. Rent a room?"

"They have a boat that makes two trips between the lodge and here everyday."

"I see. You live there?"

"Just for this summer. My father has a cabin."

Andy continued to unload his supplies. Jimmy and Lou returned to their car.

"We'll have to come back. We need to plan this out. Let's go."

They got into the car and headed back to Brooklyn.

Andy went back to the Osprey and unloaded. He noticed that the boat at the dock in front of the cabin was not there. Cheryl was probably at Walker's. Andy hoped everything was going well.

He grabbed a bite to eat, and settled down on the porch with his laptop. He read more about the magic bullet theory. He studied how young Warren Commission junior counsel Arlen Specter theorized that one bullet, one of only three shots according to Commission conclusions, had gone into Kennedy's back, exited out his throat, entered Connally, shattered his 5th rib, entered his right wrist and then hit his left thigh. Then the bullet was found on Connally's stretcher at Parkland Hospital in nearly pristine condition, a feat that even the FBI couldn't replicate.

He read how President Johnson took control of the investigation almost immediately and ordered the limousine shipped off, repaired and cleaned, (they even sent Connally's clothes right to the cleaners!) thus destroying vital evidence that could either have supported the Warren Commission's findings, or disputed them. Andy also read how the curb where the bullet or bullet fragments from the shot that had hit James Tague (one of the three shots according to the Commission) had been repaired after the shooting before the Commission had investigated it. Evidence again was either tampered with or destroyed knowingly or unknowingly. Nevertheless, if it wasn't a conspiracy, every agency, including the FBI and Dallas Police, had made serious investigation errors; an unusually shoddy criminal investigation. Andy found a clipping from the House hearings that said that the House Select Committee on Assassinations concluded that almost every agency had been seriously deficient in its activities.

About an hour and a half later, just as his head began to spin and ache with all this inconclusive and conflicting information based on either serious sloppy investigative work, or conspirators, Andy heard the boat returning. Feeling rescued, he walked down to the dock.

Cheryl pulled up and he tied the boat off. She got out while Andy steadied the boat for her. They embraced.

"You're still alive," greeted Andy.

"He's more cooperative."

They walked towards the Osprey. "He's getting around much better. I called Doc Bergholtz and he wants Walker to come in for an exam when he's able. How'd your day go?"

"Good. I found what I needed and came back early. You asked Walker if he'd go see Bergholtz?"

"Yeah. He said absolutely no."

"Perhaps the Doc could come for a house call?"

"He'll have to, although Walker said he'd shoot him if he tries."

Andy laughed and shook it off. They walked into the Osprey. Cheryl set her bag down on the table and turned to Andy. She engulfed him in a long and passionate kiss. It seemed an eternity, or Cheryl dreamt it was. She finally gave Andy some room to breathe.

"Wow," said Andy.

They stood there embracing again, until Cheryl at last lifted Andy's T-shirt off over his head. She began kissing him all about his chest, driving him wild.

He returned the favor, by lifting her shirt off and undoing her brassiere. He kissed her gently on her neck, working his way down to her breasts.

She wanted to explode. Andy led her into the main room. He placed a blanket down onto the floor and threw a couple pillows down. In the severe humidity, sweating with passion, they embraced again and kissed intensely for a couple minutes until they slowly sat down, then laid down on the blanket and pillows. They completely undressed one another and were consumed by the moment. Each felt that they were truly lovemaking, not going through the motions of young lust.

Afterwards, Andy lay there embracing her. He had never had sex like he was having it now. Not with Wendy or even the three other girls that he had had relationships with; never was it like this. Perhaps with them it had been because they were all inhibited by their inexperience. Never had any of them been as uninhibited in the way that Cheryl was.

Seventeen

His full time chauffeur/butler/bodyguard/everything guy, McCabe, drove Hank Seine up to Franklin's door. McCabe was a tall, well built thug who wore dark sunglasses to hide his eyes that usually continually scanned the area.

Seine knocked on the door.

Franklin expected him. He opened the door and let Seine enter while McCabe stood guard outside. McCabe had a shoulder holster carrying a 9mm UZI sub-machine gun, and a belt holster carrying a 9mm Glock.

When Franklin needed to contact Seine, he had to use a special unlisted number that went through McCabe and thereafter relayed to Seine. Franklin didn't know where Seine lived, but knew it had to be somewhere in the western United States because it usually took him only a few hours to get here. Seine usually contacted Franklin and informed him on short notice that he was visiting, mostly for social calls. Only on rare occasions had Franklin contacted Seine.

Franklin and Seine had had their professional and semi-social relationship all those years ago. Now, however, they rarely saw one another. Franklin was active in the senior community in Sierra Vista and had a separate life with new friends he had made in town. Seine, on the other hand, had no new friends but was, like his long lost employee O'Connell, a recluse.

"What's so urgent?" Seine asked walking past Franklin to the chair he always sat in.

"Sit first."

Seine made it to the chair. He looked up at Franklin with an impatient stare.

Franklin sat on the couch opposite him.

"Don't get excited and have a heart attack on me."

"I'm listening, Goddamnit."

"A man by the name of Gordon Krup, from the agency, came and visited. A couple of college kids hacked into their computers and were running searches on O'Connell."

Seine exploded. "I knew it! I told you you son-of-a-bitch!"

"Now calm down, you old bastard. Turns out one of the kids is the boyfriend of O'Connell's granddaughter. She's trying to find out what happened to him."

"His granddaughter? No kidding. What'd they get?"

"Nothing from the company."

"What do they know about him?"

"It appears they know nothing about where O'Connell is or could be."

"It appears? Didn't they interrogate?"

"One of the kids is dead. The one who did the hacking was struck by a bus."

"Before they got answers?"

"Yeah."

"Sloppy. You know in our day we'd have gotten answers before we whacked them."

"I know. But the other kid's father is a federal judge, Bell I believe he said."

"A judge?"

"Apparently he knows nothing about what's going on. The kid hasn't told him."

"The boy's name?"

"Andy, I think."

"Father's?"

"Just Bell is all I got."

"I don't like it. Where are they?"

"At the boy's father's cabin in a place called Beaver River, New York. I checked. It's up in the Adirondacks. What're you thinking?"

"I don't know."

"Everyone we know is dead, or dying."

"I still have contacts."

"Why am I surprised?"

Seine didn't like this at all. O'Connell's granddaughter? Perhaps she'd know things they weren't privy to, or have found things out they hadn't. "What about the company. What're they going to do?"

"Nothing. Although Krup was curious about O'Connell and why he was missing, they're too busy and satisfied with the revelation that it's only a couple kids, one of whom is the granddaughter, so they probably won't go any further."

"Yeah, but it's always been the fuckin' kids. What did Krup come up with about O'Connell in Langley?"

"That his files were omitted. But they found many cross references, including both our names."

"Damn. I thought you shredded everything?"

"Everything I could get my hands on. But, as you know, we didn't have the computers they do now. We did everything the old fashioned way, finger through manila file folders. Many files weren't cross-referenced then.

"Damn it."

"They only know he was an assassin and was contracted on several occasions. That stuff will never be made public. Relax."

"How?"

"I don't like this either, but you're talking about a couple of kids, for Christsake, Hank."

"I think we just need to watch them and find out what they know, and if they found out something."

"I want no part of this anymore."

"What're you saying, Winston?"

"I'm too old for this."

"I'm only two years behind you, you shit!"

"It's over. Everyone is dead. O'Connell is dead himself, or is right behind us."

"He's only in his sixties. He could be rambling on about what he did."

"And you think anyone would take him seriously?"

"Who knows. The point is we never finished the job. It's still unfinished work. I always finished a job."

"Well, everyone I knew in the business is dead. If you have contacts, you take care of it. But I want no part in harming kids."

"Come off it, Winston. What the fuck do you think you did all those years? Children always got killed. Caught in the cross fire."

"Okay, okay. But it's over for me."

"You're fucking delusional. You're afraid of death now and you think God will forgive you?"

"I don't know what I think. All I know is I've had it. I'm through! I'm probably one, two, maybe no more than three years away from ashes to ashes and dust to dust."

"Oh, Jesus, Winston. All right. All right. I'll take care of what needs to be done. You stay here and repent." Seine struggled to get up. He steadied himself and shuffled out the door leaving Franklin sitting there worried about what Seine might do to those kids.

He hobbled to the window and watched Seine as McCabe drove him off.

Franklin walked into his home office. He sat there thinking that he had to warn these kids some way. He pushed aside a box under his desk and lifted a patch of the carpet there to reveal a floor safe. He bent over and rotated the combination dial and opened the door. He reached down into the safe and pulled out several rubber-banded diaries. He took the rubber band off and opened up the latest book.

He had made an entry the other day when Krup had visited. He hadn't made an entry in these books for many years before that. He wrote a brief entry about Seine's visit and what he feared Seine planned to do. When he finished, he closed the book and put the rubber band around the bulk of them. He placed the books back into the safe and locked it. He folded the carpet back into place and shoved the box back over the carpet.

Franklin, like O'Connell, in his later years, was afraid to die. He tried to make peace with himself, and had rediscovered religion; religion he had lost after being drafted and serving in W.W.II. He had been raised a strict Mormon in Utah and his father had been a minister. After Franklin saw the horrors of W.W.II, he thought that either there was no God, never existed, or that he didn't care. Otherwise, how could he have let happen what occurred, despite how the Bible tries to justify God's apparent apathy with what his creatures do?

In fact, Franklin had been assigned to the detail that guarded Eisenhower as he walked through the death camps. Franklin had fought on the front lines, but never had he been abhorred by the revulsion of the thousands of malnourished and diseased bodies being bull dozed into large mass graves like that. Franklin couldn't eat a regular meal for days following his visits with Eisenhower. Many soldiers vomited even when they hadn't anything in them to expel.

Andy and Cheryl went over to Walker's cabin. He was already up and had traipsed around, dragging his oxygen tank along. Andy brought his computer, as part of his plan now to engage Walker, and was sitting on the porch while Cheryl washed Walker's dishes and tidied up in the kitchen.

Walker came from the bathroom and made his way into the kitchen, dragging his feet as he moved.

"I should change your sheets and wash them," said Cheryl.

"Yeah, whatever," said Walker on his slow pace to the porch. He sat next to Andy who had his computer engaged and resting on his lap.

Andy didn't look up. He pretended to be busy by tapping away at the keys. Walker watched him for a few minutes.

"Technology, Huh?" Walker eventually snitted.

"You've never seen one of these?"

"No."

"You can store thousands of pages in here."

"Thousands?" said Walker unimpressed.

"And retrieve anything in a fraction of a second."

"Incredible" said Walker sarcastically.

"It has a built in modem, and I can plug into your telephone and go on-line and retrieve information from anywhere it is available in the world."

Walker shook his head, looked away. "I don't have a telephone," he said matter-of-factly.

"I know."

"What do you have in there?"

"Papers from school, notes."

"Why out here, now?"

"I'm working on my senior thesis for next year. It's due in April."
Walker nodded.

Andy thought that perhaps Walker was thawing out; was more amicable. He looked back into the kitchen and saw Cheryl working. "She really wants to get to know you."

Walker didn't answer. He heard Andy, but still had trouble dealing with the fact that Cheryl was his granddaughter and had found him.

How was he to know Leonora wouldn't throw the envelopes away, much less use the money? He stewed about how much luck played a part in her tracking him down.

"She is your own flesh and blood."

Walker turned to look at him, but still didn't answer the line of questioning; rather he changed it. "What's your thesis about?"

Here it goes! Andy had to engage in more deception once again to satisfy a higher purpose. "I'm writing about Vietnam and how Kennedy's policy was different and going in one direction while Johnson changed it and took it in another."

Walker almost crapped in his pants! His heart rate increased, and his face felt warm. He had to look away to hide it from Andy. "What the hell do you mean?" he demanded.

"I mean, if you look at the policy his administration had, and the direction he was pointing to—"

"Ah...I don't know what you're saying."

"You've heard of the famous National Security Memorandum—everybody knows the number—number 263, dated October 11, 1963?"

Walker wanted to explode, but didn't answer.

"It came out in the late seventies, was declassified, made public?"

Walker continued to look at the lake. "I don't know anything about that."

"It referred to Kennedy's approval for the plan to withdraw 1,000 military personnel by the end of 1963, and be completely out of Vietnam militarily by the end of 1965."

Walker couldn't believe this. His mind went on overload. "Ah." He waved it off.

Andy pressed on with his fictitious thesis paper making it up as he went along. "Well, what would have happened if he had lived and pursued that policy? Would we really have had the war, and how would've things been different? Many have argued that it would have been the same. I don't know. Certainly if you look at the views his brother had, there's no way it would have come to that. If he had lived, he would've most likely been reelected, and Nixon might not have been as strong in '68 as he was. There're so many events that might have come out differently. We might not have had Watergate and Americans wouldn't be so cynical about their government today."

"I don't buy it. You hot shot kids and your idealism. You're changing history."

"You even said earlier how many Americans haven't been exposed to or studied Native Americans and other events, and now are reluctant to know the truth."

"This is different."

"I don't think so. You guys wrote this chapter, with your subjective slant."

"Jesus, you fuckin' kids."

"After all that this country went through with the Cold War, look at how things turned out. We made peace with the Russians after all—something Kennedy tried to do, but wasn't allowed—and Eastern Europe was freed from the grip of communism."

"What the hell does that mean?"

"What?"

"That he wasn't allowed to."

"He was murdered."

Walker shut up and thought he was going to die.

"Everything that Kennedy sought was finally achieved after trillions had been spent. My argument will focus on what would've happened if we didn't have Vietnam, and if the Cold War was ended by Kennedy, say by the late sixties, a full thirty years before it ended. Both Truman and Eisenhower like so many said that Communism would eventually fail, on its own. We wouldn't have spent all that money, and perhaps could have spent the money elsewhere more wisely and have had a better United States, internally, and the world at large for that matter."

"You sound like those idealistic naive kids of that time. Believe me, when you get into, oh, I'd say your middle forties, you'll come to realize what most do. That those thoughts of a better world are just pipe dreams."

"I don't know."

"Well I do. I'm not so sure your paper is worth the effort."

Neither did Andy, for it wasn't real. However, it was beginning to provoke Walker in the way in which Andy had hoped. Now if he could continue, he'd be able to take it in the eventual direction he planned.

"I mean, you have to ask yourself why Kennedy was killed." Andy said.

Walker couldn't believe this! Was he to be haunted by this kid, like a phantasm from his past? "What the hell are you saying now?"

"Look at all the money spent. Who got rich?"

Walker jammed his cane into the floorboard and twirled it.

"Just what Eisenhower said we had to guard against. I mean, my God! Read Eisenhower's farewell speech. Doesn't anyone think it ironic and unusual for a General, who had gone all the way to the top, and been a part of that establishment for so long, to say those things he said? No one understood what the hell he was talking about. No one wanted to believe the significance of what he was saying. Only he knew, from being on the inside, what was going on and what it all meant. I mean, it's unbelievable. He said he was worried about our democracy and the unwarranted influences of the Military Industrial Complex."

"You don't know what you're talking about."

"I don't?"

"You're better off leaving the past alone."

"You said that people were now discovering events that had been swept under the rug."

Walker gave him a cross look. "But that's different."

"You're losing me."

"Well, get with it."

"You see," continued Andy, "we're more than five trillion dollars in debt. The right says due to the social programs, but spending billions on the war and trillions on defense for the Cold War certainly has to be factored into the equation."

"It's crap."

Now Andy gave him a cross look. "Why?"

"Because."

"Why?"

"There is no why."

"What do you mean?"

"Those were different times. You don't understand."

"Please explain."

"You're talking in circles," huffed Walker.

"I'm talking in circles? What the hell are you talking about?"

"I'm talking about this is all nonsense. Its liberal fantasy."

"I don't follow."

"You want to believe this fantasy that the world would have been a better place if Camelot had survived. Camelot was a deception. A myth. Kennedy was a wealthy Harvard boy whose patriarch gangster father pulled the strings. Jack was no different than the rest of us, and in many ways was more."

"How so?"

"He pulled the plug on Diem, then encouraged the coup against him. After the Bay of Pigs he set up all those anti-Castro groups using the CIA. His private life, well, everyone knows all about that now. The man was inconsistent, a paradox. You're better off not wasting your time."

Andy watched him ferment. He wanted to push it. He could see he was getting to him. "So, it's a waste of time to study history?"

"I didn't say that. It's a waste of time to study fantasy."

"I don't want to seem disrespectful, but you're old and bitter."

"Ah…" Walker waved his cane at Andy. "Like I said, You didn't live through it and you don't know what it was like."

"And like I said I can study it."

"You're precocious, but utopian, like many of the young usually are."

"Precocious?"

"Move on with your life. Get over it."

"But you must agree that to know the past is to not repeat it, as they say."

"Yeah, but study the facts, not conjecture."

Walker got up to go.

"And you know the facts?"

Walker gave him an acrimonious glance. "Don't read into it. You're wasting your time. Going around in circles." He stormed off into the kitchen.

Andy called it quits for now. He'd work on him later. He followed Walker into the kitchen. Walker went in to lie down on his bed while Andy stood with Cheryl.

"What's all the heated discussion about?"

"History, truth, justice, and the American way."

"Oh yeah?"

"Yeah. Whatever that means."

They tucked Walker in, closed up and went back to the Osprey to have a quiet dinner alone. Andy saw that a message on the answering machine was blinking. He played it.

"Andy, its, Wendy. I'm flying into Utica tomorrow. Pick me up at two O'clock. See you then. Bye."

Andy erased the message and looked over his shoulder, aware that Cheryl had heard that. He dialed Wendy's number. Her father, the Congressman, answered in a Ted Kennedy accent. "Andy, how are you my boy?"

"Fine, sir, thank you. Is Wendy there?"

"No, she went out with friends. She's really looking forward to seeing you and spending a couple weeks at your cabin."

Shit, Andy said to himself. "I'll be in the rest of the night. Please, whatever time it is, have her call me."

"Okay, sure will."

"Thanks." Andy hung up. He felt he had to explain to Cheryl. "She's my ex-girlfriend. We broke up a few weeks ago. I told her not to come, but she never listens to anyone, including her parents. I'm not in love with her."

"It's okay."

"No it's not okay." Andy got a little too angry, and realized it when he said that tersely, that he was taking it out on Cheryl. "I'm sorry. But that's the way she is. She just imposes without asking. I don't want her to come here and mess things up. It's over."

She felt uncomfortable with his outburst. He moved closer to her. "I really feel something here," he said. "I've never felt this way before. I'll be honest with you. Wendy and I have been seeing each other for three years. Believe me, it's been a rocky road. Before Wendy, well, there were a couple others, but they weren't serious relationships."

"Stop," she said gently. "It's okay. You don't have to explain. I understand. I too feel something that I thought I had before, but now more so. I'm falling in love with you. I want you to come over and visit me in Huntsville and I want to come visit you in Cambridge. I want to see you after all this is over with. I had a boyfriend who went off into the army and screwed around. He never wrote me until one day and said it was over." She sighed. "There. We got both our past lives out in the open and we don't have to talk about them anymore."

They held each other tightly. He took a deep breath and exhaled. She could feel the tension he released. She knew now more than ever, that she did love him. A Yankee at that!

Seine sat in the back seat of the car as McCabe drove. They passed the sign welcoming them to Sierra Vista, Arizona.

Winston Franklin had remembered something about Seine's visit that he wanted to record. In the middle of packing for his trip to Beaver River to find these kids, he took out his diary and wrote down what he had remembered.

Franklin left the combination to his safe in his bank safe deposit box in Tucson. Upon his passing, his son in Los Angeles, when he came to settle Franklin's affairs, would discover the combination and a short note where to find the safe. After Franklin's passing, what did he care when the story broke? For some ironic twist in a former CIA man's endeavor, he wanted the truth to come out. He was, indeed, like O'Connell, afraid that if there really was a God, he had to come clean and make peace.

"Winston, going somewhere?"

Franklin spun around to see Seine standing at the doorway to the room. McCabe stood in front and to the side of him.

"Hank, what the hell's going on?"

"You've lost it, Winston. I knew what you planned to do by reading into your reaction and what you said."

"Don't be foolish. We're too old for that."

"I can't let you take this trip."

"Hank, you're paranoid. These are just a couple of college kids, one looking for her grandfather."

"And when they find him—"

"How the hell're they going to find him, when after all these years we couldn't?"

"Perhaps she has a lead we didn't. I can't take that chance. What's that in your floor?"

Franklin tried to stand in front of his open safe, but Seine could see it.

"Just some bank books."

Seine hobbled over to Franklin's desk. Franklin grabbed the books and wouldn't let Seine see them.

Seine stepped back and nodded at McCabe.

"Hank, what're you doing?"

McCabe pulled out his UZI and shot a burst of rounds at Franklin. Franklin fell to the floor, dropping his books.

Seine grabbed the books from the floor and fingered through them. "I knew it!"

Franklin gasped for air, held his hand up for help.

"You fool, Winston." He took out a .45 handgun and pointed it at Franklin's head. "You understand. I have to preserve the truth. Otherwise, this country would be ripped apart." He discharged a round into Franklin's head killing him. He took the books and walked past McCabe. "Burn it."

Seine waited in the car at the end of the driveway while McCabe set a small incendiary device.

Five minutes later from the end of the street in their car, Seine and McCabe saw the house go up in flames. "Let's go," Seine ordered.

They drove off.

Eighteen

The next morning Andy and Cheryl awoke side by side. He stroked her soft tan hair, and kissed her gently. Wendy never called. Andy got up and dialed her again, but only got the answering machine. He hung up without leaving a message.

Damn it. He'd have to go into Utica and meet with her. He'd explain to her that's it's over and put her back on the plane.

After breakfast Cheryl went over to Walker's cabin while Andy trudged back into Stillwater and drove down to Utica. He waited for her at the gate.

Her plane arrived and the passengers disembarked, however, Wendy wasn't one of them. Andy went to the airline counter and inquired, and found out that there was a message there for him. He took the note that said that Wendy couldn't make it today. She changed her plans and went with a friend to New York City. She said she would try again next week.

Andy crumpled the note and stormed out of the terminal. He couldn't believe it! When he got back to the Osprey he planned to either leave a message with whomever, or on the machine. He would tell her not to come and that it was over, for good. Adding to his misery, he got a speeding ticket on highway 12 on the way back to Stillwater.

Riles entered Krup's office. Krup sat at his desk talking on the phone. Krup waved for him to sit, but Riles didn't, he was too anxious about what he had to say.

A minute later Krup hung up.

"You're not going to believe this," said Riles glancing up from the papers he held.

"What?"

"Winston Franklin's house burned to the ground last night."

"What?" Krup stood as his jaw dropped. Riles handed him the papers.

"Police located his body this morning. Preliminary reports say he had bullet holes all about his torso."

Krup sat down slowly. "Someone knew we talked." He thought a moment. "He lied. He knew where Seine was. He must have told Seine about my visit and Seine killed him." Krup shuffled the papers. "We need to find this Seine and find out what this is all about."

"The Bureau?"

"Yeah, you're right. It's gone too far. I'll call them." Riles left the room while Krup placed a call to the FBI.

The FBI was informed. Special Agent Dan Fullerton found his assignment challenging and intriguing. In his late thirties, and having risen fast in the ranks, he was a workaholic who had little time for anything else, including his wife and two kids. After meeting with Krup, he returned to his office in the J. Edgar Hoover FBI building in DC.

He sat in his office reading the files that had been given to him. This Henry Seine was a mystery man just as much as this John O'Connell.

Fullerton read how Winston Franklin had worked with Seine. Obviously, Franklin had something on him and must have killed him. Fullerton had to put the pieces together and find out what.

He dug through what little information there was of this O'Connell. He read the same report that Andy had gotten from his father's computer.

Krup hadn't told Fullerton the entire story. He left out the part about the death of Patrick Hennelly and Bolt's encounter with Andy. It was, after all, illegal for the CIA to be plodding around harassing and investigating American citizens. Although they had done it in the past, that was the FBI's job.

Krup told Fullerton that O'Connell's granddaughter was in this place called Beaver River, New York and staying with the son of Federal Judge Richard Bell. However, he didn't elaborate on the computer break-ins. Krup told Fullerton that this granddaughter had made an inquiry and was denied information. Krup did tell him of his visit with Franklin after he had discovered the references to O'Connell, Seine and Franklin.

Obviously, Fullerton realized, this granddaughter didn't know where O'Connell was, that's why she had made the inquiry. So, Fullerton wouldn't waste his time going to her yet. He decided to travel to Sierra Vista and see what the local police had come up with.

Krup would give Fullerton a little time. He would send Bolt out, back to Beaver River to follow-up with Bell's kid later.

The next day, Andy and Cheryl got up and went straight over to Walker's cabin. He was already up and had gotten himself breakfast. Each day he reset his bomb and was sitting on the porch when they walked up.

"I have to say, Mr. Walker," said Andy closing the door to the porch after entering, "that you seem to be enjoying this porch."

"I have to give you that much, kid," said Walker moodily.

Andy set his laptop on the floor beside a chair and sat next to Walker while Cheryl went into the kitchen.

"I don't think I'll need the help soon," said Walker looking away.

"Can you really turn her away?"

"You two have something going?" Walker snapped. Andy was embarrassed. "Maybe." He put his right foot up on his left knee and rocked in the chair nervously.

Walker looked over at him. "I've always taken care of myself."

"I don't want to sound like a smart ass, but you're old."

Walker snorted. "Not that old."

"You weren't always this anti-social."

"How would you know?"

"You had to have been involved with her grandmother."

He didn't answer.

"And I would assume that you were married to her."

"Never assume anything."

"Then I should be blunt and ask direct questions?"

"I don't know about that either."

"I hope you don't get cross, but the term contradictory comes to mind."

"Look, what is it you want?"

"I don't know, friendship."

"I'm a hermit, besides all mine are dead.

"I'm not, Cheryl isn't."

"It's too late for new ones."

"Disagree."

Walker shook his head and looked out at the lake. Andy measured Walker's reaction, then picked up his computer. He opened a file and pretended to work on it.

Walker observed for a few minutes.

"Do you think William Colby was murdered?" Andy asked out of the blue.

Walker had read the accounts in the paper about the former CIA director's drowning, and considered it, but didn't dwell on it. "What the hell are you talking about now?"

"Well, he was station chief in Saigon and instrumental in administering the Phoenix Program. He died just before all those former Vietnamese operatives showed up and demanded back pay and compensation after the Pentagon said that they didn't exist, until they were finally forced to admit that it was true after those documents surfaced."

Walker couldn't believe this! He had known Colby and had worked for him before he became chief and before the Phoenix Program and now this kid digs up this part of his past that he has spent years trying to forget? "I don't know anything about it."

"But you worked for the government?"

"Who told you that?" Walker asked agitatedly.

"You. The military, remember?"

Walker groaned and turned his head away. What the hell, he thought, was this kid doing? "That's different. I got out after Korea."

Andy knew he was pushing it. But, he wanted answers. "What was your military specialty?"

"Specialty?"

"Everyone has a different job."

"I was just a grunt."

"Did you kill anyone?"

"What?"

"In a war you shoot to kill the enemy."

"Yeah, I guess. I don't know."

"What was your shooting status?"

"You ask a lot of questions."

"I just find it fascinating, that's all."

"Well, I…"

"Were you a marksman, expert, what?"

"I was, well…I was an expert."

"I figured you had to be."

"What the hell do you mean?"

"With all those weapons, you obviously have an interest, I figured a talent."

Walker let it slide. Yet, he was uncomfortable with where this was going.

Andy fiddled with his computer while Walker ignored him. This went on for several minutes until Cheryl joined them on the porch.

"I think I'll be fine now," said Walker.

"What do you mean?" Cheryl asked.

"On my own."

"On your own?" She went over and stood in front of him. "You think I came all this way and have done all this for you just to walk away now?"

"I didn't ask you to."

"I'm sorry, but I'm not leaving until I get the truth."

"You couldn't take the truth."

"Try me." She stood there with her arms folded.

Walker played with his cane. He finally let loose in the hope that Cheryl would run off like Nora had. "Okay, okay, Goddamnit! She divorced me."

"Why?"

"She discovered what it was that I did."

"And what was it you did?"

He'd had it! That was it! He blurted it right out. "I was a killer."

Cheryl laughed disbelieving. Andy's foot fell off of his knee!

"Right. Give me a break. A killer. What did you do, fool around on her?"

"Never! I never cheated on her."

Andy was astonished that Walker had said this. After having toyed with him, Cheryl got it right out of him.

"Just cut it out," said Cheryl still disbelieving.

Walker glanced over at Andy. Andy caught his glance, but looked away. He wasn't sure if Walker was going to kill them!

"What, were you Mafia or something?" Cheryl asked.

"I was an assassin. I killed people for hire. Why do you think I'm hiding up here like this?"

Cheryl shut up. She looked over at Andy. He nodded his head.

"What are you nodding your head for?"

"I believe him."

"What? Why?

"I think he worked for the government as a contract killer."

"Now you've gone too far," said Walker.

"What're you going to do, shoot us and bury us in the back yard?" Andy closed the top to his computer.

"If you keep up this grand inquisition."

"I think you should come clean. It's good for your soul."

Cheryl backed off, since it now appeared to her that Andy knew more than he had let on.

"I've made my peace," Walker confessed.

"I was only speculating, to engage you in conversation," lied Andy. "Many people in Beaver River have wondered all these years what you were hiding from. Some said drugs others a bank robber. Mr. father thought witness protection program."

"Well, it was a good guess."

"Wait a minute," said Cheryl pacing in front of them. "How many people?"

Walker waved his hand, not wanting to answer.

"Three, ten. More?"

He shrugged his shoulders, looked away.

Cheryl was impatient with his obfuscation. "How many?"

"I don't know."

"What do you mean you don't know?"

"I didn't keep count."

"You didn't keep count?" Cheryl backed up and sat against the railing. She was overwhelmed. "You have to turn yourself in."

Walker laughed. Andy joined in.

"What's so funny about it?" She gave Andy a look that could kill.

"You tell her smart ass," Walker instructed Andy.

Cheryl looked at him. Andy had completely cracked up. "I'm…I'm sorry." He regained his composure to explain. "My guess, is, that he worked for the CIA."

"I don't understand."

"It wasn't illegal at the time that he probably was a contract assassin."

Cheryl begged of her grandfather, "Is that true?"

He nodded and wiped the tears as a result of his laughter.

"I don't believe this." Cheryl got up and paced behind them like an interrogator would in a police interrogation room.

"Now you'll leave me alone."

"My grandfather, a murderer?"

"It wasn't murder. It was business."

"Business? Killing people is a business?"

"What did Johnson call it? In his Texas drawl, oh, `a damn Murder, Inc.'"

"I'm outraged."

"Well, get a grip. That's the way things were."

"This is sick."

"You'll have to grow up now, granddaughter."

"Don't patronize me."

Andy got up to comfort her when he saw that she wanted to cry from the shock. She pushed him away. She was as disgusted with him right now as she was with her grandfather.

"Grandmother wanted a divorce because of this?"

"She found out what I really did as a living and asked me to stop. I told her that I couldn't just stop. I was a part of a system that just doesn't let you stop. If you wanted out, they'd kill you. They'd have to protect their operation at any cost."

"But you did stop. You came here. Why not with her?"

"I kept working after the divorce. I didn't retire here in secret until I had done a job and decided that I had to get out. It was too late with her. She didn't want me after she had time to think about everything, and besides, it was too dangerous to bring her along." He paused, and actually wanted to cry. "I wanted to bring her. I did love her. But, things just didn't work out. I couldn't take the chance and have her get hurt."

"So, Walker isn't your real name."

He shook his head slightly.

Andy sat back down. He actually felt sorry for this pathetic creature.

"Jackson then isn't my grandmother's name either."

"That much I can tell you. No. I did convince her to change it after she understood that it would be too dangerous to keep it. I helped get her set up in Huntsville."

"I can't believe this." She rubbed her face in her hands.

"Andy?" Walker asked.

"What?"

"You have to keep this to yourself. I will kill you if word gets out. I have killed, without conscious, and I will do it again if I have to. I don't care if your father is a federal judge."

Andy swallowed hard. Then, he laughed.

"This ain't no goddamn joke."

"All right, all right. I won't say anything. There's nothing to gain."

"I can't leave now," said Cheryl. "This makes me want to help you all the more."

"After what I told you, you want to stay?"

"I want to understand."

"Understand? What's to understand?"

"I don't know. I'm not afraid of you."

"I almost killed you."

"What's that?" Andy asked.

"That's how he led me to you."

"You're certifiable," Andy said to Walker.

"Pipe down, Goddamnit. How can you stay now? I don't think it's a good idea."

"I'm not going to say anything," said Cheryl. "I want to spend time with you. You might not understand that, but you're still my grandfather. I couldn't abandon you. I don't care what you did. I'm not sure I still believe it. You're not going to shoot me, although him," she pointed at Andy, "I don't know. 'Seems he's not told me everything."

"I'm sorry, Cheryl," said Andy standing to face her. "I only suspected. I didn't want to tell you about my wild suspicions and get you worked up."

She looked away from him.

"I didn't have any confirmation until now."

"I don't know, Andy."

Andy leaned against the railing in front of Walker and stared out at the lake.

The porch fell silent. They heard a loon wail in the distance. A fisherman went by in his boat.

"I have nothing to live for," said Walker looking at the floor. "I have done what many would seem unconscionable. I have killed on orders from those who hired me. I have killed at most, a hundred, maybe more, I don't know anymore. I couldn't be prosecuted for something that at the time was sanctioned by the CIA, our government. Actually, there's no proof. These operations were so highly sensitive that whatever records there were are no more. The CIA routinely shredded those files."

"And what was all this for?" Cheryl asked.

"Tell her Andy."

Andy turned, faced her and sighed. "The Cold War. It was a cat and mouse game the Soviets played with us. The objective was to influence or control events in countries around the world. We'd assassinate the opposition to our puppet governments around the world, they too in kind. It was all about having favorable conditions for our markets. If you had communist states, like say North Korea is a good example, because they were so closed as a society, you couldn't get your goods and services in there to make a deal. And if you look at places like Cuba, American companies and even the Mob lost millions of dollars when Castro nationalized those businesses. So, the objective was to get rid of people like Castro. Actually, we now know, the CIA tried for years to assassinate him, actually using the mob. They admitted that they had contracted with the Mob to kill him. Unsuccessfully as we know."

Cheryl was getting lost, Andy could see that. "Not even for democracy?" Cheryl asked.

"Democracy?" Walked laughed. "It's never been about democracy. Did we set up a democracy in the Philippines? Have we set one up in Guatemala, etc.? We overthrew them in places like Argentina! I see you need a lesson in how the world works, Cheryl."

"So why hide, if it was all legal?"

"Like I just said, those I worked for had to keep you under control. As soon as you wanted to go your own way, they'd have to insure that you won't talk."

"So they'd assassinate the assassin?"

"S.O.P. Standard operating procedure."

"Why do it in the first place?"

"I was in Korea. I was better than an expert rifleman. I could pick off enemy soldiers with one shot. And when the others went running, I'd squeeze off a single shot for each one, sometimes getting a half dozen like ducks in a pond."

Amazing thought Andy. This, he expected, but it still sent a chill down his spine.

"I had quite a reputation. As anyone knows, a reputation is no secret. The CIA was created along with the entire restructuring of the military, and the entire national security apparatus. Truman signed it into law in 1947." Walker chuckled. "Later the son-of-a-bitch made a comment along the lines that he had created a monster, I think in his memoirs or someplace. I went off to Korea and was a part of an elite patrol that strategically knocked off the enemy. After the war, when the CIA began to accelerate it's covert OPS throughout Indochina—which's assassinations and the like—I was contracted. As you can guess, I was paid a lot of money." He sighed and said to himself, what the hell? He was too old now to care. Beside, these were just a couple of kids. What harm could they do him?

"Throughout the fifties I ran a gun shop in Birmingham. It was a CIA front operation. They set it up, and paid for arms to be smuggled through it. Many guns were smuggled through there to destinations all over the world. I would, of course, fly off for weeks or more at a time to do a job. Some jobs included many hits. Nora, of course for her own protection and deniability, was always told different. Oh, she knew I worked for the government, but she wasn't told the details, obviously."

He paused and thought a moment about those times. "Good guess, Andy, the Phoenix Program as administered by William Colby, actually, they had the Saigon Military Mission, oh, as early as the end of World War Two when the post war world was being cut up like a pizza pie! Actually, many jobs were conducted as early as 1945 even before the war had ended, White Cloud teams they were called. Colby, Landsdale, I knew them personally. I probably did a dozen jobs or so for these guys. You see many Americans think that Vietnam started with Kennedy. The line in the sand, to use a recent metaphor, with Vietnam actually started before the end of World War Two. The victors were salivating and dividing up the area and setting the stage for the Vietnam War then.

"I knew what was going on. I actually found out later, that Eisenhower—it's outlined in a National Security Council memorandum, I can't recall the number—wanted to 'Vietnamize' the situation in Vietnam when the French were withdrawing. It's the same approach that Kennedy proposed in 1963—astute that you are, Andy—and Nixon finally did in the early seventies when he ultimately realized that it was over."

Andy couldn't believe that he was being given all this. He sat there stone-faced. Cheryl shocked. She didn't know any of this, nor did it make any sense.

"Anyway, I was contracted by the boys—names I'm not sure you'd recognize—such as, Cabell, Aurell, Lansdale; they all worked closely with Allen Dulles."

Walker chuckled, was silent for a moment. "Arrogant sons of bitches that they were. They thought they knew better than the president did. Actually, they ran the show. The presidents, Truman, Eisenhower, Kennedy, all were misled. They all, for the most part, never were told everything that was going on."

"Those were the times." He sighed. "Yeah, I was a killing machine. I was given an assignment, and performed. I was never in on policy, or anything like that. In the military, the intelligence service, there's that ass saving term—need to know. I was only told what my target was, and given logistical support to carry it out. But, I read everything I could get my hands on. I knew policy, what their objectives were. Granted, I never ever knew what my target was until I was given the assignment, then again, many times wasn't informed until just before I pulled the goddamn trigger."

He stopped talking. He had never told anyone all this before. He couldn't believe he was telling a couple of kids all this ancient history.

"I find this all very interesting, and important," said Andy. "Truthfully, I have no intention of telling anyone. With your permission, I'd like to reserve the right to tell someone after you're dead."

Walker thought about it. Upon his death, his cabin and all that he had up in the loft would be destroyed, so who would believe Andy? "So long as you wait until after my death."

"Deal." Andy offered a gentleman's handshake.

Walker studied his hand for a second, then shook it. Walker glanced at Cheryl.

"I can't go around telling everyone my grandfather's a killer." She had a tear well up in her eye.

"I told you the truth is a bitter pill."

"I never would have imagined all this, although I guess you, Andy, did."

"I only began to put it together a couple days ago," he lied again. "I figured that you," he said to Walker, "must have been involved in something greater than drug dealing or arms smuggling. I thought that perhaps you had killed someone and moved here to hide, but never thought an assassin having killed dozens."

Walker nodded and stroked his cane. "Yep. Hell of a life. All the old boys are dead. David Phillips, Dulles. They're all gone."

Cheryl dragged her chair over next to Walker's. She sat down and lamented. "I don't understand any of this. I've never heard it before."

"Not many have," Walker said. "Partial truth—since absolute truth can never be known—comes out many years after the fact. Do you think the churches taught their parishioners about the Crusades while it was happening or immediately after? No. It's taught now, then again, not in the churches. Like I said, what about the true history of Native Americans? All the broken treaties on behalf of our government? All the murder, death marches and reallocations and slaughters in the name of the United States of America, progress or God. It's beginning to creep into the textbooks only now, to the objections of some angry white males. Look at slavery in this country. It still digs at many people today.

"Do you think some Germans and Poles are taught what happened next door in the camps," continued Walker, "or even in their own towns? There are towns in Germany and Poland where what happened to the Jews there is not taught. The people grow up and never know that those towns had large Jewish populations and that those Jews were slaughtered or turned in by their neighbors and ancestors. Maybe someday that history will be reintroduced there, but probably not, at least in the immediate future. The problem is that for those who lived through certain events, or immediately thereafter, they don't want to know, or can't handle the truth. Many of course can't believe that their own governments and people could have done those things.

"It's all there, the crusades, the Native Americans, American slavery, the Jews in Europe. You only have to research it, and incorporate it. And that doesn't happen until those who had lived through it are gone. You just said, Cheryl, that you couldn't go around telling people that your grandfather is a killer. Why not?"

Cheryl looked away.

Walker nodded his head. "It's not something to be proud of, is it?"

She shook her head slowly.

"Same thing about what I was involved in. Some of it's there, in government documents, such as NSC memoranda, CIA files, Pentagon, but most has been shredded, destroyed. It'll take years for the records that survived to be made public and released for inclusion in history, if it happens at all. That's why they wait until we're all dead. After we've been dead for fifty years or so, what does it matter then? Even after the children, and perhaps the grandchildren are gone so that they too won't be embarrassed or ashamed of what their fathers or grandfathers have done. That's the way it is."

Walker had a coughing spell. He had to take his handkerchief out and cough into it so the spittle wouldn't fly out.

Andy was speechless. Cheryl was chagrined.

"Better than any college class, Huh, Andy?" Walker said after regaining his breath. "Consider me a living history book."

"Now that it's all out in the open," said Andy, "I hope you're not inhibited to continue."

"Within bounds."

Andy suspected what that meant. So far, Walker hadn't revealed the entire story, he knew. He knew he'd have to approach that subject even more delicately.

"But that's all for today. I'm tired." Walker got up and shuffled into the main room where he laid down for a nap.

Andy and Cheryl sat there in tense silence. After a couple minutes, Cheryl demanded, "Take me back to the lodge."

Andy followed her to the boat. They motored back to the lodge's dock in rigid repose.

Cheryl got out and headed for the lodge. Andy sat there in the boat and watched her go. He saw her go straight to her room, so he decided that it was best that he leave her alone. He boated back to the Osprey.

In her room, Cheryl laid down on her bed, facing up at the ceiling. He was right, the past hurt. She lay there thinking about this revelation for the longest time until she fell fast asleep cradling her pillow in her arms.

Nineteen

Jimmy Scardino and Lou Gravino made their way north via the New York State Thruway. They had packed clothes that would disguise them as fisherman so they'd assimilate in Beaver River. Jimmy had a .357 Magnum and Lou had a 9mm.

Jimmy had it all planned. If everything went accordingly, then they should have Tommy coming home within days. Lou sat back in the car listening to rock and roll as Jimmy drove.

At a gas station in Albany, Jimmy flirted with the cashier, an attractive young woman who had no time for him. Lou sat waiting in the car impatiently.

"I'm very rich," Jimmy told the woman.

She looked at him dubiously as she counted out his change.

"Why don't you quit and come with us?"

"Thank you, please don't come again."

"Bitch!" Jimmy shouted as he sauntered off out the door. He gave the woman the creeps. Just another hood that thought he was something for being so.

Lou gave Jimmy a restless glance.

"Whaddaya you looking at?" Jimmy asked.

"Nothing. Nothing."

Jimmy peeled out onto the road.

Hank Seine sat back in his first class seat. McCabe sat next to him. The plane ascended. After a stopover in Chicago, and a plane change in Rochester, they flew into Watertown on a shuttle where they rented a car and drove to Stillwater. This Beaver River, in the Adirondacks, they both learned, was an isolated area. Like Jimmy and Lou, Seine and McCabe had bought disguises. Soon, Beaver River would be full of out of town fishermen, none of whom had ever been there, or fished.

The plan was simple: Harass the kids into telling them what they knew about the whereabouts of O'Connell.

Andy sat quietly eating some scraps for his late lunch when the phone rang. It was Pat's father.

"What?" Andy said in disbelief.

"He was killed by a bus," said Pat's father over the phone somberly. "He ran right out in front of it."

Andy was struck with silence.

"Andy?"

"A bus? Why would he do that?"

"I don't know. A witness said she saw a man chasing him. The police are saying it was an attempted robbery."

Andy sat down. He was stunned. "Did they get a description of the man?"

"The man was described as a street person, with long hair and a beard."

"A street person? Long hair and a beard? I'm sorry, Mr. Hennelly."

"Thanks. The funeral's tomorrow, at noon."

"Where?"

"Our lady of Grace in Boston."

"I'll be there."

Pat's father hung up. Andy sat and overloaded his head. A street person was chasing him? Had he gotten Pat killed over all this? Andy suddenly felt sick and was dizzy. He lay back onto his bed and tried to catch his breath. What had he done? A street person. The CIA? That guy didn't kill him the other night. Perhaps they are waiting until Andy knew more. Pat knew as much as he did. They wouldn't have killed him for hacking into government computers. Andy would have figured it out and gone to the authorities. However, who would believe him?

He lay there until he could stand. Damn! He walked over to the lodge and knocked on Cheryl's door. He waited. There was no answer.

Inside, Cheryl lay in bed. She was awake, but didn't answer the knocking. She was still taking this revelation about her grandfather hard. In a way she wanted to return to Alabama and forget all this. Yet, she wanted to stay and confront her grandfather more. Then again, she had feelings for Andy. At present, however, she didn't want to see him until she sorted through all this.

Andy went back to the Osprey and wrote Cheryl a note explaining that he had to drive into Boston and attend a friend's funeral. He taped the note to Cheryl's door.

Andy headed on in to Stillwater while Cheryl got up and ate a late lunch in the lodge after reading Andy's note. Andy told her to go ahead and use the boat to go to Walker's.

As Andy drove east on the Thruway, he passed Jimmy and Lou going the other way.

Jimmy and Lou were quite the site in Stillwater later that afternoon. They had brand new gear stacked up by the dock waiting for Dusty's shuttle boat. They had purchased a new tent, camping and fishing gear. They looked like amateurs.

McCabe drove up with Seine in their rental. McCabe unloaded their newly purchased fishing and camping gear. Seine shuffled down to the dock, dressed in baggy jeans and wearing a sports cap. He resembled Tommy Lasorda, before Slim Fast. McCabe was dressed looking like a frontiersman. Needless to say, everyone now gathered on the dock was conspicuously out of his element.

Seine looked at Jimmy and Lou as McCabe piled the gear on the dock. Dusty's river-style boat was tied off there, but he was in the local store nearby.

No one said anything to anyone. Jimmy threw Seine a pathetic glance. Seine gave him an icy stare.

A couple minutes later Dusty came from the store. He greeted the miserable assembly and collected fares. Seine inquired about the lodge and Dusty so informed him that there were available rooms.

The gear was stowed on board and McCabe assisted Seine on deck. They sat on one side of the boat while Jimmy and Lou sat on the other. Every one of Dusty's new guests wondered where the hell they were, and were going. Like Cheryl, no one had ever realized that there was such a remote place such as this in New York State.

Fullerton interviewed the Sierra Vista Police investigator of the Franklin murder. He learned that Franklin indeed had been shot to death, with 9mm rounds, twenty of them to the chest and torso. Several rounds were found imbedded in the charred wall of Franklin's bedroom. The arson investigators discovered the floor safe, but it was empty.

It was a local matter. Fullerton got a copy of the police report and gave the Sierra Vista detective some background on Franklin, then returned to DC. He decided that he should interview the judge's son in this place called Beaver River. He called the Beaver River Lodge and spoke with Ronny who explained the area and accommodations. Fullerton didn't identify himself. He told Ronny he was coming on vacation.

Krup was concerned that what he had told Franklin may have been repeated to whoever had killed him, probably Seine. So he dispatched Bolt again to Beaver River to keep an eye on Andy Bell. Krup told Bolt to change his disguise so that the kid wouldn't recognize him.

Bolt did in fact do just that. He would make himself up to look like a fisherman.

Walker wasn't feeling well today. He had had another coughing spell and hadn't even gotten up before Cheryl arrived. She managed to get him up, feed him and shuffle him off out to the porch where he sat coughing.

"Where's Andy?" Walker grunted.

"He had to go to a funeral."

Walker sat stone-faced staring out at the lake. He wondered if perhaps he had gone too far, telling these kids dangerous information. He couldn't believe it, after all these years.

Did it matter anymore? Walker wasn't exactly sure. He wanted to believe that they wouldn't say anything until after he was dead. He realized that he couldn't kill these kids to cover his past anymore. He had repented for his sins and only hoped that God would forgive him. Even some very religious people, Walker imagined, would have difficulty believing that God would forgive him now, so he certainly couldn't kill anymore.

Cheryl was depressed. Walker looked over at her as she sat down on the porch minutes later after cleaning up around the cabin. He had a short coughing spell then took out a cigarette and lit it, taking a profound drag. She watched him in disbelief.

"It's my business," he said.

"I'm just amazed how long you've lived."

"Too long."

"How long have you been smoking?"

"I started when I was in the war."

"Doc Bergholtz said your lungs looked like coal."

Walker shrugged it off.

Cheryl had to talk more about his revelation so that she could at least try and understand, not that she would ever approve. "I saw the crucifix earlier."

He scowled.

"You feel remorse?"

"I wouldn't use that term."

"What term would you use?"

"Atonement."

Now she was detached.

"You're still wondering how I could have done it."

She nodded.

He looked over at her and moaned. "It was a job. I was paid." He dragged on his smoke. "I believed that it was good versus evil. When one is so blinded by the objective, well, then, you do it without conscious. I still believe it was for the right cause."

"Murder?"

"Would you kill a tyrant who enslaves, represses?"

She looked out at the lake.

"We didn't see it any other way than that." He took another drag on his cigarette and held it deep within his polluted lungs, or what was left of them. "It was survival, the preservation of our way of life. Kill or be killed."

She wasn't convinced.

"You didn't live it. People were scared. It was a different time. It was a war. Granted a cold one, but in war, you destroy the enemy. Someone has to do the dirty work. What about the Revolutionary War? Murder? The Civil War? Again, Murder? On behalf of the Continental Congress, we killed the British. On behalf of the Union, Lincoln, we killed Johnny Reb. Should we work to prevent war at all cost? I believe so. But when war comes, you either kill your enemy, or are killed by him. Don't think for one moment that the KGB wasn't engaged in the same tactics."

"It's just different when it's someone who's related to you," she interjected.

"How do you think Stalin's daughter feels? What about Truman's daughter? Some consider both men to be mass murderers."

Cheryl stared at the fresh wood floor that made up the new porch. This was all over her head.

"I can see you have a lot to learn," he said.

"I don't think so."

"Do *you* think it was murder?"

"What's the difference, murder, killing?"

"Its not called murder in war. It's that simple."

"But you're talking about a war, I guess a hot one, not a cold one. I can see it that way, a real war."

"The Cold War was real."

"And how do you define it?"

"Only in the employment of the hardware and how the soldiers are used." His mind drifted.

She scrutinized his every facial expression. "You're Catholic?" She asked.

He nodded.

"I thought you'd have to confess to a priest to be forgiven."

"Not if there's not one around."

"How could you stand it all alone up here for so long?"

"It's nothing more than man alone with his natural environment. Alone with his God, and all the creatures."

"What about other people?"

"'Don't need it."

"Are you afraid to die?"

He shook his head.

"What about being held accountable if there is an afterlife or judgment or something?"

"There's not much I can do about that now. As I understand it, according to most, if not all religions, if one is truly repentant, then they stand a good chance of forgiveness."

She shook her head. They were quiet for several minutes.

"You and Andy have something going?"

"You can tell?"

"It's not hard to."

"Yeah. I guess we do."

"You're from two different worlds."

"In a way. But in a way not." She paused, looked over at him. "Were you from Alabama?"

"Yeah. Born in Birmingham."

"How long did you know Nora?"

He snubbed his cigarette butt out. "Twenty years. We met before I went to Korea."

"And it was only because of what you did she wanted out?"

He nodded and dropped his butt into a can by his chair. "It greatly disturbed her. She wanted me to stop, and like I said, one just doesn't stop."

"So, why did you stop?"

He froze, and went into a trance.

"Why did you stop?"

"I, ah…did a job and knew that they'd kill me to cover it up afterwards."

"I don't understand. You do all those other jobs and they didn't kill you. Why would they kill you for this job?"

He didn't answer, or rather, he wouldn't.

"Why would they kill you for this job?"

"I'm tired. I need to lay down and rest." He got up to go. She had to take him by the arm to steady his shuffle. She soon forgot that he didn't answer her question.

It was quite a convention. Jimmy and Lou checked in followed by Seine and McCabe. Ronny did think it was odd when his son checked in these people that everyone had brand new never before used equipment.

Bolt checked in minutes later. Again, Ronny, sitting at the bar, scratched his head upon seeing another patron with new equipment.

Fullerton checked in yet minutes after Bolt had. Ronny asked Dusty if he thought it was odd that all these most recent guests had new equipment. Dusty said he didn't know.

It was late in the afternoon when the convention walked around and scouted the area. Jimmy and Lou had no idea where to look, so they walked around looking for any signs of Andy.

Bolt walked past the Osprey and determined that Andy wasn't there.

Before he had left DC, Fullerton had been given real estate information for the town of Webb, Herkimer County, so he located Judge Bell's property right after Bolt had passed by. He too saw that the place was locked up and that no one was home.

Unfortunately, Seine and McCabe didn't have the information that Fullerton had. Seine sat in the bar chatting with Ronny while McCabe snooped around.

"No, I've never been here," said Seine sipping bourbon.

"It's our quiet little corner of the world."

"Nice." Seine gave it moment, then said, "An old friend of mine used to have a cabin in these parts."

"No kidding. Who?"

"Judge Bell. Do you know him?"

"Of course. His cabin is the red one about six lots over."

"Really? Is he in?"

"On the weekends, every weekend."

"Good. We'll have to catch up."

"Where do you know the Judge from?"

"I'm ah…retired from the bench myself. 4th circuit down in Pennsylvania." Good lie. Ronny had no idea where what circuit was located. "He had a boy," said Seine.

"Andy. He's around somewhere."

"Good. Good. Very well." Seine downed the last swallow of his bourbon. "Thanks."

Ronny nodded as Seine sauntered out the door. He sat on a bench waiting for McCabe to return.

Later that night it was an unusual gathering. The gaggle, in search of Andy, sat in the dining room dressed in their novice fishermen gear. Cheryl came in, sat down and scanned the crowd that included a young family, a father, mother and three kids, ages 5 to 10, or so she figured. Assortments of other guests were scattered around. An unusual busy night for Dusty and his wife, Marge, who was cooking in the kitchen. Marge was a doting wife who helped out in the kitchen and the lodge.

Seine and McCabe—just back from discovering that no one was at home in the Bell cabin—sat chewing on their dinner. Jimmy, restless and perturbed, had finished while Lou cleaned his plate. Bolt was by himself on one side of the room. Fullerton was still out scouting.

One at a time, when they finished, the crowd disbursed and wandered off down the road, except Seine who was too tired. He retired to his room. He was incensed. This Judge's son, Andy, never showed. He didn't want to be here any longer in this God forsaken place than he had to be.

Everyone else hovered in the vicinity of the Osprey. It almost looked like the keystone cops on a stakeout.

Jimmy and Lou finally went back to their room later that night. Jimmy played with his handgun while Lou watched a silly re-run of *Full House*. His childish laugh agitated Jimmy who at one moment pointed his gun at him and told him to "shut the fuck up."

One by one the other snoops returned to their rooms at the cabin, all disappointed, and agitated.

Twenty

After Pat's funeral the next day Andy drove into Cambridge and went up to Pat's dorm. He met Pat's brother, Randall, there. Randall was two years younger than Pat and still had one year on his current enlistment in the Navy.

Andy meandered around the room. Randall sat on a bed looking through Pat's things.

"Do you mind if I look through his computer?"

"No. Not at all," said Randall. "I don't understand this."

"I know what you mean," said Andy sitting down and firing up the computer, although, he suspected.

"I mean, what's he running from a homeless man for? Most of them won't bother you if you leave them alone."

"It doesn't make any sense." Andy searched through an entry log, but saw nothing significant. He opened and closed several files, but couldn't see anything related to what he had asked Pat for. No O'Connell files or any others. He presumed Pat had panicked and ran and was hit by a bus. It had to be that CIA man. Why had he chased him? Andy was furious and would confront that man if he ever saw him again; Andy could kill him!

He cut off the computer. "I'm sorry, Randall. Pat was a good friend." Andy was torn up inside. *He* had gotten Pat killed. He was certain. He didn't know if he could ever tell Pat's family. Hopefully, someday he could.

She wanted to surprise him. Wendy was an attractive 22 year old with medium length blond hair. She was the type of girl that many young men Andy's age would fight over. She had several bags with her and she hired a porter to transport them to her rental. She tipped the man five dollars and drove off towards Stillwater. She hadn't ever been here before, but from what Andy had told her, and the map she carried, she found her way.

In Stillwater, she boarded Dusty's shuttle boat.

In Beaver River, she told Dusty that she was Andy's girlfriend. Dusty thought how lucky this kid was having more than one beautiful young woman. What's he got going on over there?

Wendy found the Osprey but discovered that it was locked up and no one was there. She went back to the lodge and checked in for the night.

Andy drove all night. He wanted nothing more than to be with Cheryl and help her through this. He had fallen for her and believed he was in love, perhaps true love. He stopped for coffee along the way to aid him as he drove.

They certainly had gotten a lot out of Walker. The obvious pieces of the puzzle were falling into place. He wondered if he should push it. Damn! He had to know if his suspicions were correct. As he drove, listening to a top forty station, he decided to go for it. What would Walker do, but deny it?

It was two O'clock in the morning when he got to Stillwater. The boat was at the dock where he had left it. The moon provided just enough light so he went back to Beaver River and the Osprey to sleep. Oddly enough, his father hadn't left a message to pick him up any earlier this weekend, so it would be the usual Friday afternoon this time.

Everyone rose early the next morning: Jimmy and Lou, Cheryl, Fullerton, Seine and Bolt. They ate their breakfasts at the lodge. Everyone scanned the crowd at one time or another. Each trickled out into the area and began spying about the neighborhood before Andy dragged himself out of bed at nine O'clock and sat on the porch unaware he was being watched from almost every angle.

He saw Cheryl walking towards the Osprey's dock on her way to Walker's.

"Cheryl," he called out.

She heard him and turned to see him standing on the porch in his underwear. Her heart fluttered when she turned and saw him. She traipsed up to the porch. He opened the door to allow her entry. He hugged her, but she was slow to reciprocate.

"I missed you," he said.

"I have to admit, me too."

"Let's talk."

She nodded. He motioned for her to sit on the porch, which she did.

"I suspected something along those lines, about your grandfather."

"I understand. You don't have to explain."

"I felt I should have the facts first."

"You're right. I'm sorry. I was in shock and just couldn't believe this. We had a long talk yesterday. I'm not so sure I buy all his justifying his actions and all, but it was that stupid cold war stuff that I don't understand. He's having more spells and is getting worse. The Doc is coming to check."

"Let me get dressed and we'll go over there." He wiped a tear from her cheek. She walked down to the boat and waited.

Andy watched her go and went back into the Osprey.

"Guess who?"

Andy was in the process of putting one of his legs into his shorts and was standing on one foot when Wendy startled him. He fell over backward and crashed onto his bed.

"What the hell are you doing here?" He jumped up and finished pulling his shorts up to his waist.

She walked right over and threw herself upon him, knocking him back over onto the bed. She tried to kiss him, but he struggled to get up and pushed her away before she could.

"Dammit, Wendy! Didn't you get my message?"

"Andy, I decided to get back together with you."

He buttoned his shorts and looped his belt. "It's over."

"I broke up with you. So I'm the one who can put it back together."

"What're you, Humpty Dumpty? Well, it's too late now. I'm breaking up with you."

"You can't break up with me."

"Oh? Why not?"

"Because."

He grabbed a T-shirt from his drawer and put it on, tucking it in his shorts. "No, I don't like you. As a matter of fact, I never liked you. You were only going with me because it was fashionable and you've always been stuck on yourself. You need a Bill Maher 'Get Over Yourself Award.'"

He sat down on his bed and put his sneakers on.

She stood there fuming. "I come all the way up here for you and this is how you treat me?"

"How I treat you? I drove all the way down to Utica the other day and guess who left a message there that she wouldn't be coming?"

"Well, I changed my mind. What's the big deal?"

"The big deal is that you were supposed to have been the hottest girl on campus. The one all the guys wanted. Well, I have to tell you, you're not that good."

"Andy! How dare you."

"It's the truth. And you know that you have always just gone through the motions. You've never opened up and enjoyed our relationship."

"Whaddaya mean enjoy?"

"Sex. You've never enjoyed it."

"How do you know what I enjoy?"

"Come on, Wendy."

"Wait 'til I tell my father about you."

"Your father? This is between you and me. It has nothing to do with your father. What are you going to have him do? Open a sub-committee and investigate? What is this, national security?"

"I can't believe you're doing this to me. I love you." She tried to move closer, but he got up after tying his sneakers and was leaving.

"No you don't, Wendy. It's never been about love. It's been about popularity." He stopped and turned to her on the porch. "Look. I have someone else."

"That's what this is all about?"

Jimmy perked up when he saw Andy standing on the porch with this girl. He and Lou had been walking by when they heard the arguing that was just a little too loud and had carried beyond the confines of the cabin.

He put out his arm and stopped Lou dead in his tracks. They hid behind a tree. "It's him. Must be his girlfriend." They watched.

"Who is she?"

"None of your damn business. It's over, Wendy. If you would've checked your machine you would've heard me say the same thing. Go home."

"You haven't heard the last of me."

"You've heard the last of me."

She stood there by the cabin as he locked it up and headed down to the dock to join Cheryl. Wendy watched as Andy got into the boat with her and motored off.

Wendy stormed off.

"Follow her," Jimmy said to Lou. "I'll watch to see where he goes."

Lou tailed Wendy back to the lodge. Jimmy watched Andy and Cheryl boat off across the lake. He lost sight of the boat after it had gone a distance. He hurried back to the lodge and joined Lou.

Wendy quickly threw her belongings back into her suitcases and went to check out. Dusty told her that the first excursion wouldn't leave for more than an hour, so she told him to bring her things down to the dock at Grassy Point and that she would go ahead and walk it. She was so steamed that she needed to work out her anger.

Jimmy and Lou started to follow her down the road, but Jimmy stopped. "I have an idea," said Jimmy. "She's gonna go back to the dock. This'll work out just as good. Let's go back and get our things."

They double timed back to the lodge and scooped up their new camping equipment.

Wendy was half way to the landing when Jimmy and Lou, with all their gear in their backpacks headed for the landing.

A few minutes later Wendy was sitting on a log near the landing when Jimmy and Lou marched upon the scene. Jimmy had already instructed Lou what to do, and he got to it going straight down to the boats that were docked there. He surveyed them.

Jimmy went over to Wendy. "Going back?"

She looked up at him, not wanting to engage in conversation.

"You can go over with us."

"I have to wait for my things."

Jimmy grew impatient. "We'll take you over."

"Are you deaf or just plain stupid?"

"Fuck you bitch!" He pulled out his handgun and pointed it at her face. "You're going with us!"

"What are you doing? Are you crazy?"

He reached out and slapped her across the head with his free hand. "Go!"

She recoiled from the blow. "You don't know who you're dealing with."

"No, you don't know who you're messing with." He gave her a nudge. She wouldn't budge! Damn, did that piss him off! He pistol-whipped her. She fell to the ground and blacked out.

Lou had already hot-wired someone's boat. It was simple. He had been hot-wiring cars since he was 12. A boat was actually easier because the wires were easier to locate behind the panel.

Jimmy hoisted Wendy up and held her under her armpits. Her feet scraped along in the dirt as he dragged her down to the dock. Lou helped load her into the boat. She was coming around, moaning slightly.

Lou fired up the boat after Jimmy was on board. The boat motor hit a few stumps as it went through the Grassy Point area. They finally were out onto the reservoir.

Seine sat on the bench outside the lodge while McCabe went snooping around the Osprey. Fullerton and Bolt had already done the same, and from their respective hiding posts near the Osprey, had seen Andy leave with Cheryl.

McCabe walked past Bolt who was sitting on a stump across the roadway. Neither said a word to the other.

Bolt and Fullerton headed back to the lodge while McCabe ducked into the woods to hide.

Bolt passed Seine on the bench when he entered the lodge. Seine looked at him, but said nothing. Bolt thought about the old man, sitting there dressed like a wretched old fisherman with a cane who could barely walk. Not an ideal place for the feeble.

Seine returned to his room to rest. He was seriously too frail for this cloak and dagger stuff anymore.

Fullerton was a couple minutes behind Bolt. He entered the lodge and stood behind Bolt who was in the process of renting a small boat from Dusty. After Bolt had signed for his boat, Fullerton did the same.

McCabe returned to Seine and informed him that there was no activity at the cabin. McCabe hung out around the lodge while Seine rested in his room.

The visit with Walker was uneventful. He was deteriorating. The surgeons had done their best, but the cancer had spread and it was just a matter of time.

Andy and Cheryl boated over to the beaver dam and in a secluded area in the sweltering moonlit night, laid a blanket down on the beach and made love. The only interference they encountered was from a nosy otter that seemed to protest the invasion of his territory. Afterwards, the young couple laid perfectly still and played dead while the otter sniffed Andy's feet. He scurried on his way after realizing that these two humans didn't have anything of substance for him.

"What're you thinking?" Cheryl asked.

"What a life, and how much of a different time your grandfather lived in."

"You don't agree with him?"

"It's too complicated. Agree isn't the right word."

"I don't know what then could be the right word. He assassinated people."

"Yeah, he did that. I don't know, Cheryl. In the real world of spooks, what're the rules?"

She didn't answer.

"Are there any rules? I mean, what goes on behind the walls of the clandestine world? There's no way we'll know. Sure, there've been books written by ex-agents and all, but do they really get into the details? What's funny about this whole mess is that I've read how when you go to other countries, especially third world countries, that they know more about what our CIA's doing or has done than we know. It's interesting how our supposedly mainstream, many would say liberal press, doesn't tell us what goes on. Makes you wonder."

"The problem is that most Americans aren't interested."

"Aren't interested in what their government does on their behalf?"

"It's too complicated. They don't want to deal with it. I was certainly that way. Who has time?"

Andy nodded. "You're right. You're absolutely right."

They laid there for a long while not speaking. Neither one wanted to rush into a relationship, although they felt something more than just casual sex.

Walker had a rough time. He vomited blood and coughed his lungs out. When morning came, he was delirious and couldn't get out of bed. He laid there shivering in a cold sweat. He forgot about resetting the bomb beneath the floorboard like he had been doing each morning. When the alarm went off he accidentally knocked it off its stand. It broke.

Andy and Cheryl tried to get Walker up, but he acted childlike waving his arms and whining. Cheryl got some medication and Andy had to hold him down while Cheryl forced it down Walker's throat. He lay there whimpering like an animal.

"I've got to go call Bergholtz," said Andy.

"I'll stay."

He hurried down to his boat and started across the lake.

Going in the opposite direction, fifty yards from Andy's port bow, was a disguised Bolt. Bolt saw that it was Andy, so he cut his engine and drifted, pretending to get ready to fish. He picked up his fishing pole and cast it into the water. It got caught on a stump and he had to cut the line.

As Andy pulled up to his dock, Fullerton went by in his boat. He recognized the fact that this kid pulled up and docked in front of the Bell cabin, so he turned around and went straight over there.

Andy went in and called Bergholtz. Bergholtz informed Andy that he would be there as soon as he could. He'd have Dusty bring him over to Walker's cabin. Andy hung up the phone.

"Andrew Bell?"

Andy turned to see Fullerton standing at the door. "Oh shit."

"Dan Fullerton, FBI." He offered his credentials.

"Great. I don't have time for this."

"Well, you better make time, Kid. I've got a lot of questions." Fullerton let himself in, an act not at all comforting to Andy.

"Yeah? Well, I've got some questions. FBI you say? My friend was murdered by the CIA."

"What? I don't know what you're talking about."

"Of course you don't. But the CIA has already been here and found me on account of my friend, Pat Hennelly, whom a shadowy CIA guy chased down or so he said. He didn't have to die."

"I'll have to look in to that."

"Yeah, you do that. And when it goes no where, then what?"

"Look, I'm investigating the murder of a former CIA man who was found shot to death in his burned out house in Arizona."

"Whoa. What's that have to do with me?"

"The man was an acquaintance of another former CIA man who has been listed as missing since the early sixties after he was fired for his mishandling in the Bay of Pigs invasion of Cuba."

Andy's face turned ashen. Fullerton read him. Andy was thinking O'Connell, but Fullerton said, "Seine was his name."

"Wait a minute. I don't know any Seine." (Although he did know the name).

"Seine worked with another man on several occasions. This other man has been listed as missing for just as long as Seine."

Andy sat down slowly because he felt light-headed. He took a deep breath as Fullerton stood over him.

"You're involved with his granddaughter."

"O'Connell."

"John O'Connell."

"John O'Connell," said Andy nodding his head. "We've been trying to find out what happened to him. That's all. You know, I was thinking about applying to the FBI after graduation. Now, I'm not so sure I like the way you guys operate."

"You're the son of a federal judge."

"And if I weren't?"

"That came out wrong."

Fullerton stood beside Andy like a bird of prey. "I suspect that this man who said he was from the CIA may be working for Seine."

"Great. What's he want with me?"

"What does your friend, Pat, have to do with all of this?"

"Did." Andy paused. "You really don't know?"

"No."

"I'm supposed to believe that?"

"We don't know everything."

"Yeah, and the CIA doesn't tell you everything either."

"It's a different agency."

"You're on the same team."

"Get to it."

"Pat was a computer hacker who broke into the CIA's computer looking for O'Connell for me."

"For his granddaughter."

"Cheryl."

"Why did you think he would be in the CIA?"

"We tried the Pentagon first, but found omitted files."

"I'm not following. Why Pentagon?"

Andy was quick on the trigger. "We found reference to him being in the military."

"Why the progression to the CIA's files?"

"Because it seemed his files were shady or in question and I knew how many military people in those days did double duty for the intelligence services."

Fullerton thought about Andy's explanation. He wasn't convinced, yet he let it go.

"What does your father know?"

"Nothing."

"You've got to tell him."

"I got Pat killed."

"What else have you found out about O'Connell?"

"Not much. What did he do that someone is after him?" Andy knew the answer, clearly, but toyed with Fullerton.

"I don't know."

"You're lying."

Fullerton nodded his head. His lips curled up slightly when he realized that this kid had it together. "Okay. All right. O'Connell, this man in Arizona, and Seine worked together. Apparently O'Connell has something on them. O'Connell would be in his late sixties. He may not be alive."

He almost isn't, thought Andy.

"I have to go back to Washington. If this Seine makes contact with you, don't engage him. He's dangerous."

"Out here, what do you expect me to do?"

"Just get away and call me at this number." He handed Andy his card.

"Should I arm myself?"

"No. That could be more dangerous."

"This is crazy. This guy is a former spook who must know a trick or two and I'm just not supposed to engage him?"

"Where's your father?"

"In court."

"Tell him the whole story."

"Can you call me if you find O'Connell? For Cheryl's sake." Andy played with him.

"The FBI isn't a private detective agency."

"I thought you work for the American people?"

"A little cocky, aren't we?"

"Don't insult me."

Fullerton threw him a nasty look and split.

"Fuckin' asshole…" Andy stood there pissed at how these guys treated the people who paid their salaries.

Fullerton checked out and had made the shuttle that would pick up Bergholtz. On his way out he stopped in Lowville and informed the State Police who he was and what he was looking for: Seine. He told them Seine was wanted for questioning in the death of Franklin. He went back to DC and continued the investigation from there.

Jimmy and Lou had set up camp near Independence River in a spot not authorized for camping. The camp was, however, secluded behind some trees around a bend, so no one should notice. They had tied Wendy up and placed her in the tent. She never came around from the blow to her head until late morning.

Lou went out and collected firewood while Jimmy guarded Wendy. She came out of her stupor and moaned faintly. Jimmy went into the tent and kneeled down next to her. He took a long look at her, recognizing the fact that she was very attractive.

"My head hurts you asshole," Wendy managed to force out through her lips. "You're in big trouble."

Jimmy remained silent. He had an urge. He was actually turned on by girls who challenged him. His breathing rate increased and he looked over his shoulder to see if Lou was near.

"My father is a congressman. You'll never get away with this."

"Shut up, bitch!"

She struggled with the twine that bound her wrists. Her ankles were bound also.

"You're not going anywhere until I get what I want." He unzipped his shorts and took them off.

"What're you doing, you pig?"

She struggled to resist as he pulled her shorts down to her ankles and tore her panties off. She protested so he stuffed the panties in her mouth.

He slapped her across the face. She squirmed in place as he forced himself on her. She tried to roll over, kicking at him, but he held her.

Lou returned to the campsite and heard her muffled screams. He rushed into the tent. "Jimmy!"

"Get in here and hold her down!"

Lou did as instructed. He pinned her shoulders to the floor of the tent.

Jimmy raped her while Lou held her firmly.

When Jimmy was finished, Wendy laid there in stunned silence. She had no expression on her face whatsoever, yet, a tear welled up in her eye and rolled down her cheek.

She was the most attractive woman Jimmy ever had. He put his shorts back on and left her laying there in his filth. Lou sat there on his legs not knowing what to think. He had never been a part of something like this before. He began to wonder if Jimmy had gone too far.

Twenty One

Andy returned to Walker's cabin carrying the Warren Commission volumes he had borrowed. Cheryl sat beside the bed and saw him carry them in. She said nothing, but watched in curiosity. Walker was fast asleep, out cold from the medication.

Bolt had watched Andy from his boat on the lake through high-powered binoculars. He saw that Andy docked at the island. He waited until Andy was inside the cabin before he went for a closer look.

Andy and Cheryl heard Bolt's boat pass by the front of the island. Andy peered out the front window and saw the fisherman go by. "We need to talk," he sighed.

"About what?"

"Let's go out here." Andy led her to the porch. "There's more than I've told you."

"I'm listening," she whispered.

"Your grandfather's real name is John O'Connell."

"O'Connell?"

"Before he confessed, I had a friend at Harvard, a computer hacker, run a search in some government files."

She looked away at the lake.

"I had learned very little from the files, simply because they were missing or destroyed or something. It all makes sense now. I couldn't tell you all this until I was sure he is who he was."

She shook her head. "How did you know who to look for?"

He motioned for her to follow. She trailed him into the kitchen. He got the key for the chest and led her to it. He opened the chest and allowed her to search the contents. She read the dog tags there and saw the name: John O'Connell.

She sifted through the other contents while Andy glanced back at Walker who was fast asleep. Andy closed and locked the chest after she had finished.

"But did you know what he had done before he told us?"

"I suspected." Andy pointed at the trap door to the loft. "I'll get the key." He got the key and returned. "You go up and look around and I'll keep guard in case he comes out of it. The board on the window comes off to let in light. There's a hammer there. It just peels off."

Cheryl took the key, climbed the ladder, opened the loft and went up to look around.

Andy went over to investigate the cache of weapons that were stacked against the wall. He grabbed an AR-15 and found some corresponding rounds. His father did have a .22 caliber Remington rifle and had taught Andy how to use it years ago however, these guns were out of his league. Nevertheless, it didn't take a brain surgeon to figure out how to load this civilian equivalent of the military M16. He examined a round in a nearby clip. He discharged one and discovered that they were full-metal-jacket rounds. "Jesus."

He put the round back into the clip and jammed the clip into the rifle. He checked to insure that the safety was on. It was.

Cheryl stayed up in the loft for quite some time. He decided to go up and see what was going on. He grabbed the books and climbed the ladder where he discovered Cheryl standing skimming through a file by the window.

"How's it going?"

She just shook her head and kept on reading the file. She found a file that was intriguing to say the least. It had one name she recognized and another she did not.

"I know who Nixon was, but who's this?"

Andy stepped closer to look. "Allen Dulles. He was a director of the CIA—all through the Eisenhower years. Kennedy fired him after the Bay of Pigs disaster. He was appointed to the Warren Commission to investigate the assassination of President Kennedy."

"He was fired?"

"Yeah. Can you believe it? I mean, they didn't exactly get along, many said hated. Disagreed on policy. Kennedy always felt that Dulles set him up and let him down. So, Kennedy forced him to resign—in government that's what they call it, but it's really a firing—then Johnson appoints him to the Commission to determine if Oswald was the lone nut. Can you believe it? Could you be objective after someone fires you? Some say Johnson put him on the Commission as a spy for the agency, at least to protect it."

Cheryl slowly shook her head.

Andy sat down in the office chair. He grabbed Volume 3 and opened to the testimony of Bonnie Ray Williams, a Texas School Book Depository employee who was laying new plywood flooring on the sixth floor that day. He said that the floorboards had holes in them and light shown in from above.

> Mr. Ball. Did you see Oswald on the sixth floor that morning?
>
> Mr. Williams. I am not sure. I think I saw him once…. But he wasn't in the window that they said he shot the President from. He was more on the east side of the elevator….
>
> Mr. Ball. This morning, when you think you saw Oswald on the sixth floor, can you tell us about where he was?

Mr. Williams. Well, as I said before, I am not sure that he was really on the sixth floor....

Mr. Ball. What time did you knock off for the lunch hour?

Mr. Williams. Between 11:30 to 12....

Mr. Ball. Now, did you go downstairs?

Mr. Williams. We [the men working with him] took two elevators....

Mr. Ball. Now, did something happen on the way down—did somebody yell out?

Mr. Williams. Yes; on the way down I heard Oswald...Oswald hollered, "Guys, how about an elevator?...And Charles said, "Come on, boy," just like that. And he said, "Close the gate on the elevator and send the elevator back up."

Mr. Ball. Are you sure it was Oswald you talked to?

Mr. Williams. I am sure it was Oswald. I didn't talk to him.

Mr. Ball. But you heard him?

Mr. Williams. I heard him.

Mr. Ball. You went down to the first floor. What did you do?

Mr. Williams. We went down to the first floor.... I washed up, then I went into the domino room where I kept my lunch, and I got my lunch, came back out and went back up....

Mr. Ball. What did you have in your lunch?

Mr. Williams. I had a chicken sandwich....

Mr. Ball. You say you went back upstairs. Where did you go?

Mr. Williams. I went back up to the sixth floor.

Mr. Ball. Why did you go to the sixth floor?

Mr. Williams. Well, at the time everybody was talking like they was going to watch from the sixth floor....

Mr. Ball. Did anybody go back?

Mr. Williams. Nobody came back up. So I just left.

Mr. Ball. Where did you eat your lunch?

Mr. Williams. I ate my lunch…the third or the fourth set of windows….

Mr. Ball. What floor?

Mr. Williams. Sixth floor.

Mr. Ball. You ate your lunch on the sixth floor?

Mr. Williams. Yes, sir.

Mr. Ball. Were you all alone?

Mr. Williams. Yes, sir.

Mr. Ball. Did you see anyone else up there that day?

Mr. Williams. No, I did not.

Mr. Ball. How long did you stay there?

Mr. Williams. I was there from—5, 10, maybe 12 minutes.

Mr. Ball. Finish your lunch?

Mr. Williams. Yes, sir. No longer than it took me to finish the chicken sandwich.

Mr. Ball. Did you eat the chicken?

Mr. Williams. Yes, I did.

Mr. Ball. Where did you go when you left there?

Mr. Williams. I went down to the fifth floor.

Mr. Ball. How did you get down there?

Mr. Williams. I took an elevator down.

Mr. Ball. You didn't go down the stairs?

Mr. Williams. No, sir….

Mr. Ball. When you got to the fifth floor and left the elevator, at that time were both elevators on the fifth floor?

Mr. Williams. Yes, sir….

Mr. Ball. Approximately what time was it?

Mr. Williams. Approximately 12:20….

Mr. Ball. Were you at what window?…

Mr. Williams. We was on the east side of the window….

Mr. Ball. How did you know the President was shot at this time?

Mr. Williams. We heard the shots, and we assumed somebody had shot him....

Representative Ford. Why didn't you go up to the sixth floor?

Mr. Williams. I really don't know.... James Jarman said, "Maybe we better get the hell out of here."

Representative Ford. Mr. Williams, when did you first know that the President's motorcade would come by the Texas School Book Depository?...

Mr. Williams. Friday morning, we was on the sixth floor, and I think some fellows mentioned it to me....

Representative Ford. You did not know the motorcade was coming by your building until Friday morning?

Mr. Williams. No, sir....

Mr. Dulles. When you were on the sixth floor eating your lunch, did you hear anything that made you feel that there was anybody else on the sixth floor with you?

Mr. Williams. No, sir; I didn't hear anything.

Mr. Dulles. You did not see anything?

Mr. Williams. I did not see anything.

Mr. Dulles. You were all alone as far as you knew at that time on the sixth floor?

Mr. Williams. Yes, sir.

Mr. Dulles. During that period from 12 o'clock to—10 or 15 minutes after?

Mr. Williams. Yes, sir. I felt I was all alone. That is one of the reasons I left—because it was so quiet.

Mr. McCloy. When you saw Oswald that morning, was he carrying any package? Did you see any bundle or package with him?

Mr. Williams. No, sir; I didn't see anything other than the clipboard with the orders on it that he was filling....

Mr. Ball. Did you hear anything upstairs at all?

Mr. Williams. No, sir; I didn't hear anything.

Mr. Ball. Andy footsteps?

Mr. Williams. No, sir....

Mr. Dulles. Did you hear either of the elevators going up or down while you were eating your meal?

Mr. Williams. No, sir; I did not.

Mr. Dulles. You didn't hear the elevators at all?

Mr. William. No, sir.

Mr. Dulles. Were they noisy elevators? The operation of the doors and so forth?

Mr. Williams. Yes, sir....

Mr. Ball. Now, when you were questioned by the FBI...they reported in writing here that you were standing at the west end of the building on the fifth floor, a policeman came up on the elevator and looked all around the fifth floor and left the floor. Did you see anything like that?

Mr. Williams. Well, at the time I was up there I saw a motor-cycle policeman. He came up....

Mr. Ball. What did he do?

Mr. Williams. He just came around, and around to the eleva-tor....

Mr. Ball. You told them on the 23rd of November that you...were standing where they would have seen anyone com-ing down from the sixth floor by way of the stairs. Did you tell them that?

Mr. Williams. No, sir....

Mr. Ball. Did you hear anyone going up or down the stairs?

Mr. Williams. No, I didn't....

Mr. Ball. As you were standing at the window, did you hear any footsteps?

Mr. Williams. No, sir....

Mr. Ball. After you stood at the west window for a while, what did you do?

Mr. Williams. After we stood at the west window for a while, we decided to go down. Then we left.

Mr. Ball. How did you go down?

Mr. Williams. By stairs....

Mr. Ball. There were some people on the fourth floor?

Mr. Dulles. Looking out the window?

Mr. Williams. Yes, sir.

Mr. McCloy. Which stairway did they take, west or east?

Mr. Ball. There was only one stairway, and that is the one in the corner. Did you run downstairs?

Mr. Williams. Yes, sir; we ran....

Mr. Ball. Did you go out of the building shortly after you came downstairs?

Mr. Williams. They wouldn't let anybody out of the building....

Mr. Dulles. Did you see Lee Oswald at any time during this period?

Mr. Williams. No, sir....

Andy found a copy of a FBI report of Carol Arnold, another employee of the Depository. It was dated November 26, 1963. The FBI statement said:

She had left her office on the second floor of the building to go downstairs and stand in front of the building to view the Presidential Motorcade. As she was standing in the front of the building, she stated she caught a fleeting glimpse of Lee Harvey Oswald standing in the hallway between the front door and the double doors leading to the warehouse. Mrs. Arnold said she "left the Texas School Book Depository Building at about 12:25 PM...."

"So how the hell did he get back up there in time?" Andy said out loud.

"What?" Cheryl asked.

Andy shook his head, "Nothing." He read how Dallas Patrolman Marrion Baker, in his FBI report, said that he had run into the building within seconds of the shooting along with building superintendent Roy Truly. Baker said "On the second floor where the lunchroom was located, I saw a man standing in the lunchroom [the words drinking a coke were scratched out but legible]." Baker said he asked if this man was an employee, and Truly said that he was. Both Truly and Baker identified the man later as being Oswald.

So, thought Andy, this Oswald was in at least two places at the same time, or was faster than Speedy Gonzales at getting around that no one saw him move. He rubbed his eyes and opened to the testimony of Mrs. Robert Reid. Oh, realized Andy, I read this already, the lady who saw Oswald with the coke two minutes after the shooting on the second floor. Drinking a coke? Andy couldn't make sense of it. He found another section that Walker had highlighted. It was from Appendix XI of the Warren report. It was from a FBI report taken from Oswald's interrogation with Dallas Police:

> Oswald stated that on November 22, 1963, at the time of the search of the Texas School Book Depository building by Dallas police officers, he was on the second floor of said building, having just purchased a Coca-Cola from the soft drink machine, at which time a police officer came into the room with pistol drawn and asked him if he worked there.

Andy read another FBI report Walker had there. Lillian Mooneyham, clerk of the 95th District Court, told the FBI:

> It was about four and a half to five minutes following the shots fired by the assassin, that she looked up…and observed a

man standing in the sixth floor window behind some cardboard boxes.

Walker had a section highlighted by the House Select Committee on Assassinations that concluded: "There is an apparent rearranging of boxes within two minutes after the last shot was fired...."
Andy was stunned. How could Oswald have been on the second floor drinking a coke immediately after the shooting, yet be on the sixth floor standing by or rearranging the boxes in the sniper's nest? He scratched his head.

He finished reading these passages and wondered why Walker had highlighted them. He put the book back on the shelf and grabbed one he hadn't yet looked at. It was volume 26 and had many Commission exhibits. Walker had a page marked. He flipped to page 467. It was a copy of a letter, several pages long, from Leon D. Hubert and Burt W. Griffin, Staff members, President's Commission on the Assassination, to, Richard Helms, Deputy Director for plans, CIA. It was dated February 24, 1964. Walker had selective highlighted areas. Andy Read:

Jack Ruby returned to Chicago.... He also continued to engage in ticket scalping. [He] had been employee[d] at various Chicago night clubs.... Ruby returned to Dallas.... He eventually purchased the Vegas Club and operated it with Eva after early 1959. In 1960, he purchased the Sovereign Club, changed the name to the Carousel Club, and continued to operate it and the Vegas Club until his arrest on November 24, 1963.

He is known to have brutally beaten at least 25 different persons.... While living in Dallas, Ruby had very carefully cultivated friendships with police officers and other public officials. At the same time, he was, peripherally, if not directly connected with members of the underworld.... Ruby also is rumored to have been the tip-off between the Dallas Police and the Dallas underworld, especially in regard of the local liquor laws. Ruby is said to have been given advance notice of prospective police raids on his own club and other clubs.

His associations with stripteasers and cheap entertainers brought him into contact with people of questionable reputations. Ruby operated his businesses on a cash basis, keeping no record whatsoever—a strong indication that Ruby himself was involved in illicit operations of some sort.

When it suited his own purposes, he did not hesitate to call on underworld characters for assistance.

At the time of his arrest, Ruby was found in possession of various radio scripts issued by H.L. Hunt, a prominent American right wing extremist.

In about 1959, Ruby became interested in the possibility of selling war materials to Cubans and in the possibility of opening a gambling casino in Havana.... Ruby is also rumored to have met in Dallas with an American Army Colonel and some Cubans concerning the sale of arms. A Government informant in Chicago connected with the sale of arms to anti-Castro Cubans has reported that such Cubans were behind the Kennedy assassination....

His primary technique in avoiding prosecution was the maintenance of friendship with the police officers, public officials, and other influential persons in the Dallas community.

It is possible that Ruby could have been utilized by a politically motivated group upon the promise of money or because of the influential character of the individual approaching Ruby.

Andy skipped down to part B.

B. *The Following groups and places seem significant in looking for ties between Ruby and others who might have been interested in the assassination of President Kennedy.*
Ruby had a contact with Barney Baker, reputed to be close to Hoffa.

Andy seemed to recall that it was the Kennedy brothers who brought down Hoffa, who subsequently was sent to prison, then finally pardoned by Nixon. Hoffa had been a generous contributor to Nixon's several campaigns.
Andy continued reading:

Ruby also frequented the Cabana Motel in Dallas, alleged to have been built with Teamster money.
[Of] the Las Vegas gambling community, Ruby was particularly close to Lowie J. McWillie.... Ruby visited him in Havana.
Musician [Billy Joe Willie] employed by Ruby at Carousel Club, lives in Irving, Texas, across the street from Mrs. Ruth Paine (friend at whose home Marina Oswald resided).

Wait a minute! Andy said to himself. Paine was the lady who got Oswald the job at the Book Depository. More unusual coincidences!
From Walker's clues, he read from the Commission's report:

The evidence indicates that he [Ruby] accepted an invitation from gambler Lewis J. McWillie, who subsequently became a violent anti-Castroite, to visit Havana at McWillie's expense.

He saw a note Walker had scribbled there that said "See page 466." It was copies of two letters. One was from J. Lee Rankin, General Counsel, to Richard Helms. It was dated May 19, 1964 and read:

At a meeting on March 12, 1964, a memorandum prepared by members of the Commission staff was handed to you which related to the background of Jack L. Ruby.... At that time we requested that you review this memorandum and submit to the Commission any information contained in your files regarding the matters covered in the memorandum, as well as any analyses by your representatives which you believed might be useful to the Commission.

As you know, this Commission is nearing the end of its investigation. We would appreciate hearing from you as soon as possible....

Andy read the other letter from Thomas H. Karamessines, Acting Deputy Director for Plans, CIA. It read:

...An examination of Central Intelligence Agency files has produced no information on Jack RUBY or his activities.

...Our records do not reflect any information pertaining to these persons [Ruby and his acquaintances].

The letter was dated 15 September 1964, nine days before the Commission submitted its report to President Johnson, who upon receiving the report, only said, "It's heavy."

Andy was dumbfounded, to say the least.

He placed the book back onto the shelf and picked up volume 11. Walker had a scrap piece of paper marking a spot. It was the testimony of Sylvia Odio. There weren't any highlighted sections, so Andy skimmed it.

Odio said Lee Harvey Oswald had come to her home in September of 1963 in Dallas. He was with two men and that they were either Cuban or Mexican. She was told that Oswald could help in the underground in its war opposing Castro.

A pencil notation made by Walker said, "See 26, p. 595-597." Andy found that section. It was a letter written by General Counsel Rankin to J. Edgar Hoover, dated August 28, 1964. It read:

> Please conduct whatever additional investigation you deem appropriate to determine the possible validity of Mrs. Odio's testimony. We think it might be in order to determine Mrs. Odio's veracity in other areas by checking on some of the testimony she gave concerning her background. We note that she claims to be acquainted with Manaolo Rey, an anti-Castro leader in Puerto Rico, and that her father is a political prisoner of Fidel Castro.

Another scribble there by Walker said, "See p. 838." Andy flipped over to 838. It was a reply from the FBI dated September 8, 1964. It read:

> Mr. Ray stated he continues in his position as leader of JURE [Junta Revolucionaria Cubana]. He said he is personally acquainted with Sylvia Odio of Dallas, Texas, by virtue of the fact that her parents had visited him and other members of the anti-Castro organization, Movimiento Revolucionario Del Pueblo (MRP) in Cuba.... He said that eventually both parents of Sylvia Odio were arrested and imprisoned by the Castro regime for the help given to the MRP...Mr. Ray stated that he regards Sylvia Odio to be intelligent, and a person of good character.

The FBI also said:

> Rogelio Cisneros, a leader of JURE, said he "Was aware that both her mother and father are imprisoned" in Cuba.

Another note scribble there said: "See p. 363." It was Odio's sister's account to the FBI. It said that she had answered the door for the three men and that the man who came to Sylvia's residence with the two Latin Americans was Oswald.

Andy went back to Odio's testimony. He scanned the testimony and learned that Odio said that one man that had visited her said, "You are working in the underground." They had said that they "were good friends of your father."

Another scribbled note there said, "WRC, p. vii." Andy found it and a section was highlighted. It was from the Commission's final report. It read:

> While the FBI had not yet completed its investigation into this matter at the time the report went to press, the Commission has concluded that Lee Harvey Oswald was not at Mrs. Odio's apartment in September of 1963.

Andy wondered why when each time a credible witness pointed the situation in the possible area of a conspiracy, that the Commission chose to conclude the opposite, when even the FBI had concluded the validity of most of those witnesses.

Andy sifted through a pile he hadn't paid too much attention to before. He found a file near the bottom that grabbed his attention. It was labeled: CIA-sponsored operational bases. Andy learned how, following Kennedy's secret deal with Khrushchev not to invade Cuba, Kennedy closed down the very anti-Castro CIA operations that he had set up. And, when many recalcitrant anti-Castro groups and CIA agents continued to secretly operate despite orders to desist, Kennedy had them arrested and closed down.

Two names Andy discovered were linked to groups that continued to operate: David Sanchez Morales and Antonio Veciana. Another name

Andy thought he had seen before was linked to these two men: Maurice Bishop.

He learned how Morales had been a `mechanic' for the Agency and had been contracted all over the world, from Vietnam to Laos to Latin America. The file detailed Morales' adventures in those countries including several assassinations he had been involved in.

Andy found another file on the bottom of the pile that was labeled: Phillips.

The file consisted primarily of photocopies from the House Select Committee on Assassinations. It involved Phillips' testimony, staff reports and Committee conclusions.

Andy learned how Phillips was all over the Western Hemisphere, could speak Spanish fluently, and was closely associated with several assassination attempts at Castro. Phillips was also instrumental in the CIA sponsored campaign to overthrow Argentinean President Allende. Andy also learned that Phillips was a `Master' dis-information officer.

Andy learned how the Committee believed that Phillips had committed perjury. However, the Committee let it ride because they were out of money, and had to close down their investigation and didn't have the resources to dig deeper into the archives of the CIA. Actually, Andy realized, the Committee didn't want to "open doors" when they should be "closing doors."

Andy found two intriguing points: One, that Phillips was the CIA agent in charge of the Mexico City operation who was responsible for showing the Warren Commission that "Oswald" had visited the Cuban and Russian diplomatic entities there. It was Phillips who after the Kennedy assassination had sent the FBI the photograph of a man the CIA said was Oswald, but in fact, as the CIA later admitted, was not Oswald.

Under oath to the House Committee, Phillips was asked what proof the agency had that Oswald was indeed in Mexico City that short time before the assassination, as the Warren Commission concluded. Phillips said that their cameras and recording devices weren't working that day, but their informants said it was Oswald.

Walker had a newspaper clipping there from the *Dallas Morning News* that quoted Cuban operatives at the Cuban consulate who said the CIA's camera and recorders "were always working."

Andy's mind whirled. Wait a minute, he thought. Oswald, according to the Warren Commission, had been in Mexico City just two months before the assassination trying to get visas to go to Cuba and the Soviet Union. However, there's no photographic evidence to support this fact, and, as Andy recalled, even J. Edgar Hoover had written a memo to the State department just a couple years before this episode that someone was using Oswald's identify.

Andy scanned more of Walker's highlighted sections and discovered that several witnesses in Mexico City said that the man arrested in Dallas identified as Oswald, was not the Oswald they saw in Mexico City. Hence the photograph the CIA had of a man they said was Oswald at the Cuban and Russian missions who was not Oswald. That makes sense, yet, Andy was well aware of, the Warren Commission took the CIA on faith that Oswald was in Mexico City and had gone to the Russian and Cuban diplomatic missions.

In the middle of the file Andy saw the photograph of the Oswald in question, as displayed before the Warren Commission. He could plainly see that the man in the photograph was not Oswald. Walker had scribbled a note there that said, "Man never identified."

Andy shook his head.

At the back of the file Andy found a sketch that was given to the House Committee by Antonio Veciana of the man who he said was Maurice Bishop. Veciana, the virulent anti-Castro Alpha 66 founder, had worked for many years with Bishop who was introduced and identified to Veciana as a deep-cover agent of the CIA who coordinated the CIA's anti-Castro operations. Behind this sketch was a House Committee photograph of David Atlee Phillips. Andy instantly realized that he was looking at the same person. Walker had scribbled a note there: Bishop=Phillips. The `Master' slips-up!

On the next text page, Andy almost fell over when he read it. Veciana, when in downtown Dallas at the Southland Center building to meet with Bishop concerning the Alpha 66 operation in September, had waited until Bishop had concluded his conversation with a young man. The young man departed and Veciana and Bishop then discussed their operation. The day Kennedy was killed, Veciana recognized the young man that Bishop had had a conversation that day with was Lee Harvey Oswald.

A newspaper clipping from the *Miami Herald* told a story that Veciana was shot at, but survived after he had spoken to House Committee investigators.

Another clipping from the *Herald* had a story about the murder of mobster John Rosselli. Rosselli had disappeared in July 1976. Senate sub-committee chairman Senator Schweiker in secret had questioned him on April 23, 1976. The article explained how Rosselli was "the link" between the CIA and the mob assassination plots against Castro. Rosselli's body was found in a 55-gallon drum floating in Biscayne Bay. He had been "shot, cut open from his chest to his navel, and his legs had been cut off."

Andy sighed, closed the file and dropped it on top of the pile. He didn't care about rearranging things in the order he had found them. It all didn't matter anymore. Nothing mattered.

"I don't understand all this," said Cheryl. "Let's go back down."

Andy nodded and followed her down the ladder. He locked the trap door after exiting.

"That certainly confirms what he's been saying," she grumbled. "All those guys looking at you like they're ghosts."

"That's exactly how I felt."

She saw that Walker was still sleeping. "This is too much for me to handle. I still can't believe it."

"I have to pick up my dad. Bergholtz should be here soon. You want to stay here, or go back?"

"I'll wait."

"You going to be okay?"

"Yeah. Go ahead."

"I'll see you when I get back." He kissed her and ran out the door.

Jimmy had already left the message at the stoop of the Osprey. He had returned to the campsite when Andy found the plastic bag that contained Wendy's panties, her driver's license and a short note that said:

> We have your girlfriend. Tell your father the Judge to reverse
> his decision about Tommy Scardino, or else she will die! If you
> call the police, she will die. We are watching.

Andy's jaw dropped open. "We have your girlfriend?" Andy said out loud to himself. "Who are we? Scardino?" Andy didn't know what to do. He did know that his father was on his way to Stillwater, so he headed off frantically in that direction.

McCabe spotted him! He lost him however when Andy drove off towards the landing. McCabe hurried back to inform Seine.

"He came in off that boat and left for the landing," said McCabe.

"He's around then," said Seine. "We need to get a boat, have it ready so we can find out where he goes."

McCabe darted out of the room. Seine sat there hoping that this kid, and his girlfriend, had something on O'Connell.

Bolt had also watched Andy leave Walker's island. He docked and walked up to the door. "Hello?"

Cheryl came to the door. "Yes?"

"I was wondering who lived here." He edged up the steps.

"Who're you?"

"Ken Small."

"I'm sorry. I don't know you."

"I come up here and fish. I saw the island and wondered whose it was."

"It belongs to my grandfather. He's ill."

"I think I met him. May I see him?"

"I don't think it's a good idea, Mr. Small."

He pushed his way past her. She didn't like this at all. He saw Walker out cold on his bed. He looked around and saw all the weapons against the wall and now knew that he had found John O'Connell.

"I think you should leave."

"I just wanted to see him. Thanks." Bolt departed leaving Cheryl wondering what that was all about.

Bolt returned to the lodge and placed a call to Krup.

"Okay," said Krup over the phone. "Stay close, but out of sight near the island. I should be there later tonight. Pick me up in Stillwater at nine."

Bolt hung up and grabbed a snack from the bar. He got back in his boat, and pretended to fish near the island.

Andy met Bergholtz at the dock in Stillwater. "She's with him now. I'll be over later."

Bergholtz took off on Dusty's boat a few minutes later. Andy paced back and forth in front of the Black Bear until his father pulled up twenty minutes after Bergholtz had left.

Andy ran over to his father's car when he pulled into the parking lot. "Wendy came for a surprise visit yesterday. I told her to go home and I found this a couple hours ago."

The Judge read the note and looked at her identification. He threw Andy a shocked glance then walked into the Hotel. Andy followed.

The Judge placed a call. "Bob? Its, Richard Bell. Listen, my son's girl-friend has been kidnapped. I'm in Stillwater at the Hotel. She's Congressman Kern's daughter."

"Kern? Wonderful," said a gruffy man's voice over the phone.

"It's related to a case where I sent a drug dealer up for life. The note says they'll kill her if we go to the police. You better notify the congressman."

"Okay. Wait there and I'll assemble a team."

"Listen, You'd better do this undercover."

"We'll pose as fishermen. We'll see you in few hours."

Judge Bell hung up and turned to Andy. "Bob Williams, FBI."

Oh no, thought Andy. "I left Cheryl at Walker's. I'm concerned about her too."

"Take the boat and go. I'll get Top to take us over when they get here."

Andy hustled back to Beaver River. When he drove up to the Osprey, McCabe was watching. He saw Andy get into his boat, so McCabe ran to get into the one he had just rented. He followed from a distance and saw that Andy docked at this island near South Branch. There were two other boats already docked there. He watched Andy run up to the cabin. Obviously, realized McCabe, there was something going on there. He waited from a considerable distance and watched through high-pow-ered binoculars.

Amazed at the cache of weapons, Dusty stood examining them as Bergholtz explained how Cheryl should administer Walker's medica-tion. Andy rushed in out of breath.

"What's wrong?" Dusty asked.

Andy tried to catch his breath. "Wendy, my ex-girlfriend came to visit yesterday. I told her that I didn't want to see her and that she should go home. She was kidnapped on her way out. It has something to do with a case my father presided over."

"That's the girl who never showed at the landing yesterday," said Dusty.

"Yeah. What happened?"

"She told me to take her bags down and meet her at the landing, and wasn't there when I got there. I had no idea. Wait a minute. The Miller's boat was stolen from the landing."

"Then whoever kidnapped her stole the boat. They're still in the area."

"Have you called the police?"

"They said they'd kill her if we did. My father's in Stillwater waiting for some undercover FBI men, I guess from Syracuse. So, we have to keep this to ourselves."

"Well," said Bergholtz breaking the tension, "I gave Cheryl the instructions. He's dying, slowly, but is too sick to transport. He needs plenty of rest. Someone should stay with him."

"I'm the obvious choice," said Cheryl.

"I'm staying too," said Andy. "Dusty, can you inform my father what's going on here and keep me updated on what's happening with Wendy?"

"Sure. I'll come back with news just as soon as I get some."

Bergholtz closed his bag and signaled to Dusty, "Let's go."

Andy walked them down to the dock. McCabe and Bolt, from their respective boats on the lake at opposite sides of the island, watched the activity.

Andy saw Dusty and the Doc off and returned to Cheryl. Walker began to stir after the medication that Bergholtz had given him started to take effect. "I don't think we should tell him any of this," said Andy. Cheryl nodded.

"I'm thirsty," said Walker. Cheryl fetched some water.

He tried to sit up, but didn't have the strength. Andy helped him up so he could sit on the edge of his bed.

"What happened?"

"You have some kind of jaundice that made you delirious," said Cheryl returning with the water. "Bergholtz came by and gave you some medication to lessen the effects."

"Great," said Walker sipping the water. "Son-of-a-bitch sets foot in here again trying to save my life and all and I'll take him with me." He coughed. "I need a goddamn cigarette."

Andy looked at Cheryl. She shrugged her shoulders. Andy grabbed Walker's pack and lighter from the stand. Walker lit up and seemed to feel better after a few puffs.

Andy strolled out onto the porch. Cheryl followed. They were silent as they saw a boat going across the lake towards the lodge. From their angle, they couldn't see Bolt.

"A man popped in here a few hours ago."

He spun around. "What man?"

"Said he was a fisherman who had met Walker before. He just pushed his way into the cabin and looked at him sleeping there."

"Damn." Andy huffed. "What did he look like?"

"Middle age, short hair with a fisherman's jacket. He wore baggy pants."

"His face?"

"White. Thin. He did have a stocky neck."

"Like he works out, with weights?"

"Yeah. Who is he?"

"Shit."

"Andy?"

"I think he's CIA."

"What!? What else haven't you told me?"

"He came to visit me last week. There's more."

"Damn it, Andy!"

"This CIA man chased after my friend, Pat, at Harvard who did the computer hacking and got him run over by a bus. That's the funeral I went to."

"Oh my God!" She collapsed into the chair.

"We may have to protect ourselves."

"But he didn't kill you."

"Not yet."

"You trust them?"

"The CIA? 'You kidding?"

"How're we going to protect ourselves?"

Andy motioned with head towards the main room of Walker's cabin.

"I don't know the first thing about all that stuff."

"What's to know? You just put in a clip, pull the cocking handle and pull the trigger."

"Oh, fine. So we're supposed to become like him?"

"If someone comes at you, you defend yourself."

She ran her fingers through her hair nervously. "I can't believe this."

He leaned over and put his hands on her shoulder.

"I'm sorry," he said.

"For what? This is the old man."

"But because of my curiosity, I tipped off these guys."

"Forget it. I don't want you to think about that."

They checked on Walker and found him hunched over on the edge of his bed finishing his smoke. "You look miserable," said Andy.

"I feel miserable. How am I supposed to look if I'm dying?"

"You can live a little longer if you try."

"Come on, what's the point?"

"How about for me?" Cheryl said.

He grunted and snubbed out his cigarette.

McCabe had a trying time with Seine. Seine almost fell over when he tipped the boat too far to one side. McCabe had to go slower because Seine weighted the boat down and the water level was almost up to the gunwale.

The sun was beginning to set and a stiff breeze kicked up.

Twenty Two

Bolt had no other way to get to Stillwater to pick Krup up, so he had to drag his rental over the culvert that separated Beaver River Lake from Stillwater Reservoir. It was a long journey back to Stillwater in a small outboard. Bolt had a strong flashlight to use upon his return trip with Krup.

FBI agent Bob Williams set up a command post at the Hotel in Stillwater. Williams was a clean-cut no nonsense career agent looking for that break. He had just found it; Congressman Kern's daughter! His advancement was being handed to him. He used a room upstairs and left two agents there. In the helicopter ride from Syracuse, he had called the Congressman who demanded the FBI fly him in also. Needless to say, Wendy's father blew his stack.

Williams, two more agents and Judge Bell, went to Beaver River and set up a sub-station at the lodge. The Park Ranger, Hank Fisher, grabbed Top and together they began searching the reservoir.

Having found no new evidence or notes back in Beaver River, Williams decided to get a search underway there. Dusty gave two agents a boat to search Norridgewock Lake while Williams and the Judge searched the reservoir in the Judge's boat.

Jimmy and Lou were already running out of supplies, most notably food. They certainly weren't campers, or had been boy scouts, and hadn't properly prepared. Someone would have to make a run into Stillwater. Jimmy decided to send Lou. Lou would have to break into the small store there.

Jimmy tried to force feed Wendy because even though they untied her hands, she was frozen in some sort of trauma. She laid on the floor of the tent in the fetal position and wouldn't feed herself. She only stared at the side of the tent. Jimmy tried, but it was futile. She wouldn't eat. Her mouth remained closed and she didn't move.

"The hell with you then, bitch," said Jimmy. He threw the bag of potato chips on the ground. He met Lou outside the tent getting ready to leave for Stillwater. "She won't eat."

"She actually said she's a congressman's daughter?"

"Yeah, so. What about it?"

Lou shut up.

"So, we bury her here in the woods and no one ever finds her."

"Maybe you shouldn't've raped her."

"I'll do whatever the fuck I want."

"I don't know. I mean, I've hurt guys, in the business. But not a girl, like this."

"Don't go soft on me or I'll bury you out here next to her you asshole."

"You would too, wouldn't you?"

"Just do what the fuck I tell you and there's no problem."

"Okay, okay, but I can't kill her."

"You've killed before."

"Guys who deserved it."

"All right you pussy. I'll do it then when the time comes, after they release Tommy."

The sun had completely disappeared behind the trees. The moon slipped behind a cloud and didn't poke out again. The night wind had a slight bite to it. Andy put on a dark colored windbreaker he had brought along and Cheryl put on a light sweater. They ate on the porch by candlelight while Walker rested in his bed after eating a small bowl of chicken soup. He dozed off.

They heard a boat approaching, but couldn't see a light. Andy went down to greet it, thinking it was his father or Dusty. After circling the island to make sure that no one was around, Seine and McCabe decided to go ashore.

Andy stood on the dock and could see that it wasn't Dusty, but two men he hadn't seen before.

McCabe slowed the boat. Seine called out, "Andy Bell?"

Oh great! Each time someone started off like that it meant either the CIA or FBI. "No," lied Andy.

"We just want to talk."

"I don't know any Andy Bell."

"Nice try, but we've been watching." The boat was several yards away and approaching.

Andy turned and sprinted back to the cabin. "Lock the door and blow out the lights," he said to Cheryl as he flew inside and grabbed an AR-15. He pulled the cocking handle back allowing a round to be chambered.

"Who're they?"

"I think another former CIA guy who's been looking for O'Connell."

"I don't like this, Andy."

He threw a glance of agreement, but what could he do? She locked the door and blew out the candles. He handed her the rifle and snatched up the Cobray M11 sub-machine-gun. He found the holster that Walker had used the night he went after Cheryl and strapped it on. Andy jammed a clip in and holstered it on under his windbreaker. He grabbed another AR-15 for himself and shoved a clip into it. He pulled the cocking handle back and said, "Use it if you have to." Cheryl looked down at the rifle she was holding like it was a snake or something. She watched Andy who crouched down by the front window. She imitated his move.

McCabe helped Seine out of the boat and up the path. It took a few minutes because of Seine who hobbled along with his cane, but they finally made their way to the porch door. McCabe opened it and Seine stumbled up the steps.

Andy opened the front window. "Stop!"

They froze and listened.

"I have a rifle pointed at you. I suggest you leave."

Seine looked at McCabe. Seine didn't take Andy seriously. He started to shuffle across the porch.

Andy reacted by squeezing off a burst of rounds.

Several rounds, ten at least, splintered the porch at their feet. McCabe hit the deck, but Seine just stopped in his tracks.

"I'm not kidding!"

"Listen you punk," yelled Seine, "I'm coming in there!" He looked at McCabe. "Get up and break it down."

Walker was awake and alert. "What the hell's going on?"

"Intruders," said Andy.

They heard McCabe break the window in the door. Andy sneaked out into the kitchen and hid behind the door.

Walker forced himself to sit up, but couldn't negotiate his body to get out of the bed. He tore the oxygen tube off his head in frustration.

McCabe reached in and unlocked the door. Andy waited until he was just inside and had the right angle. He swung the rifle around by holding the barrel—still a little warm from the firing—and struck McCabe in the side of the head. McCabe fell backwards out the door and crashed to the floor of the porch. He was rendered unconscious.

When Andy bent down to see if he was out. Seine smashed his cane down onto the back of Andy's neck. Andy fell to the floor injured, but was not out. He grabbed his neck in agony.

Cheryl acted fast. She rushed into the kitchen and pointed her rifle at Seine. "I'll use this if I have to."

"You won't have to." He moved towards her.

She winced and squeezed the trigger. Several rounds discharged and impacted all about the ceiling above Seine's head.

He froze, but kept his cool.

Andy kneeled, then slowly got up. His neck hurt. He secured his rifle and pointed it at Seine. "You son-of-a-bitch! That hurt!"

"How do you think he feels," said Seine pointing to McCabe with his cane. "You've never killed anyone son, and you're not about to start." Seine started to move.

"No, but I will." Walker sauntered in from the main room struggling to hold his wretched body up. "Give me your rifle," he said to Cheryl.

"Don't do it," said Andy. "Everyone just stop!"

"Andy shut up! This man's a killer."

"And what the hell does that make you? Stop, Goddamnit!"

Everyone froze. "You, sit down over there," Andy said to Seine pointing at the kitchen chair.

"Fuck you, kid," said Seine. He moved for him.

Andy squeezed off a burst of rounds, several of which struck Seine in his right foot.

Seine roared in agony and dropped his cane. He steadied himself against the wall.

Walker and Cheryl couldn't believe he did it. "Andy," said Walker, "give me the goddamn gun."

"You sit down there or I'll do the same thing to you!"

"I'm dying. You'd just put me out of my goddamn misery."

"You can still feel pain."

"Why you, shit."

Everyone stared one another down. Walker finally capitulated and hobbled to the kitchen table. Seine huffed to himself, limped to the table and sat opposite Walker.

"Cheryl," said Andy, "wrap his foot."

He snatched up Walker and Seine's canes and tossed them in the main room.

She fetched a towel and did what Andy told her to do. Seine grimaced in pain as she took his shoe off and cleaned the wound. His foot was shattered and bloody. She wrapped it tightly in the towel.

Andy stepped through the door and checked on McCabe. He started to moan a little. Andy returned to the kitchen and found some twine in the drawer. He bound McCabe's wrists, ankles and then took a piece and tied a line from the wrists to the ankles; hog tied. He returned to the kitchen, grabbed paper towels, returned to McCabe, stuffed a wad into McCabe's mouth, and tied some twine around his head to hold it in place.

Andy returned to the kitchen and locked the door behind him. He pulled the shade down over the broken window.

"You don't know who you're messing with, kid," said Seine.

"Yeah, I do. An old bastard who's lost touch with his senses." Andy prepared an ice pack and held it to his sore neck.

Walker went into a coughing spell, wheezing and spitting.

"You're in good shape, O'Connell," said Seine.

"Shut the fuck up," said O'Connell catching his breath. "Give me my goddamn cigarettes, Cheryl."

She fetched them, trembling slightly after this event.

O'Connell lit one up and felt better. "So what happens now, Andy?"

Andy grabbed another chair and sat a few feet from the end of the table. "Get me another clip, Cheryl."

She didn't hesitate, for she saw a maniacal Andy that she hadn't seen before. This wasn't the gentleperson she grew to love. She gave him two clips. He dropped the spent clip from the rifle and inserted another. He wedged another in-between his shorts and his hips.

"Cheryl, light some candles," ordered Andy. She did as instructed and lit three around the kitchen, including one on the table.

"Well, this is a fine mess, Andy," said O'Connell blowing smoke. "Now what do we do?"

"What we do, my old and distinguished gentlemen, is talk."

"What the hell do you want to talk about now?" O'Connell asked.

Fullerton was in his office at the J. Edgar Hoover Building in DC when he was notified that there had been a kidnapping of Congressman Kern's daughter in a remote area of the Adirondack Park called Beaver River. He made a couple calls and discovered that this girl was the ex-girlfriend of Judge Bell's son Andy. The wheels in his head were turning as he got on a flight immediately to Syracuse. What the hell was going on up there? He planned to meet up with the Syracuse agents and at least explain what he could without going into too much detail.

Bolt and Krup were on their way back to Beaver River. Krup sat in the front of the boat and held the flashlight. Krup tried to formulate questions he would ask O'Connell. From what Krup could determine, O'Connell hadn't done anything illegal, disappearing the way he did. All that he had done for the agency during his time, being what they termed a `Mechanic,' was forever buried in the files of the CIA. Yet, Krup had as much curiosity as anyone, and had to talk with this guy.

Lou was on his way to Stillwater. He motored along in his stolen boat down the reservoir and passed by Krup and Bolt going the other way. Krup didn't see Lou's boat until he heard it off the starboard side by about forty yards. Lou's wake rocked their small craft and almost caused a spill. Bolt cussed, "asshole."

Lou did what Jimmy told him to do, but he was uneasy about the situation. He left Jimmy alone with her.

Jimmy raped Wendy again. This time, however, she didn't struggle or fight back. She was dazed and unresponsive. Jimmy did his thing then went out and sat by the fire. He had never raped anyone before, but there was something about the way this "bitch" reacted and made him feel that he had to put her in her place. No girl Jimmy had ever been with had ever talked to him that way! It was more about teaching a lesson to this bitch, than sex, although she was very attractive! He roasted a hotdog on a stick and gulped a beer.

Judge Bell and Agent Williams motored east on the reservoir in Judge Bell's boat. Judge Bell had a relatively strong spotlight that Williams used to scan the shoreline. They had already stopped at several campsites where families and buddies were camped out. They asked a few questions, explaining that they were looking for a young woman who was missing. No one had seen anything relevant.

They gave each site they visited a description of Wendy that the Judge had provided the agents and then went on to another site.

Twenty Three

"I know more than I've let on," said Andy. "And I think, Mr. O'Connell, you know what I'm talking about."

O'Connell blew smoke in Andy's direction. Seine sat there struggling to control the throbbing pain in his foot.

"It's time to come clean."

"You're messing in things you have no idea about," said Seine.

"I have a right to know the truth."

"Fucking kids. It's always been the fucking kids. The decline of this country is due to the lack of respect by kids towards their elders."

"You're so full of it."

"How dare you, you insolent little fuck talk to me like that! I should get up and kick your ass!"

"You move and I'll make you suffer and beg for mercy. You'll want me to kill you and put you out of your misery."

"Andy, you'll become like them," said Cheryl who was standing behind him holding the AR-15 and shaking slightly.

"These are extremely dangerous men, Cheryl. It's time you knew the truth." He snapped at her, and she didn't know him.

"What, that they were assassins?"

"And then some." He gave O'Connell a look that could kill.

O'Connell glanced at Seine who gave him an irate look in return. O'Connell took a deep drag, then blew the smoke out. "You looked up in the loft, didn't you Andy?" O'Connell coughed.

"I had to."

"You know what they say about curiosity."

"Just cut the crap."

"You kept a diary?" Seine asked pointedly.

"No."

"What then, goddamnit?"

"Research."

"What kind of research?"

"I wanted to know just as anyone."

"You stupid asshole."

"What difference does it make up here?"

"You see the outcome."

O'Connell shrugged his shoulders.

"And look what happened," Seine stewed.

Andy grew impatient. "Start talking."

"You going to torture me?" Seine smirked.

"If I have to."

"Well, then," quipped O'Connell, "since you know it all, you tell it smart ass."

Andy nodded his head. "Okay. All right, I will. Remember that picture of Kennedy on the wall, Cheryl?"

"Yeah."

"It was a memorial."

Seine fidgeted. He wanted to stop this.

Cheryl looked confused. "A memorial?"

"Your grandfather was involved."

"What? How so?" She didn't believe it.

"He was at least one of the shooters. Tell her the rest, Mr. O'Connell."

O'Connell looked at Seine. "Stop it," said Seine. "Don't do it, you old bastard."

O'Connell blew smoke in Seine's face. "Who're you calling old? I'm only in my late sixties. You're at least eighty."

"You look older than me. We'll have to kill them."

"We? I'm not doing anymore killing. I don't work for you anymore."

"I'll kill them then goddamnit!"

"In case you forgot, I'm holding the gun," said Andy.

"That's only for the moment."

"No, after you come clean, I'm going to turn both of you in."

Seine laughed uproariously. "There's no evidence anywhere. No one'll believe you. There's no one left. It's over."

"All except one."

"No one would believe a dying old fart."

"Speak for yourself you decrepit piece of shit," said O'Connell.

They sat looking at each other wanting to rip one another apart.

Finally, Seine nodded slightly. "How'd you know?"

"I didn't," said O'Connell.

"But you suspected."

"The way in which the whole operation was conducted, from the beginning, suggested how large a hit."

Seine shook his head. "Fuck. You got whiskey?"

"In the cupboard, Cheryl," said O'Connell.

She got a bottle of Jim Beam and a shot glass and gave them to Seine. He poured a jigger and downed it. He feared that it was going to be a long night.

"I'm waiting," said Andy.

O'Connell took a drag, then snubbed it out. He exhaled and looked at Seine. "You-son-of-a-bitch. I worked for you for fifteen years, and you couldn't trust me?"

"It wasn't personal. It was business."

"All the others are dead?"

"Most within days, some took longer. One other got away."

"Jesus Christ I was right. Who's the other? Sampson?"

"Dead."

"You killed Sammy?"

"Not personally."

"Damnit, Hank, he was one of the best." O'Connell shook his head in disgust.

"You understood the scope of it. This country would've been torn apart during a crucial time."

"Who's alive?"

"Harrelson."

"No shit?"

"He's not talking, despite joking about it while being high on cocaine when they got him for killing a Judge."

"He killed a Judge?"

"A federal judge. He got sloppy. Son-of-a-bitch slipped away and was elusive all those years."

"He got life then."

"Yeah. I'd get him if I could, but it's not like the old days."

"Fucking Harrelson. He was good."

"When did you get all this?" Seine asked indicating the cabin.

"On that last pass. I suspected a couple months before that, but didn't get all this finalized until October."

Cheryl, who had been pacing the floor behind Andy, pulled up a chair and sat beside him. She didn't know what to do about Andy. He was acting crazy. She was actually scared of him at this moment.

"Were you behind the grassy knoll?" Andy asked.

O'Connell laughed. "No."

Seine slammed his fist down onto the table. "Enough!"

O'Connell lit another Pall Mall. "Eat shit, you asshole."

"I should kick your pathetic ass too."

"Don't waste you precious energy. It might kill you."

"Who was behind the fence?" Andy demanded impatiently.

"I don't know. Who was, Hank?"

Seine looked up and shook his head. "I'm through. I'm not talking. You'll have to shoot me. I'll never say anything."

"I can arrange that," said O'Connell. "Still got that cloak and dagger mentality, I see."

"There were shooters." Andy said.

"At first I thought no," said O'Connell.

"What do you mean you thought? Look at all the testimony."

"I was told there would be two guys as spotters with walkie-talkies and to create a diversion, but apparently another shooter was behind the fence to get him if I missed, which was unlikely."

"A diversion?"

"And it worked. I had all the time in the world to slip away."

"What're you talking about?"

"Look at all the police and witnesses who ran in that direction looking for shooters immediately afterwards. The majority of the attention was focused there, not on the book building. They didn't close off the building for almost ten minutes."

"But they shot from there."

"Someone did. Both to create a diversion as well as to get a shot off."

"Wait a minute. You're saying you were up there on the sixth floor?"

"I had a spotter behind me. The commission was wrong, actually about a lot of things, but wrong about when the first shot was fired. It was sooner than they had concluded."

"So why didn't you shoot when they came up Houston?"

"I was told to wait until they were headed down Elm, so that everyone would be looking away from the building and wouldn't see the rifle sticking out the window. Coming up Houston, they might have spotted me beforehand. I was told that the diversionary shots would come from the fence and that they would have disguises so as not to stand out in any fashion out of the ordinary."

"Look," O'Connell said as he chain-smoked (if anyone were to walk by the cabin, they'd think it was on fire) "there were four teams for training, two men on each. We were told that one team, the best would be used as the primary, and one other team used as the secondary one, for the diversion. We practiced for six months. Teams A and B—that was the team I was on—we were chosen to concentrate our efforts on a moving target."

He took a drag. "I later learned, through the research, that the White House had announced the trip on September 26. Anyway, we had this elaborate setup. Teams C and D were let go. Wait a minute. You didn't, Hank?"

Seine didn't respond.

"Jesus Christ." O'Connell shook his head, too a drag. "We were given a final pass in October, and that's just after I began to figure this out. I had never been in on something so secret as this, and under such isolated and controlled conditions—we were kept on a base in the Texas desert. Anyway, I finally decided that after this job it was over, that I should disappear for a while. Well, after it was over, I knew that I would have to stay hidden for the rest of my life. I never planned on this being a permanent arrangement. Anyway, I figured it had to be a big political figure.

"Then," he continued, "the day before B team was informed that it was chosen as the primary and I was chosen as the main shooter, they separated the teams and we never saw each other again." He paused and looked over at Seine. "After the shit had hit the fan, I knew why I was picked, because I knew that I wasn't the best."

"Stop!" Seine struggled to get up. Andy jumped up and jabbed his rifle muzzle into Seine's chest, pushing him back into his seat. Cheryl jumped up behind Andy. O'Connell calmly sat in his seat and took yet another drag.

"You little punk. I'll—"

"You'll what? You're in no position."

"You'll have to kill me then."

"Don't tempt me."

"Andy!" Cheryl said.

"Cheryl, he's right. He'll never go alive."

"I don't like this."

"Well, you'd better get hold of yourself."

Andy stood there and stared at Seine for the longest time. Seine didn't give a crap if Andy killed him, yet he still felt obligated to do his part and keep his oath to his former employer in particular and the Agency in general.

Cheryl finally sat down defeated. She was scared to death, more of Andy than the two old helpless men were. Andy calmly sat.

"Let's get back to the diversion. I don't understand the diversion," said Andy. "How can that be?"

O'Connell took his time answering. "We were told that there was to be a diversion and that some plants would draw off the authorities in the immediate aftermath."

"Okay, but the wounds."

"The wound in the neck was mine, I'm positive. The first shot was a complete miss and hit the curb. My other shot I think hit Connelly and was the so-called magic bullet they found under that stretcher at Parkland. I was damn lucky to get off those three shots. That piece of shit Mannlicher-Carcano was in bad shape."

"How did it get there?"

"I don't know. I was trained to sight and quickly adjust fire to any weapon that was poorly sighted. My guess, Oswald, remember the Manchurian Candidate?"

Andy nodded.

"The what?" Cheryl asked.

"Manchurian Candidate," said O'Connell.

"I don't understand."

"Tell her, Andy."

"The *Manchurian Candidate* was a movie, made about the same time of the assassination, just before I think. It was about a Korean War soldier who was brainwashed by the Chinese Communists to go back to the States and kill a major political figure so that a puppet president could be installed. It came out about the same time of the assassination and when the CIA was experimenting in mind-altering drugs to use on enemies or captured spies and individuals in the spy world. It starred Frank Sinatra who was a close friend of Kennedy and he pulled the film from the theaters just after the assassination."

"Prophetic to say the least," said O'Connell. "So my guess was that Oswald was used all along like the character in the *Manchurian Candidate*."

"Okay, so what about the shots?"

"Well, I had practiced with an identical Mannlicher-Carcano since about the same time that Oswald ordered his using his alias in Dallas. I, of course, had to practice with these specially constructed skintight gloves. That was so I wouldn't leave any prints and that Oswald's palm print would show of course since it was his weapon. The authorities made such a big deal out of the fact that they found Oswald's finger prints on some of the boxes there, but he worked there filling book orders moving boxes."

"The shots," demanded Andy.

"Yeah, well, to hit a moving target, and sight in the cross hairs for each shot, it takes time. I got that weapon only fifteen minutes before I fired it. You see I was very good at sighting in weapons. I did it for years in my shop in Alabama. Well, I knew that first shot missed and I had the general area of where it went, so I adjusted fire. Let's see. The sight I believe was high and to the right, so I adjusted accordingly, that was the shot that hit the curb, so my second shot hit in the neck. My third shot, I think had to be the shot that hit Connelly, since he was still holding his hat after the impact of the neck shot. The Commission said that his wrist had been shattered by that neck shot, but that's impossible. The head shot wasn't mine, I'm sure of it. The impact, as seen on that home movie is all wrong."

Cheryl was disgusted. She shook slightly.

"Goddamnit, John. You've gone way too far," said Seine downing another shot of Whiskey.

O'Connell looked at Seine and blew more smoke. "Cool it, Hank, you son-of-a-bitch. I'll see you in Hell."

"So then some of those other seven wounds were from team two," said Andy thinking aloud.

"I don't know, I'm not a forensic scientist. They still fight over it today."

Andy shook his head. "Okay, so you were on the sixth floor."

"Right where they said the patsy was."

"You saw him?"

"I never saw him."

"How did you get out of there without anyone seeing you?"

"The building was having its floors refurbished and there were many men in there that week doing the work. We were dressed like workmen. We actually walked down the stairs right after those two ladies had, ah, the ones on the fourth floor. We walked right on out the door, apparently like Oswald had later on after his Coke."

"And you never saw him?"

"No."

"Where was he?"

"I guess he was on the second floor like those people said he was drinking his Coke."

"You guess. You guys didn't have anything to do with that?"

"I didn't. Not a thing. I was only a 'mechanic.' Recruited by him," O'Connell pointed at Seine, "and trained during the 50's in the 'village' in the Mediterranean. This was all after Korea."

"Wait a minute. What about E. Howard Hunt the Watergate guy? And that Sturgis?"

O'Connell took another drag and held it deep. He nodded and blew out the smoke. "I had met them both many years earlier in Florida during the Alpha 66 days. Hunt was always very cordial to me. I thought he was a clandestine genius. I don't know what, if anything he had to do with this. Hank?"

Seine shook his head. Slowly, he said, "Fuck you."

"But he and Sturgis were the transients," demanded Andy, "as the diversion so you could get into place before the shooting or something."

"It looks pretty convincing to me," said O'Connell. "Transients, Hank?"

"You all go fuck yourselves. Unlike you I honor my oath, I'm sworn to secrecy. I'd never betray them." Seine now drank from the bottle, the hell with the shot glass.

"What the hell does it matter?" Andy demanded.

"That's right, kid. What the hell does it matter? It doesn't anymore. It's ancient history that has nothing to do with the present."

"You're pathetic!"

"This is the kind of company you keep?" Seine asked of O'Connell.

"Andy, you had better take a step back and think about what's going on here," O'Connell admonished.

"Finally some truth."

"Things aren't that simple."

"You know, I'm tired of all this double speak crap."

"I thought Cheryl had a lot of growing up to do. You're just as naive."

"Shut up!" Andy pointed his rifle at O'Connell who blew more smoke. "I'm getting sick of your pollution."

"It's my goddamn house."

Like Cheryl, O'Connell saw an Andy he hadn't seen before. He studied him.

"Yeah, shut up." Seine said to O'Connell.

O'Connell laughed. "He's right, Hank. You're pathetic. Pathetic old piece of paranoid shit."

Seine shoved the table at O'Connell. O'Connell stopped it before it rammed into his belly.

"What did he do?" Andy ordered.

"Just a bureaucrat," said O'Connell. "An administrator." He paused. "He put together teams, trained and provided logistical support."

"You weren't working for the CIA?"

"I worked for him," he nodded at Seine. "I don't know who he worked for. Hank?"

"No," Seine finally acknowledged. Defeated, he finally admitted, "I retired in sixty one."

"Not fired with the rest of them?" Andy asked.

"Fired is too strong a term."

"And you had no revenge?"

Seine shook his head. "No. I made more money on the outside."

"Okay, but you knew the target."

"I've said more than I should."

"But you killed him," said Andy to O'Connell.

"Look, it was just another job."

"Killing the president isn't just another job." Andy shifted in his seat. He had to rest the rifle on his knee.

"I told you. Once you're in, you can't get out." O'Connell snubbed out his cigarette and lit another.

Andy had a thought flash through his head. "Cheryl, look at that picture you have of your grandmother with O'Connell."

She did.

"Look closely at that young O'Connell and tell me what your impression is."

She studied the photograph. "Like I've seen him before, but I just can't figure out where."

"Looks like Oswald, doesn't he?"

"Oh, my God. That's it. I knew he looked familiar. I mean, he is skinny, short hair and similar features, but it isn't him."

"But looks similar."

She nodded.

"That's why they chose you."

O'Connell took a deep drag. "Yeah, I knew something was amiss, because at least three others were better than I was."

"Didn't you worry that you could have been set up?" Andy asked.

"They're going to frame a hit-man? It would show as a conspiracy for sure."

"But why go to all that trouble and frame Oswald, when you could just have done it and walked away?"

"I wasn't just to walk away, like Oswald. If they didn't have the perfect assassin, then there certainly would've been chaos. They needed the perfect assassin. A professed Marxist for Christ's sake. But, on the flip side, it didn't make any sense. Look, he defects to the Soviet Union and tries to renounce his American citizenship, but he goes to the embassy on a weekend when the embassy is closed. He stays for a couple years and returns to Dallas and is befriended by an anti-Communist, George de Mohrenschildt and his family, a white Russian immigrant, the son of a Czarist minister. Does that make any sense? Then, after getting friendly with the anti-Communist community of White Russian immigrants in Dallas, he goes to New Orleans and hands out pro-Castro leaflets in front of Guy Banister's office, with the address of the building that Banister uses on the leaflets. He then gets into a scuffle with an anti-Castroite and goes on the local television station and professes his Marxism, then, after that incident, disappears for awhile. Even the Commission couldn't account for him for about two weeks."

"An interesting detail, to say the least," he continued, "was that this character Oswald spoke the Russian language fluently. How many people you know, back in those days before all these self-help audiotapes, could teach himself Russian? Even his wife said when she met him in Minsk that she thought he was a Russian, except that she thought he was from a different region because he spoke the language so well.

"You have to look at this de Mohrenschildt character. He was an oil-man who was friends with Texas oilman H.L. Hunt—incidentally Ruby took one of his employees to Hunt's son for a job interview. Anyway, de Mohrenschildt showed up at a training base for anti-Castro Cubans getting ready for the Bay of Pigs in Guatemala. He said he was on a walking tour with his wife through Latin America.

O'Connell chuckled. "Then he got this letter from Richard Helms thanking him for providing the agency with valuable foreign intelli-gence. The letter's in the National Archives. Of course this memo didn't come out until those Church hearings in the middle seventies, again, information kept from the Warren Commission. The son-of-a-bitch even testified for the Warren Commission, but, like so much that the Commission failed to investigate, they said that there was no evidence that de Mohrenschildt had any connection with American intelligence. And I'm the fuckin' Queen of England! That memo proved he had.

"He befriends Oswald. They even give his wife gifts when the first baby arrived. After Oswald gets back from Russia, de Mohrenschildt gets him a job in Texas at a map making company that did aerial photo analysis and map printing for the US Military. Go figure how the hell a defector, who said he was a Communist, gets a job working for a defense contractor. Doesn't make any sense to me. Check the record. Neither the FBI nor the CIA, according to them, interviewed Oswald upon his return from the Soviet Union, a common practice for people traveling there during the Cold War. Remember that we executed the Rosenbergs. However, de Mohrenschildt almost immediately befriends him? Sounds like a debriefing to me.

"It gets better. The day before de Mohrenschildt was to be questioned by an investigator for the House Assassinations Committee, according to the Miami Police, de Mohrenschildt puts a shotgun in his mouth and blows his fuckin' head off. He had a similar picture in his garage of that famous one of Oswald holding his rifle in the backyard.

"No, Oswald was a monster created by somebody, my guess he was that monster right of the *Manchurian Candidate*. Even the CIA and other government agencies as we have learned lately, were heavily into mind-altering drug experimentation during the Cold War.

"But, at every turn, the Warren Commission looked the other way. You have to ask yourself why. What would have happened if the secrets that came out in the middle seventies had come out at the time of Kennedy's death? Chaos. Maybe anarchy."

O'Connell took a drag; wheezed a bit.

"What about that French guy?" Andy said. "The one who was expelled the same day?"

"Jean Soutre. He was on the other team that wasn't used. I never saw him again after training camp the day we departed for the hit. I don't know what became of him. Hank?"

Seine sighed and laughed softly to himself. He took another swig. "Okay. Okay, goddamnit!" Seine laughed again. "'Almost blew it." He shook his head. "They had him right in their hands."

"What do you mean?" Andy demanded.

"The CIA had him and they expelled him."

"Yeah, I remember reading that," said O'Connell. "So what did you do with him, Hank?"

Seine nodded slightly. "We got him in Mexico. He's buried out in the desert somewhere."

"Holy shit," said Andy softly to himself. He sighed. Everyone was quiet for a moment.

"I was relieved," said O'Connell, "when that Specter came up with the magic bullet theory."

"Wait a minute, that worker was eating his lunch there."

"That was a problem. Bonny Ray Williams, I later learned who he was. We decided to wait only a couple more minutes, but he finally left. Good thing for him."

"You would've killed him?"

"This operation was six months in the planning and too much money had been invested. We were supposed to do whatever it took."

Silence. Everyone wondered what would happen next.

"So Oswald was a patsy," said Cheryl disbelieving, "or a *Manchurian Candidate*."

"Any fool would question why he'd do it, not to think he wouldn't be caught and everything would point to him. He leaves the rifle; he works there. He'd know they'd discover all this."

"Do you think he could've killed Tippet?"

"There's inconsistency because of the distance he traveled in such a short time frame, and that the key witnesses couldn't identify Oswald. That one witness, Markham, had to be re-interviewed because they found that she had been inconsistent, some said lying. Despite all that, the Commission chose to believe her and discarded all the others. And several Warren Commission witnesses placed Tippet in Ruby's club on more than one occasion talking with Ruby himself. Ruby was incoherent when asked if he knew Tippet when Supreme Court Chief Justice Warren was present in the jailhouse. He said he knew a Tippet."

"Did you know Ruby?"

"Not personally. I had seen him twice, once on a base in Louisiana and once in Florida. He was only at each briefly, then left. He had something to do with running arms, jeeps or something to the island."

O'Connell shifted in his seat. "Look. More than one credible witness said that they knew each other, Ruby and Tippet. Everyone down there knew that Ruby had a lot of connections with the Dallas Police and he treated them all very well in his club. Not a night went by that didn't have several cops in his club watchin' the girls having a drink. And the Commission never adequately explained how Ruby had gotten into the garage to kill Oswald when the garage was secured by at least 70 cops who were there. One Commission counsel member even called one of the cops who testified a 'Damn liar.' And, if you watch and listen to the video of Oswald's killing by Ruby, what do you hear at the exact moment that Ruby lunges forward into view?"

Andy shook his head.

"At the exact moment, when Oswald appears, you hear a car horn once, then again, and in a split second, Ruby rushes forward and shoots him. My god! How coincidental is that? I mean, this Oswald character, as far as the Dallas Police are concerned, not only presumably to them, killed the President of the United States of America, but a Dallas cop, one of their own. And everyone in those days knew what happened to cop killers if there was a chance. Anyone knows the old 'code of silence' rule that still pervades our police departments yet to this day. There's testimony in the report that the Dallas Police were warned of the possibility that Oswald was going to be killed. So, the hierarchy had all those cops there to protect Oswald. Only authorized personnel were allowed in there. Yet, Ruby waltzes right on in and walks up that close. No one figured, or did someone, that a cop would let Ruby sneak in there and then give a signal for him to get the hit. It's too obvious, yet the Commission didn't dig to explain this. They conceded that they couldn't exactly establish the fact as to how Ruby got access.

"So, it suggests to me," continued O'Connell, "that Tippet was cruising in the area of Oswald's house within a mile, outside of his normal patrol area, looking for what? Oswald, before—as the Commission even points out—that Brennan supposedly gave a description of him, me; before the APB went out. It was about this same time that Sorrels was talking with Brennan and then Truly. Tippet was sent to kill him, only perhaps Oswald figured it out first, if he was even there, and shot him. But I'm not so sure he did. When that didn't work, Ruby is sent in to get into the garage to do the job. Ruby ended up doing the killing of Oswald, after Tippet failed to do so. Sounded like a hit to me.

"Those Dallas boys were tight," O'Connell went on. "It's no great secret that many of them in those days were very right-wing, KKK and the like. This country was split on what Kennedy was doing, ever so slowly I grant you, with civil rights for minorities and all, and trying to make peace with the communists, and the whole Cuban disappointment from both the Bay of Pigs, to the missile crises where Kennedy had made a deal with Khrushchev and sold them out—the anti-Castroites. Then read the Ruby testimony, if you can call it that. He rambles on about that the Commission has to take him to Washington so he can talk, because he can't say anything in Dallas because he's not safe. He rambles on and on about that and never directly answers the questions asked of him."

"It's so complicated," said Andy. "There's so much information."

"Wait a minute," said Seine. "So where'd you go? We were waiting in the car on Commerce."

"I laughed when I read how the Commission explained Oswald's travels after the shooting. I walked to the Greyhound Bus Station at Lamar and Jackson Streets. My car was parked there in the lot. I must have been there at about the same time they said Oswald was. I drove all night."

Silence again, as everyone was lost in thought.

"Well, you've gone too far," said Seine. "Either they die, or we die."

"I wouldn't worry about that."

"It really doesn't matter for you anymore," said Andy to Seine.

"What the hell do you mean?" Seine roared.

"You don't have much longer to live, I mean your age."

"What would you know?"

"Just tell me who hired you?"

"I don't know," said Seine.

"Come on, you're not going anywhere," said Andy.

"I never knew. Most of the jobs we did I never knew."

"You worked for the CIA."

"I reported to various people throughout my career but they were just contacts, deep-cover agents, not the employers themselves."

"How would you know?"

"To tell you the truth, I guess I didn't."

"'Sounds like double speak."

"Pretty good with your terminology, Huh?"

"You're patronizing."

"You've got a lot to learn, kid."

"Even President Johnson, like O'Connell said earlier, admitted later in an interview that the CIA had run a Murder, Incorporated, and worked with the Mafia to kill Castro."

"But it was all clandestine. If, by chance we were caught, we would've been a dead end. I couldn't identify the deep-cover agents. I was the last link in the chain. Plausible denial they call it, and that's exactly what I had, we all had, up and down the line. Everyone only knew what his 'need to know' was. Everyone had plausible denial about what everyone else did."

"But you must've suspected who did what."

"And my suspicions were my own. I never shared them with anyone."

"Why don't you share them with us?" Andy raised the rifle slightly and pointed it at him.

"Fuck you."

Andy shook his head. "I can't believe it. Johnson said in that interview in the Atlantic Monthly—in 1973—he said that it had been a conspiracy and he believed—even after his own commission reported to him that Oswald acted alone—that Oswald hadn't acted alone. Nobody paid any attention."

"Because it just doesn't matter anymore. It's that simple. People don't give a damn. All they care about is if they have their daily bread, a roof over their head, and a little extra money to have a good time with, be entertained. Can't you ever get that, kid?"

Andy was flustered. He actually wanted to shoot the old bastard for being so cynical.

"So, did they order the mop up or did you?" O'Connell asked.

Seine nodded and smirked. "It was SOP, John. You know that."

O'Connell laughed. "I was the link in the chain just below you."

"And after you were dead, and I had gotten Harrelson, it ended with me. I couldn't take that chance. After that I could've relaxed and died of old age. Harrelson, now, doesn't matter. They say he's insane now and talking like a raving lunatic." He paused. "You only had half the money."

"I wasn't a big spender. I'd made so much on all the other jobs, and invested wisely, that I could retire. The stock market did very well over thirty years."

"I've heard it all, or most of it, and I still can't believe it," said Andy.

"You're kidding," said Cheryl. "If you've heard it all and can't believe it, then how am I supposed to make any sense out of all this? I have no idea what this is all about. I've never heard any of this."

"What about the security that day?" Andy continued.

"At the time," said O'Connell, "I was told not to worry about it. Later, after I had done all the research, I discovered that there was virtually none that day. There should have been Secret Services agents on those buildings, and most certainly all those windows would've been closed. All the agents were riding in the damn motorcade and some should have been posted along the route."

"And the hobos and epileptic seizure?" Andy asked.

O'Connell looked at Seine who took a swig of Jim Beam. "Again, I don't know. I do know that we did move into the building from the rear about the same time that happened. A coincidence?" O'Connell shrugged his shoulders. "My guess is that it was the perfect diversion. We walked right up through the stairway when everyone was on his or her lunch break. Like I said, they were refurbishing the floors there in the building and we were told that there were many workers who were not regulars working there at that time and that we would fit right in and that nobody should challenge us. And nobody did. The building was almost empty as everyone was out in front of the building getting ready for the arrival of the motorcade. There were a couple people on a couple floors, but no one there when we moved into position on the sixth after Williams had left."

"So you were to kill anyone in the way."

"Yeah."

"How?"

"Old 'black OPS' move with a knife. It's called the silent kill. You stab the victim in the carotid artery. They bleed to death almost immediately. We were to leave the knife and told that it would be traced to the fall guy. Luckily, we didn't have to do that, although, if Williams hadn't left, he would have been the first victim."

"Where was he?" Andy asked pointing his rifle at Seine.

"He got us to the building, then I don't know. But I know he drove a white Chevy Impala during the training phase."

"Just like Bowers, the railroad supervisor, said he saw driving around in the rail yard near the fence before the shooting."

"I guess he was there checking out the area."

"Enough!" Seine slammed his fist down on the table, startling everyone, except O'Connell.

"You already had your tirade," said O'Connell. "It doesn't matter anymore, Hank. Just let it go."

Seine's face was crimson. He could have a stroke at any moment. "It's over," he said. "It won't change anything to know everything. Besides, people don't give a goddamn about what happened so long ago in a different time."

"I think it's important," said Andy.

"People will get up and go to work tomorrow and never give it another thought."

"You're pretty arrogant about what the people will do or what they won't do."

"And you're just another kid stirring up trouble."

"Thank God your generation is dying off. Perhaps attitudes will be different."

"People don't change. Someday you'll become like us."

"I don't know about that. I'd rather kill myself before I become like you."

"You're living in a fantasy land."

Andy shook his head. Everyone was quiet for a long moment.

"Let's get back." He pointed his rifle at O'Connell who raised his eyebrows at Andy's audacity.

"Well, what do you want to know?"

"The Commission."

"The Commission, of course, discounted so much. They had to." He took another drag, coughed a bit. "And, you have to admit, that the FBI had a complete detailed background on Oswald within minutes after the shooting, given how the Bureau is so screwed up most of the time how could they have had all that together so quickly if they didn't know about him beforehand, as they testified, or were involved somehow? I think we all were used. Every one of us up and down the line. If anything, the FBI had signals about this and certainly was an accessory after the fact, probably for self interest, C.Y.A."

"What's that?" Cheryl asked.

"A term that's used everyday in the government. Cover-your-ass."

"Aren't most of the files on Oswald still unavailable to the public?" Andy asked.

"The ones not destroyed. They destroyed most of his military records, they say, routinely a few years later, coincidentally when researches were filing Freedom of Information lawsuits. I mean, would you, as a clerk or another higher up who ran across Lee Harvey Oswald's military records, not preserve them for the sake of history after the officials concluded that he was the assassin? It's preposterous! Those files would have been invaluable for history's sake. The only military records now available are the ones that were included in the Warren Report. And those are sketchy. So why is it that the files in the

National Archives that were saved before being destroyed are unavailable yet to this day?"

Andy shrugged.

"Look, a trial is a public matter, the public has a right to sit in on a trial. If Oswald had lived, and went to trial, then all those still yet classified, top secret files, both his CIA and FBI files on his activities, would have been made public in that trial, let alone he would've sang. A defendant has the constitutional right to put on his defense—and face his accusers, the government—and to subpoena that evidence necessary for his defense, which in this case includes what he may or may not have done for, or to the government.

"However, as we all know," continued O'Connell, "all those files, in their entirety, are still, for the most part, classified and not available to the public. If you study the Warren Commission, you'll see that they reviewed only some of that evidence—because the FBI later admitted it withheld some. But they discounted, for whatever reasons, Oswald's shady activities, alias and acquaintances. I mean, this guy walked around and did more than the average citizen could have gotten away with at that time when the red scare was in full swing. He defects to the Soviet Union and is there during the shoot down of U2 Pilot Powers, after having been assigned to a radar unit in Japan in 57, that monitored those flights, then returns, supposedly disappointed in the Communist system. And then he goes to work in the depository in October? Like I said, the FBI finally admitted, during the House hearings in the middle seventies, that they had withheld evidence from the Commission. They knew that Oswald was in Dallas before the shooting, and Special Agent Hosty destroys the letter after the assassination that Oswald wrote to the FBI before the assassination. An informant even told the Texas Attorney General and the Dallas Prosecutor Wade that Oswald had intelligence connections, they said an informant."

"And then he was killed by Ruby," said Andy.

"And look at his connections."

"The mob?"

"They all knew each other. Ruby, Marcello. David Ferri was Marcello's personal pilot and Guy Banister had worked with him. Ruby had connections with the underworld, even the Warren Commission admitted that. And Richard Helms finally admitted that Clay Shaw had worked for the CIA during those days. And, incidentally, or coincidentally, Shaw was associated with the international Trade Mart, as a Director, which had a subsidiary in Dallas where Kennedy was to give his speech that day. The CIA admitted in that Senate hearing that they'd hired the mob to get Castro, so that proves they were all connected, and Oswald had crossed paths with Ferri and other anti-Castro Cubans in New Orleans, yet again, the Commission discounted this evidence."

"There's no way to know who hired you?"

"I have no idea. Look, most of all these names we throw around now, the bodies attached to those names, are all dead, died shortly thereafter. Hank?"

"Not by me."

"Everyone knows Kennedy shut down the anti-Castro Cubans, cleaned out the CIA. He had a lot of enemies. Like you pointed out, Andy, it seemed he was getting ready to pull the plug on Vietnam, and make peace with the Soviets."

Andy stared at Seine who looked down at the table. "It's so intertwined," said Andy.

"And I don't think anyone will ever be able to untangle it."

"That's why you guys need to come forward. You could begin to unravel it."

Seine and O'Connell looked at one another. "No chance in hell," said Seine. "The chain is broken with me."

"Then you'll have to kill yourself," said Andy. "Or swim to the mainland. I'm taking the boats."

"No one would believe you," said Seine.

"That guy from the CIA who came looking for O'Connell might like to listen."

"You're wasting your time, Kid."

"I just think that the people have a right to know the truth!" Andy was mad as hell.

"You need to get a grip, kid. Move on with your life," said O'Connell lighting yet another cigarette.

"You guys messed with history."

"And it doesn't matter," said Seine. "Like I said, People don't give a crap what happened thirty, forty years ago. It doesn't have any relevance to their lives today. Most people don't want to hear about the dirty work. It's over their heads. Too ugly. Many wouldn't believe it even if we were to tell them. Many on that Church Committee were appalled. How did they think things were done in the real world? Did they actually think you walked around and played nice guys with your enemy who was out to destroy you? It doesn't matter anymore what we did all those years ago. So just get over it."

"And that's the kind of thinking that's screwed up this country," said Andy. "You know as well as I do that everything was down hill after Kennedy was killed. Vietnam, Watergate. This country's never recovered."

"It will. Get over it and get a life."

Silence. Andy steamed a moment. Everyone was pissed in one way or another.

"That man saw you, didn't he?" Andy asked.

"Brennan? Yeah," said O'Connell, "he saw me, and described me quite accurately. He didn't identify Oswald in that line-up, because it was me, who resembled him, but if you saw the two of us together, or closely together in time, then you would see and note those differences, so that's why he didn't identify him. All that crap about him being afraid of a communist conspiracy and afraid for his family was gibberish."

"And they used Brennan as the source of the APB."

"That's what the Commission concluded despite the fact that the time frame is all out of whack. I've studied that carefully. It's all there in the Warren testimony. All those contradictions the Commission either discounted, or said people were mistaken. They always sided with the FBI's conclusions, and it didn't take a genius to realize that J. Edgar Hoover hated both brothers. Hoover's job was on the line. Hoover screwed with Kennedy even during World War Two when he spied on the young Navy officer. He showed his father Joe documentation where young Navy man Jack was sleeping with that German spy. Jack Kennedy never forgave Hoover for spying on him in those days. And then, Johnson and Hoover were good friends, after having been neighbors in Washington all those years when Johnson was Senate Majority Leader.

"Anyway," continued O'Connell, "Brennan says that he told Sorrels the description within ten, fifteen minutes. However, in Sorrels' testimony, he says he was in the motorcade and went to Parkland first, before he came back to the scene well after one O'clock. Again, the commission, being the Gods they were, decided that the witnesses were all mistaken about their sequence of events and or the timing."

"That man saw Ruby then?"

"Probably. What a clown. He was probably standing there watching near the front of the building."

"They didn't investigate that?" Andy asked.

"The problem with the investigation was that there were too many witnesses and evidence that the Commission simply had to include some, and discard some. Look, they had to prove Oswald did it, and lead only in that direction. All this other extraneous stuff, well, it would have pointed in another direction that they didn't want to go. They agonized over that, and people like Boggs were worried about this. The others, either they didn't want to go that way, or they couldn't, for whatever reason or motive. They never adequately followed all their leads, because they had to totally rely on the investigating arm they had at their disposal, and that was Hoover's boys who were either so embarrassed by their miscalculations and sloppy oversight in preventing this when there were signs beforehand, all over the place, or they were incompetent. The House Committee pointed out many mistakes that the Commission made, the autopsy and elsewhere. It was just a big mess, for our fortune I must add. I tell you, Andy, after all my research, I still don't know who ordered it, and he really doesn't either. That's just the way we operated, again, plausible denial on the part of everyone involved."

"You could speculate, even if he won't."

O'Connell smiled. "I suppose. If I had to guess, based upon all that I've read, and my experience, I'd have to say it was the anti-Castro Cubans either alone, or with Mob support, they had mutual interests in Cuba. And again, I would say that either the CIA or the FBI or both, had either warnings or indications before the fact, and were complacent for whatever motive, and had to cover up their oversight or sloppy work after the fact. My best guess—Ferri was a very persuasive character. I think it's possible that he used his connection with Oswald and had Oswald deliver the weapon there as like the character out of *The Manchurian Candidate*. Oswald just followed directions, either knowingly, or as a *Manchurian Candidate*. We were probably hired by powerful and influential anti-Castro forces, with or without the help of Marcello and the New Orleans mob. I believe Maurice Bishop, who I believe was David Atlee Phillips, and who was the money man and the influence behind Alpha 66, probably outside the overall domain of the Agency (a lot was in those days) was involved. The man was a dis-information genius.

"Did you know Bishop, or Phillips?"

"Not personally. I saw the man they called Bishop at the JM/WAVE station in Florida. I later saw the House photo of Phillips and knew they were they same man. Antonio Veciana, Frank Sturgis and E. Howard Hunt were all connected in more ways than one with Bishop. How about it Hank?"

Seine nodded his head slightly.

"What was that?" Andy demanded.

"Come on Hank," said O'Connell. "Spit it out for Christ's sake."

Seine glared at him.

"Is that who it was?" Andy stood up and pointed the rifle directly at Seine.

"Quit pointing that goddamn thing at me unless you intend to use it."

"Jesus, Hank. Just lighten up."

"I don't know, goddamnit!"

"You can guess," said Andy.

"I'm not sure."

"Not sure what?"

"Goddamnit! I don't know. I think so."

Andy lowered the rifle.

"I never saw him."

"Who?"

"Bishop."

"So I was right," said O'Connell.

"It was Bishop. I don't know who he was."

"Wait a minute," said Andy. "I don't understand. You just said it was Bishop."

"Bishop was a fictitious name. Not his real name."

"I'm not following."

"I never saw him. Everything was handled deep-cover and in clandestine ways, never more than that. The money was always deposited in safe deposit boxes waiting for my retrieval."

"Damn spooks," said O'Connell.

"You never saw him?" Andy was frustrated.

"I just said no. I never saw him. Never. He ran everything from the shadows."

"But you heard his voice?"

"Thirty five, forty years ago and more. I wouldn't recognize it today."

"Besides," said O'Connell. "Phillips died of cancer in the late eighties. A lot of people involved in this died of Cancer, come to think about it."

Seine took a swig, Andy fidgeted, O'Connell blew smoke and Cheryl sat in stunned silence.

"But, when did you know when you were to do it?"

"I didn't know when it would be." O'Connell looked at Seine. "We're listening, Hank."

Seine was now feeling the buzz of all that booze. "Okay, okay goddamnit!" He took another swig from his bottle. Slowly, he revealed, "They always said it was to be in Texas, but they hadn't decided on what city. They were planning on a roof hit and when they knew the route, they would have a situation to exploit. The White House announced it would go to the trade mart in Dallas, with a motorcade through downtown via Main, which meant they had to turn and go down Elm, because you can't make the turn onto the freeway from Main. I was told that operatives had placed a patsy in a job in a downtown building who would be set up for the fall. They also told me to get O'Connell as the number-one man because he closely resembled this patsy."

"Okay. What about your escape?" Andy asked O'Connell.

"That was all planned out too," said O'Connell, "but I knew better."

"How so?"

"I was supposed to link up on Commerce Street with him and be whisked away like the rest, they sped off in a car there, but I slipped away in the crowd. We were supposed to be flown out somewhere, but, Hank, I was one step ahead of that plan."

"David Ferri, the pilot was to fly you?"

O'Connell shrugged his shoulders. "I don't know. I didn't know him."

"I didn't either," said Seine, "but I had heard the name in Miami at the JM/WAVE Station and he was to fly him out to the desert somewhere where we'd be waiting to whack him."

"I read that somewhere, the JM/WAVE," said Andy thinking aloud.

"The CIA's operation in South Florida to overthrow Castro," said O'Connell, "actually set up by Kennedy himself. It was a CIA front operation officially called Zenith Technical Enterprises Incorporated. Its sole purpose was clandestine operations against Castro's regime. It was an enormous operation that spawned many ardent terrorists who attacked Cuban and Russian ships. Those guys had some balls. I spent one whole summer down there training those bastards to shoot straight. Hot as hell."

Andy shook his head. Cheryl stared at him. Everyone sat quietly for the longest time; O'Connell smoking his cigarette and coughing, Seine downing Jim Beam.

"One more thing, Andy," said O'Connell. "Think about it. Read your constitution. It says something to the effect that a crime committed in a particular state shall be tried in that state. Congress didn't pass a law until the following year, because of these events, making it a federal crime to kill the president and other federal officials. Therefore, technically, the federal government had no legal jurisdiction to assume control of the investigation, certainly not at least until the Commission was set up days later. But what happened? As we said, Johnson took control immediately, and they ran off with the body before an autopsy was completed, and we now know how that turned out. The National Archives even says that Kennedy's brain is missing, some say Bobby Kennedy got it through his secretary a few years later and destroyed it because he didn't want his brother's brain on display someday for people to gawk at. I don't know. Anyway, most of the evidence is locked away until you're my age."

"But what about Lincoln?" asked Cheryl.

"What about him?"

"The army took control of that."

"But that was in the District of Columbia, a city run by the federal government still today. It's their jurisdiction there. Dallas wasn't."

"Okay, but the Commission was made up of men, men who were respected."

"Reputable and all. Look, Cheryl, we all know, it's been established, that they were misled by the FBI, and certainly the CIA, as it stands, doesn't admit to its secrets and policy. Dulles even admitted that. And Dulles? A spy on the Commission for his friends in the agency. You know, they say, and I can attest to this, once in the CIA, always in the CIA. Yes, the Commission had a monumental task and when witnesses and evidence pointed them in a direction that was contrary to what the FBI or the CIA was telling them, the Commission repeatedly discounted, rejected and overruled the testimony and evidence even after so much of that testimony checked out and wasn't disputed, sometimes, ironically, by the FBI. When you read the report, the Commission uses hundred of times the words: 'probably mistaken,' 'could have been easily mistaken,' 'probably did not see' this or that, 'was in error,' 'was incorrect.' Then, so many statements taken by the police and other officials were excluded from the report. Yet, they unevenly chose to believe the testimony of witnesses that pointed to what the FBI concluded to them, that Oswald had done it, and done it alone. Remember when you asked about Colby, Andy?"

Andy nodded slightly.

"Did you know that when Colby began to sing to Congress in the middle seventies about many of the CIA's closely held secrets, that President Ford (a Warren Commission member) fired him and appointed George Bush who put the lid on the information coming out in all those hearings?

"This stuff can't come out. You see, Cheryl, like I said we were in difficult times. One year prior to the assassination we went literally to the brink of war. Nuclear war. The majority of Americans were afraid of Communism. The Commission was under pressure by not only the President, but also other forces to put this matter to rest, and conclude what they did. This country would've been torn a part during this crucial period if it was either a conspiracy by external forces, which Johnson always believed, or anti-Castro Cubans from within, or the mob or Right-wing extremists.

"But now," he continued, "it doesn't matter anymore. We survived that time, and it doesn't matter what really happened almost forty years ago. It doesn't change anything now. That's why all that material is locked away in the National Archives. By then, everyone will most certainly be dead, and all the secrets that those records hold, won't mean anything anymore, including the conspiracy and who was involved, which I believe will never come to light."

"But don't you think," said Andy, "that it robbed this country, and the world, of the chance to get over sooner all that we went through, with Vietnam and the Cold War?"

"Maybe, maybe not. No one can say definitively."

"Why did you highlight the sections and material that you did?"

"Because, like I told you, I wasn't told anything other than what my job was to be. I didn't know all those cast of characters. Hell, I had never even been to Dallas before, and most certainly haven't ever been back there. I was brought in and used for a specific task, and was only trained to do one thing. And that was pull a trigger and hit a target. Everything else was completely peripheral. I was just as curious as anyone about what really happened."

"Where'd you get it all?"

"The research?"

Andy nodded.

"Syracuse University. Twenty five years worth."

"And all the files from the agencies?"

"I got my hands on a lot of them while I was employed by them. I was a paper freak. I always believed in having a copy of papers with my name on them to cover my ass."

"You did hits for the CIA. You weren't an agent?"

"No. Just a contract employee."

"What's the difference?"

"Semantics."

Andy was silent. He shook his head. He didn't have anything more to say. Somehow, he had to get these two old bastards to the authorities and hopefully the truth could yet come out.

O'Connell now didn't care. He knew it was over. Somehow he had to get the kids out of here and finish Seine off. Seine had similar thoughts. However, he had to kill them all.

Cheryl was in shock. She had always thought that this was all ancient history. Actually, she hadn't heard any of this before.

For the longest time, everyone sat in silence. Andy figured he had heard all that they were either willing to tell, or knew. Yet, Andy had this burning desire to tell the whole world.

Twenty Four

McCabe had managed to untie the twine. He crashed through the kitchen door.

Cheryl and Andy jumped up and turned. McCabe had his UZI out. He pointed it at Andy, but just as he squeezed the trigger, Cheryl deflected his aim by thrusting her rifle upward knocking McCabe's arm.

Several rounds struck the ceiling. Andy leveled his rifle and let a burst of rounds go.

McCabe was hit, but not before squeezing off another series as he fell backwards out the door. A few rounds from McCabe's gun hit Cheryl in her stomach. She went down.

Seine pushed the kitchen table over onto O'Connell and tried to stand up. He fell over onto O'Connell who burned him with his cigarette butt in his face.

Andy was so enraged at the sight of Cheryl falling to the floor that he emptied the entire magazine from his rifle into McCabe, killing him. Andy dropped his rifle and kneeled down to cradle Cheryl in his arms.

Bolt and Krup portaged their small boat over the culvert when they heard that burst of rounds from Andy's rifle off in the distance. They stopped for a quick interlude, then went back to the task at hand.

They quickly got situated in the boat on Norridgewock Lake and headed to the cabin, full steam ahead.

Fullerton had stopped in Stillwater and made contact with the two agents there. Top had returned from his run so he took Fullerton over to Beaver River where Ronny picked him up. They had just arrived at the lodge when they too heard the burst of automatic weapons fire coming from across the lake.

Ronny prepared a boat. Despite his age, he was handling the excitement well. He was transporting a special agent of the FBI!

He and Fullerton took off across the lake moments later.

Lou docked the boat in Stillwater. He sneaked up to the general store. He broke the glass and went inside. He stocked up with all that he could carry and loaded up in the boat. He stopped to gnaw on some beef jerky. He opened a beer and took a swig. Moments later he set off for the campsite, hoping like hell he could find it in this darkness.

One of the two agents at the Stillwater Hotel had looked out a window and saw Lou breaking into the store across the way. He quickly summoned the other agent and together they commandeered a boat and followed Lou.

Andy could care less about O'Connell and Seine who were beating each other up on the floor. Cheryl's injuries required his immediate attention. He got some towels from the bathroom and applied them to her wounds.

"We have to get you out of here," he said.

"I don't feel very well."

"John O'Connell?" Krup called out from outside on his way up the path.

"Oh no," said Andy. He grabbed Cheryl's rifle and stuck it out through the broken window in the door. He panicked and let off a burst of rounds.

Krup and Bolt hit the dirt.

Fullerton had just arrived at the dock. Ronny could have a heart attack at any moment. Fullerton took out his cell phone and placed a call.

O'Connell had managed to get the upper hand and had Seine beaten. O'Connell crawled into the main room and located his cane. Seine regained his faculties and crawled after him.

O'Connell grabbed his cane and hoisted himself up onto his bed. He got up and whacked Seine about the head and shoulders. O'Connell shuffled over to the weapons rack and grabbed an M16 and three fragmentation grenades.

Fullerton made his way up the path to Krup.

"What the hell are you doing here?" Fullerton demanded.

"The same thing you are."

"Great."

"We're not here."

"Just back me up," Fullerton barked. He low-crawled closer to the porch.

Inside, Cheryl was fading. Andy was preparing to move her.

"This is special agent Fullerton of the Federal Bureau of Investigation. Put your weapon down. I'm coming in."

O'Connell broke the front window in the main room with his rifle and slung it over his shoulder. He stuck the .50 caliber Browning machine gun through the opening. "The hell you are!" He engaged the weapon and let loose a burst of rounds.

Fullerton hit the grass and rolled. "Holy shit! The nut has a fucking machine gun!"

Seine managed to reach O'Connell's feet. He bit O'Connell at the ankle. O'Connell was more annoyed than he was in pain.

"You old fool!" O'Connell barked. "You couldn't let it rest."

Seine went for a deeper bite, but O'Connell swung his rifle down and pointed it at Seine's head. He let fire a quick report and Seine's head exploded.

O'Connell slung the rifle again. He yelled as best he could for a sick man of his age. "Anyone tries to come in here will wish he hadn't." He threw a frag grenade out the window. It rolled down past the porch and exploded. Luckily, both Krup and Fullerton had cover behind a tree so no shrapnel got them.

However, Ronny fell out of the boat. Shrapnel landed in the water around him. He treaded water and held onto the dock.

O'Connell made his way back into the kitchen and blew out the two remaining lit candles.

Andy sat holding Cheryl. Tears streamed down his face. She was now unconscious.

"Get her to the bed," ordered O'Connell.

Andy looked up at him.

"Now goddamnit!"

Andy picked her up and carried her to the bed. O'Connell followed.

"Let me see," said O'Connell. Andy backed off a little while O'Connell bent over and felt for a pulse. He couldn't find one! But he wasn't about to let Andy know.

"Look. She needs medical attention. You have to go out there and tell them we need a helicopter."

"Me? They'll kill me."

"They don't want you. They want me."

Andy knelt down to Cheryl again. He wiped the tears from his face with his shirtsleeve. Cheryl was pale. Andy took her hand and stroked it.

"There's no time," snapped O'Connell.

Andy kissed her on her forehead and headed for the door. "I'm coming out," he called out. "Don't shoot!" He edged out through the porch and crept down the path.

Fullerton stood up from behind a stump.

"We need an airlift. Medical attention!" Andy shouted.

Fullerton took out his cell phone and flipped it open like Captain Kirk from Star Trek would. He called for the chopper he had flown in on at Stillwater.

O'Connell locked the broken kitchen door behind Andy. He went back into the main room. He stood there panting against the wall for support. He looked at Cheryl's body, then away. He shuffled over to a chair near where his memorial had been. He sat down, then slid down onto the floor. He positioned himself under the table. He opened the trap and took out the bomb. He reset it.

"We need to go in," insisted Fullerton.

"He'll shoot you." Andy was hysterical. Tears streamed down his face.

"You need to convince him we don't want to arrest him. He hasn't done anything wrong."

"Ha. You don't know the half of what he's done, but he thinks you know."

"Look, Andy, we just need to calm everyone down."

"Where's the helicopter?"

"It's on its way."

Andy turned and ran back to the porch. He discovered the locked kitchen door.

Inside O'Connell had gotten himself back up into the chair. He was on his way back to the bed where Cheryl laid when Andy pounded on the door, so he rerouted.

"O'Connell! Open up the door!"

"Andy, it's over. She's dead."

"No! You're lying." He reached through the broken glass and struggled to unlock the door. O'Connell saw what he was doing and made his way over there.

Andy just got the door open in time.

"Stop." O'Connell pointed his rifle at him.

"I'm coming in!" Andy pushed the rifle muzzle O'Connell was pointing at him to the floor. Andy rushed in and fell to his knees. "Damn it! Cheryl, please." Andy could barely see through his tears that he had to continually wipe away.

O'Connell shuffled in. "Andy, goddamnit! It's over. You have to go."

Andy held Cheryl's hand and dropped his head to her breast. "I can't leave her. Jesus, I can't. What have I done?" He looked up at O'Connell. "You bastard! Look at all you've done. You killed her! You killed everyone!"

O'Connell didn't have time for this. He'd killed too many. He couldn't stand the sight of Andy crying over his dead granddaughter. He said to himself, I hope this doesn't do you damage. He clocked Andy in the back of the head with the butt of his rifle. Andy moaned as he fell to the floor.

O'Connell went back to the window and yelled, "One man. In here now, unarmed!"

Fullerton passed off his handgun to Krup and hurried up the path. He entered and saw O'Connell who had his rifle trained on him.

"Drag the kid out, now. The girl's dead. It's over."

"Listen, O'Connell, we can work this out."

O'Connell fired off a burst of rounds above Fullerton's head. "Now! Out goddamnit!"

Fullerton hoisted Andy up and fireman carried him out the door. He got back to the dock and felt for a pulse. He found one. Andy started to come out of it.

Inside, O'Connell sat down next to Cheryl on the edge of the bed. He set his rifle down by his side. He cradled his granddaughter's body in his arms, holding her tightly. He stared at the spot where the bomb was beneath the floor.

Tears welled up in his eyes. As he spoke, the tears streamed down his face. "Forgive me Father, for I have sinned." He paused. Then, "Our father, who art in heaven, hollowed by the name, they kingdom come; they will be done, on earth as it is in heaven. Give us this day our daily bread; and forgive us our trespasses as we forgive those who have trespassed against us; and lead us not into temptation, but deliver us from evil. For the kingdom, the power and the glory are yours, now and forever."

Andy's head hurt. He tried to get up, but Krup held him. "I gotta get back in there."

"There's nothing you can do. You might have a concussion."

"I've got to!" Andy struggled, but Krup held him down.

"He's by the bed," Fullerton said.

"He'll shoot you," said Andy.

"I've got to stop him." Fullerton started up the path.

O'Connell repeated the Lord's prayer and asked for forgiveness again. His wretched old face was soaked with tears. He heard a click, and stopped talking. He looked at the floor.

Andy managed to stand up, but Bolt had to steady him. Andy screamed, "No!"

A terrific explosion rocked the entire lake. The fuel oil and fertilizer in the barrels beneath the floor ignited and sent a large raging fireball up towards the stars. The small crowd that had gathered near the lodge felt the shock wave. They had to shield their faces from the glow of the blast.

Fullerton was knocked backwards from the shock wave. His head rang and he had an instant headache.

Ronny had pulled himself up onto the dock, but the blast knocked him back into the water.

Debris flew all over the small island and some of it landed in the water.

Bolt and Andy also had fallen to the ground.

Krup stood up and had to shield his face from the intense heat from the fire that now consumed what was left of the cabin. Another explosion from the ammunition erupted and knocked everyone to the ground again.

Krup crawled forward and dragged the dazed Fullerton back to the dock.

Everyone, all over the entire area, from as far away as Stillwater, heard the blast and saw the fireball rise into the air.

Judge Bell and Williams changed course and headed that way. The other two FBI agents on Norridgewock Lake did the same.

Jimmy stood by the campfire and wondered what the hell had happened.

Lou was lost, going around in circles on the reservoir. He saw the plume rise skyward.

The helicopter from Stillwater was almost on scene when they saw it. The pilot had to steady the bird against the blast's percussion.

The two agents spotted Lou as he finally located the camp and went ashore. One radioed Williams.

Andy got up and walked around in a daze. The cabin burned. Andy, Krup, Bolt and Fullerton had minor flash burns on their faces, but everyone was too disquieted to feel the pain.

A crowd of boats had gathered on the lake. Judge Bell pulled up with Williams. Fullerton had come out of his minor stupor and took charge of the situation.

The helicopter came in and hovered near the dock, the blades from it fanned the flames of the fire.

"We've located the camp with the girl," Williams called out over the noise of the chopper.

Fullerton waved the chopper off. "Get them out of here. Tell them to stand by at Stillwater."

Judge Bell ran up and comforted his son.

The chopper swooped off.

The area was quiet again save the sound of the crackling from the inferno.

Andy sat on a nearby stump. He shivered.

"We'll need your boat, Judge," said Williams.

Judge Bell nodded. "Okay. Just a minute."

"What is it?" Andy asked in a monotone voice.

"They found Wendy. It's a couple of hoods."

"Wendy." He said that distantly. "Cheryl's dead."

"I'm sorry."

"I loved her."

His father said nothing.

"I'm coming with you."

"Where?"

"Wendy."

"I think you should wait for me at the Osprey."

"No. I can't. I'm responsible."

His father wasn't sure. He could see that Andy was in shock. "All right. Let's go."

They chased after Williams. "What is it?"

"My son, Andy. Wendy's his girlfriend."

Andy heard it, but didn't think about that comment.

They went down to the Grassy Point Landing and jumped down into the Judge's boat.

The Judge opened it up. They rendezvoused with the two other agents about a half-mile from the camp. Williams mapped out a strategy.

Andy sat in the back of his father's boat in a daze. He was confused, and in some way, it hadn't sunk in that Cheryl was really gone. He couldn't accept that fact. He was so angry. His tears had long since dried, yet he just stared off into space.

The two boats separated and each went in towards the camp from a different angle.

The two agents jumped ashore and headed in towards the campfire. Williams jumped off of the Judge's boat and ran for the camp.

Andy watched him go. He reached up and felt the Cobray that was still in the holster under his windbreaker. He was thinking, but not rationally. He jumped up and hopped out of the boat and was off into the woods quickly before his father could say, "Andy!"

Andy was gone.

Lou sat with Jimmy eating cheese balls and drinking beer.

"What do you think those explosions was?" Lou asked.

"I don't know. I don't care."

"What should we do?"

"Sit tight and wait. You keep watch."

The two agents held back upon seeing the two perpetrators near the fire.

Williams moved in from the other side.

"You hear something," said Jimmy.

"I don't know."

Williams called out, "FBI, you're surrounded. It's over."

Jimmy sprinted off in one direction and Lou in another like chickens missing their heads.

The two agents chased Lou on the one flank, and Williams took off after Jimmy.

Andy held back and saw Williams in pursuit of Jimmy.

Down the path, Jimmy jumped down into a ditch and rolled under a log. It was too dark for Williams to see him as he jumped over the log and kept running.

Andy ran towards the tent. "Wendy?" He whispered.

"Andy?" She said in a mumbled tone.

Andy burst into the tent and found Wendy lying bound on the floor of the tent.

"Oh my God," He fell to his knees and untied her. Her face was badly bruised and her mouth was bloody. She had a gash above her eye where Jimmy had beaten her.

She was in shock. Andy horrified. "What kind of animals did this to you?"

She cried, couldn't speak. He held her in his arms. Judge Bell poked his head into the tent.

Andy helped her up and out of the tent. She couldn't walk straight and collapsed outside the tent.

"They raped me," she managed to cry. "The short one. It hurts so."

"Take her, dad."

He passed her off to him.

"Andy, no. That's an order."

Andy threw his father a deranged look and sprinted off in the direction Jimmy and Williams had gone.

Jimmy had gotten up after Williams had passed. He decided to head back and take Wendy as a hostage. He turned by a tree and came face to face with Andy, standing only several feet from one another.

Andy recognized the face as the one he had seen in Stillwater. He put his hand inside his jacket and clicked off the safety of the Cobray. He slowly slipped the Cobray out of the holster. He didn't blink and kept his hard eyes focused on Jimmy. His eyes bore a hole through Jimmy who had stopped frozen in his path.

"Make your move, asshole," said Jimmy.

Andy said nothing.

"I dry humped your bitch. Taught her a thing or two."

Andy's eyes seemed to have turned into black marbles.

"You're fucking crazy! Fuck you," shouted Jimmy. He pulled out his .357 and leveled it at Andy.

Andy was quicker and it took Jimmy by surprise. He thought Andy was bluffing. Andy emptied the entire clip, all 36 rounds into Jimmy, striking him about the chest and torso.

Jimmy writhed in agony as he fell to the ground in a contorted dance. He died like so many of his gangster ancestors.

Williams happened upon the scene. Andy looked at him and slowly dropped the Cobray to the ground.

Williams saw Jimmy's weapon by his side. Yet, he stood there in disbelief.

The other two agents had apprehended Lou without resistance. They returned to the campsite and attended to Wendy.

Judge Bell rushed into the woods and found Williams and Andy facing one another. The Judge surveyed the scene. He couldn't believe it!

Twenty Five

The sun rose over Beaver River a couple hours later. Fullerton had set up O'Connell's entire island as a crime scene and waited for the Sheriff to come and assume control.

Andy hadn't spoken a word since the shooting of Jimmy. He returned to the island and sat on the ground leaning up against a stump looking at the smoldering cabin. There was absolutely nothing left but ashes.

His father stood over him with Fullerton.

"Wendy's in the hospital in Watertown," said Fullerton. "Her father is there now and is screaming at everyone. He's threatening hearings."

Andy said nothing, but continued to stare at the hot coals.

"She's unresponsive and incoherent," continued Fullerton. "They've done a rape kit."

"You can't blame yourself, Andy," said Judge Bell. "Any of this."

Andy slowly stood, threw his father a vacant stare and walked up to the crime scene yellow tape that surrounded the cabin. He lifted it and walked towards the ashes where his newly built porch had been.

Judge Bell and Fullerton exchanged worried glances.

"What was it that Walker had done?" Judge Bell asked of Fullerton.

"His name was O'Connell, John O'Connell. He had at one time been a contract assassin for the CIA."

The Judge nodded, said nothing.

Epilogue

Later when the Sheriff investigators searched the area they discovered that there were no human remains. All four bodies were completely consumed in the inferno. It was as a crematorium. O'Connell had planned well.

During the investigation the investigators found the will in the shed. Walker had bequeathed the island to the State of New York, which later decided to erect a marker and left the island as a permanent gravesite, as part of the park system. It was not to be bought or sold ever again.

The Judge retired three years later, sold his home in Syracuse and lived at the Osprey full time. He had, in a way, become like Walker.

Andy graduated from Harvard and helped with Wendy's recovery. She slowly came around and he felt obligated to look after her, and that included marrying her. She was never the same again, however. She held onto Andy like a child holding onto a parent. He protected her and she practically never left his side.

Andy got his law degree and passed the bar three years later. He went to work for his father-in-law, eventually becoming his chief of staff.

Andy and Wendy bought a home in Massachusetts and rented an apartment in DC for Andy's use when he was in Washington.

Andy never returned to Beaver River again, and never spoke about what had happened or what he had learned.

About the Author

This is J. C. Arlington's second novel. His first novel, Dance With The Devil, can be purchased from Barnes & Noble bookstores, from Barnes & Noble.com, or from Amazon.com. He teaches and lives in California with his wife.